Tong Yi glanced over his shoulder, back toward the scream.

Then looked again.

A huge bird, easily twice the size of a human, raced after him.

Its feathers were the color of wet concrete. The beak of an eagle filled its snake-like face. Its head twisted from side to side, showing just how long and sinuous its neck was. Sickly white feet resembled a rooster's, thick and scaly, with razor-sharp black talons.

God *damn* it. Where had that *huang* come from?

Judging by its color, or lack of it, it must be a female. She blended in well with the granite gorge walls. The *feng*, the male of the *fenghuang* pair, had a white-death face, reddish wings, and blue legs. And it spat poison, which the female couldn't.

Tong Yi dared another glance back. Evil mountain *shan* and other non-humans sometimes used the *fenghuang* as mounts. However, the giant bird was riderless.

Maybe he had a chance. Maybe he could make his way out of Taroko Gorge alive. Make it back to Hualien City, back down the east coast of Taiwan.

Except, the female's nest was probably close by, judging by how well she knew the road, drawing back her wings when the car-and-a-half width dropped down to a single lane over a bridge.

Was she defending her young? Or looking for a snack for them?

It didn't matter. Tong Yi had to get the hell out of there.

The Immortals' War
A *Huli* Transport Novel

Leah Cutter
Copyright © 2016 Leah Cutter
All rights reserved
Published by Book View Café Publishing Cooperative
by arrangement with Knotted Road Press
www.BookViewCafe.com
www.KnottedRoadPress.com

ISBN: 978-1-61138-635-6

Artwork:
© 13902474131 | Dreamstime.com - Qianyang Ancient Town In China Photo
© Neotakezo | Dreamstime.com - Explosive Escape Photo

Cover design and interior © copyright 2016 Knotted Road Press

The Immortals' War

Leah Cutter

Also By Leah Cutter

The Cassie Stories:
Poisoned Pearls
Tainted Waters
Spoiled Harvest

The Chronicles of Franklin:
The Popcorn Thief
The Soul Thief

The Seattle Trolls:
The Changeling Troll
The Princess Troll

Contemporary Fantasy:
Of Myst and Folly
Siren's Call
When the Moon Over Kualina Mountain Comes
Zydeco Queen and the Creole Fairy Courts

Historic Fantasy:
Paper Mage
The Caves of Buda
The Jaguar and the Wolf
A Sword's Poem

The Shadow Wars Trilogy:
The Raven and the Dancing Tiger
The Guardian Hound
War Among the Crocodiles

The Clockwork Fairy Kingdom:
The Clockwork Fairy Kingdom
The Maker, the Teacher, and the Monster

THE IMMORTALS' WAR

Leah Cutter

Book View Café
www.BookViewCafe.com

Dancing with Tong Yi

The piercing scream rolled through the canyon of Taroko Gorge, in the northeast mountains of Taiwan, reverberating over the sound of Tong Yi's motorcycle.

Tong Yi swerved, startled. He fought to straighten out the handlebars, straining his biceps. He kept up his speed, forcing his wheels back onto his side of the highway.

Luckily, he'd been going down a straight-ish piece of road, not taking a curve, so he kept the bike upright.

Plus, he was driving the bike that his boss, Ren Wu, called "Bing Xi"—the name meaning bright and happy—a sleek red-and-black Yamaha Street Rally. She was always steady, gripping the road well.

Tong Yi glanced over his shoulder, back toward the scream.

Then looked again.

A huge bird, easily twice the size of a human, raced after him.

Its feathers were the color of wet concrete. The beak of an eagle filled its snake-like face. Its head twisted from side to side, showing just how long and sinuous its neck was. Sickly white feet resembled a rooster's, thick and scaly, with razor-sharp black talons.

God *damn* it. Where had that *huang* come from?

Judging by its color, or lack of it, it must be a female. She blended in well with the granite gorge walls. The *feng*, the male of the *fenghuang* pair, had a white-death face, reddish wings, and blue legs. And it spat poison, which the female couldn't.

Tong Yi dared another glance back. Evil mountain *shan* and other non-humans sometimes used the *fenghuang* as mounts. However, the giant bird was riderless.

Maybe he had a chance. Maybe he could make his way out of Taroko Gorge alive. Make it back to Hualien City, back down the east coast of Taiwan.

Except, the female's nest was probably close by, judging by how well she knew the road, drawing back her wings when the car-and-a-half width dropped down to a single lane over a bridge.

Was she defending her young? Or looking for a snack for them?

It didn't matter. Tong Yi had to get the hell out of there. Neither his leathers nor his helmet would protect him from the beast. At least the company's colors—*Huli* Transport, brown and yellow—weren't bright enough to make him a flaming target in the misty gray, pre-dawn light.

Possibly, though, just because he worked for *Huli* Transport was why the *huang* had targeted him. *Huli* Transport specialized in delivering messages, as well as transportation services, for non-humans. Tong Yi didn't understand the politics between the human and non-human races. He wasn't sure he even wanted to.

The *huang* screamed again. The sound bounced off the closed-in canyon walls.

Tong Yi leaned left, into the next curve, not daring to slow down. Bing Xi took the curve like a dream.

The bird folded her wings and dove after him, sliding like an eel through the air. She didn't lose any speed either.

Tong Yi had only driven Taroko Gorge once before, and that had been before he'd started working for *Huli* Transport. He didn't know the road well enough to recognize where he was, or how many *li* he had to survive before he got out.

He also didn't remember the road being this narrow, the rough rock walls so close, or how few of the turns had guardrails.

Why hadn't someone warned him that the *fenghuang* lived here? It made sense, actually. The gorge's steep walls and tight curves made an excellent hunting ground.

Tong Yi should have realized that delivering a message to Zhang Guo Lao, one of the Eight Immortals, was never going to be that easy.

Still, he hadn't been the only one who'd stepped up and happily volunteered when Ren Wu had asked who was available for a run. Once he'd been chosen, though, the other two messengers had giggled at him, the new recruit, getting the job.

Of course, neither of them had offered any advice or warning. Wan Cho had gone back to eating her Ramen and playing games on her phone, while Han Di had walked away, going outside to smoke another sweet clove cigarette.

One less messenger meant more jobs for the other messengers. *Huli* Transport had only recently branched out from mainland China into Taiwan, and into delivering messages as well. For more than a year, it had only been Wan Cho and Han Di. Though *Huli* Transport had hired Tong Yi, the expected growth of their services had yet to catch up, so the messengers had to compete for what little work there currently was.

The road curved to the right. A yellow warning sign flashed by, showing a black series of S-curves.

Shit.

No straightaway in sight.

Tong Yi kept up his speed. At least it was too early in the morning for a damned tourist bus to be coming the other way, taking up the center of the road.

The blacktop at the next curve shone darkly, coated with a fine slime of water from the picturesque waterfall tumbling down the gorge wall.

Tong Yi felt his back wheel start to go out from under him. Cursing, he backed slightly off the accelerator.

The *huang* saw her chance.

Instinct made Tong Yi slow more and duck.

The *huang's* talons clicked together in the air where Tong Yi's head had been. She screeched angrily as she coasted over him. Then she unfolded her wings and flapped, heading back up toward the sliver of blue sky above the dark walls of the canyon.

Tong Yi held Bing Xi on the road through sheer will as the backdraft pushed against him. She was heavy enough to take it, though. A lighter machine would have been blown off the road.

How the hell was Tong Yi supposed to find Zhang Guo Lao when he was going at this speed? Tong Yi was certain he'd recognize him: like the rest of the messengers, Tong Yi had apparently been born with a higher level of *sight* that had then been enhanced with the training all employees of *Huli* Transport received.

The old man was known for resting with his white mule along the Liwu River that rolled through the bottom of the gorge. Tong Yi had hoped to find him as the road opened up into one of the main highways.

He'd assumed none of the other messengers had fought to get the job because Zhang Guo Lao was known as a trickster. Finding him, delivering the message, as well as getting his response, was sure to be, well, tricky.

Tong Yi glanced up again. No sign of the *huang*. She was probably winging her way behind him again.

Or lying in wait in front of him.

The *huang* couldn't be the immortal Zhang Guo Lao in disguise, could she?

That didn't feel right to Tong Yi. According to all the legends, Zhang Guo Lao was much more likely to misdirect his "victim" by appearing as a human, maybe as a bum or old prospector, in order to test the kindness of someone. Not to attack as a completely different creature.

Another scream pierced the air.

Tong Yi shivered.

Damn bird was back.

How was Tong Yi going to get out of the canyon alive? Then find the immortal? He didn't want to drive past Zhang Guo Lao by accident, then have to come back and face the *huang* again.

The road flattened out and Tong Yi found himself climbing.

Great, just great.

The road was bringing him closer to the sky where the stupid bird was. The canyon walls dropped away.

Tong Yi glanced back when he dared, but he didn't see the creature. He knew she was close, though. Stalking him.

The road continued to climb. Tong Yi negotiated another steep curve. If he hadn't been being chased, he would have enjoyed how Bing Xi handled turns. How she took hills at speed.

Hell, he might have even appreciated the beauty of the rocks.

Up ahead, fog and clouds rolled across the road. It was another reason why so many tour buses would clog the road later in the day: the tourist brochures for Taroko Gorge promised not only beautiful rolling whitewater at the bottom of the gorge, but also that the would draw closer to heaven where the road rose up above the low hanging clouds.

Tong Yi plunged into the damp whiteness. Bing Xi's growling engine reverberated between the rock walls. He couldn't see a damned thing through the fog. What sweat had gathered under his leathers suddenly cooled. He flipped up the faceplate on his helmet as the moisture beaded up, making it even more difficult to see.

The next screeching cry seemed to come from all around Tong Yi.

Shit.

Where was the damned thing?

A talon appeared directly in front of Tong Yi.

He ducked and swerved.

Bing Xi fishtailed on the wet road.

The claw missed him by mere inches.

Tong Yi slowed and fought to keep Bing Xi upright. He had a few seconds (he hoped) before the bird made its way back around.

Suddenly, Tong Yi popped out above the clouds. Clear blue sky opened above him. Higher peaks, the gray rocks laced with snow, appeared on either side. Below him stood a lake of white fog.

Tong Yi slowed the bike and pulled over to the panoramic overlook. He tried to slow his breathing. Damn it. That had been close, but he'd escaped. At least for now. The damned bird wouldn't come after him up here, out in the open.

Only after Tong Yi stood Bing Xi up and swung his leg over the seat did he realize just how badly his entire body shook.

He couldn't rest long. He had to negotiate the rest of the gorge road before the tourist buses started rolling.

The buses wouldn't stop the *huang*. No, instead, Tong Yi would be trapped, unable to escape. The humans riding the buses wouldn't see the great bird hunting him: their mundane eyes missed all manner of things. They'd only see another young man accidentally driving off the gorge road when he tried to pass them. They'd never notice the great beast who attacked.

But how was he going to find Zhang Gua Lao and deliver his message? Without dying in the process?

After stretching and jogging in place, Tong Yi still had no idea how he was going to get through the rest of the gorge alive. The cool morning air invigorated him. Bright sunlight made the gravel at his feet sparkle. He wished he could stay there. Fetch a lovely cup of light green tea from his thermos and watch the day roll past. Read more about the history of the gorge on his phone, learn more about this beautiful place.

Tong Yi had always been fascinated by his homeland. He'd thought more than once about becoming a historian or geologist. He didn't have the grades, however, to get into a good college. After serving his one year of military service following high school, Tong Yi still felt he'd been lucky to get the job with *Huli* Transport.

Even if it was turning out to be more than he'd anticipated.

However, Tong Yi couldn't waste any more time up here on the top of the mountain. He had a message to deliver. His contract clearly stated that he would make heroic efforts to deliver all messages entrusted to him.

At least his family would receive a very large insurance payout from *Huli* Transport if he was killed while on duty today.

Tong Yi didn't want to die. He wanted to live, grow old and venerable, like his grandpa. Have his own family. Raise a son.

His older brother, Quan Lo, the eldest sibling in the family, was the one with the death wish, wanting to flame out and leave a beautiful corpse.

Tong Yi wouldn't abandon his family that way.

He wondered sometimes if his brother also had some sort of *sight*, which was why he'd started drinking so heavily and shooting heroin, rather than deal with the red-faced ghosts, fox fairies, and even stranger creatures that co-existed in the world, generally hidden to most humans.

When the representative from *Huli* Transport had approached Tong Yi, telling him that he had great potential, he'd seen the opportunity to help his family out of the debts generated by the eldest son.

Shaking himself all over like a dog, Tong Yi climbed back on his bike and started it up. The purring of Bing Xi's engines sounded pitifully small in the open air, spread out and thin.

But the vinyl seat had warmed in the sun, and the clean winds had cleared Tong Yi's senses.

He just had to go like hell, get out of the gorge, and not slow down until the very end. Hopefully he could time his approach to the immortal with the *huang's* attacks, be able to slow down between the monster's strafing runs, actually see the old man and not blow by him.

Tong Yi rode the bike slowly to the edge of the wet fog. It smelled like a thunderstorm, that sharp scent of ozone piercing through his sinuses to the back of his skull. Tong Yi revved the engine once, twice—a challenge to the creature—before he shot forward into the blinding whiteness, hugging the canyon wall.

The *huang* waited just on the other side.

Tong Yi was glad he'd chosen the right side, and not the center, where the bird had been. Her talons clicked empty a couple feet to his left.

Ha! Tong Yi sneered. He could do this.

A second claw manifested right in front of Tong Yi. He swerved to the left.

Damn it! Now there were two of them. Had the bird's mate joined her? The fog was too thick for him to be able to see.

He wouldn't be able to predict the attacks. If the damned birds coordinated well, he wouldn't have any rest between them, either.

The road curved as it dropped down. Above the muffled roar of the engine, Tong Yi heard the splash of a hidden waterfall. He slowed suddenly, but still fishtailed across the wet road. Claws brushed against his back, throwing him forward, making him swerve harder to the right.

Tong Yi knew better than to put his foot down to help stop the fall. He threw his weight to the other side, forcing Bing Xi up straight, though the front tire wobbled.

Goddamn it. He wasn't going to get out of this day like this. Not without some serious road burn.

The next curve climbed again.

Tong Yi torqued the accelerator, leaping forward. Maybe there was another break above the clouds up ahead.

Of course, that might just give the damn bird the chance to recruit yet another of its kind for the free lunch.

After another curve, the fog thinned out. Tong Yi saw an opening.

But it wasn't the road going above the clouds again.

No, a bridge rose up from the road.

Not a human bridge. He didn't need any extra *sight* to tell him that.

Was this an escape route? Or a trap?

Tong Yi had never heard of a bridge like this. Solid bleached-wood planks ran down the center of it, while shining strands of spun glass held up the looping arches. The foot of the bridge spanned almost the width of entire road.

He saw that he had a choice. A skinny sliver of road curved to the left of the bridge. Tong Yi could stick to the road and not take the bridge if he wanted.

Two piercing screams rang together behind Tong Yi.

He swerved to the right, then to the left, hoping that the erratic path he took with his bike would protect him.

Bing Xi flowed easily in and out of the curves, like she was dancing.

At least the road went straight for a short while before the foot of the bridge. Tong Yi sped up, pushing the engine to a roar. He swerved one more time, then righted the bike and struck the foot of the bridge straight on.

The bump tossed both wheels off the ground. He flew.

Tong Yi held on tightly, forcing the front fork to remain pointed straight ahead, not turning in the least.

He landed on the bridge with a solid *thump.*

The entire bridge dipped and bucked.

Tong Yi fought to keep Bing Xi upright. His already sore arms strained more.

The screeching call of the *huang* faded as Tong Yi climbed the bridge. He slowed, risking a glance back.

The *huang* and her *feng* mate wheeled at the far end of the bridge, frustrated, unable to follow him.

Tong Yi slowed the bike further, pausing. The bridge lifted up, off the road, across the gorge. Nothing but steep walls and endless rocks lay beneath it.

Up ahead, the other edge of the bridge disappeared in more thick fog.

Out of the frying pan and into the fire?

Possibly.

Tong Yi didn't have a choice, though. He just pushed on.

The fog on the far side of the bridge was wetter and colder than the clouds Tong Yi had pushed into earlier. He thought about pulling down the visor of his helmet, but decided not to. He didn't need wet condensation on the visor obscuring his vision. He needed to be able to really *see.*

Nothing but whiteness surrounded Tong Yi. He strained his ears over Bing Xi's rumble, but couldn't hear anything beyond it.

The fog tasted of calm and snow. Tong Yi didn't relax, however. He had no idea where he was, or what was ahead of him.

The bump at the far end of the bridge tossed Tong Yi back up into the air, despite the slow speed. Both wheels left the ground again.

This time, though, he landed on gravel. The tires spun. Tong Yi skidded and fishtailed, but kept the bike upright.

Where the hell was he?

After only a few yards, the fog dissolved.

Tong Yi found himself still riding on a peak. Clouds covered the valleys between him and the mountains on either side. The blue sky above him was much brighter and sharper, while the winds were thinner, needling him.

The road itself wasn't much more than a dirt trail. The sides of the mountain spine dropped abruptly on either side of him.

If he swerved or fell, it was a long way down.

If there was a bottom at all.

The trail forked. Another solid bank of cloud loomed ahead.

Tong Yi had no way of knowing which way to go. He stopped, considering. Then he walked his bike down along the right-hand path, stuck his nose into the fog, then down the left-hand one.

There had been that movie once, where the wise wizard had said to follow your nose.

But one side didn't smell sweeter than the other, or more sour.

Tong Yi tried again. This time he caught the faint call of a seagull from the right-hand side. Plus, Bing Xi seemed to roll more easily along that path.

Zhang Gua Lao was known as a fisherman....

Taking a chance, Tong Yi started down the right-hand side. Maybe he could climb back up if it turned out to be the wrong path, though in all the myths he'd ever read, it was the second (or third) person faced with a choice who ended up choosing correctly. The first person never got a chance to correct course.

Hopefully, Tong Yi had chosen correctly.

The fog here wasn't as thick. Tong Yi still rode on a dirt trail, cut into the side of the mountain. Sharp rocks pushed out from the left. To his right, the land abruptly dropped off. Far below, he heard a stream rushing by.

A rumbling to Tong Yi's left made him hang on more tightly to Bing Xi. What was that? Earthquake? Or…

Waterfall.

The path swerved hard to the left. Tong Yi barely made the turn. The waterfall fell off the overhanging cliff, while the trail went behind it. Wet dirt made Bing Xi's back wheel slide.

And keep sliding.

Tong Yi swallowed down the bile that suddenly rose as he fought to right the bike.

He was *not* going off the damn cliff.

The wet stone directly behind the waterfall wasn't an improvement. Tong Yi continued on his barely controlled skid. Bing Xi started turning sideways, until the rear wheel was inches away from the edge of the cliff.

With an abrupt jerk, Tong Yi managed to right himself. He stopped Bing Xi on the hairpin turn, panting.

What the hell had Tong Yi been thinking? Why had he believed he could do this job? Why had he signed up for *Huli* Transport in the first place? Did he really want to keep going? He'd signed a contract, but still…

However, the company had already given him such great training. Not just in *sight*, but magic, as well as martial arts. *Huli* Transport had opened up the world for him, teaching him both about the human and the non-human worlds.

And the pay was Western scale. Much higher than any other job he could hope to qualify for.

That was, if he could manage to live through the next few paychecks. He should probably sign up for motorcycle trick-riding lessons.

With a sigh, Tong Yi edged forward again, the trail dipping sharply.

He also might ask for combat pay with the next message he delivered.

Tong Yi felt like getting off his bike and kissing the ground when he finally reached the bottom of the mountain.

However, he was afraid his legs would shake so badly he wouldn't have been able to walk, or even have the strength to get back on Bing Xi.

In front of Tong Yi ran a long stretch of white sandy beach. The ocean, just beyond, looked strangely calm, a flat dark blue, burping little waves onto the shore. A solid, blacktop road ran out from the foot of the mountain, then turned and cut across the sand.

To Tong Yi's left, on the far side of a stream that ran down from the mountain and out into the ocean, an old man dressed in plain white robes sat cross-legged on the ground, his fishing pole dipping into the water. Beside him, a large white mule stood, nodding its head to its own internal rhythms.

Finally! Here was Zhang Gua Lao. Tong Yi was certain of it. He eagerly turned Bing Xi that direction.

As soon as Bing Xi's front wheel touched the sand, she stopped.

Frustrated, Tong Yi kicked the starter pedal.

Nothing. The engine didn't even click.

When Tong Yi backed up, so both wheels stood firmly on the blacktop, the engine turned right over.

Tong Yi looked over his left shoulder, to where the immortal sat, and then back up, along the road. As far as he could tell, it didn't curve that direction at all, just ran straight along the beach, with tall mountain cliffs on the left and the ocean on the right.

It didn't go anywhere near the old man.

With a sigh, Tong Yi backed Bing Xi up onto her kickstand, turned off the engine, and took off his helmet. In the sudden quiet, the waves sounded louder. Seagulls squawked in the distance. A quick glance told Tong Yi that despite how loud they'd grown, the waves hadn't increased in size.

Yet.

Tong Yi put down his helmet on the seat of his bike and swung his leg over slowly, happy that he could stand. He stomped his feet a couple of times into the ground, driving feeling back into his toes. From his saddlebag he grabbed the red envelope he was supposed to deliver to Zhang Guo Lao. He kept on his gloves, not touching the paper with his bare fingers out of respect.

How far across the sand was it to the immortal, really? Would the distance grow as soon as he put his first foot down? Would he ever reach the old man?

It didn't matter. Tong Yi had to try. He was so close. He couldn't fail now.

Luckily, it only took Tong Yi about thirty minutes to cross the few dozen yards from the road to the stream where the immortal still sat, fishing.

Unfortunately, the wind and waves had built up unnaturally fast during that time. A storm brewed just off the coast. Dark clouds tumbled over one another, flashes of lightning sparking through them. The air smelled of ozone and rain.

If Tong Yi had any luck remaining, he'd get at least halfway up the mountain trail before the storm struck the coast.

Knowing how this day had gone, though, the storm would hit before Tong Yi even left the blacktop for the mountain trail.

Tong Yi approached the old man silently, afraid that he might drive away any fish that swam in the stream if he was too loud. There was no way across the stream that Tong Yi could see. It was too wide for him to try to leap across. And he knew that if he tried something stupid like walking into the water, well, it would be like the beach, and suddenly turn into an endless lake. He'd probably drown.

Zhang Guo Lao looked up a couple minutes after Tong Yi had reached the far side of the stream. "*Ni hau*," he said, nodding his head.

"*Nin hau*," Tong Yi replied, bowing low, using the more formal form of greeting, relieved that his patience had paid off and he wasn't going to have to wait longer.

The immortal gave a toothy grin to Tong Yi. He put his bamboo fishing pole to the side, sticking the end into the sand. Then he stood, smoothing his plain white robes. A large, brown-leather belt held them together. Many oddly-shaped pouches and bags hung from it.

"Have you come to join me fishing today?" Zhang Gua Lao asked.

"No, sir," Tong Yi said. "I have a message for you."

Tong Yi raised the envelope up, resting it on both of his open palms above his head as he offered it to the old man. He knew better than to grab hold of the envelope as a sudden wind whisked it away, out of his grasp, across the water, and to the immortal.

When Tong Yi looked back up, the old man had already opened the envelope and drawn out the letter.

The immortal's face darkened as he read.

Tong Yi looked away, back out toward the now angry water. He really wasn't looking forward to the trip back.

"This means war, you know," Zhang Gua Lao said softly.

"Excuse me?" Tong Yi asked.

War? What did that mean? Between who?

"Ah, never mind," Zhang Gua Lao said with a heavy sigh. He gave Tong Yi what looked like a forced smile while he slipped the letter inside his robe.

Then the immortal began to fold the red envelope.

Tong Yi remembered the old stories, about how the sturdy-looking mule standing beside the old man was actually made of paper and would fold up neatly into one of the pouches hanging off Zhang Guo Lao's belt.

When the immortal had finished, a beautiful red lotus flower sat in the palm of his hand.

The lotus was a symbol of purity, though it was mostly used by Buddhists.

Was it a declaration of peace? Or maybe pacifism, indicating that he wouldn't be joining this war? Or was there some other message trapped inside the clever folds?

Zhang Gua Lao raised up the flower in both palms, presenting it to Tong Yi, then he blew on it.

Tong Yi reached out his open hand and accepted the lotus after it floated back across the stream. He assumed this was Zhang Gua Lao's response to the letter. Still, Tong Yi waited to hear if there was anything else.

The old man looked down at the stream, seemingly lost in thought, before he glanced up again. "Give Bi Qi some extra attention from me, would you?" the old man asked.

"Excuse me, sir," Tong Yi said after a moment. "Who?" He had no idea who the immortal was talking about.

"Bi Qi," Zhang Guo Lao said. He looked over Tong Yi's shoulder. "Your steed."

Tong Yi glanced over his shoulder, then whipped around. Where his motorcycle, Bing Xi, had once rested, now stood a graceful black mare, with red ribbons braided into her mane and tail. She shook her head at Tong Yi and whinnied, pawing at the ground.

"She wants you to hurry back," Zhang Guo Lao said. "She wants to dance more. She really enjoyed this morning's ride. She likes dancing with you."

"Dancing?" Tong Yi asked. *Dancing?* All the slides and fishtailing and nearly falling off the cliff? Those had been her idea of *fun*?

Did fishtailing equal dancing to Bi Qi?

"She likes you," Zhang Guo Lao confided. "She may even let you ride her in her natural form someday."

Tong Yi and Bi Qi were going to have to have a long talk at some point. But for now, Tong Yi had another message to deliver, bringing Zhang Guo Lao's reply back to his boss, Ren Wu.

And more dancing with Bi Qi to survive.

War On All Fronts

Here is Zhang Gua Lao's reply," Tong Yi said, pulling the perfectly-folded paper lotus out of his messenger bag. The immortal had folded the flower out of the envelope that had held the message Tong Yi had delivered to him.

The red paper flower flared in Tong Yi's palm, as though lit by an internal flame. It suddenly felt heavy and warm, and the smell of the ocean filled the room.

Damn it, why had Tong Yi taken off his gloves? He should have kept them on. Hurriedly, he reached past the piles of papers and put the flower down on the desk of his boss, Ren Wu.

Ren Wu merely grunted. He stared at the red flower, lost in thought. His flat cheeks smoothed out, making his jaw seem more defined. His black eyes remained hooded under his broad forehead.

Was Ren Wu actually a native, one of the Amis tribe, and not Taiwanese? Tong Yi had never asked, but sometimes wondered about his boss's heritage. The Amis tribe were the largest group of natives in Hualien City, but Tong Yi had only met a couple in his high school. They mainly lived north of the city, up along the east coast of Taiwan, and kept to themselves, separate from the Taiwanese. He wouldn't have ever thought that one of the Amis tribe would end up in such a responsible position.

Tong Yi took a deep breath, sinking into one of the uncomfortable vinyl chairs on the other side of his boss's desk. He tried to relax, rolling his shoulders, still tense from his long ride. He could only see Ren Wu through a slim opening between the stacks of papers, folders, and books piled high on the desk.

The rest of the office felt just as cramped. It was a tiny room, barely big enough to hold the long, dented, two-drawer metal filing cabinet that filled the entire wall under the window behind Ren Wu, plus the desk, and two chairs.

Despite how closed-in it felt, the office still soothed Tong Yi, in part because it *was* so plain, so ordinary, with its shabby and scuffed yellow paint and the faded calendar that was two years out of date hanging on the wall.

The ride back to the office on Bing Xi—his motorcycle—had been just as harrowing as the trip to deliver his message. She'd transformed while he'd struggled across the sand, leaving the immortal to his fishing, changing from a beautiful mare into a sleek motorbike.

Which was her natural form? The horse? Or the bike? Tong Yi had a suspicion there was much, much more to her.

Plus, Bing Xi had wanted to "dance" some more, causing him to nearly wipe out more than once as he made his way back through Taroko Gorge.

But she was just playing, right?

Tong Yi hoped that was the case, that she wouldn't actually hurt him, though he wouldn't put it past the big beast to give him a bad case of road rash.

The air conditioner in the window kicked on suddenly, rattling the metal horizontal blinds. Tong Yi shivered in his brown-and-yellow company uniform, the air suddenly cold and clammy. He found himself yawning, exhausted from all his riding.

Finally, Ren Wu looked up, his brooding dark eyes staring into Tong Yi. "Something else you want?" he asked, his voice more gentle than Tong Yi was expecting.

Tong Yi debated not saying anything, but he was too curious. "Zhang Gua Lao. When I gave him the message. He said it meant war."

But war between whom? And why?

Ren Wu nodded slowly. "You'd think they'd know better. Being immortals and all."

"But what does it mean?" Tong Yi asked.

Ren Wu suddenly smiled. "It means the Hualien City branch of *Huli* Transport might be expanding sooner than planned. War is good for business."

"Really?" Tong Yi asked, surprised. He'd figured that war might shut down the transportation company. They specialized in carrying messages and packages for non-humans, as well as providing transport for the more sensitive clients.

Wouldn't war just make folks…leave?

Ren Wu turned a serious stare at Tong Yi. "We are neutral," he said. "*Neutral*. We deliver message for *all* sides."

"Okay," Tong Yi said. He hadn't thought being neutral was possible.

Then again, until recently, he hadn't thought that fox fairies and giant man-eating birds and every other legend he'd ever read about were real either.

"We will *not* take sides," Ren Wu emphasized. "That's the only way *Huli* Transport has survived previous conflicts. You understand?"

"I do," Tong Yi said, nodding. "We work for everyone." He'd actually heard that before as part of his orientation. It didn't matter what type of creature needed their services, they'd still deliver.

All of the messengers pledged that they would deliver their message, taking serious oaths, swearing their lives.

In Tong Yi's case, if he died during the course of doing his duty, his family would be well paid.

If his older brother didn't get hold of the money first.

"Anything else?" Ren Wu asked as he scooped up the paper flower.

Another sharp spike of light burst from the flower, the red color splashing across Ren Wu's face.

For a moment, Ren Wu's eyes flared red as well.

Tong Yi pushed back in his chair.

He'd always assumed that his boss was human.

As quickly as it had come, the light diminished. Ren Wu looked perfectly ordinary.

When Tong Yi had started with *Huli* Transport, he'd gone through three months of training, learning how to distinguish humans from non-humans, as well as how to see beyond the everyday, mortal world. He could recognize all of the magical things around the office. Though he might not know what they did, at least he knew they weren't mundane. The training had emphasized that it was for his own protection as much as anything else.

Maybe it was time for a refresher course. Or maybe he should ask the other messengers what they thought of the boss.

"Nothing else," Tong Yi said when he realized that Ren Wu had asked him a question. He stood up quickly.

"See you tomorrow," Ren Wu said, dismissing Tong Yi. "Take off the rest of the day."

"Tomorrow," Tong Yi said, nodding. Though it was still early afternoon, he'd already had his adventure for the day. He was grateful that his boss recognized that, and didn't work any of the messengers too hard.

Tong Yi left the office, walking downstairs to the first floor of the building and out the back. God, even his legs hurt. Sleeping for the rest of the day sounded like a better idea all the time.

Huli Transport took up a double-wide space in the middle of a block in western Hualien. The vehicles maintained by the company were kept inside on the ground level, the motorcycles on one side, with the three other vehicles primarily for transporting clients on the other: a pedal cab, a tiny electric car that seemed to be made completely out of plastic parts, and a luxurious golden sedan.

Bing Xi, the sleek red-and-black Yamaha Street Rally, waited in the company stall.

The other two bikes were gone, both Han Di and Wan Cho out delivering messages. Han Di always took a long time delivering his messages. He claimed it was because the clients wanted to chat. It was much more likely that he had spent the time jabbering at them. Wan Cho was always much faster, but then again, she rarely said anything to anyone. Though Tong Yi had watched her flip her long hair back with one of the cuter fox-men who had come, instead of hiding behind it.

Tong Yi stared at the motorcycle. He'd already wiped her down, removing the spattered sand from her exhaust pipes so she was clean.

When Tong Yi had been at the ocean in that other world with the immortal Zhang Gua Lao, for a moment, he'd seen Bing Xi's true form—the great steed Bi Qi, a black horse who'd towered above Tong Yi, with red ribbons braided into her mane and tail.

Zhang Gua Lao said that Bing Xi may let him ride her in her native form someday.

But Tong Yi couldn't see anything different about the motorcycle. It seemed like a regular machine. Nothing magical about it at all.

Just like Ren Wu had seemed ordinary.

Just how incomplete was Tong Yi's training? He'd been led to believe that he'd always be able to tell if something was magical or not.

Obviously, that was wrong.

What was missing from his training? What else had his employer not told him?

Tong Yi and his mother and father sat around the tiny table in the kitchen, eating the fried rice that Dad had brought home. It was generally easier for them to have carryout than to cook. Dad worked in an office in downtown Hualien, selling insurance, while Mom tutored students in business English at Tzu Chi University.

The night was warm and cozy, just the three of them. A single light was on over the table, while the rest of the kitchen was dark. The scent of garlic and chicken filled the air, though the room always held the smell of the barley tea that his mom liked to drink. They sat around the table, holding their bowls up as they ate, so they wouldn't impolitely spill any.

Tong Yi couldn't really tell his parents about the messages he delivered. So he merely grunted and nodded when his father asked how his work was going.

When a second question didn't follow, Tong Yi put his rice bowl down and told his father, "It's going well. Very well." He couldn't say he'd actually gotten a promotion, with Bing Xi showing her true self to him, though it kind of felt that way.

"Are you being careful?" his mom asked. She'd been worried about the complicated insurance policy that came with the job. His dad had gone through the papers carefully, making sure there were no tricks, that the policy was legitimate and would actually pay out.

"Always, Mom," Tong Yi assured her. Again, he couldn't really talk about how he'd been "dancing" with his motorcycle earlier. She wouldn't understand.

He didn't fully understand either, why Bing Xi liked almost dumping him, but he'd survived without falling or hurting himself. At least so far.

"I still wish you'd go into something safer," Dad said. "I don't understand why you can't get an office job."

"And with that Chinese company," his mother added. They didn't trust the mainland.

Tong Yi shrugged. It was an old argument. He'd never had the grades, though, to go into banking or something more lucrative. Plus, his family didn't have the connections, the necessary *guan xi*—that network of favors owed and given, that generally started before a child was born—to even get him an interview.

He didn't tell his parents that there was another side to *Huli* Transport, the salesmen who negotiated the contracts with the non-human clients. The people in sales worked in a different part of town, nicer, closer to the water.

Tong Yi was pretty certain he didn't want an office job. At least not now. He liked the freedom to come and go, not to be stuck behind a desk like Ren Wu.

Plus, though Tong Yi was fully human, he loved learning about the non-humans. There was so much more to the world than what his parents saw. Tong Yi had found himself actually studying hard to learn more about the non-humans and their place in the human world. He'd started trying new tea shops and noodle houses in order to be among the non-humans more, fascinated by the depths they added to his beloved city.

That knowledge of the others made him feel special. Different. He wasn't sure he'd ever want to work at a regular place, not after seeing what he'd seen.

Even if it meant sometimes tangling with giant man-eating birds.

"Maybe you could go interview again," Mom suggested.

Tong Yi just shrugged. He didn't want to actually argue with his parents about this again. Then he added, "I am making a good wage."

Mom sniffed. "You know Tau Yien's son? He just started as a banker. I'm sure he's making more than you are."

Tong Yi didn't let himself reply. He *was* making a lot of money, particularly with the hazard pay he'd receive after a job like the one he'd done that day.

So much money that he could afford his own apartment, if he wanted to live on his own.

But he wouldn't do that. He couldn't just abandon his parents that way.

Before his mom could continue, the door to the apartment crashed open.

Quan Lo, the eldest son, was home.

Tong Yi didn't like the look his parents exchanged: part worry, but also, part fear.

Silence followed.

"I'll go see—" Tong Yi said, starting to rise when Quan Lo came into the kitchen.

"There you are! All my lovely people! How are you? I am fine, I am!" Quan Lo said, speaking rapidly as he danced in.

Though the lights in the kitchen weren't bright enough for Tong Yi to see, he knew that his brother's pupils would be mere pinpricks. Tong Yi had no idea what his brother was high on, but it didn't matter.

All that mattered now was protecting his parents from their eldest son.

Again.

Because he couldn't report his brother to the police. Not without destroying his family. His parents would kick him out and never speak to him again if he turned against his brother.

Tong Yi rose all the way and stepped in front of Quan Lo.

God, where had Quan Lo been? He smelled rank, like urine and rotted fish. How dare he come in smelling like that? It was so rude. So disrespectful for everyone living in the tiny apartment.

At least the T-shirt Quan Lo wore looked clean, faded gold letters on black, advertising some American band. His eyes shone with manic delight, peeking out from between greasy strings of black hair. The light threw his sharp cheekbones into contrast. He'd always been thin, but the drugs had made him even more skinny.

Tong Yi hated that he still had to look up to meet his brother's eye. Though Tong Yi had had a growth spurt in his late teens, he was still shorter than his older brother.

"Why don't you sit down and join us for dinner?" Tong Yi suggested, though what he really wanted to do was to kick his brother out of the house, barring the door to him until he sobered up.

"It's too marvelous a night to sit and eat," Quan Lo said. "Not when I feel like dancing!" He put his hands on Tong Yi's shoulders, trying to push them back and forth to a beat that only Quan Lo heard.

Tong Yi resisted. At the very beginning, his brother's manic moods had felt freeing to Tong Yi, particularly given the strict rules their parents had always made them follow. They'd spent long afternoons giggling and dancing like mad fools, jumping on the chairs and sofa, even going so far as to hide the statue of Confucius that usually sat on the family altar.

Now, Quan Lo's disrespect just angered Tong Yi.

While his parents were disappointed in Tong Yi's employment, at least he *had* a job. Slowly but surely, he was making a dent in the credit card debts his brother had incurred.

Quan Lo had stopped stealing the family's things for the past three months. They had the same TV, his father's scooter hadn't been vandalized, and his mother still had all her jewelry. Tong Yi wasn't sure how Quan Lo was paying for his drugs. Maybe he had stolen credit cards from someone else.

Or maybe he was paying for them with his body. He'd hinted at that, once. Tong Yi really didn't want to know.

God, if only he could get his brother locked in a jail forever. But he couldn't. Not if he still wanted a home.

"Sit. Eat," Tong Yi said sternly, staying ramrod straight and still.

"You're no fun," Quan Lo complained. "Don't you want to dance with me?" He continued shoving at his brother, the feeling less playful, more forceful, now.

Tong Yi stepped back and stared hard at Quan Lo. Tong Yi had been "dancing" most of the day with Bing Xi. But Quan Lo couldn't know about that, could he?

Tong Yi had always wondered if Quan Lo could have worked for *Huli* Transport as well—if one of the reasons he'd turned to drugs had been because he could also see all the *other* creatures who existed.

But Quan Lo was off in his own world, bopping his head and dancing in circles with himself now.

Mom and Dad finally unfroze. "I'll get you a bowl," Mom offered, standing up.

"Sit," Tong Yi directed.

Too late. Mom had already gotten up from the table, skirting around the two brothers, heading for the cabinets.

Quan Lo grabbed her arm as she passed.

Tong Yi cursed under his breath. He didn't want this to get worse.

"You'll dance with me, won't you, Mommy?" Quan Lo wheedled, as though he were six years old.

To Tong Yi's surprise, his mother didn't acquiesce. "I'll get you a bowl for rice," she offered instead.

Was his family getting as sick of his older brother as he was? Were his parents finally getting past the fact that Quan Lo was the eldest son, and therefore, the one they'd pinned all their hopes and dreams on?

But Quan Lo wouldn't be denied. "Come here," he said, yanking his mother closer.

"Ow!" Mom said.

"Let go of her," Tong Yi growled, getting up into his brother's face.

The rotten smell of Quan Lo's breath swam over Tong Yi.

Quan Lo snarled and raised his free hand, as if he'd strike his brother.

Tong Yi didn't flinch. He glared at Quan Lo, daring him.

The training from *Huli* Transport hadn't just been about seeing other creatures, but learning how to defend himself if necessary, lessons that Tong Yi had continued on his own.

However, before Quan Lo could get a taste of what Tong Yi had learned, he let go of their mother. She was crying, rubbing her arm. She'd probably have a bruise there, and would wear long-sleeved shirts for a week.

Tong Yi hadn't understood what had happened the first few times. He'd just been perplexed at his mother's wardrobe change, particularly in the middle of summer when it had been so warm.

When Tong Yi had finally figured it out, he had raged at Quan Lo even more. But his parents wouldn't hear of him reporting their eldest son to the police. And Tong Yi tried to be the good son, and not go against his parents' wishes.

"I'm not hungry," Quan Lo said. He looked over at the table. "At least, not for that." He held out his hand to Tong Yi. "I want noodles. Not rice."

Tong Yi sighed. If he gave his brother some money, who knew what he'd spend it on?

Then again, at least he'd leave. And probably wouldn't come back for the rest of the night.

"Here," Tong Yi said, drawing some New Taiwanese dollars out of his wallet.

He was prepared for Quan Lo to snatch at his wallet, trying to take all of his money, as he had before.

This time, Tong Yi held onto the wallet tightly.

When his brother grabbed onto his wrist, Tong Yi turned his arm sharply, twisting and breaking the hold.

Quan Lo narrowed his eyes at his brother. Then looked at the dollars in the proffered hand. "That will barely buy me tea," Quan Lo pouted.

"Too bad," Tong Yi said. "Take it. And go."

"Mommy, you love me more, don't you?" Quan Lo said, turning toward their mother who'd inched away, back toward the kitchen table.

"I don't have anything more," Mom said, shaking her head and looking at the floor.

Tong Yi cursed silently again. Had Quan Lo already gotten money from Mom earlier that day? That week?

"Fine," Quan Lo said. He flounced out of the kitchen. "I'll just help myself to the lamps out here."

"You will not," Tong Yi said, storming out of the kitchen.

Quan Lo stood in the open doorway leading outside, laughing at his brother. He had a set of keys in his hand. "See ya!" he said as he slammed the door shut.

Tong Yi rapidly patted the front of his jeans, then groaned.

While they'd been fighting, his brother had pickpocketed his keys.

He took a deep breath, followed by another. He listened for the familiar sound of his scooter driving away.

Then he reached for his phone, calling the police. He *was* going to report it this time, no matter how much that might anger his parents. Of course, they considered it a family matter, too shameful to involve outsiders. That was their way.

Too bad. Quan Lo had gone too far this time.

Tong Yi didn't expect that the police would be able to do anything. They'd never find his scooter, as Quan Lo would sell it for parts. Money for more drugs.

Just like he had with Mom's scooter.

Tong Yi would have to get a ride from his dad in the morning.

He wouldn't be able to borrow Bing Xi, not for personal use. But he was going to have to get another scooter. He had a job to do. Work he enjoyed, despite how low his parents thought his current position was.

Both Mom and Dad were seated at the kitchen table, their rice bowls raised in front of their faces, eating as if nothing had happened.

Tong Yi's rage boiled up. He knew he couldn't choke down another bite. "Thank you for dinner," he said formally. "I'm not hungry anymore."

Then he turned and stalked up the stairs to his room, slamming the door.

He couldn't abandon his parents. Couldn't leave and go for a ride. Could only sit and stew and dream about escape.

"Dude. You've got to be joking," Han Di said as Tong Yi got off his dad's ancient Vespa in the lane behind *Huli* Transport.

Han Di was already in his *Huli* Transport uniform—brown shirt and pants, with the yellow fox icon on the shirt pocket—standing next to his own ride, a sweet Honda Fireblade motorcycle, smoking yet another of his obnoxious clove cigarettes.

Tong Yi just shrugged. At least his dad had loaned him some wheels. He'd have to call his dad later, to see if he needed to be picked up or if he'd found his own ride.

"What happened to your own piece of shit scooter?" Han Di asked as Tong Yi looped a chain through the front tire of the bike and connected it to the steering handles, as he'd promised his dad. It wouldn't actually secure the Vespa—it was just to deter someone from walking up and taking the bike.

Not like Tong Yi was worried. The lane never had much traffic, just the occasional resident going about their business. Plus, the fancier vehicles just inside the garage were all magically protected—anyone trying to steal one of the official transport vehicles would be instantly paralyzed. He figured those wards would probably warn off any would-be thief.

Tong Yi regretted once again that he didn't have any magical abilities. Or he might have been tempted to put such a spell on his own vehicle, tuned specifically to his brother.

"Stolen," Tong Yi said. Which was true enough. The police hadn't found the bike right away, which meant that Quan Lo had probably sold it to buy more drugs.

Quan Lo never kept any drugs at the apartment. The first time Tong Yi had found that bag of pills, he'd flushed them down the toilet. Quan Lo had listened to Tong Yi's warnings that time, and had never brought drugs home again. Otherwise, Tong Yi might have taken them to the police and gotten his brother arrested.

"You know, I got a cousin. Works at a dealership up the way," Han Di said, stopping Tong Yi before he could escape into the *Huli* Transport office.

Tong Yi just snorted. Han Di had cousins *everywhere* in Hualien. As far as Tong Yi could tell, the other messenger was related to at least half the city.

"I doubt you can afford something as sweet at Bing Xi," Han Di said, nodding toward the other motorcycle. She still stood where Tong Yi had parked her, resting in her stall, with a gleam on her black and red body that didn't come just from the overhead lights. "But you could probably get something nice enough to make her jealous."

Tong Yi shot a sharp look at Han Di. What did he know about Bing Xi? And her true form? The messengers supposedly shared the transport motorcycles for delivering messages, as well as the other vehicles the company maintained.

If Tong Yi was being honest, though, he did feel possessive of Bing Xi. If he made her jealous, would she be nicer to him? Stop trying to dump him in the name of "dancing" with him?

Han Di added, "We can go over there at lunch."

"Okay," Tong Yi said after another moment. He needed a new scooter. And though he had his brother's debts to pay off, he could probably still afford something nicer than what he'd been driving.

Maybe he could get something "sweet" enough to make Bing Xi jealous.

The lot Han Di drove Tong Yi to was tiny. Instead of being on the outskirts of Hualien where all the car dealerships were, it was close to the coast, in a residential district. It looked to Tong Yi like a house that had had its front yard paved and turned into a retail space. A chain link fence surrounded the yard, with faded limp plastic flags hanging from it.

Motorcycles and scooters stood in three neat rows, maybe two dozen vehicles in all. Of course, there wouldn't be a price tag on any of them. Tong Yi would have to negotiate that.

At least they were all newer models, and they gleamed in the sunlight.

Back behind the bikes and scooters stood a garage, not a house. The smell of fresh oil wafted from it. Boxes of parts filled at least two of the walls of the garage. Two motorcycles were resting there, one in pieces. A short man squatted next to it, then rose when they came up.

"Hello! Hello!" he called in greeting, wiping his hands on a cloth. He wore a light blue shirt stained with grease, a pair of dark blue pants that were probably just as stained, and sandals. He didn't look at all like Han Di, who had a sharp nose, rock star cheekbones, and thin lips. This man looked more like Ren Wu, with a flat face, prominent jaw, and tiny eyes. His skin was dark, looking like he'd spent a lot of time out in the sun. His hair was roughly cut, as though he'd hacked it off himself with a knife.

"Let me do the talking," Han Di warned.

Tong Yi nodded slowly. Wasn't this supposed to be a cousin?

When the man came up, Tong Yi was surprised at just how short he was. Tong Yi wasn't that tall, 5'6", but the man barely came up to his chest.

However, he was easily twice as wide as Tong Yi, and his hands were huge. He nodded his head when he recognized them, his grin filling his face.

"Han Di! Hello! Hello!" he said. "Good to see you. This is friend, yes?"

Han Di nodded. "This is my friend Tong Yi."

"Good! Good!" the man said. His accent was strange, as though he weren't actually Taiwanese. Was this another of the Amis tribe? "I am Monkey Man."

Tong Yi looked more carefully at the man in front of him. He seemed fully human.

"Monkey Man provides bikes and services for a lot of the foreigners," Han Di explained.

"I practice my English with them," Monkey Man said, in English.

"*Hau*," Tong Yi replied. Though he'd learned to speak English in high school, he'd prefer to keep speaking in Taiwanese.

"Come. Come. You must have tea with me," Monkey Man insisted, leading them back toward the garage.

Hidden from the street by the rows of scooters sat a tiny table with a teal-green teapot and half a dozen matching cups. The set was stained and cracked with age, though it looked clean. A mosaic of red, green, and blue glass pieces set in concrete, in the shape of a many-pointed star, decorated the top of the table. Next to the table stood a portable cooking burner, with a metal water kettle on it, the sides scorched.

Monkey Man squatted down next to the table and started preparing the tea, stuffing the teapot full of leaves from an unmarked black tin that looked as though it had once stored pasta. Han Di squatted down beside him, looking as comfortable as any peasant.

Tong Yi grimaced and squatted down as well, though he knew he wouldn't be able to maintain that position for long before his feet and legs fell asleep.

"Tong Yi's scooter was stolen," Han Di told Monkey Man. "And he needs a new bike."

"Ah. Ah," Monkey Man said, pouring the already boiling water into the teapot. He immediately poured the water back out of the teapot and onto the ground, saying, "Never drink the first tea. That just wakes the leaves up." Then he refilled the teapot and set it to the side to steep.

"Young man like you, need a fast bike, right?" Monkey Man said, turning his gaze on Tong Yi.

Tong Yi shrugged. Though he'd never admit it to Han Di, and his parents wouldn't believe it, he was more cautious than that. He really wasn't looking for speed. He got that with Bing Xi.

Reliable, on the other hand…so that he wouldn't be stuck pushing his motorcycle when the monsoon rains started and he was still many *li* from home.

"He needs a fancy bike," Han Di told Monkey Man. "Something to make his other girl jealous."

"You messenger, for *Huli* Transport, right?" Monkey Man asked.

"I am," Tong Yi said.

"You have fancy bikes there. Fancier than mine," Monkey Man said, nodding. He started humming to himself as he poured the tea, offering the first cup to Tong Yi.

Tong Yi politely took the cup, holding it between his two palms. It warmed his hand and his legs suddenly felt better. The smell of black tea came from the cup, bitter and strong.

The first sip splashed against Tong Yi's tongue. There were surprising strands of vanilla and cherry mixed in with the taste of smooth black tea.

"This is good," Tong Yi told Monkey Man. "Very good."

The man grinned at Tong Yi, showing all his teeth like a foreigner. "You have good soul," he replied. "I have bike for you."

"Good," Han Di said. He took a sip from his own cup, obviously savoring it. "That's very good. I knew you'd be able to help."

"I have perfect bike," Monkey Man said. "Dependable and fast. Not cost too much. Plus good lock. So it can't be stolen again."

"Thank you," Tong Yi said. However, he still wasn't certain he wanted to buy a bike today. Shouldn't he look around more? Try to get a good deal? Tong Yi didn't completely trust the other messenger. They did compete for jobs, sometimes.

Though if Tong Yi was being truthful, he did trust Monkey Man. Tong Yi's training might not have been as complete as he'd first thought, but he also knew a good soul when he met one.

"But I'm not sure—" Tong Yi started to say.

"I know. I know. You need to meet the bike first. Take a ride. You sit. Stay. I will get," Monkey Man said. He hopped up and went through the garage, out a door in the back.

As soon as their host was gone, Tong Yi stood up, groaning and stretching his legs.

Han Di grinned up at him. "You should get used to squatting like this," he said. "Sometimes clients will want to talk, take you out for tea."

"Really?" Tong Yi asked. He stomped his feet, forcing circulation back into them. "I didn't know that." He'd only delivered packages so far, not clients.

"Yup," Han Di said. "Practice every night."

Tong Yi sighed and nodded. He felt as though there was still so much he had to learn, about his position, *Huli* Transport, the other beings, and so on. A whole new world had opened up to him, and he had only scratched the surface of it.

Monkey Man came back through the garage pushing an FZ8 Yamaha Streetfighter motorcycle. The gas can was a cool blue, and the lines of the bike sleek. The metal around the headlight flared out, with red lightning bolts painted onto the black, like some kind of laser. As it drew closer, Tong Yi realized that the bike was this year's model.

"Try it," Monkey Man said. He pushed the bike out into the street.

Tong Yi slung his leg over the bike. It was surprisingly heavy. He'd build muscles pushing it around. That was probably a good thing.

The engine started right up, purring nicely.

Tong Yi knew he was in trouble already, before he'd driven a single block.

This was going to be the perfect companion for him.

And probably sweet enough to make Bing Xi jealous.

"Listen up," Ren Wu said, coming into the employee break room where Tong Yi, Han Di, and Wan Cho were hanging out between jobs. It had been about ten days since Tong Yi had brought back Zhang Gua Lao's message. The three of them had never been busier. It was a rare occurrence now for the three of them to be hanging out together.

Ren Wu paused and sniffed the air, wrinkling his nose.

The air stank of the eggs cooked in tea that Han Di insisted were good for his health. Tong Yi hoped that Ren Wu would say something.

A TV hanging in the corner of the room silently showed Japanese anime with Chinese subtitles. The table the three of them sat at was littered with Sudoku and English-language crossword puzzles.

Ren Wu looked more tired than Tong Yi had ever seen him. Dark black circles under his eyes marred his flat cheeks. His cream-colored polo shirt, with the emblem of a fox on the left-breast pocket was wrinkled, as if he'd slept in it.

"You're all required to take additional training. Tomorrow morning, 10 a.m. At the sales office."

"Why?" Han Di asked. "What training?"

"You'll find out tomorrow," Ren Wu said. Then he handed out assignments for all of them, sending them each to the far ends of Hualien, so Tong Yi couldn't talk with the other messengers about the training.

Seemed as though the war had been good for business. When Tong Yi asked Han Di and Wan Cho about it, they had no idea who would be fighting whom, or why. That hadn't stopped Han Di from speculating, while Wan Cho had silently listened, as usual, her long hair half-hiding her face.

Tong Yi had spent one entire day ferrying heavy envelopes back and forth between the sales office near the pier to the east and two of the non-human offices close to the train station in west Hualien. He'd had to sign for each envelope, then prick his thumb and give them his print in his own blood. Normally, he had to deliver such a confidential message once a week. Having to do it several times in one day left his thumb sore and swollen.

At 10 a.m. the next day, Tong Yi drove to the sales office on his new bike—Mei Fuang. He wasn't certain the name fit her—though the blue of her gas can and her clean lines did remind him of the beautiful flowers she'd been named after.

If she had another name, he was certain she'd tell him at some point.

Bing Xi hadn't tried to dump him for more than a week as well. If Tong Yi had to guess, he'd say she seemed distant.

Was she jealous of Mei Fuang? Or angry? Or was she also tired, doing all the deliveries that they'd been on in the last week?

The sales office for *Huli* Transport was much nicer than the messenger office. It was there to impress clients. The offices resided in a ten-story building, taking up two entire floors. The front lobby looked like the entrance to a private men's club. A small, white reception desk stood in the foyer, modern and sleek, with a single receptionist standing behind it.

Tong Yi hadn't dared ask for the receptionist's name. She was model-pretty, with a stillness about her, like a statue. She wore her black hair in soft curls up on top of her head that day, her nose small and cute, slightly upturned, perfect for kisses. Her eyes were broad and intelligent. She had soft cheekbones and a knowing smile, as if she held all the secrets.

Today she wore a navy blue dress with a tiny fox emblem on the left breast. She gave Tong Yi a warm smile and told him, "Third floor, conference room 314-E."

Tong Yi hesitated. Maybe he could at least ask her for her name, but then she looked over his shoulder at the next person coming thru the door.

The receptionist's smile grew distinctly less warm. "Han Di," she said, her melodic voice suddenly harsh. "You'll be with Tong Yi, third floor, conference room 314-E."

"Thanks, babe," Han Di said as he slid up to the reception desk. He leaned on it, while the receptionist leaned back. The smell of Han Di's clove cigarettes flowed from him. "So whatcha doing later tonight?"

"Not seeing you," the receptionist said frostily. "You need to go now, or you'll be late for your training."

"Come on," Tong Yi told Han Di. He also resolved not to ask the receptionist's name, or to hit on her, not if she was already tired of dealing with Han Di.

"Later, sweetheart," Han Di told the receptionist, blowing her a kiss as he pushed off her desk and sauntered over to Tong Yi.

"I think she's warming to me, don't you?" Han Di asked as he slipped his arm inside Tong Yi's.

Tong Yi smiled and shook his head. Though the receptionist obviously was immune to Han Di's charms, there weren't many who were.

"What do you think the training's all about?" Han Di asked as the elevator rose.

Tong Yi shrugged. "No idea." He'd wondered about it the previous night. Maybe the bosses had realized that their employees couldn't see everything that was magical and so they'd decided to address it. Or maybe it was time for a refresher course.

Though the building was new and modern, the third floor was old-fashioned. Wood paneling covered the lower half of the walls. The lights were all recessed, soft and unobtrusive, not harsh fluorescent bulbs. Thick brown carpet covered the floor, with waves of red dancing through it.

The artwork lining the walls showed fanciful paintings of temples, all red and gold. Tong Yi didn't recognize any of the buildings, or the gods, but he wasn't about to ask.

The door to the conference room was firmly shut when they arrived. Tong Yi glanced at Han Di, who just shrugged and indicated that Tong Yi should open the door.

It didn't swing in automatically, or even open easily. Tong Yi felt as though he was pushing the door open against a strong wind.

The inside of the conference room was dimly lit. Dark clouds gathered across the ceiling, obscuring the lights there. A plain wooden conference table took up most of the center of the room.

At the far side of the room stood a whirling gray oval, the center of it black and deep. If Tong Yi had to guess, he'd bet it was a portal to…somewhere else.

"Shut the door," a tall man standing near the corner instructed.

Tong Yi stepped inside the conference room, then waited until Han Di also came in before he pushed the door shut. It still felt as though he was fighting against a strong wind, though there was none in the room. The gray swirling mass at the far side was oddly silent. The room smelled of its most recent cleaning, harsh chemicals and fake flowers. Tong Yi tasted something bitter, like burnt sugar, at the back of his throat.

Wan Cho was already there. She sat in one of the conference room chairs, leaning back, playing a game on her phone, ignoring all of them, hiding behind her hair as usual.

The man stepped forward. "You will call me Uncle Bei. Today you're here to learn about portals." He didn't look or sound like a kindly uncle at all. Instead, he appeared to be a businessman—probably a lawyer—in an expensive black suit and crisp white shirt, with a red-and-black striped tie. The cufflinks at his wrists were gold with red jewels and powerful enough that Tong Yi felt their magic even without concentrating on them.

Tong Yi felt his eyebrows climb. "Portals? To where?"

Uncle Bei gave him a chilling smile. It fit his sharp face with its chiseled cheekbones and harsh jaw. "To the battlefield, of course. There is a war starting. And *Huli* Transport is the messenger service of choice for all sides. Please, have a seat."

All sides? Were there more than two sides fighting? Tong Yi had so many questions, but knew that this wasn't the person he should ask them of. Instead, he nodded, sitting stiffly, with Han Di beside him.

Ren Wu had been right. It appeared that war was going to be very profitable for *Huli* Transport.

"You've all signed your non-disclosure agreements, with the non-compete clauses, correct?" Uncle Bei started off, addressing them from the far side of the conference room, next to the whirling portal.

All three messengers nodded. The agreements had been included in the mountain of paperwork Tong Yi had signed when he'd first started with *Huli* Transport. He wouldn't be able to work for another messenger company for at least two years if he left *Huli* Transport.

What kind of competition did *Huli* Transport have? Were there a lot of transportation and messaging companies that did what they did? Tong Yi had been under the impression that they were unique, but after he'd signed all that paperwork, he hadn't been certain.

From an expensive, black leather briefcase, Uncle Bei pulled out three stickers, handing one to each messenger. Each was embossed with a gold fox sitting in the center, about the size of a flattened out dumpling, taking up most of Tong Yi's palm. The gold sparkled in the dim light of the conference room. "Place this on your helmet," Uncle Bei instructed. "Then wear your helmet at all times in the warzone."

The magic in the sticker made Tong Yi's fingers tingle. "What is this?" he asked, handling it gingerly.

Uncle Bei gave him a calculating smile. "You can feel the magic?"

Han Di, Wan Cho, and Tong Yi all nodded slowly.

"Good. This sigil marks you as non-combatants. No one will attack you while you're wearing it," Uncle Bei said.

"But war's messy," Han Di pointed out. "What happens if we get attacked accidentally?"

"The fines are astronomical," Uncle Bei assured them. He looked very satisfied with himself. "If you're injured while delivering messages in the warzone, believe me, they'll pay for it."

Tong Yi wondered how much of that money would go to his family. He assumed that while Mom and Dad would be set for life, *Huli* Transport would also get a very good chunk of cash.

Hopefully, that would make the messengers less of a target.

"For now, you need to hold onto the stickers. They were very expensive to make, so do not lose them," Uncle Bei said.

Tong Yi hesitated, but still put the sticker in the front pocket of his jeans. The magic would protect him, and he figured extra protection down there wouldn't hurt.

"Now," Uncle Bei said, indicating the large gray swirl of clouds at the far end of the conference table, "this is an active portal. Note the color of the clouds surrounding it."

Tong Yi peered closely at the gray swirling mists. They kind of looked like the mists that he'd gone through on Bing Xi, when he'd crossed over onto the bridge that had taken him to Zhang Gua Lao. This portal was darker though, more dense.

"Notice the blue veins of light," Uncle Bei said. He pulled out a red laser pointer and traced light through the mist.

Now that Uncle Bei had pointed them out, Tong Yi realized he could see them, stretched out like a delta of riverbeds, circling the entire portal.

Tong Yi looked away, as he'd been taught, then looked back, trying to "see anew."

The magic of the portal suddenly struck him, pulsing with its own heartbeat of power. Before, he'd known it was magical, but it was more of an intellectual realization. Now, he *felt* it, with that deep sense that his trainers had awoken in him.

Did the other messengers go through the same realization? Or had they come in feeling the magic?

"None of you have the power to create such a portal as this," Uncle Bei said after a few more minutes. "If you did, well, you wouldn't be sitting on that side of the table. At least, not for long."

Tong Yi leaned back, surprised. He didn't think he had any magical ability at all. Sure, he could see things, and once he'd started his training, he could see a lot better.

But he couldn't *create* magic, could he?

Uncle Bei hadn't used the word *ability* though.

He'd used the word *power*.

Did that mean that with more training, Tong Yi could develop more magical ability? Maybe become a wizard, or whatever Uncle Bei was?

It was worth asking Ren Wu about sometime. Maybe during Tong Yi's annual review, though that was more than half a year away.

"The portals to the warzone will be generated here, at headquarters, whenever there's a message that needs to be delivered. The portal will be maintained for a single hour. You'll need to watch your time."

"What happens if it takes longer than that to deliver a message?" Tong Yi asked. When he'd finally found Zhang Gua Lao, the immortal had appeared to be only a few feet away from him. However, time and distances were funny in that place, and it had taken Tong Yi over thirty minutes to cross a very small stretch of beach.

"The portal will only be open an hour," Uncle Bei said firmly. "If you miss it, you'll have to get back on your own. Through the badlands."

"But sometimes it takes more than an hour," Han Di explained. "Particularly when you're trying to deliver to a figure of legend or myth. They're tricky that way, and don't always want to be found. Or make it easy."

Tong Yi nodded. So did Wan Cho.

"Portals are expensive to maintain," Uncle Bei said finally. "It isn't practical for us to keep them open for much longer than an hour."

"But that's not practical for us," Wan Cho said.

Tong Yi raised his eyebrows in surprise. The female messenger rarely said anything. He hadn't expected she'd speak up like that.

"You won't want to spend any longer in the warzone than you have to," Uncle Bei assured them.

"We're supposed to deliver our messages. Or die trying," Han Di said. "What happens if the recipient doesn't want the message and is hiding? We can't just give up in an hour."

Uncle Bei pressed his lips together in disapproval, glaring at the three messengers.

They glared back at him. It struck Tong Yi as a typical job situation, something he'd heard his father complain about often: how his dad's bosses in Taipei would make a decision without really thinking through the consequences, or how that decision would affect the people actually doing the work.

"Fine. I'll check with headquarters to see if we can extend the open portal for an additional half an hour," Uncle Bei finally said.

"And you'll send out a search team if we don't return?" Han Di asked sweetly.

"How are we supposed to find you?" Uncle Bei asked. "It's a warzone."

Tong Yi dug his sticker out of his pocket. It glowed even more brightly now. "Through these."

Uncle Bei opened his mouth, then closed it again. He gave Tong Yi a thoughtful look. "That's actually a very good suggestion. I will inquire."

"Now," Uncle Bei continued, obviously trying to get back to business. "Are you ready to go through the portal? I want you to experience the land of the warzone now, before you have to be rushing through it to deliver a message. Plus, the land is currently empty of combatants."

He paused, then added, "I can't tell you that you'll get used to the warzone. It was deliberately created so that no one would be comfortable there. It can be very disorienting at times. But you need to have an understanding of what you'll be facing. Ready?"

Tong Yi looked at the other messengers. Han Di shrugged, while Wan Cho said nothing, as usual.

Slowly, the three of them stood up.

Tong Yi had been excited about more training, learning more about magic. Knowing about the non-humans and their places.

Now, he wasn't so sure.

The fact that most of the sky of the warzone was covered in nasty, boiling clouds somehow didn't surprise Tong Yi. The dreary gray instantly pressed down on him, trying to force out all the joy of life.

Just underneath the clouds, visible on top of the far ridge, lay the naked sky that was a peculiar shade of purple, like a bruise.

It was *wrong*. The sky was never that color. Not even during a sunset. There was too much red in it, like old blood. It looked thin, like a mere layer of color painted over the dome of the earth. As if, just beyond it, was something much worse, though Tong Yi didn't want to spend time imagining what that might be.

The land was open, denuded of trees. Rough terrain made up the ground, rutted and full of dangerous holes, covered with weeds and dying grass. The air itself smelled of dried bamboo, bitter and musty.

To the right (North? South? There was no way to tell) stood a ridge, that looked as though it stretched to either side for miles.

Tong Yi stomped his feet, trying to get a better feel for the earth. It seemed solid enough, like packed dirt. At least that would be better than sand or clay.

He didn't trust the clouds above him at all, though. They looked angry, like they'd enjoy opening up and dumping rain on him, without any warning.

The land wasn't comfortable, as Uncle Bei had told them. However, it wasn't that uncomfortable, either.

Uncle Bei looked at the three of them, assessing them for a moment, before he said, "Follow me."

Han Di caught Tong Yi's arm and gestured for Wan Cho to go first. She rolled her eyes at them and strode off.

"Weird, huh?" Han Di asked Tong Yi quietly. He was rubbing the back of his neck and glancing around as if expecting some kind of ambush.

Was that how Tong Yi was supposed to be feeling? Paranoid?

"Weird," Tong Yi agreed, tripping. Then he tripped again, just a few steps later.

There was something wrong with the light. He kept misjudging the ruts. Normally, he was very sure-footed. Was that part of the uncomfortable quality of the warzone?

He wasn't looking forward to driving Bing Xi across this terrain. Particularly if she was feeling playful and wanted to "dance" with him. He was sure to wipe out.

After about five minutes' walk, Uncle Bei stopped and turned around. "Now, look back. Find the portal."

Tong Yi turned.

Panic spiked through him. Where were the gray clouds? The swirling mass? The portal should be right there. They'd walked in a straight line. How was he supposed to find it?

He took a deep breath and forced himself to scan the area slowly, one small section at a time.

It *had* to be there. But where?

He remembered the blue veins running through the mist. Could he use those to direct his eyes?

Still nothing.

He was too far away to feel the magic of it, though it had pulsed as strong as a heartbeat.

He couldn't feel anything. Or rather, he couldn't feel the portal.

But now, he *could* feel the land, could feel its malignity, how hate emanated from it in soft waves.

The land didn't want anyone there. It would have them all leave now, and quickly. Or die. Spill their blood to water it. It wasn't picky.

Tong Yi now understood why Uncle Bei had described the warzone as uncomfortable. That soft, underlying, continual background radiation of *hate* and *leave now*.

Suddenly, Tong Yi saw the portal. Or felt it. Or saw and felt it, though it wasn't with his regular sight.

It was the one spot that was *different* from the rest of the land in the warzone, the one place that wasn't pushing him away. It appeared darker than the rest of the landscape, strong with its own magic.

Finally, Tong Yi looked back at Uncle Bei. He was watching Tong Yi with a speculative look on his face, as if he'd like to spend some time dissecting him.

"You found it?" Uncle Bei asked Tong Yi.

"I did," Tong Yi assured him.

"Are you certain? It took you a long time," Uncle Bei asked.

"I'm certain," Tong Yi said. He knew exactly where the portal was now.

Uncle Bei pointed at Wan Cho. "You locked into it first. You lead us back."

Wan Cho shrugged and started walking in a direct line to the portal.

Was Uncle Bei afraid that Tong Yi wouldn't be able to find his way back? Or was he testing Wan Cho?

All during the return to the portal, Tong Yi felt Uncle Bei's eyes staring holes into his back. He wasn't sure why.

Tong Yi had passed the test. He'd found the portal. He could find his way back when he came here to deliver a message.

Though if he was being honest, Uncle Bei wasn't the only one worried about Tong Yi being able to do it a second time.

The smell of burnt rice hit Tong Yi when he opened the door to the apartment he shared with his parents.

Was something wrong? He hurried through the living room, quickly scanning for anything out of place as he went. However, the gray couch along the one side was still there, and still needed a new cover, the large, flat-screen TV was still standing opposite it, and the white bookshelves holding some books but mostly knickknacks that constantly needed dusting, were still overly full. The family altar table still stood quietly tucked away in the corner. Tong Yi would have to get a fresh dish of uncooked rice for it soon.

As far as Tong Yi could tell, everything was there. Quan Lo hadn't stolen anything more. Tong Yi also knew that when he finally moved out and had a family of his own, that he'd keep his place much cleaner and less cluttered.

Down the hallway from the living room were stairs leading up to the bedrooms. Just past the stairs the hallway continued, past a small bathroom and leading to the kitchen.

Crash!

What the hell?

Tong Yi burst into the kitchen, then pulled up short.

Of course.

Quan Lo stood in the middle of a disaster area. Pots and pans lay strewn across every counter. Burnt rice still smoldered in Mom's good wok. It looked as though Quan Lo had tried dismantling an avocado then had forgotten to open the garbage can, instead tossing the skin and pit on the floor beside it. Along with burnt noodles and other things Tong Yi couldn't easily identify.

"What are you doing?" Tong Yi asked.

Quan Lo turned from where he was standing at the sink. "I was going to make dinner for everyone!" he exclaimed. He wore the evidence of his attempt, his cream-colored polo shirt smeared with relish, hot sauce, and avocado.

"Bullshit," Tong Yi declared as he stepped closer, reading the failed attempt. The big rice cooker wasn't on the counter—just the small one, the one that made only a single serving. "You were trying to cook something for yourself and were too fucking high to succeed."

Quan Lo gave him a wide grin. "Caught me. Now, won't you help?" he wheedled.

Tong Yi pressed his lips together, willing himself not to explode.

Help you? Sure, I'll help you. Right through the door. Don't come back.

But instead of saying anything, Tong Yi silently picked up the wok full of burnt rice from the stove.

He then nearly dropped the pan. Was the rice *moving*? Was the pan actually full of maggots instead?

He blinked his eyes and looked again. No, it was just normal rice. Burnt to a crisp. On all sides, not just the bottom of it.

Had Quan Lo burnt the rice accidentally? Or on purpose? Had the rice looked like maggots to Quan Lo as well, and had he tried to kill them?

Tong Yi turned toward Quan Lo, but he wasn't paying attention. Instead, he was trying to precisely slice that damned avocado.

"Got to get it just right," Quan Lo told Tong Yi. "So the pieces will mash together."

Tong Yi shook his head as he ran water in the wok. "When are you going to grow the fuck up?" he asked quietly. "Start acting like the eldest son? Take on some responsibility?"

"I have you for that!" Quan Lo announced happily. "So I don't have to."

Tong Yi dropped the wok into the sink with a loud clank. "You're wrong," he said. "Mom and Dad don't treat me like the eldest son. I'll always be the second son to them."

"Sounds like I'm not the one who needs to grow the fuck up," Quan Lo commented.

Tong Yi glared at Quan Lo, who just shrugged at him. "You're making good money," Quan Lo said. "Why don't you get a place on your own?"

"Because I'm not an asshole who just abandons his family," Tong Yi shot back.

"You can't save everybody," Quan Lo said darkly.

"What the fuck does that mean?" Tong Yi asked. "I'm not trying to save anyone. Particularly not you. And besides, Mom and Dad don't need saving."

"That's what you think," Quan Lo said.

What the hell? Oh, right. Quan Lo was high. He wasn't supposed to be making sense.

Tong Yi picked up the wok again, then set it to the side to soak.

"So, little brother," Quan Lo said as he abandoned his avocado and sidled up beside Tong Yi. "Since you are making so much money, surely you can afford to loan your big brother some?" He draped a heavy arm across Tong Yi's shoulders.

Tong Yi pushed Quan Lo away with his hip. "Bug off," he said. "You're not getting another dollar from me."

"Please?" Quan Lo said, wrapping both his arms around Tong Yi's chest and pressing into him like a lover.

"Get off me," Tong Yi said. He got one hand underneath Quan Lo's arm, ready to twist and do damage, while he kept his weight solidly on both feet, ready to push to one side or the other and kick backwards.

Quan Lo just laughed in Tong Yi's ear. His breath smelled like rotten fish.

Tong Yi exploded into action. He twisted Quan Lo's arm as he pushed down, freeing himself. At the same time he stomped on the arch of Quan Lo's foot.

Quan Lo hopped backwards, his face showing total shock. "Ow! Asshole. I was just playing." He stayed on one foot, bringing up the other to massage the arch. "If you'd been wearing boots, you could have broken my foot," he complained.

"Awww," Tong Yi said, flush with victory. "And that would have meant a trip to the hospital and the opportunity to dry out. Want to try your luck again?"

Quan Lo glared at him. "You don't want to do this," he warned.

"What? I don't want *you* to grow the fuck up? I don't want you to stop being an asshole to Mom and Dad? I don't want you to dry out and get a decent job? I don't want you to start being my older brother again?" Tong Yi shouted at him, the words exploding out of him like his movements had earlier.

"You do *not* want to declare war between us," Quan Lo said darkly.

"You know what? Fuck you," Tong Yi said. "You're the one who declared war on us when you decided you'd rather start shooting up than become an adult."

Quan Lo shook his head. "You're the one who chose sides. Not me." He put his weight on his foot gingerly, then turned and left.

"Don't bother coming back!" Tong Yi shouted after him.

That was it. He was just going to change the locks on the doors. Mom and Dad would be angry, but they would understand as well. And the next time Quan Lo came back, high, well, Tong Yi *would* call the police. His parents would just have to understand that it was not healthy for their elder son to return. Despite what the rest of the family would say.

Tong Yi turned back to the mess in the kitchen when he heard the familiar sound of a motorcycle being kicked to life.

He reached down to his pocket, but his brother had taken his keys.

And his wheels.

Again.

Bing Xi ran quietly through Hualien that morning—almost subdued. They were on their way to the sales office. Tong Yi needed to deliver his first message to the warzone, to the famed archer, Houyi, who had shot down the nine other suns when they'd threatened to scorch the earth.

Though it was early, and the sky still held the shadows from the night, droves of scooters accompanied Tong Yi. It felt as though everyone who'd needed to drive someplace that morning was taking the same route as him. He passed an entire family on a larger Vespa, putting along—Mom, Dad, three kids, the dog, and a bag of groceries all carefully piled up. There was a schoolgirl in her uniform sitting sidesaddle behind her boyfriend, her head resting between his shoulders. There were men in suits, who reminded Tong Yi of his dad. Women, also, in fancy business clothes.

It felt ordinary. Normal. The smell of the exhaust. The buzzing sound of so many scooters. The quietness of the streets. Almost like a dream.

If Tong Yi could, he would have spent every morning like this. Learning about the ordinary ways of people, how they traveled, what they did. Though he loved his growing knowledge about the non-humans, he liked learning about his fellow humans as well.

Tong Yi took the long way to the sales office, driving along Hai'an Boulevard, next to the ocean for a ways. Mostly the water was hidden by port offices and piers. But every once in a while he caught a glimpse of it, shining with the new dawn.

Would he make it back? Han Di, when he'd returned, had seemed shaken. He'd taken a day off, then spent the next sitting in the messenger kitchen staring at his phone and not talking, not joking. He wouldn't even rise to the bait when Tong Yi teased him about his stinky eggs.

Wan Cho hadn't said anything, either. Then again, she never did. But she had taken three days off, then come in with her long hair chopped short and styled in a manner that made her look younger and much cuter. She still didn't say much, but she now looked directly at Tong Yi.

It made him uncomfortable, those knowing eyes staring at him.

The sales office sat in the middle of the block. Instead of driving directly to it, Tong Yi followed his instructions, and took the street just north of the office and turned down the lane along the back.

It was a typical lane, barely wide enough for a single American-made car, made more narrow by the number of scooters and planters that residents had placed on the edges of their property. The houses and flats back here looked run down, with paint peeling off the faded green plaster in chunks, the pavement cracked and full of potholes.

About one-third of the way down the block, the lane was cut off by a brick wall. A tall waxy plant with broad green leaves grew along the base of it, and the dead remains of strands of ivy hung from it.

Tong Yi paused. Had he read the instructions wrong? The brick wall was old, solid, and completely blocking his path.

He looked away, then looked back at the wall. No, it wasn't solid. There was an entrance, just to the left of center, camouflaged by the leaves.

He strained to see better. It *was* magical. But the magic was very faint.

Tong Yi didn't get off Bing Xi. He just started walking her forward.

The engine died.

Tong Yi restarted the engine and revved her. She sounded so loud in the quiet alley.

He tried walking the bike forward again.

The engine died a second time.

She obviously didn't want him approaching the entrance slowly.

With a sigh, Tong Yi wheeled the bike around in the tiny lane, barely missing the dingy white scooter with a missing rear tire. When he got to the end of the lane he gunned it.

Bing Xi leaped forward, racing toward the wall.

Here goes nothing.

Tong Yi pushed his helmet down harder on his head and then leaned forward.

Maybe today he'd find out just how good that insurance policy was.

Then he was through the wall. He hadn't felt anything, no cold mist running over him, no shift in awareness. He had been in one place, then suddenly, he was in another.

The neighborhood beyond the wall was also old and quiet, but it was rich. Tall trees lined the lane. Fancy iron gates taller than Tong Yi were set up between them. As Tong Yi drove forward slowly, he saw marble squares nestled into tall grass, leading the way to…somewhere.

Just a few gates down stood a gray, swirling portal on the left. Uncle Bei stood beside it, wearing a charcoal gray suit and gold tie. He still looked human, though his sharp features appeared even sharper now, his nose as pointed as any anime character's, his eyebrows mere lines.

"Do you have the message?" Uncle Bei asked as Tong Yi drove up.

Tong Yi nodded slowly, though he made no move to show the envelope to Uncle Bei. They'd been told often enough to deliver their messages to the recipient and no one else.

Uncle Bei didn't press the matter. "Here," he said, holding out a pocket watch. "You'll need this."

Tong Yi looked at the watch carefully. It had a plain white face with Roman numerals on it, no brand name or date function or anything else. The back of it was gold, with swirling vines and leaves engraved into it. It was set to 11:00.

Was that what time it was here? It had been barely 7 a.m. when Tong Yi had reached the lane.

The pocket watch didn't appear to be magical in the least.

"Your phone—most anything electronic—won't work in the warzone," Uncle Bei explained. "This will be the only way for you to keep track of time. It has only mechanical parts."

Tong Yi hadn't thought about that. He'd figured he'd just set an alarm on his phone, as usual. He carefully placed the watch in his jacket pocket, vowing to get a chain for it.

He couldn't afford to lose it, that was for certain.

"I'll hold the portal for at least an hour," Uncle Bei told him.

Would Uncle Bei hold the portal for longer than an hour? After careful consideration, Tong Yi decided that he would—as long as nothing more pressing came up.

Tong Yi tightened the strap down on his helmet and revved Bing Xi one last time.

"Good luck!" Uncle Bei called.

Tong Yi nodded.

Bing Xi leaped forward.

And they were through.

Tong Yi pulled up on Bing Xi abruptly. The land was still awful, the sky bleeding a peculiar shade of purple, the clouds threatening to drop a deluge of water and wash the lands clean.

However, between Tong Yi and the ridge in the distance now stood an army of men.

No, not men. Not regular men.

Mole men. *Zhi ren.*

Their blind eyes were tainted a yellowish white, like pus. They held their faces up to the air, as if worshipping the sky, while with their claws they tore at each other, skin and fur and blood flying everywhere. They wore dirty black loincloths and sometimes brought an enemy's arm closer to bite, but they didn't wield swords or spears or guns.

Tong Yi hadn't realized that gore had a smell, but it did, like rotten cabbage cooked in rancid oil.

He was glad he'd skipped breakfast.

Though some of the mole men closest to Tong Yi raised their heads, sniffing in his direction, none of them came any closer.

Behind Tong Yi, the portal still burned. Beyond it, more empty land, covered in scrub and burnt grass.

Tong Yi had been told that Houyi, the archer, would be in the command camp, close to the ridge, directly opposite the portal.

Thousands of mole men fought in a giant river of rabid destruction between Tong Yi and the ridge.

How was he supposed to get there and deliver his message?

Tong Yi checked the watch that Uncle Bei had given him. It was just slightly after eleven.

It probably wasn't coincidence that the portal just behind him would disappear at twelve—noon or midnight, it didn't matter.

Though Tong Yi *really* didn't want to be here when there was no light.

Curious, Tong Yi kicked Bing Xi back to life. She started right away, her engine growling quietly. He turned on her headlight. Instead of the blue-tinged halogen light he was expecting, it was tinted with yellow, a much warmer color.

Uncle Bei had said that most electronics didn't work here. Tong Yi pulled out his phone and checked. It was completely dead.

How much of Bing Xi was electronic? And how much of her was magical? She still didn't appear magical, no matter how many times Tong Yi studied her, or for how long.

But now wasn't the time to try to answer those questions. He had a message to deliver.

Or die trying seemed much more real that morning.

Tong Yi picked a direction at random, going right, keeping the army to his left. He had to find an opening. Before his time ran out.

After twelve minutes of reckless driving, going as fast as he could, the army of mole men appeared to be thinning. Instead of a solid mass of fighters, there were merely groups of ten to twenty, broken off from the main group, battling.

Tong Yi wasn't sure how much further he'd have to go to completely clear the army. The terrain under Bing Xi's wheels hadn't been smooth, but she hadn't been trying to "dance" too much with him either—had only tried throwing him off a couple of times.

He decided to cut across, dodge between the screaming combatants.

He hadn't planned on the bodies.

"I'm sorry!" he couldn't help but call out as Bing Xi drove over a fallen mole man's arm.

The pair of them swerved and wove, trying to avoid both the fallen and the fighting. The mole men growled at Tong Yi when he swerved too close, clawing at him before returning to their foe.

Which appeared to be each other. Tong Yi couldn't see any difference between one group and the other. No colors divided the combatants into sides.

The last group they drove past took too much interest in them, so Tong Yi couldn't slow down, couldn't take a breath. He had to keep driving, now with the snarling army on his left, the ridge on his right. Large boulders marked the bottom of the hill, yet more obstacles for Tong Yi to swerve around.

However, he was finally rewarded by the sight of brown tents up ahead of him. Above the pavilions hung flags, something red and green, though Tong Yi couldn't see the design as no wind filled them or lifted them up.

The entire camp seemed out of place, though the brown canvas blended into the dry landscape and burnt weeds.

It took Tong Yi a moment to recognize that the tents didn't belong to this land, not like the rocks and the mole men. They didn't pulse at him with malevolence, telling him to leave.

They were a welcome refuge.

No wonder he felt as though they didn't belong here.

Two guards stood at the gate. Tong Yi turned off Bing Xi and backed her up onto her kickstand, though the metal points sank deep into the soft dirt. He stomped his feet when he got off the bike, realizing just how badly his legs were shaking.

The ride to the tents had been…harrowing. In some ways, worse than having a man-eating monster bird attacking him.

Tong Yi understood now why the other messengers had been so changed after they'd done deliveries to the warzone.

He handed his messenger badge to the guard on the right, while the guard on the left side of the gate continued to scan the horizon.

The guard wore ancient armor, the kind Tong Yi had only seen in history books, with dull gray metal bands tied together with colorful red and green ribbons. His helmet had black peaked wings along either side. He wore a long sword strapped to his back, along with smaller swords and knives tucked into his wide brown belt. Instead of traditional sandals, he wore modern black leather boots, scuffed and worn, workman boots, probably with steel toes.

His face was as round as a full moon, with a matching large nose and flabby lips. He was missing his two front teeth and a large scar ran across the bottom of his chin, making his face seem even wider.

"So who are you here to see today?" the guard asked as he continued looking at Tong Yi's badge. His voice was much higher pitched than Tong Yi had been expecting.

"Houyi," Tong Yi replied.

"Ah," the guard said, finally looking up. He studied Tong Yi for another moment before he handed back Tong Yi's badge.

The plastic was extra warm. Tong Yi was expecting that—the guard had some kind of power, and had scanned his badge not for the characters printed on it, but for the magic encoded within it.

The second guard spoke up. "Houyi's in the general's tent," he said.

"The general's tent?" Tong Yi asked. Though there weren't many tents, he didn't have time to get lost. He barely had time to deliver his message and get back.

The first guard told him, "Large one in the middle. With the red door."

"Thank you," Tong Yi said. He turned to go get Bing Xi.

"You can leave her there," the first guard said. "We'll look after her."

"No harm will come to her," the second guard assured him.

Tong Yi debated for a moment. He could get through the camp faster on foot. "Thank you," he said as he rushed through the gate.

Most of the men inside the compound were dressed similarly to the guards, in ancient armor, with swords and helmets. A few wore traditional sandals, though most had on modern boots.

None had any emblem or flag on their chest, which Tong Yi found strange. Shouldn't they be wearing the symbol of their leader? But most of them did have on red and green, which he guessed were the troop's colors.

The big tent was easy to find. It appeared to be in the center of all the other tents. Tong Yi made himself race toward it, though a part of him just wanted to relax and take it easy. He suspected that was part of the magic of the compound, to get the soldiers to rest.

The guards standing on either side of the red flap covering the door of the tent barely glanced at Tong Yi's badge before drawing the flap to one side.

Inside the tent, light glowed in all the corners, making it brighter inside than it had been outside. Plain rugs of brown and green covered the dirt floor. An old fashioned writing desk sat in the corner, while a large table covered with maps took up much of the middle of the room.

A tall woman stood on the far side of the table. She had the flawless skin and perfect beauty of a goddess. Her face was heart shaped, with a broad, intelligent brow, clear eyes, the cutest nose, and a rosebud mouth. Her long black hair hung straight down, almost to her thighs, like a silk curtain.

She wore similar armor to the guards, except that the iron bands were made from a bright, silver metal instead of dull and gray. She had the same red and green ribbons as everyone else, intertwined with ribbons of the purest light blue, like a summer sky.

Tong Yi pulled up short. "Excuse me," he said, looking around.

She appeared to be the only person in the tent. There weren't any additional curtains partitioning off other areas, at least none that Tong Yi could see.

"Can I help you?" she asked. She only gave him a small smile, but he could tell she was laughing at him.

"I have a message for Houyi," Tong Yi said.

The woman held out her hand expectantly.

"I must give it to Houyi directly," Tong Yi explained.

"I *am* Houyi," the woman said. Her amusement filled the room.

"But Houyi is a famous archer!" Tong Yi blurted out. "He was born with his left arm longer than his right, so he could shoot the greatest bow."

The woman held up her arms.

The left was at least a hand's length longer than the right.

"But…" Tong Yi said. He knew she was a magical being. Had she just made one arm appear longer? He did glance at her chest. She had no breasts to speak of, nothing to get in the way of a bow.

"The ancient legends occurred before humans became so ossified," the woman explained. "Before the roles of men and women became so fixed."

Tong Yi still hesitated. Every legend he'd ever read had talked of Houyi as a man. Not as a woman.

The woman before him smiled. "Lieutenant!" she called out.

One of the guards who'd been standing at the door came rushing in. "Sir?"

"Who am I?" she asked, still smiling.

"You are Houyi, the greatest archer to ever live," the man replied stiffly.

"Thank you. That is all," Houyi said.

The man nodded curtly and marched back through the door.

"I apologize," Tong Yi said, reaching into his messenger bag and pulling out the message.

The red envelope warmed between his fingers, another sign that he was in the presence of the correct recipient.

"No need to apologize, young man. What is your name?" Houyi asked.

"Tong Yi," he replied. He held the envelope up above his head, resting in both of his palms, before bringing it down and presenting it to her.

"Thank you for your tenacity," Houyi replied. "I'm glad we have such principled men as you."

Tong Yi bit his lip. He wasn't about to remind the archer that he was merely a messenger, and therefore, completely neutral.

Maybe she didn't realize that they also delivered messages to the other side. Or sides. Tong Yi and the other messengers had never been able to determine exactly who was fighting. Or why.

Houyi read the message with a thoughtful expression on her face. "Give me a moment to compose my reply," she said. She went and knelt smoothly at the writing desk in the corner.

Tong Yi nearly groaned when she started shaving ink from her ink stone. He didn't have time for all this! The portal was going to be closing soon.

And he'd be stuck here forever.

Houyi finished her missive, writing it out with a beautiful, pearl-handled brush. She blew on the paper before folding it and putting it back into the red envelope Tong Yi had delivered the original message in.

Then she wrote a name on the front of the envelope. The characters flared as she wrote them, as if they were being burned into the paper.

"This needs to be delivered to Sun Hou-tse," Houyi told Tong Yi as she handed him the message.

The Monkey King? Tong Yi swallowed. "I must go back to my office first," Tong Yi told her.

"I know. However, it must be your next delivery," she instructed.

"*Huli* Transport will ensure that it's delivered," Tong Yi replied. He wasn't about to guarantee that he would be the one to deliver it. Going to the warzone earned him at least one full day off, maybe two. With pay.

Though both Han Di and Wan Cho had taken off extra time after their first trip, without any repercussions, except that the remaining two had worked extra the entire time.

Houyi didn't look pleased, but she merely nodded.

"It's good to have such professional messengers," she said as Tong Yi packed away her missive. "If you ever get tired of being a delivery boy, I always have need for more soldiers."

"Thank you, sir," Tong Yi said. "I appreciate the offer." He wasn't about to tell her that there was no way in hell that he'd take her up on it.

Delivering to the warzone was bad enough. He really didn't want to live or fight there.

Let alone die there.

"Excuse me," Tong Yi said just before he left. "Is there an easier way through the battle?" He figured if anyone knew, Houyi might.

"You had to drive all the way around it?" Houyi asked. She seemed surprised. She went back to her writing desk and scrawled a few characters across a page. "This will help," she said, handing it to him.

The characters basically translated into "Safe Passage."

"It may or may not stop the *zhi ren* from attacking. But they might not kill you, bearing that," Houyi explained.

"Thank you, sir," Tong Yi said. That wasn't really going to help.

He gave the archer a deep, formal bow, then walked quickly from the tent.

He was running out of time.

Tong Yi discovered that the *Safe Passage* paper was sticky on the back of it. He gingerly applied it around Bing Xi's headlight before he started her up.

Her engine still sounded smooth and quiet, making Tong Yi feel more secure. It might be a horrible land, but he had a friend here.

He swung out, and Bing Xi fishtailed her rear end.

Okay. So he had a friend here whose idea of "fun" was dumping him on his ass. At some point they were going to have to have a really long conversation about that.

At least it kept him on his toes.

He started down along the ridge, going back the way he'd come. He had just under thirty minutes to make it back to the portal. It had taken him twelve to get to the end of the army and twelve to get back to the tents, which happened to be almost directly opposite where the portal had been.

Why couldn't Uncle Bei have set up the portal closer to the camp? Was there a magical reason? That would make sense, actually—Houyi and the others wouldn't want magical portals suddenly appearing in the middle of their "safe" zone.

Bing Xi suddenly swerved, heading toward the army of fighting mole men.

It took Tong Yi a few moments to get her headed in the right direction again, but he'd noticed something.

The mole men closest to them had shifted away when he'd approached, not merely growled at them.

Maybe the *Safe Passage* sticker had some power.

Tong Yi tried again, easing his way toward the battle.

Those nearest shied away.

Maybe he could go directly through. And it wouldn't take as much time.

He slowed to a stop, standing with the bike, examining the field.

This was *not* his idea of fun. Swerving around battling mole men. And their bodies.

Houyi hadn't said the *Safe Passage* would stop them from attacking him.

But maybe it would give him enough of an edge to get through them…

"Here goes nothing!"

The mole men fighting directly in front of Tong Yi appeared too involved with each other to pay any attention to him. Up above, the sky had darkened, the clouds growing thicker. At least they hid the awful sky.

Even through Bing Xi's wheels, the earth of the warzone beat at Tong Yi, wearing him down, wanting him to leave.

He felt like screaming that he was trying to leave—however, he was in the middle of a fucking battle at this point.

Why had he decided to drive through the battlefield? Instead of around?

Oh yeah. That's right. Because his motorcycle thought all the obstacles were *fun*.

Tong Yi drove as slowly as he thought was safe, though Bing Xi would sometimes race her engine and make him go faster.

It was just so damned hard keeping track of everything coming at him so fast. It was worse than any video game, because he wasn't trying to slay the monsters, but avoid them.

And their bodies.

Fortunately, the company leathers that he wore protected him from the few creatures who had managed to claw at him.

Unfortunately, he was probably going to have to buy a whole new suit, given the tears. Plus, he'd never get the stench of the battlefield out of them. Even through his helmet, the stink was unbelievably bad, like fish rotting in a heap of bad melons.

By the time Tong Yi got to the far side of the battlefield, he felt completely wrung out. He slowed down and brought Bing Xi to a standstill, before killing the engine and resting for a moment, gaining his bearings.

He was *not* going to do that again anytime soon.

If he had a strong belief in the gods of his parents, he might have said a thankful prayer. But he was no longer sure who he'd pray to.

Once they'd cleared the battlefield, it was much easier for Tong Yi to pinpoint the location of the portal.

It was still there. He hadn't saved that much time by going through the battlefield instead of around it. He checked the watch—he had maybe ten minutes before it would wink out of existence.

Not like he was planning on sticking around here.

He paused for another moment, looking out over the awful terrain, the still bleeding sky, the mass of mole men rabidly fighting.

He didn't care if war was good for *Huli* Transport. He didn't ever want to come back here.

Just as he was about to start Bing Xi up again and get the *hell* out of there, he heard the whine of another engine.

Wait.

There was only supposed to be one messenger from *Huli* Transport at a time in the warzone. Wasn't there? That was what Ren Wu had implied. And Tong Yi hadn't missed his portal, it was still there, that single point of sanity.

Were there other messengers? Tong Yi and Han Di had speculated about it. Did *Huli* Transport have competition? The non-compete clause in their contracts hinted at such.

It didn't matter. Tong Yi could ask those questions when he got back.

The other motorcycle's engine ran up before the rider changed gears. It had a familiar sound to it, then it caught between second and third gear.

Just like Mei Fuang, his old motorcycle had, when he'd first started riding her, before he'd figured out how to ease between the gears.

That couldn't be Mei Fuang, could it?

The only person he knew who'd be driving her would be his brother.

The other motorcycle settled into its fourth gear, a low, very familiar growl.

Tong Yi hesitated. He had about ten minutes. It wouldn't hurt to take a quick look around, would it?

He started up Bing Xi. Revved her engine in response to the one in the distance. Then he bent over and took off, racing toward the sound.

Since she didn't balk, or instantly direct him toward the portal instead, he figured she agreed with his choice.

Or at least that was what he hoped.

That she wouldn't instead find it "fun" to be stuck here.

Tong Yi was, but wasn't, surprised to see his brother on Mei Fuang, his stolen motorcycle. Quan Lo wore a stained, long-sleeved white shirt under a chest plate. It wasn't like any of the armor Tong Yi had seen so far: instead of being long strips of metal tied together with ribbons, it appeared to be made out of a single piece of metal. The center of the chest plate had a hard, sharp line to it, and the metal was silver and shiny, even in the dim light of the warzone.

Quan Lo wasn't wearing a helmet. His hair hung down, limp and oily. Madness crouched in his eyes, not just the craziness brought on by drugs, but something else, something that Tong Yi had never seen before.

What the hell was Quan Lo doing there? How had he gotten there? He hadn't come through Uncle Bei's portal, had he? Were there other portals to the warzone? Who maintained them?

"Brother!" Quan Lo called out.

"What are you doing here?" Tong Yi asked as he flipped up the visor to his helmet.

"I could ask the same of you," Quan Lo replied. "But I see you have your Dudley Do-Right costume on."

Tong Yi sat up more stiffly on Bing Xi. "I have a job, you know. A reason to be here."

Quan Lo nodded sagely. "You've chosen sides."

"I did *not* choose sides," Tong Yi said firmly. "*Huli* Transport is neutral. *Neutral.* We deliver messages to all sides."

Quan Lo shrugged. "That's also a side, you know."

"Bullshit," Tong Yi said. He glanced at his pocket watch. "While I hate to break up this little family reunion, I have to get going." It had only taken him three minutes to get here. Three minutes to get back, and he'd still have four minutes to spare.

"You're wrong, brother mine," Quan Lo said. "That *is* a side. Law versus chaos."

A chill went down Tong Yi's spine.

A society couldn't live without rules and order.

He'd grown up in a very Confucian home. A small statue of the great scholar sat on the family altar table, next to the statues of Xi Wang-mu and Weng Chang.

Quan Lo had grown up in the same home. But he'd decided to take a different path. He'd chosen the side of chaos, if that was a side in this war.

"I see," Tong Yi said.

He couldn't save his brother. Not until he'd made a different choice. It wasn't just the drugs. His brother had turned into a foreigner, an alien in their very midst.

An enemy.

"Goodbye, my brother," Tong Yi said formally.

"So you've decided to go to war against me," Quan Lo said. "Not smart, little brother."

Tong Yi flipped down the visor of his helmet. He was done talking. He'd never get through to Quan Lo.

And he had to get back to the portal on time.

Quan Lo lifted his helmet off the back of his bike. It wasn't a normal motorcycle helmet. It was white with shredded white wings sticking straight up from the sides. The front was like an ancient war helm, with a metal grill instead of a visor. Quan Lo fitted a pair of dark, wraparound sunglasses over his eyes.

He looked like a demon. Who the hell had given him his armor?

Tong Yi started Bing Xi up and curved to his right, going back to the portal.

Suddenly, Quan Lo was there, cutting him off.

"Asshole," Tong Yi muttered, swerving.

Quan Lo wasn't deterred. He turned and made another run at Tong Yi.

Was Quan Lo trying to run Tong Yi over?

Of course he was. He'd decided that they were on different sides. He'd decided to become the enemy.

At least he didn't have a damned pike or something. That would be all that Tong Yi needed.

Tong Yi seriously didn't have time for this. Uncle Bei wouldn't hold the portal for more than an hour. He wouldn't hold it for any less than an hour either—he, too, was on the side of law.

Bing Xi swerved around Mei Fuang. The other bike growled at them.

Had Mei Fuang always been magical? Though Tong Yi hadn't seen anything magical about her, he'd suspected she was.

Had she always been corrupted, though? Or had that been Quan Lo's doing?

It didn't matter. Tong Yi would have to ask Han Di about it later, or maybe he'd go pay another visit to Monkey Man himself.

In the meanwhile, he had a madman on a motorcycle that was as fast as Bing Xi, who'd declared war on him.

Tong Yi continued to move the fight with Quan Lo closer to the portal. If he could have hightailed it out of there, he would have. However, Mei Fuang proved to be a worthy opponent. She growled and swerved at Bing Xi on her own, determined to take the other bike out.

Quan Lo, on the other hand, was just an asshole. He laughed as he drove Tong Yi off his original course, forcing him to tack instead of making a straight run to the portal.

At least Bing Xi seemed to understand the importance of Tong Yi's haste. She didn't try to dump him or fishtail more than necessary. She kept her "dancing" to their fight.

But time was running out.

At least the portal was in sight.

Quan Lo realized that was Tong Yi's destination and seemed more determined than ever to keep him away.

Finally, Tong Yi had had it. He spun Bing Xi through the dirt, putting out a leg to catch him as he cranked his circle tighter.

Then Tong Yi headed straight for Quan Lo.

He wanted to play chicken? Fine. Tong Yi could crash into Mei Fuang, wreck Quan Lo, and run to the portal if necessary. He didn't want to leave Bing Xi behind, but he might not have any choice.

Bing Xi, however, had other ideas. She swerved at the last minute, throwing dirt up at Quan Lo's laughing face.

They passed close enough to touch. Quan Lo shoved at Tong Yi, forcing him to wobble and turn further away from the portal.

He wasn't going to make it.

Tong Yi turned and raced toward the portal again.

Again, Quan Lo got in his way, thwarting him from getting closer.

Tong Yi didn't think he'd get any sympathy if he got off his bike and ran. Quan Lo seemed determined to do him harm.

What had happened to his brother? Had it just been the drugs? Or had those been a gateway to something else?

Had he really joined the side of chaos? It almost made sense, as a rebellion.

Quan Lo really did need to grow the fuck up.

But neither of them were likely to see their next birthday at this rate.

Tong Yi made another run toward the portal.

This time, he got past Quan Lo.

Finally! Tong Yi pushed Bing Xi as fast as she would go, racing toward the portal.

Quan Lo appeared beside him. He shoved Tong Yi again, making him swerve, but not driving him off course.

They only had a few more feet to go.

Tong Yi bent forward, over Bing Xi's gas can. He vowed he'd take even better care of her than he had.

Quan Lo suddenly shoved at him again. How had he gotten onto the other side? Mei Fuang wasn't really faster than Bing Xi, was she? Or did the other motorcycle "belong" here more than Bing Xi? Had Mei Fuang also chosen the side of chaos?

Tong Yi straightened out his bike and turned back toward the portal.

Too late.

The portal started shrinking, the magic leaching out of it. It was half the size of a door now.

"Stop!" Tong Yi screamed. He could still make it through if he stayed bent over Bing Xi.

The portal winked out of existence.

Tong Yi drove desperately toward where the portal had been. Maybe there was still some residue of magic left there. Maybe it would sense him if he approached. Come back to get him.

Quan Lo shoved at him again, driving him further away.

"Damn you!" Tong Yi shouted at Quan Lo.

Quan Lo just laughed. "Next time!" he called. He turned Mei Fuang and drove straight at the army of mole men still fighting. He entered the fray, driving over any and all who turned on him, still laughing, striking out at the beasts.

What the hell was his brother doing there? Why was he in the warzone? Had he been sent to stop Tong Yi from getting back? Was he part of some opposing force? Was chaos really that organized?

Had Mei Fuang also chosen a side? Quan Lo over Tong Yi? Or was it Mei Fuang's jealousy of Bing Xi that had changed her? Corrupted her?

Tong Yi drove slowly to the site where the portal had been. Nothing remained. No magic. No light.

No hope.

Would the next portal open up right here? Tong Yi turned off Bing Xi, backed her up onto her kickstand, then got off, stomping his boots.

What was he going to do? He doubted that Uncle Bei would send someone to look for Tong Yi. They wouldn't open up another portal until there needed to be another message delivered.

He could wait here. At least for a little while. Before the land turned him crazy. It pulsed at him more strongly, now that he was touching it with his own feet, not shielded by Bing Xi's tires.

He didn't belong here. No one did. Not even Quan Lo, though he acted as though he did.

Should he go back to Houyi's camp? She would welcome him as a fighter. However, she wouldn't help him leave.

All Tong Yi wanted to do was go home.

Suddenly, the ground under Tong Yi's boots trembled.

Earthquake?

He looked around, trying to see what was causing the trembling.

The mole men were on the move. They'd stopped fighting each other. The entire mass of combatants now raced to Tong Yi's left.

It certainly would be easier to get to Houyi's camp if the armies had moved on.

There appeared to be more mole men than Tong Yi had first encountered. The river of racing figures went on and on. They trampled their dead, their claws digging up the hard-packed ground.

Eventually, though, the last of them raced past Tong Yi.

He stood back up and looked out over the empty stretch of land.

Of course, nothing stood between Tong Yi and the far ridge.

Houyi's camp had moved as well.

The day dragged on. Tong Yi felt more and more antsy. The land pulsed strongly at him, until he felt like it drenched him with hate. The clouds overhead continued to threaten—any time now, they were going to open into a complete deluge.

No one was coming for him. Except possibly Quan Lo, but he would only come back to fight Tong Yi again. Possibly kill him.

Tong Yi was going to have to get out of here himself.

Uncle Bei had said that they could leave through the badlands.

Given how the warzone felt, Tong Yi wasn't certain he wanted to drive through land that was going to make him feel worse.

He had no choice.

But where the hell were the badlands?

Tong Yi stood up and closed his eyes, trying to feel his way there.

Everything felt bad, awful, hateful.

Was there any direction that felt worse?

After turning in a complete circle twice, Tong Yi opened his eyes.

There. Just to the left of where the archer's camp had been. A slight cleft was apparent in the ridge. Was it a pass to somewhere else?

With a sigh, Tong Yi got back on Bing Xi. She started up right away, her growl a comforting sound.

Time to leave, whether he had a portal or not.

Going across the expance of land where the mole men had been fighting was easier this time. The passing army had trampled most of the bodies into the ground.

Sometimes, though, Bing Xi's wheels spun on the blood, or Tong Yi bumped over an arm or a leg.

They finally reached the far side. No friendly magic remained in the place where the archer's camp had been.

The hate from the warzone was now stronger where the camp had been. Was it rebelling against the neutral zone the tents had created? Surging to fill that void?

Bing Xi climbed around the boulders of the ridge easily enough. The grass here was tougher, longer, causing her tires to skid now and again.

Tong Yi directed them toward that opening in the ridge, where the land felt worse.

They tacked back and forth across the ridge as it grew steeper. Tong Yi looked back once they'd gained some altitude.

Was there another way out? If he went the opposite direction?

However, it appeared as though the planes of the warzone went on forever. There was no escape that way, not unless he drove off the very edge of the earth.

No matter how badly Tong Yi wanted to escape, he didn't want to die.

As they neared the crest of the pass, the boulders grew more massive, going from the size of his dad's Vespa to the size of a car, then bigger, maybe the size of a bus.

Still, Tong Yi found a path through the rocks. Bing Xi didn't like going so slowly, but Tong Yi didn't have a choice. He sometimes had to back up and try another trail when the boulders completely blocked him.

Finally, though, he couldn't find a path.

On his own, he could squeeze his way through the slit of an opening between two house-sized boulders.

He couldn't squeeze Bing Xi through as well. Her handlebars made her too wide.

He tracked back again and again, but he couldn't find another path.

This appeared to be the only way up.

And he was going to have to make it out alone.

"I'm sorry," Tong Yi whispered to Bing Xi as he removed the keys and her saddlebags. "I will come back to get you. I swear." He laid his head down on her gas can, his arms wrapped around her.

Tong Yi wasn't going to cry. The dust made his eyes water, though. He squeezed them shut, then stood back up, palming away the water from his eyes.

Though he felt stupid doing it, Tong Yi placed a kiss on the top of Bing Xi's headlight.

"I will come back and get you," he promised again.

Then Tong Yi shouldered his bags and started back up the trail. He wasn't looking forward to the badlands without the comforting growl of Bing Xi, her companionship, the way she shielded him.

He'd only taken a few steps when he heard a strange sound from behind him.

Was that a horse's neigh?

Tong Yi turned back around.

Instead of Bing Xi, the motorcycle, Bi Qi, the horse, stood there. She was tall—Tong Yi's head barely cleared her shoulders. Her hair was all black, with bright red ribbons tied into her mane and tail.

She shook her head at him and neighed again.

Tong Yi took a cautious step toward her. "Of course! You can get out of here on your own. But I would have come back for you. I swear."

Bi Qi merely shook her head again and bent down, lowering herself.

It took Tong Yi a few moments to figure out what she wanted.

"Do you want me to ride you? Are you granting me that honor?" he asked, breathlessly.

Tong Yi had the impression of Bi Qi rolling her eyes at him.

She lowered herself a bit more.

"Thank you," Tong Yi said, bowing low to her. He stepped onto a nearby rock, then swung a leg up and over her back.

Bi Qi nodded, then turned, going back down the trail.

Had Tong Yi missed the actual pass? Was Bi Qi going to show him a different way?

Then she turned. Tong Yi felt her muscles tense under his legs.

Oh shit.

She was going to make a run at the boulders. Maybe even jump over them.

Tong Yi bent over and held on for dear life.

The beauty of the badlands haunted Tong Yi. It was an endless sea of gray rocks, sometimes tall and wind-blasted into strange shapes. Nothing lived there. No moss or grass or trees. Not even insects. Death pulsed at him from horizon to horizon.

It also mesmerized him, more than he wanted to admit. The starkness sang to a deep part of his soul.

He would have to get Uncle Bei to tell him more about this place. Learn all that he could.

He was glad he rode Bi Qi. That she knew where to go.

Because if he was honest with himself, he might have been tempted to stop. To touch the land. And that probably would have been deadly.

Tong Yi's thighs ached. He felt sore in places he didn't know could be so painful. He wasn't certain he'd be able to walk once they reached civilization.

How long had he been riding? He wasn't certain. The watch Uncle Bei had given him had stopped at the border. How many days had passed? His throat was as parched as the ground under Bi Qi's hooves.

Finally, a dark cloud appeared on the horizon. Bi Qi had been steadily walking; now, she picked up her head and began to trot.

Tong Yi bounced on Bi Qi's back, trying to hold on with his sore legs. God, he missed her as a motorcycle. At least her ride was a lot smoother then.

The dark cloud spread across the horizon, blocking out everything behind it.

Was that another portal? Tong Yi wasn't sure. Lightning sparked suddenly, traversing the blackness.

It wasn't natural, not as if anything here was.

Bi Qi changed from a trot to a gallop. Her stride lengthened.

The smell of ozone blew from the cloud, cold and acrid.

Tong Yi bent over again, clasping his hands together under Bi Qi's neck. Her muscles worked under his legs, tirelessly.

How was he going to thank her properly when they finally got to the other side?

They plunged into the darkness. Tong Yi couldn't see a thing. He tried to take a deep breath but his lungs had frozen. The sound of screaming reached his ears—was that Bi Qi? He added his own voiceless screams, trying to encourage her, to loan her what strength he had.

Tong Yi felt Bi Qi starting to transform under his legs. His thighs no longer pressed so far apart. His feet suddenly had something to rest on. He unclasped his hands, letting them float back up, naturally finding Bing Xi's handlebars.

Suddenly, they shot through the darkness. Tong Yi found that they were airborne, Bing Xi's engine racing, with the ocean to their right and sand beneath them.

Tong Yi leaned forward again, bringing Bing Xi down as carefully as he could, keeping her wheels perfectly aligned.

They bounced off the sand, then reconnected, still going full tilt.

Tong Yi threw back his head and howled with delight when he realized they weren't too far from the sales office of *Huli* Transport, just down the beach from downtown Hualien. It was late afternoon, though what day, he wasn't sure.

He'd made it.

"Thank you, Bing Xi," Tong Yi said. "Thank you. Thank you. Thank you."

The bike swerved and fishtailed.

"We will go dancing again soon. I promise," Tong Yi said.

And he meant it.

Tong Yi sat in Ren Wu's office. The air conditioner in the window appeared to be working overtime given how chilly the room felt. Tong Yi was exhausted, body and soul. Ren Wu had taken one look at him, opened up a desk drawer, pulled out an unmarked tube and handed it to Tong Yi.

"What's this for?" Tong Yi asked.

"Your legs. Use it when you get home tonight," Ren Wu told him.

"Thanks," Tong Yi said.

He handed over his message from Houyi.

Ren Wu sniffed it, then put it to one side of his still overcrowded desk.

"Why did you miss the portal?" Ren Wu asked.

Tong Yi sighed. He wasn't certain how much he should tell Ren Wu. It was a family matter.

A chill ran down his spine.

Damn it. Now he sounded like his parents.

He suddenly understood why they'd never wanted to turn Quan Lo in to the police.

Still, Tong Yi had to say something. "Someone delayed me," he said eventually.

"Who?" Ren Wu asked.

Tong Yi pressed his lips together.

"Someone you know," Ren Wu guessed.

Tong Yi nodded, guilt washing over him. Maybe he should tell Ren Wu. However, his parents would consider him a bad son if he did.

"*Huli* Transport is *neutral* in this war. You cannot choose a side," Ren Wu warned.

"I know," Tong Yi said. Was choosing law a side? He didn't think Ren Wu thought in those terms.

Then again, no one really understood who was fighting whom.

Ren Wu just stared at Tong Yi.

"I haven't chosen a side. I will continue to deliver messages impartially," Tong Yi promised.

After several long moments, Ren Wu finally nodded. "Just see that you do," he said. "Now, get out of here. Take the next three days off. You've earned it."

"Thank you," Tong Yi said, standing wearily.

Just as he was leaving, Ren Wu added, "Girls like flowers, you know."

"Excuse me?" Tong Yi said, turning back.

"Girls. Like Bing Xi. Sometimes they like it when you bring them flowers," Ren Wu explained.

"I see," Tong Yi said, though he didn't. Not at all.

He wasn't dating Bing Xi, was he? But he did need to show his appreciation for her. He vowed to find her the prettiest bouquet he could when he next came into the office. Then maybe set it up in the stall for her? Or put it in her saddlebags? Or somehow strap a rose to her headlight?

He wasn't thinking straight. He'd have to figure it out later.

For now, he was going to catch a cab home and sleep for two days straight.

Then, and only then, would he think about how he'd just lied to his boss.

He had chosen a side. As had *Huli* Transport.

They were both on the side of law.

And against all those who weren't.

The Sweet Shop

Tong Yi carefully slid the golden sedan into the only visitor's parking place open in front of the sales office for *Huli* Transport, between two other fancy black sedans. It was his first time actually transporting a client. Normally, he carried messages, important papers, and packages from one location to the next. He much preferred driving the motorcycle Bing Xi over the sedate sedan.

Even if the seats were white leather and felt as smooth as silk against his rough palms. And the dashboard had a heads-up display that was as futuristic as the fighter-pilot video games that he liked. The engine itself purred with hidden power. Air conditioning was also a plus, particularly during the summer monsoons in Taiwan, when the hot pavement literally steamed after a cool rain.

Okay, so maybe the sedan was a sweet ride. Tong Yi still resented having to wear a monkey suit—white shirt with a skinny black tie, black suit with a tiny brown fox on the breast pocket, black socks and polished shoes. It made him feel stiff and unnatural. He was used to his bike leathers, or jeans, or shorts, even, given the recent temperatures.

Tong Yi blasted the air conditioning while he waited in the car. The instructions had been very specific about him staying in the car, not waiting outside, and keeping the car running. His client would need to go as soon as he arrived.

Of course, no one showed up for at least ten minutes after Tong Yi had parked. He wasn't surprised. Taiwan didn't have "island time" as foreigners sometimes called it. There were occasions where time meant something, like the start of a class. However, arriving ten to fifteen minutes after a scheduled appointment wasn't generally considered late.

Tong Yi knew better than to get out his phone and start playing a game. As soon as he did that and was in a spot where he couldn't save his score, the client would arrive. His luck was usually just that awesome.

Plus, he wanted to look good. He wasn't on probation, not exactly, with *Huli* Transport. But all the good delivery assignments kept being given out to the other two messengers. Ren Wu, his boss, hadn't sent Tong Yi back to the warzone either.

Not that Tong Yi really wanted to go back. The battlegrounds had been deliberately created so that no one wanted to stay there. That land *hated*, and hated a lot.

Was this non-probation probation because Tong Yi hadn't made a definitive decision yet about his brother, Quan Lo, as well as Tong Yi's own position in the war? He thought he knew what side he was on, even if *Huli* Transport was officially neutral.

But it made Tong Yi's head hurt just thinking about it.

So instead, Tong Yi waited, watching the traffic passing behind him through his rearview mirror. The street wasn't congested with traffic, just a constant stream of scooters. It was mid-afternoon. A clutch of teenagers buzzed along, students, all wearing identical school blazers with white shirts and gray pants, probably going home from classes. There were the usual families—Mom, three kids, the dog, and half-a-dozen bags of groceries all loaded onto an ancient green Vespa. Plus secretaries in short skirts running errands for their bosses.

When the backdoor opened, Tong Yi started. He hadn't seen anyone crossing behind him, or come up from the front.

He didn't turn around, but caught his passenger's eye in the mirror.

It was Uncle Bei. The wizard—spell caster—shark lawyer—looked the same as the first time Tong Yi had met him: a short, skinny Chinese man with a sharp nose. He wore an expensive gray suit with a very subtle white pinstripe, along with a crisp white shirt and a yellow-and-brown striped tie, *Huli* Transport official colors. He wore the same cufflinks he always did, gold with red, faceted, diamond-shaped jewels that were powerful enough that Tong Yi could feel the magic in them without concentrating on them.

Was this a test? Tong Yi had the impression that Uncle Bei had never trusted Tong Yi, not after the first trip to the battleground.

"Where to, sir?" Tong Yi asked. Even though Uncle Bei worked at *Huli* Transport, Tong Yi decided to treat Uncle Bei as a most important client and not as another employee.

Uncle Bei gave Tong Yi his very shark-like smile, showing all his dazzling white teeth.

"*Si si si si Ba Guan jie,*" Uncle Bei said with great satisfaction.

Tong Yi couldn't help his shiver. *Si*, the number four, was always considered unlucky. Though it had a different tone, it had the same phoneme as the word for *death*. Buildings frequently didn't have a fourth floor. If a baby was born on the fourth, his parents generally celebrated his birthday on the third or fifth.

What kind of business would keep such an address? Either they considered themselves very lucky and didn't care about their address, or they courted such bad luck.

Plus, for Uncle Bei to say the address that way, that series of fours, instead of forty or four hundred…Was Uncle Bei deliberately trying to make Tong Yi uncomfortable?

Ba Guan Street was just north of the downtown area. It had many business offices along it, with only a few retail shops. Tong Yi also knew of a *Ba Guan* Lane, a *Ba Guan* Court, and a *Ba Guan* Alley. Tong Yi paused, thinking about the best way to get there.

Tong Yi realized that Uncle Bei was waiting for Tong Yi to respond. "Right away, sir," Tong Yi said. He carefully checked all his mirrors, and even half turned to look behind him, to make sure that the way was clear before he backed up.

He didn't want to mess up anything today. Not with Uncle Bei.

Was this a test of some sort? A way for Tong Yi to prove his worth? So he could be sent back to the warzone, given better assignments again?

Or was this just a normal drive?

Tong Yi eased into traffic. He had better luck than usual, and got to *Ba Guan* Street without incident. He didn't watch Uncle Bei in the rearview mirror, just every once in a while glanced at him.

His passenger wasn't watching the road or where they were going— instead, he kept his head turned to the side, watching the buildings passing by. He looked contemplative. Maybe formulating a new spell.

Or maybe he was calculating all the ways he could kill someone. Tong Yi wasn't sure.

"Turn left here," Uncle Bei suddenly instructed Tong Yi. "Then turn right into the parking lot behind the building."

Tong Yi turned smoothly. A tall electronic gate barred the entrance to the parking lot, made of solid black-painted metal with strong, gray-iron bars running up and down.

The door started sliding open silently as the sedan got near.

Was there a sensor in the car that the gate recognized? Or some kind of spell?

Tong Yi hadn't felt any magic, but that didn't mean there wasn't something there.

He knew that his magical training was far from complete. But when he'd asked about it, Ren Wu had been evasive, and the other two messengers didn't know any more than Tong Yi.

The lot only held two dozen spaces. The few cars already parked there were expensive and modern, the kind that would cost Tong Yi an entire year's worth of salary just for the bribes and licenses to maintain.

After Tong Yi parked the car, he caught Uncle Bei's eye in the mirror again. "Should I keep the car running and wait for you, sir?" he asked.

Uncle Bei looked forward again. It was fascinating how his eyes changed, going from looking long distance to suddenly here, now, with a laser focus on Tong Yi.

Tong Yi gulped but didn't look away.

"I think you should come with me," Uncle Bei purred.

"Certainly, sir," Tong Yi said. He stopped the car and hopped out, coming around to the side to open Uncle Bei's door for him.

As Uncle Bei stood, he threw his head back and sniffed the air. He appeared to be searching for something.

Tong Yi kept his own head down, but he sniffed as well. He didn't smell anything beyond the usual pollution, soy and garlic from the noodle shop up the street, and very subtly, under everything else, the constant scent of the nearby ocean.

When Tong Yi looked back up, Uncle Bei was looking at him. "It'll do," he said.

What would do?

Tong Yi closed the door after Uncle Bei, then pressed his thumb on the lock under the door handle. A light flared for a moment, seeming to coat the car, then disappeared.

Any untrained human who'd happened to be looking at the car at just the right second still wouldn't have seen anything.

Someone with training would realize that Tong Yi had just enabled the car's magical protections. Any thief would be instantly paralyzed the moment he touched the car.

Tong Yi hurried across the parking lot after Uncle Bei. They left through another tall gate that opened when Uncle Bei waved his hand in front of it.

So, the lot was magically protected. Tong Yi still was glad he'd locked the car. Just in case.

Tong Yi wasn't a bodyguard, despite the martial arts training he'd had, first as part of his messenger training, then on his own, keeping up his time at the gym. He still kept a careful eye out as they walked down the sidewalk to the corner and turned up *Ba Guan* Street, a much busier street, watching the cars and scooters pass, the few pedestrians.

Golden Roman numerals above the glass doors were the only indication they were in the right place. The doors themselves were made out of silver metal, with dark and slightly mirrored glass in the center, so Tong Yi couldn't see inside. The handles were long and also made out of silver metal, polished to a strong gleam.

Tong Yi reached forward to open the door for Uncle Bei.

"Wait," Uncle Bei said, stopping Tong Yi before he touched the door.

"Sir?" Tong Yi asked, straightening up. What had he missed?

"What do you see?" Uncle Bei asked, indicating the door.

Tong Yi asked, "Is this the wrong door?"

At Uncle Bei's sigh, Tong Yi continued. "I see the building numbers, right there." He pointed at the golden numbers above the door. He didn't repeat the number himself. All those fours.

For a moment, the numbers wavered, as if a sudden wash of water had poured over them.

Was Tong Yi wrong?

Then the numbers solidified, gleaming with a light that Tong Yi instantly recognized as magical.

Huh. What had just happened?

"You know, the girl…" Uncle Bei started.

"Wen Cho?" Tong Yi supplied. The only female messenger for the Hualien City branch of *Huli* Transport.

"Her. She couldn't find the door, even after walking up and down the street half a dozen times. Han Di found it, but again, he had to search."

Tong Yi shifted from one foot to the other, uncomfortable under Uncle Bei's scrutiny.

"Sir?" Tong Yi finally asked after the silence had dragged on for more than a minute.

"Your boss, Ren Wu, was wrong about you," Uncle Bei said conversationally.

Had Ren Wu told Uncle Bei that Tong Yi wouldn't be able to find the door? That he didn't have what it took?

Uncle Bei nodded to himself, then gestured toward the door.

Tong Yi took a deep breath and grasped the handle. The metal burned cold against his palm.

He didn't know what was behind this door, and now, he really wasn't sure he wanted to find out.

A tinkling bell went off as Tong Yi opened the door to the shop for Uncle Bei. Then he followed the lawyer inside.

Sound assaulted Tong Yi first. J-pop blasted from speakers in the ceiling. Electronic riffs scaling up and down—the siren's trill of a video game—competed with the bouncy beat. The familiar sounds of pachinko underlay everything else—the drop of metal balls, followed by the higher-pitched pings of the balls hitting metal pins as they made their way to the bottom of the game board.

The air smelled of milk chocolate, light and sweet, his favorite type of chocolate. Tong Yi also smelled the tartness of sweet-and-sour balls, the kind he'd gotten as a kid from the corner store just down the street from his parents' apartment. Mixed in with that was the darker scent of black licorice, and the pure sweetness of rock candy, sweets his dad and mom enjoyed.

Wooden cases lined the walls and created a maze in the center of the room, each just a little over waist height. The shop was about twice as big as the break room at *Huli* Transport. It gave Tong Yi a closed-in feeling, though he thought he could see everything. The floor under his feet felt cold and slick, even through his fancy shoes. It was made of some type of stone that he'd bet never warmed, even in the heat of summer.

Clear plastic covers went over the top of each individual case. Some were open, showing their curved sides, almost like an old fashioned roll-top desk.

Paper signs about the size of Tong Yi's palm, made out of neon yellow, pink, and orange were stuck to some of the cases, proclaiming "Best Quality!" "Limited Supply!" "Buy Now!"

The walls themselves were decorated with posters of the most popular J-pop boy bands, as well as Hello Kitty and anime movie posters.

Tong Yi glanced at Uncle Bei as the magical presence of the shop made itself known. Suddenly, all of Tong Yi's skin itched. The acrid taste of magic coated the back of his tongue. The sweet smells of candy remained, though now tainted with something darker, less innocent.

The hidden contents of the wooden cases pulsed brightly with spells. The jars lining the far wall held a blacker magic, brooding and *aware* in a way that made Tong Yi not want to look too closely. Even the tall plastic columns that contained what looked like different types of brightly-colored hard candy on the wall just to the right of the door were enchanted as well.

"Welcome to The Sweet Shop," Uncle Bei said with a sly grin.

The person who stepped up behind the counter on the left side of the door was not what Tong Yi had been expecting. Then again, he wasn't sure what exactly he was expecting. Not given a magic store that looked as though it had been hit by a Japanese pop-culture bomb.

The guy was probably in his early twenties, only a couple years older than Tong Yi. He had long, shaggy black hair that kept falling over his eyes like he was some kind of rock star. He had a flat nose and thin lips, along with a ready smile. He was Taiwanese, not Japanese.

He also wore cat ears. They weren't real as far as Tong Yi could tell. They were brown fur and stuck up from a black band the guy wore over his head. Of course, he wasn't wearing the band to keep the hair from falling in his face—he kept flinging his head back.

Weird.

His shirt was at least kind of tame, white with wide green stripes running down it, along with a brown embroidered vest that buttoned up to his chin. It made him look more like an old-fashioned proprietor of a pub, than… this place.

"Hey! Welcome!" he said. "Hi, Uncle Bei. Who's your friend?"

Tong Yi blinked and stayed perfectly still, waiting for Uncle Bei to tear this guy a new one.

While the lawyer insisted on being called the same name as a lovable children's character in a local cartoon—a white rabbit—he was anything but cuddly.

Uncle Bei gave a long suffering sigh. "Ge Deng, this is Tong Yi."

"Howdy!" Ge Deng said in English.

"Hello," Tong Yi replied in the same tongue.

"So what can I do for you today?" Ge Deng asked Uncle Bei, beaming, switching over to Mandarin Chinese.

"Client needs a rather complicated protection spell," Uncle Bei said.

"Got a new shipment in just last night," Ge Deng said proudly. "Though you probably already knew that, as *Huli* Transport delivered it. What in particular are you looking for?"

Huli Transport also did regular shipments? Tong Yi had no idea.

Uncle Bei started listing off ingredients. Petrified chicken's feet. Fresh birch wood. Black marbles made from Mount Vesuvius glass. Octagonal amber.

Tong Yi's head spun as he listened. He wouldn't have been able to remember such a list, let alone even recognize half the ingredients.

Then again, he'd felt the same way when he'd first started training with *Huli* Transport and had had to learn the names of all the mythical creatures who were actually real and wouldn't mind eating him for lunch. Like the *huang* and its mate, the *feng*, two giant man-eating birds who'd tried to snack on him in the Takoro Gorge.

There must be books or scrolls of spells that listed the necessary ingredients. Maybe he'd ask one of the other messengers about them. He couldn't imagine Uncle Bei volunteering the information.

More to learn. The prospect both thrilled him and made him tired, though he suspected the latter was just a hangover from being in school and being forced to study things that didn't interest him.

Ge Deng nodded thoughtfully as Uncle Bei finished his long list. "Got most of that," he said. "But the orange Scottie hair. Have you ever thought about changing that to dried bass thread?"

Tong Yi tried to follow the ensuing conversation, but he didn't understand half the terms they used. Bass thread wasn't actually thread, but scales from a bass fish tied together?

Uncle Bei seemed completely preoccupied with talking ingredients with Ge Deng—who didn't register as that magical to Tong Yi, but it might have been because the shopkeeper was in such a magical setting—so Tong Yi slowly walked off, looking at the other cases.

The first held a display. Only half of it was in bright light, a distinct spotlight on the wooden shelf.

In the center of the circle of bright light sat a bowl of what looked like polished blue stones, each about the size of a regular marble. A thin wire net covered the top of the bowl.

The other half of the cabinet had a purplish black light shining on a cage made out of the same wire net, full of black creatures scrabbling at the edges. They were spider-like, but with only six legs and much larger mandibles.

Did these creatures turn to stone in the light? Tong Yi didn't even have a name for them. He'd have to go looking through the reference library at *Huli* Transport. But they were very expensive. The price, per ounce, was more than he made in half a year.

He had the urge to poke the cage with a pencil, but resisted.

Besides, that wasn't really the type of thing that he did.

That was more Quan Lo's, style. Who Tong Yi hadn't seen for a month, not since he'd run into his brother in the warzone.

Tong Yi moved on to the next cabinet. It held what looked like silk bags in every color he could imagine—red, pink, white, blue, green, brown, black, and so on. He'd bet they were for holding charms and amulets. They had their own magic, just a touch. They were all plain, without decorations, but the bright pink sign next to them exclaimed that custom embroidery was just a few Taiwanese dollars extra.

Next was a cabinet filled with spools of ribbons, with magical scissors to cut them. More crystals and rocks and enchanted gems. Powders that Tong Yi didn't look too closely at, not when they appeared to be all different states of bone—charred, ashed, pulverized, slivered, and grated.

When Tong Yi circled around a set of cases all back-to-back, with more large containers holding bright, magical candies, he finally found the pachinko machines. They appeared to be playing themselves, the balls sliding down to the bottom, then rising up back up to the top in a clear plastic tube, gathering into a cluster then releasing again.

Tong Yi found himself mesmerized by the fall of the balls, the sound like tinkling water dropping down a waterfall. It took him three tries to physically turn his body away: his head kept turning back, attracted by the sound.

He started when he realized that a girl now stood beside him. She had long black hair down to her waist, and was dressed similarly to Ge Deng, with a crisp white-and-red striped shirt and a very similar brown vest. Her nose was cute and pert, and her smile, charming.

However, her cat ears were real, growing up from underneath her hair on either side of her head. If Tong Yi had to guess, he'd bet they were lynx ears as they were covered with soft white-and-gray tufted fur.

Her human face appeared Japanese, not Chinese or Taiwanese.

"First time here?" she asked quietly, speaking accented Mandarin.

Tong Yi had to listen hard to understand her. "It is," he replied, nodding.

"You find door on your own?" she asked, tilting her head to one side. Her eyes were mostly normal, a green-gray color with a normal, human pupil. As she examined him, though, they shifted to brighter green, growing more round as well.

"I did," Tong Yi said.

"Interesting," the woman said. "Most are shown. You must be strong magician."

"I'm not," Tong Yi assured her. "Not a magician at all. Just a messenger boy." He swallowed suddenly, the words bitter in his mouth.

Hadn't Quan Lo called him that?

"You more than that," the woman assured him. "I am See-tza." She put her hands together in front of her chest and bowed her head.

Tong Yi repeated the gesture, well aware that most of the other races, the non-humans, preferred not to touch humans. "I am Tong Yi."

"You not training?" See-tza asked. "Not apprentice?"

Tong Yi tried to figure out what she was asking. "I'm not an apprentice magician," he finally said. "I work for *Huli* Transport, delivering messages."

"Ah," See-tza said. "Shame. Many things you could learn. Many things I could teach you." She gave him a wink. "You come back anytime you like. I put your name on door."

"Thank you," Tong Yi said, his back stiffening. He'd been warned about the *Heimao*, how they liked to seduce human men.

Though that was the Chinese myth. Was the Japanese version the same?

And while Han Di would be totally jealous of Tong Yi scoring some, Tong Yi wasn't sure he wanted that sort of encounter.

"I have to go find my client," he said, hastily bowing again.

Her bright giggles filled his ears as he hurriedly took off.

Tong Yi hadn't realized that he could blush so hard that his cheeks burned.

Uncle Bei was almost ready to go by the time Tong Yi returned to his side. When Tong Yi had first entered The Sweet Shop, he'd thought it wasn't that big. But there were long hidden corridors, and aisles that went on forever. It had taken Tong Yi some time to figure out how to find the signs that pointed to the exit.

Ge Deng was still trying to convince Uncle Bei to substitute some of the ingredients for his spell. Though Ge Deng was nothing but courteous, Tong Yi could tell the shopkeeper was frustrated.

Were the ingredients that Uncle Bei insisted on old-fashioned? Or was Ge Deng trying to push more expensive, *hip* things on Uncle Bei?

Tong Yi decided it was probably a little of both.

Ge Deng finally presented the long, hand-written receipt to Uncle Bei, who, of course, barely glanced at it before handing over a black credit card. The card itself held some kind of magical protection, and it seemed to suck in all the light in the room.

Tong Yi bet it was cold to the touch.

Ge Deng delivered the merchant slip to be signed on a tray that held two small candies, in bright, red-and-white striped wrappers.

Tong Yi had no idea what they were, but he took the one Uncle Bei handed to him.

"Good for the soul," Uncle Bei said as he unwrapped what appeared to be a very pale-yellow candy and popped it in his mouth. Then he gestured for Tong Yi to do the same.

Slowly, Tong Yi unwrapped the hard candy. It was a pale green, not pale yellow like Uncle Bei's treat. It smelled faintly of green apple ice cream, more tart than sweet.

With even more hesitancy, Tong Yi put the candy on his tongue, prepared to spit it out immediately if it was nasty or made him feel ill.

The creamy taste surprised him, like caramel coated apples, the kind that tourists bought in the fall at great expense because apples weren't native to Taiwan and had to be imported. Tong Yi closed his mouth and sucked. A second taste came through, something that made his throat tingle and cleared out his sinuses, like a strong ginger candy.

Then came the final taste, that milk chocolate that he'd first smelled when he'd walked into the store, though it tasted like the hot chocolate he'd get at the little shop down the street from his parents'. It was creamier than the caramel, coating his tongue and his throat, disappearing as he swallowed, leaving him wanting more.

"What was that?" Tong Yi asked as he gathered up Uncle Bei's various bags, all brightly striped with pink, red, and white, ready to carry them out to the car.

"Fall," Uncle Bei told him.

Tong Yi nodded. That made perfect sense, despite the fact that Tong Yi had never really lived through a fall, not like what the movies showed, with beautiful leaves and cool, crisp air. Taiwan was a sub-tropical island. It barely had winter or spring—more like summer and monsoon season.

Tong Yi opened the door for Uncle Bei as gracefully as he could (given that his hands were full of bags), then followed him out into the street.

Tong Yi blinked and shook his head when he stepped outside. How long had they spent in the shop? He wouldn't have said more than thirty minutes, max, but the sun had already mostly set and the evening air darkened around them.

Had Tong Yi been caught at the pachinko games for a really long time? Or had he just been wandering aimlessly in the store? Now that he thought about it, despite how small the shop had seemed, it had also held nooks and crannies, side hallways and rows of cabinets that he hadn't noticed when he'd first walked in.

The store had been numbered with four fours, supposedly the most unlucky of all numbers.

Was it really that unlucky?

Or was it just unlucky for some, who wasted hours and days in there, never finding the way out?

Tong Yi dropped Uncle Bei back off at the marketing office of *Huli* Transport, then carefully drove the sedan back to the messaging office. All the motorcycles and other vehicles were already parked in their designated slots, the garage brightly lit.

After Tong Yi parked, he took one of the specially prepared chamois cloths and wiped down the sedan's bumpers and around the rims of her tires. Though she'd been a sweet drive, and he'd really liked how comfortable she was, he was still looking forward to getting back to Bing Xi.

He patted the motorcycle on the seat as he passed, taking a few minutes to make sure that her fenders were gleaming as well. He'd brought her flowers, once, at Ren Wu's suggestion, but he'd felt stupid leaving them there in the garage for her.

If he was going to do that kind of thing, it needed to be more private, when it was just the two of them.

Maybe he'd make sure to get something for her the next time they went out.

Tong Yi went back inside the building, to the locker room, changing out of his monkey suit and into his considerably more comfortable shorts, T-shirt, and sandals.

As Tong Yi was leaving the room, he saw his boss, Ren Wu, in the hallway. The other man had finally started sleeping again—at the start of the war, Tong Yi figured that Ren Wu only slept at the office, and only for a few hours at a time.

But his face was no longer as gaunt as it had been, and the dark circles were finally starting to fade from under his eyes.

Business, however, was still hopping. Tong Yi and the two other messengers rarely had time to hang out together in the break room anymore. They were always on the move.

Tong Yi still wondered from time to time about his boss's heritage. His face was so flat, and his eyes weren't almond shaped. Was Ren Wu actually from the Amis tribe, and not Taiwanese? The Amis tribe were the largest group of natives in Hualien City.

"Glad I caught you," Ren Wu said, nodding at Tong Yi. Then he turned around and went back to his office, indicating over his shoulder that Tong Yi should follow.

Fear stalked down Tong Yi's back as he walked. He wouldn't put it past Uncle Bei to have already written up some kind of report about Tong Yi and how he'd done.

Was Tong Yi about to lose his job? Despite having long message runs and clients who didn't tip (or worse, weren't human and gave him nightmares, like those goblin-y things down by the docks, or the tall reptiles at the north end of the city), he really did like what he did. And it paid well. No matter what his parents might think, it was a very good job for a boy just out of high school who'd finished his mandatory year of military service with no hopes of anything bigger.

Ren Wu's office hadn't changed. It was still as tiny and cramped as ever, barely big enough to hold the long filing cabinet, the desk, and the two visitor chairs. If anything, the room felt even smaller, with even more papers and folders piled high on Ren Wu's desk. The rattling air conditioner worked overtime, pumping in chilled air. Tong Yi expected to see ice forming on the faded yellow walls. The calendars hanging there were almost three years out of date, now.

"How do you feel about your trip this afternoon?" Ren Wu asked, his dark eyes serious, boring into Tong Yi.

Tong Yi shrugged. "I think it went fine," he said. "I found the shop without any help," he added, remembering that Uncle Bei had said that Ren Wu hadn't thought he'd be able to.

Ren Wu nodded. "I knew that could," he said.

Tong Yi blinked. What? Had he misunderstood Uncle Bei?

"I've been…delaying, additional magical training for you," Ren Wu admitted.

"Why?" Tong Yi asked. He'd been right! He wasn't as trained magically as he'd first believed.

For example, was Ren Wu a wizard, like Uncle Bei? There were certainly times when he appeared to be so. However, Tong Yi couldn't detect anything magical about his boss at all. He also didn't have cufflinks like Uncle Bei, or anything else.

Even now, when Ren Wu's eyes had a red tint to them that worried Tong Yi.

"I delayed your training in order to protect you," Ren Wu said. He held up his hand. "Hear me out. Magic has a cost. A great one. It eats at your soul. The great magics, the really tough spells, can dissolve your humanity. Possibly even make you go mad."

Tong Yi sat, blinking. He'd had no idea. No one had ever talked to him about the cost of magic before. Uncle Bei had merely talked of it taking great power.

"You weren't ready yet. You needed time to think, not just to learn about your place in the world, but to make decisions about it as well." Ren Wu cleared his throat. "We are *neutral* in this war. *Huli* Transport. But not everyone has that luxury. I wasn't about to let you get more powerful until you had figured out your place."

"What do you think I've chosen?" Tong Yi asked. Because while he'd thought about it—a lot—he still wasn't one hundred percent certain. Was he on the side of order? Like his parents? Was he really against his one and only brother, who'd clearly chosen chaos? Or was there a way for him to stay neutral through all of it?

Ren Wu gave him a tight smile. "I think you're close to a decision—closer than you were a month ago. But the frog hasn't landed yet."

Tong Yi nodded. His boss was a lot wiser than Tong Yi had first suspected.

"Uncle Bei…" Ren Wu paused, his mouth pressed together as if he'd just tasted something sour. "Uncle Bei wants you to train more. To learn more. He'd push you into the war, if he could."

"But *Huli* Transport is neutral, right?" Tong Yi clarified.

"It is," Ren Wu said. "You would have to quit your job if you joined the fray. Uncle Bei could promise you much greater rewards than I could, however, if you went to work for him as a mercenary. Or in some other, possibly magical, capacity."

Tong Yi shivered. The archer, Houyi, had also tried to recruit Tong Yi. But Tong Yi had no interest in being a soldier, or killing people for money, or even living in the warzone. That place gave him the creeps.

"So I have your next assignment. A message to be delivered. In the warzone," Ren Wu said. He pushed the red envelope across the desk. "You should take Bing Xi home with you tonight. Treat her well. Tomorrow, you need to be in the alley behind the *Huli* Transport sales offices for the portal at 7 a.m."

"I will," Tong Yi said. He picked up the envelope, looking at the designated recipient.

King of the South Gate.

The warzone had gates? As well as kings? People who ruled there, presumably with enough subjects who lived there permanently that a king could rule?

Tong Yi shivered.

This didn't sound like anyone he wanted to meet.

"I will ensure this is delivered," Tong Yi said formally, using the *Huli* Transport ritual that all messengers gave.

Or die trying seemed more and more likely all the time.

Bing Xi seemed glad to see Tong Yi. She purred as he started her up. Had she been jealous of him driving the sedan earlier? She didn't try to dump him, though, as they glided through the streets.

However, when he would have turned right to go back to his parents' apartment, he felt Bing Xi nudge at him, trying to turn the handlebars to the left.

With a sigh, Tong Yi let the bike guide him. It didn't surprise him that they ended up on the beach. The sun was just setting on the other side of the island. The water shone black and cool. Large ships waited off the shore, transport for goods from the east side of the island to the west side. Strong winds blew in the smell of fish and the salt of the water, carrying away the constant scent of pollution.

Tong Yi wasn't sure he was up for "dancing" with Bing Xi—her idea of fun seemed to be trying to dump him and cause him a severe case of road rash. Besides, he was tired, more tired than he should be from spending the day at The Sweet Shop.

But if they were going to the warzone the next day, he wanted to give Bing Xi her head now, to run off any excess energy she had, here, where it was safe, or at least much safer than it was in the warzone.

He revved Bing Xi's engine and took off across the sand. Bing Xi roared beneath him. It felt to him as though she was stretching her long legs, the legs of the huge black horse that was her true form.

The ocean spread out like black glass to Tong Yi's left. To the right ran a highway, and beyond that, the lights of Hualien City. Bing Xi cut through the night air like a knife, racing as if to catch a dream.

Huge rocks made up the end of the beach, boulders larger than Bing Xi. The motorcycle ran up to the very edge of them, as if challenging them. Tong Yi spun her around, sending a spray of sand across the base of the rocks, as if dissing them for being unable to move.

After they'd raced across the sand again, Bing Xi allowed Tong Yi to go back up the long driveway leading from the beach to the city streets. She seemed to have gotten out whatever had been in her system.

When they paused at a streetlight, Tong Yi looked over at the little knick-knacks shop on the corner. It sold everything from metal lunch buckets to painting supplies, electrical wire to yarn, woks to greeting cards.

Just inside the door, Tong Yi spied a tall cooler that held tiny bouquets of fresh flowers.

Should he get Bing Xi flowers? That was what Ren Wu had told him to do.

Tong Yi remembered the red ribbons braided into Bi Qi's mane and tail. He parked the bike and ran into the shop.

In a tiny section at the back, next to all the graduation cards and red envelopes for cash, lay spools of ribbons. He bought red and black ribbons, a meter of each, then spent time wrapping them around Bing Xi's handlebars, intertwined, looking almost like braids. He let the ends dangle, so they'd blow in the wind.

When Bing Xi drove sedately the rest of the way to Tong Yi's parents' house, he assumed he'd done the right thing.

"Noodles are in the fridge," Mom said as Tong Yi came into the kitchen.

"Thanks," Tong Yi said.

Mom and Dad already sat at the table eating. Tong Yi had texted them earlier that he was on a job and wasn't sure when he'd be getting home. They were still in their work clothes, though Dad had taken off his tie and opened his collar, while Mom still wore a nice blouse.

Tong Yi heated up his noodles, chicken, and beansprouts in the microwave, then joined them.

The night closed in around them as the three of them sat comfortably in the little kitchen nook. There was the one light directly above them, as well as the light on over the stove.

"How did your day go?" Dad asked, as always.

Tong Yi shrugged. He still thought the entire afternoon had been some sort of test. And though he might have passed, what Ren Wu said about the cost of magic had left him wondering. "It was fine. Had to transport a client this afternoon, not just messages. Drove one of the fancy sedans."

That was a safe topic for them. Tong Yi could tell his parents all about the car.

He'd never mention the passenger, or where they'd gone. How could he explain The Sweet Shop? Or even magic, in general?

"Did he tip well?" Mom asked.

"Not at all," Tong Yi said sourly. It hadn't even occurred to him to hint that Uncle Bei should have given him a tip.

Well, he'd certainly acquire some hazard pay in the next day or so for going to the warzone. "Tomorrow I have to go to the far side of the island," he added.

Mom looked up from her noodles, worried. "I don't like you having to drive that far," she said. "Particularly on just a motorcycle. Can't you use one of the company cars?"

"I can't," Tong Yi said. "And besides, my bike will get there and back better than a car would." How could a car go through one of the portals? And where would it drive in the warzone? The ground was all rutted. Plus, electronics didn't work in the warzone. And Bing Xi wasn't really electronic, not her true form.

No, Bing Xi would take much better care of him than the sedan.

"Have you heard from your brother?" Dad asked cautiously as he finished his noodles.

Tong Yi shook his head. No one had heard from Quan Lo, not since Tong Yi had seen him in the warzone.

He shivered. If there was a king in the warzone, someone who had subjects, Quan Lo would probably be there. Maybe that was why Quan Lo hadn't returned.

How sane would Quan Lo be if he'd spent the last month in the warzone?

Tong Yi wanted to warn his parents, but he wasn't sure how. "If Quan Lo does show up…" Tong Yi started, then hesitated.

"I'm not just going to turn him over to the police," Mom chided. "And neither should you. He's still your brother."

Tong Yi stiffened. He'd never get anywhere with his parents, never convince them that their eldest son was no good. They were too traditional.

Hell, as the youngest son, he had very little value in their eyes. Despite the fact that he was sensible, reasonable, and had a good job that was chipping away at the debts the eldest son had incurred.

"I'm not going to promise that I won't call the police the moment I see him," Tong Yi said as he stood. He was suddenly no longer hungry. He dumped out the remainder of his noodles in the garbage, then turned back to face his parents.

On the one hand, Tong Yi hadn't wanted to rat on Quan Lo to Ren Wu. Hadn't wanted to admit seeing his brother in the warzone. The problems they had should be kept inside the family. So he understood his parents a bit more, now. Sympathized with their stance about not calling the police.

On the other hand, Quan Lo was a junkie and the family was much better off without him. They all were finally starting to relax now that he'd been gone for a month.

"Have you called the police? Told them that he's missing?" Tong Yi asked, challenging his parents.

Mom looked uncomfortable. So did Dad.

They both knew that their eldest son was trouble. However, they weren't about to admit that. There was too much baggage, too much culture, too much importance placed on the first born for them to let go easily.

Tong Yi wasn't going to push the matter.

"He'll come back. He always does," Dad said, though he sounded uncertain if that would be a good thing or not.

Tong Yi nodded. Quan Lo probably would turn up again, like a bad penny.

And maybe, maybe, Tong Yi would have made a decision about him, and decided for certain if he was with his brother or against him.

When Tong Yi left the apartment the next morning, he found that Bing Xi had changed the ribbons he'd wrapped around her handlebars. The crisscross pattern across the front was tidier, forming cool-looking diamonds between the black and red ribbons. The ends of the ribbons were tied off just before the grips for the handlebars, then braided into short pieces.

Tong Yi breathed a sigh of relief. If she'd kept the ribbons, even braided them, then maybe he'd be able to stay on her good side, and she wouldn't try "dancing" with him so much in the warzone. She had seemed to like them going to the beach the night before, the pair of them racing across the sands.

Tong Yi suddenly snorted. Han Di would totally tease him about dating his motorcycle if Tong Yi told him about it.

Maybe Tong Yi could find a girlfriend someday. That would certainly make his parents happy. Or it would give them one more thing to complain about, which honestly, some days Tong Yi felt was the same thing.

On the way to the sales offices of *Huli* Transport, Tong Yi passed lumbering trucks out delivering noodles, chopsticks, rice, and everything else small shops needed. There were only a few scooters out, businessmen on their way to their offices, and college students probably on the way back home from being out all night.

What would the truck that made deliveries to The Sweet Shop look like? Would it be running now? Or would it have completed its deliveries at midnight?

Tong Yi shook his head. He needed to focus on the here and now and not daydream.

Get to the warzone, deliver his message, and get out again before the portal closed in just an hour's time.

The alley behind the offices still looked as though it was blocked by an ancient, red-brick wall. Tong Yi drove slowly toward it, just to get a better look at it. From the end of the alley, it appeared completely normal, not magic at all.

There. Down along the base of the bricks. He finally saw a tiny thread of magic that ran the length of it, much of it hidden and broken up by dying grass. When Tong Yi leaned over to touch the rough bricks, he didn't feel any magic, not even when he pushed deeply, breathing in the still morning air, trying to catch a scent of *something*.

When he leaned back, the glimmer was still there, but stronger now.

So the wall was magical. Tong Yi couldn't push his way through. But Bing Xi could cross it.

Of course, Bing Xi wanted to ram into the wall at full speed.

With a heavy sigh, Tong Yi drove to the end of the small alley, then turned the great bike and revved her engine.

If she'd been in her native form, Tong Yi would have bet she'd be tossing her head, shaking her ribbons, neighing and snorting.

He let Bing Xi race at a crazy speed directly toward the wall.

It dissolved just as they were about to hit it, fading away like summer mist.

Tong Yi slowed Bing Xi as soon as they were through the wall. The neighborhood beyond the wall looked the same, with tall trees and ornate iron gates leading to quiet courtyards. It felt quiet here, more peaceful than he remembered. What was this place?

Uncle Bei waited for him just a short distance down the concrete lane. He wore a light brown, camel-colored suit that morning with his usual starched white shirt and magic cufflinks. His tie was the darkest black. Tong Yi didn't spend a lot of time looking at it—the dark color made him uncomfortable, as if it was sucking all the light away.

"Glad to see you're on time this morning," Uncle Bei said as Tong Yi pulled up.

Tong Yi bit his tongue. Just because he'd been late getting to the portal when he'd been in the warzone, and had had to make his way back through the badlands, did *not* mean he was not dependable.

Or even generally late.

Uncle Bei sighed when he realized Tong Yi wasn't going to rise to the bait. "Come help," Uncle Bei said, gesturing for Tong Yi to follow him.

Only then did Tong Yi realize that the portal hadn't been set up yet, not like it had been the first time.

He reluctantly turned off Bing Xi's motor, though he had the feeling that she didn't like this one bit either. He kept the keys in the ignition, just in case he needed to take off in a hurry.

Though if it came to that, she would no longer be his bike, as he'd probably be fired as well.

A long, concrete patio ran between two lines of trees, to the left. The gray bricks were settled perfectly against each other, forming a solid floor. Uncle Bei had drawn the character *men*, meaning gate, in bright red chalk, in the center of the patio. The character was about the size of Bing Xi. Other characters, some modern, some much older, circled the center character, each of them about the size of Tong Yi's hand.

If he could have, Tong Yi would have taken a picture of the characters with his phone. It was probably an incantation.

Maybe one that he could learn someday.

If he had the power. That was what Uncle Bei had told him, the first time Tong Yi had met the lawyer: it wasn't skill or ability, but *power* that held a portal like this open.

"Here," Uncle Bei said, handing Tong Yi a gray felt bag, about the size of his head.

Tong Yi took it automatically, though the magic in it made his fingers tingle. It was filled with some sort of powder, something that slid easily.

"Sprinkle this around the outside edges of the characters. Try not to get any on your clothes," Uncle Bei said without looking up, his attention focused on the ancient folded book he held reverently.

Was that a spell book? Tong Yi thought that was kind of neat. It wasn't like a western book, with a spine, but a series of folded pages all attached, like an ancient folio. Wild characters sprawled across the page, most of them written in the ancient form of Chinese that looked more like pictures.

But that book wasn't for him.

Not yet.

Tong Yi weighed the bag in his hand. The slippery quality of whatever was inside worried him. He would bet it was ash of some sort, which always felt greasy to him, the times he'd had to deliver quantities of it to clients.

Tong Yi carefully knelt down outside the circle of characters. He untied the bag with one hand while keeping the other choked tightly around the neck of the bag in case something decided to pop out at him.

When nothing happened, Tong Yi tilted the bag and let a fine drizzle of—yes, ash—out of the bag.

The ash quickly arranged itself into a curved line, so Tong Yi kept pouring. He didn't hurry. He took his time to pour very carefully as well as very neatly. When he could, he would pause and look at the characters going around the circle, trying to memorize them.

When Tong Yi finished, he closed up the bag tightly before he stood again. Then he swayed, dizzy and surprisingly tired. He'd been really concentrating.

How long had that taken? He took a deep breath and tried to settle himself. Wow. He needed some tea or something.

Uncle Bei watched him with a steady look. "Very well done," he said, holding out his hand for the bag.

That surprised Tong Yi. He'd expected either a smart remark, or to be told he'd been too cautious.

"Thank you," Tong Yi said. "What else can I help with?" Though honestly, all he wanted to do now was ride home and take a long nap.

Uncle Bei gave him that shark smile, the one that showed all his teeth. "You've done more than enough," he said.

Worry coursed through Tong Yi. What else had he done? He'd just poured the ashes, like Uncle Bei had asked him. Hadn't he?

Tong Yi looked back at the circle. Though mists were now swirling in the center of it, a familiar blue and black, and winds now pushed and pulled, the ash stayed exactly where he'd poured it, as if it had been painted on.

When Tong Yi looked more closely, he could see that the ash had melted into the ground, anchoring the circle in place.

Had he done that?

Uncle Bei started chanting.

Tong Yi tried to follow, but the words kept slipping away from him. Was that part of the training that he still needed? So that he could hold onto magical spells, actually hear them and remember them?

When Uncle Bei finished his incantation, a portal sprang up. It was a whirling gray oval, the center of it black and deep. Blue veins of light ran through the mists, sparking more brightly than Tong Yi remembered.

Was the portal itself stronger? Or was Tong Yi just better able to see the magic in it?

"I've tried to get you as close to the palace of the southern king as I could," Uncle Bei told Tong Yi as he handed over a large man's watch.

Tong Yi nodded. Right. Nothing electronic worked in the warzone—he couldn't rely on his phone to tell time, like he usually did.

"The portal will close in ninety minutes," Uncle Bei announced. "At twelve o'clock."

Tong Yi looked at the watch. According to it, the time was currently 10:30.

"So I have an hour and a half?" Tong Yi asked, confused. Uncle Bei had said that it took too much power to keep a portal open for longer than an hour.

Uncle Bei nodded, still giving Tong Yi that sharp smile. "The containment circle that you poured will hold up longer than that."

"Oh," Tong Yi said. He had no idea what else to say. He hadn't meant to do any magic when he'd poured out the ash. Or had it just reacted to him? And was that why he was so exhausted?

It wasn't smart, him going into the warzone like this. He should be well rested.

Was this yet another test?

Tong Yi shook his head. He wasn't about to ask Uncle Bei about it. He carefully tucked the watch into an inner pocket in his leather jacket, zipping it shut, then went back to Bing Xi.

After Tong Yi had started up the engine and buckled on his helmet, after he'd started slowly driving the bike into the portal, he thought he heard Uncle Bei say, "Say hello to your brother for me."

But he had to have imagined that, right?

The warzone looked very similar to the first time Tong Yi had seen it: the sky was still that awful, unnatural color of purple-red, like a bruise. Boiling gray clouds hung threateningly on the just in front of him, looking as though they were about to drop buckets of rain, or possibly acid. Dying grass covered the rutted and uneven ground. The air smelled bitter and dry, like the tomb of an ancient apothecary. No trees grew here, or even bushes. The land stood completely open. Darker, black clouds laced with lightning filled the horizon off to the west. (North? South? Impossible to tell. Tong Yi had yet to see either the sun or stars.)

On the opposite horizon ran a large ridge, full of barren rocks. Beyond them were the badlands, a desert that was incredibly dangerous, as well as indescribably beautiful. Tong Yi marked the ridge as east, because that way lay home if he didn't make it back through the portal on time.

The portal burned beside him, swirling gray and blue. Tong Yi tried to memorize its location as well as he could, noting the differences between it and the land around it.

The land *hated*. It didn't want any humans there, or really, anything living.

The portal wasn't alive, not exactly. But it wasn't of the land. Tong Yi felt the difference much more acutely this time.

Was it because he had more awareness of magic, now? Or was it because he'd helped to build the portal?

It didn't matter. He figured no matter where he was in the warzone, he'd always be able to sense the portal.

Now, which direction lay the king and the southern gate? Tong Yi looked around, studying the horizon.

There *was* something there, in the direction he'd arbitrarily assigned as south. A mound in the far distance. He had no idea how far away it actually was, or the size of it.

Tong Yi directed his attention back to Bing Xi. The ribbons across her handlebars had subtly changed yet again. The pattern had grown tighter, the diamond shapes between the ribbons smaller. In addition, the ribbons themselves had taken on a metallic sheen.

Tong Yi knew he didn't have time. He needed to get his ass in gear and get down to the palace of the southern king.

He still paused, putting the middle finger of his glove in his teeth and tugging it off so he could touch the ribbon. It felt cold to the touch. It also felt more like metal and less like ribbon. His impression was that it now formed some sort of shield.

Tong Yi patted Bing Xi's headlamp with his bare palm. It felt warm, warmer than it should. Hopefully that was normal. "Let's go do this," he told her, tugging his glove back on.

He was glad that she was better protected.

Maybe next time, he'd tie some ribbons to his own jacket as well.

Tong Yi knew better than to expect that the king of the southern gate would have built a road to make it easier to get to his castle. The ground was rutted, like huge moles lived underneath it, who were always expanding their tunnels. Sudden holes opened up as well, making Tong Yi either swerve or drop down into them, spinning his tires and fishtailing out.

At least Bing Xi wasn't purposefully trying to dump him. She probably was fishtailing a bit more than was absolutely necessary, but Tong Yi didn't try to strictly control her. He'd rather she was happy. He depended on her too much.

Finally, the shape on the horizon started resolving. Tong Yi headed straight for it, driving as fast as he could and only pausing when he was almost on top of it.

The castle, if he could call it that, looked like a child's nightmare made out of trash. No stone wall surrounded it; however, even from several meters away, Tong Yi smelled the moat. It lay hidden behind a mound of dirt that circled the castle. But it smelled like rotting, brackish water, as if filled with lotus blossoms gone rank.

Only one tower stood on the left side of the castle. It appeared to be made out of refrigerator doors, old stovetops, microwaves, and kitchen cabinets. Creatures looked down from the top of its crenulated roof. They looked like the *zhi ren*, the mole men, who'd been fighting a great battle the last time Tong Yi had been in the warzone.

Tong Yi didn't see any weapons pointed at him. Then again, if the creatures up there were spell casters, they wouldn't need something as crude or obvious as a gun.

Much of the rest of the castle also looked as though it was made out of recycled bits, like metal filing cabinet drawers, table tops and desks, as well as old stone. Chair legs stuck out at odd angles. Picture frames held bits of steel and were wrapped around the walls.

The castle itself was only two stories high. The gate leading in opened as a great black maw, the top of the left side drooping, as if it might fall suddenly.

Tong Yi stopped right next to the foul moat. The water moved sluggishly. Yellow-green slime coated the top of it. He didn't look too closely to see what sort of creatures might live in that sewer.

A dirt bridge had been built across the moat, leading directly to the open door of the castle. Tong Yi couldn't see anything beyond the black opening.

Tong Yi didn't want to just leave Bing Xi out there, in the courtyard of the castle, all alone. He turned off her motor and started walking her across the moat.

However, as soon as her front wheel touched the bridge, she stopped.

Tong Yi pushed hard, but she wouldn't budge.

Either she didn't want to go into the castle, or she wasn't allowed to.

With a sinking heart, Tong Yi turned Bing Xi around so she was facing directly toward the portal. It surprised him that he still felt the vague pulse of it on the horizon. Then he backed her up onto her kickstand.

He wanted to keep the keys in the ignition so he would have a quick getaway. But he was too afraid that someone might just steal her. He didn't have any way of locking her, either.

Or did he?

Tong Yi took off one glove. He patted Bing Xi's gas can, ran his fingers along her handlebars, then pressed his thumb against the ignition switch.

Was that just his imagination, or did a spark of blue light arc up when he removed his thumb? Just like it did when he activated the magical protection system for the golden sedan?

No matter. Any of the creatures watching him would understand that Tong Yi had just tried to protect his ride.

And maybe, just maybe, had the magical ability to do it.

Tong Yi walked straight through the dark gate of the castle. He'd checked his time—it had taken eighteen minutes to get to the castle. He wasn't planning on using the whole ninety minutes. He told himself he only had twenty minutes to find the king of this castle, deliver his message, and make his way back.

Easy, right?

A vague light sprang up in front of him. Was the light itself gray? Or was it shining through gray fog?

Tong Yi walked toward the light. The ground under his feet remained dirt, soft under his boots. The walls, what he could see of them, appeared to be carved out of rough stone, dark and dank, though here and there he spotted leftover bits that had been stuck into the rock: a blank computer screen, the dashboard of a car with the dials missing, three wire-rim motorcycle tires in an awkward triangle.

Another light came on further down the hallway as Tong Yi reached the first one. Tong Yi walked toward that one. He figured whoever ran this place was trying to direct him, show him where to go. At least the air in here didn't stink of the moat outside. Instead, it smelled dried and desiccated, like the parched frogs' legs he'd seen at the apothecary.

Every once in a while, Tong Yi passed either a closed and barred door, or an opening onto a side passage. He never wavered from following the lights ahead of him. He didn't have time to explore, and honestly, he wasn't sure he wanted to.

The whole castle was magical, though. There wasn't as much residual magic in the castle as had been in The Sweet Shop, but Tong Yi still tasted the bitterness of it at the back of his throat. His boots made no sound along the soft dirt floor. He tugged his gloves back on so he wouldn't be tempted to touch something he shouldn't.

In less than five minutes, Tong Yi heard a muttering sound, like the ocean talking to itself.

The light just ahead of him shone much brighter, spilling out into the tunnel from a larger room.

Tong Yi patted his breast pocket, inside his leather jacket, where he kept the red envelope that he was supposed to deliver. Good. It felt warm against his chest.

That meant he was getting closer to his intended client.

The noise in front of him grew louder. Now it sounded as if someone was throwing a raucous party, given the shrieks, shouts, and insane giggles.

Tong Yi didn't pause to brace himself. He didn't have time. He'd already wasted enough time walking through the castle. He had to get back to the portal.

So he walked straight out from the tunnel into a broad, circular room. Four tiers of seats rose on all sides, like a stadium. The floor here was made out of black-and-white checked marble, like a huge chessboard.

Tong Yi assumed that the man seated in the front row directly opposite the door, the one wearing a towering silver crown made out of tinfoil, would be the king. In addition to the crown, the king was also wearing a giant, red-velvet cape and a white poet's shirt.

Tong Yi marched across the floor, ignoring the hoots and hollers, as well as catcalls he heard. Just a glance told him that there were few humans here.

He wasn't sure what type of beings sat in the stadium. It looked to him like the king had raided a knick-knack store, one of those that carried a little bit of everything, and used all the items he'd found in there to create his subjects, mixed with dead animals found in a hunting lodge.

There was the thing with all the wooden spoons sticking out of its head and down its back, like a crest of feathers, with wooden coasters for eyes and cellophane holding the rest of the parts together. Another looked as though it had started off as a white-plastic garbage bin, then had wire wrapped around it to form its arms. Bright red lights bobbed at the ends of wire sticking out of its head—eyes, probably. It also had the beak of a bird of prey, hungry and sharp.

Tong Yi couldn't name any of the beings—they were newly created, not creatures from myth.

Whoever this southern king was, he had the power to be able to imagine and create such things.

The envelope in Tong Yi's jacket grew hotter still. That was unusual. Tong Yi ignored it. He knew who his client was. Despite how the southern king appeared to be ignoring him, talking to the catlike creature sitting on his left. It wasn't a *Heimao*, not like See-tza.

Tong Yi couldn't have said for certain why he felt that way, except that See-tza, for all her catness, had a human side to her. She was warm and would still purr. This creature, despite her cat face and paws for hands, was more ice than fire, and had no human in her at all.

Tong Yi stopped immediately in front of the king, looking up. "Are you the king of the southern gate?" he asked formally.

"I am," the man said. He turned his head and finally looked at Tong Yi, "brother."

Tong Yi blinked rapidly, unsure of what to say.

Quan Lo? Here?

No wonder he'd never come back.

Tong Yi finally remembered to shut his mouth. Who had made his brother king? Had he just declared himself a sovereign? Tong Yi looked at his brother, turned his head to the side, then turned back, trying to "see anew," to see if he could detect any magic.

The tinfoil crown his brother wore sparkled as if it had been spritzed with oil, making it glimmer with an unnatural light. It had half-a-dozen spires twisting out of it, giving Quan Lo an additional two feet of height. The crown wasn't symmetrical, the spires not in any kind of order.

Quan Lo himself appeared completely mundane.

Then again, so did Ren Wu, even after Tong Yi had seen his eyes flare red with an inner light.

Tong Yi barely recognized his brother. Though he had the same dark eyes, the same long, greasy hair that fell down to his shoulders, the same sharp features, there was something *off* about him.

It felt to Tong Yi as though someone else wore the mask of his brother's face. That inside, his brother had long since vacated.

The manic grin was familiar—it was the same one Quan Lo had when he'd been tripping for days.

Quan Lo was no longer there.

Finally, Tong Yi remembered himself.

This was a *client* for *Huli* Transport.

Nothing else mattered. Not any of the questions Tong Yi had about why Quan Lo was here, how he'd gotten here, how he'd become king.

"I have a message for you, sir," Tong Yi said. He unzipped his jacket just far enough to fish out the red envelope, then zipped it right up again. The heat from the envelope warmed his fingers, even through his gloves. He held the envelope up over his head with both hands so that Quan Lo could take it.

"Sir. I like that," Quan Lo said as he leaned away, indicating that the cat woman should take the message.

Tong Yi quickly stepped back.

"I can only deliver the message to you, sir," Tong Yi said. It didn't matter what he called Quan Lo, he told himself. Quan Lo was merely a client.

Only a client, if Tong Yi was honest. Nothing more.

"And if I refuse?" Quan Lo asked.

Tong Yi simply stood there without moving. He knew that the envelope was spelled to fly directly to the correct recipient if they explicitly refused. He wasn't about to say anything about that, however. If Quan Lo actually had magic, he might be able to block the envelope if he knew it was coming.

Silence pooled through the rest of the stadium. Tong Yi counted his heartbeats. He didn't have time for this. He had to get back to the portal.

He wouldn't budge, though. Wouldn't make it easier for Quan Lo.

"Fine," Quan Lo finally said, reaching out.

Tong Yi took the necessary steps forward so his brother could reach the message. Then he waited, curious, while Quan Lo read the words intended only for him.

The look of sheer annoyance that crossed Quan Lo's face warmed Tong Yi's heart, but he made sure that no emotion showed on his face.

Then Quan Lo balled up the message, tossed it into the air, and caught it in his mouth, swallowing it whole.

His jaw seemed to extend large enough for him to swallow it, like a snake's. It made Tong Yi shiver.

This really wasn't the brother he'd grown up with. Not anymore.

"My friends!" Quan Lo called as he rose up. "We've been invited to another ball! Who's ready to dance?"

A great roaring filled the room. Based on the cheers and taunts the crowd tossed out, Tong Yi assumed that they'd been asked to join a battle, one that Quan Lo's subjects felt they could win.

When the noise died down, Tong Yi asked, "Do you have a response, sir? That you'd like for me to carry back?"

The room stilled again as Quan Lo studied Tong Yi. "What if I wanted to send your head on a pike as a response?"

Cheers erupted.

Tong Yi waited again until the noise had died down to a dull roar. "The fees would be astronomical, sir," he said as blandly as he could manage.

He wasn't about to say that at least his death would serve some purpose, that Mom and Dad would be set for life.

Quan Lo gave him a sly smile. "I could just delay you again. Make you cross the battlefield. I wouldn't be directly responsible for your death, then."

Tong Yi nodded. "Again, sir, a client delaying a messenger would result in extremely harsh fees."

Quan Lo's face puckered, as if he'd just been sucking a sour melon. "So you're going to keep playing goody-two-shoes while the rest of us do the *real* work."

Tong Yi shrugged, not rising to the bait. *This is a client.* Huli *Transport must remain neutral.*

"I warned you not to declare war between us," Quan Lo said.

"*Huli* Transport has not taken sides in this conflict," Tong Yi pointed out. "We are *neutral* in this war."

"I don't mean you, messenger boy. I mean my brother," Quan Lo pointed out.

Tong Yi pressed his lips together. He wasn't about to say the words. But they slipped out anyway. He couldn't stop them.

"I have no brother," Tong Yi said distinctly. "Sir."

The silence that grew after that had its own teeth, nibbling away at Tong Yi's conscience, making him feel guilty.

He stood his ground though. He refused to take back the words. This person in front of him, this King of the Southern Gate, was a client.

Nothing more.

"You will regret this, brother," Quan Lo said. He pointed a fist at Tong Yi. A bright, red-faceted diamond ring on his middle finger flared.

The jewel looked suspiciously like the jewels in the cufflinks Uncle Bei wore.

A blast of power bowled Tong Yi over, sending him tumbling across the white and black marble floor.

"Sir, you *will* regret harming a *Huli* Transport messenger," Tong Yi told Quan Lo hotly as he got to his feet, brushing himself off.

"You have no powers," Quan Lo sneered. "No training. Nothing to protect you but that little messenger badge on your helmet."

Tong Yi stood and faced Quan Lo again. "If there's nothing else, sir, no message, I need to go."

Another blast of power rammed into Tong Yi, pushing him into the hallway that he'd first come through. He tumbled over and over, until he slammed into a wall hard enough to take his breath away.

Shit. Quan Lo was just insane enough, as well as angry enough, that he might not care about the cost, the huge fees *Huli* Transport would charge.

He might just want to kill Tong Yi.

Shaking, Tong Yi rose to his feet. *Damn* it. Why had Uncle Bei made sure that Tong Yi was weak before he'd come to the warzone?

Had Uncle Bei wanted Tong Yi to fail?

After another shaky breath, Tong Yi started jogging back through the hallway. The lights all stayed lit this time, so he could see where he had to go.

Was that so he could escape? Or to make it easier to hit him?

Tong Yi stayed close to the left wall at first, then crossed and stayed closer to the right wall.

Just as he was about to zigzag again, a blast of power surged past him. It would have caught him hard if he'd been going down the center. As it was, it grabbed his shoulder and threw him against the wall.

Damn it! Tong Yi had to survive this. Just so Uncle Bei could charge Quan Lo for attempting to kill a messenger. He didn't know what the fees actually would be. The way the contracts were worded, he knew it wouldn't just be money.

And it wouldn't be pleasant.

It didn't take long for Tong Yi to finally reach the entrance to the castle. Outside, the warzone waited. As soon as Tong Yi stepped beyond the castle he felt the land pulse with hate again, pushing at him, slowing him down.

Did Quan Lo have some power? Was he the one who had built the castle? Who had muted the warzone, making the place at least vaguely habitable?

Tong Yi ran to Bing Xi, throwing a leg over her and backing her off her kickstand before he reached for his keys.

For a terrible moment, Tong Yi couldn't find them.

Had Quan Lo stolen them? Like he had before?

But no, there were the keys, buried deep in his outside pocket.

Before Tong Yi could start up Bing Xi, he heard shouts and jeers from behind him. He risked a glance over his shoulder.

There, in the tower, stood Quan Lo, the catwoman, and several other beings.

Tong Yi quickly kicked Bing Xi to life and took off. But not in a straight line, no. He swerved to the right, then to the left.

Huh. Maybe all that earlier "dancing" with Bing Xi had been a good thing. Tong Yi knew exactly how far he could skid and fishtail and not end up on his ass.

Maybe all that "dancing" had been to teach him how to really ride.

Blasts of power exploded in the ground beside Tong Yi. The dirt kicked up into his face, hard pebbles striking his facemask.

Tong Yi kept riding like a madman, dancing between the blasts, finally getting out of range.

He didn't stop then, but continued straight to the portal, gliding through it after spending only fifty-six minutes in the warzone.

Uncle Bei looked disappointed when Tong Yi appeared.

Tong Yi made himself stop, though he kept Bing Xi's motor going.

"Back so soon?" Uncle Bei asked, false sympathy dripping from his words.

"I am," Tong Yi said curtly.

"Any message from Quan Lo?" Uncle Bei asked.

So Uncle Bei had known that the king of the southern gate was Tong Yi's brother.

"None," Tong Yi said. "Unless you view threatening to return my head on a pike as a response."

Uncle Bei gave his shark's smile at that. "How angry was he?"

"Angry enough to blast a *Huli* Transport messenger with magic," Tong Yi said.

Uncle Bei raised a skeptical eyebrow.

"And I have the bruises to prove it," Tong Yi added hotly.

"I see," Uncle Bei said slowly. "Do you want to press charges against this client?" he asked, suddenly formal. "You don't have to decide today," he added. "But I'll need to know your answer by morning."

"What exactly does it mean to press charges?" Tong Yi asked. "And what would be the penalty he'd serve?"

"Well, you'd both have to appear before a mediator. Of my choosing," Uncle Bei assured him, again with that very mean smile. "Any physical damage to you would be calculated and taken out of Quan Lo's flesh."

"So, since he hurt me, you'd hurt him?" Tong Yi asked. That didn't seem satisfying.

"Not at all," Uncle Bei assured him. "Your pain would be measured, calculated, then pound for pound, *removed* from his flesh. There's quite a bit of muscle that can be carved out of a body before you do fatal damage."

Tong Yi shivered. Did he want that kind of punishment for Quan Lo? An eye for an eye sort of judgment? It didn't seem very ordered. It certainly wouldn't sit well with their parents.

"And the other?" Uncle Bei inquired casually.

Tong Yi looked sharply at him. Casual didn't sit well on Uncle Bei. "The other?" Tong Yi asked, though he suspected he knew exactly what Uncle Bei was asking about.

"The magic," Uncle Bei said. "I assume you will be wanting to learn more."

Tong Yi stiffened. Uncle Bei sounded greedy. Much more greedy than Tong Yi would have expected.

He remembered Ren Wu's words.

Was agreeing to learn magic from Uncle Bei giving the man access to Tong Yi's soul?

"Let me think about it," Tong Yi said.

As he drove away, Tong Yi knew these were the final steps for him. He would finally have to make a decision.

He did want to learn magic, though possibly not at the cost Uncle Bei would insist on.

As for the other…

Was it finally time to declare war on his brother?

Tong Yi drove slowly through the streets of Hualien City. He knew that he should be going directly back to the offices of *Huli* Transport. Not because Ren Wu would make him work more that day—after delivering any message to the warzone, the messengers always got the rest of the day off. Or even a couple of days, if the experience had been particularly harrowing.

Without meaning to, Tong Yi found himself back on *Ba Guan* Street. Could he find The Sweet Shop all on his own? See-tza had said that she'd put his name on the door. He assumed that would make it easier for him to find the shop.

Recklessness drove him to find a place to park Bing Xi on the street just up from where he thought the shop would be. He also did the same thing that he'd done outside of the castle: patted the gas can, ran his fingers along the handlebars, then pressed his thumb against the ignition switch.

This time, the blue spark was more noticeable.

Huh. So maybe Quan Lo wasn't the only brother who had magic.

Tong Yi slid his motorcycle helmet off as he walked up the street.

He found he didn't even have to look for the numbers. He *felt* the shop. The entrance was right there, on his left. The numbers, however, were no longer in Roman numerals, but Chinese characters.

The doors themselves looked the same as the first time he'd found the shop. Silver metal doors framed darkened, mirrored glass. The handles still felt cold to the touch. The same tinkling bell announced his presence in the shop.

A slower ballad played on the store's speakers instead of J-pop, but the band was still some sort of Japanese boy band. The smell of chocolate and licorice and bubblegum reminded Tong Yi that he hadn't had anything to eat since breakfast many hours before. Magic still pressed against him from every direction, making his skin itch.

Possibly more, now.

The guy—Ge Deng—wasn't waiting behind the counter to the left of the door. Instead, See-tza was there.

Tong Yi looked carefully at her. She looked back, just as solemnly.

Tong Yi had been right. See-tza wasn't the same as the cat creature who had been at Quan Lo's right hand. That being had a lot more cat features, as well as a feral look to her eyes. She was cold. See-tza was warm.

See-tza also looked less wild, though Tong Yi wouldn't have said she looked innocent. She had a knowing look to her that Tong Yi wasn't sure he trusted.

"Can you help me?" Tong Yi found himself asking. "Can you teach me magic?"

See-tza nodded, grinning. Her smile warmed Tong Yi's heart, like sudden sunshine after a storm.

"I can help you," she said. "Learn many kinds of magic. Good magic, too, that fills the soul. Not just bad."

Tong Yi blinked. Did Uncle Bei know good magic as well? Or did he consider it beneath him?

"What is the price?" Tong Yi asked. Everything sweet—or maybe it was just everything—had a price.

See-tza laughed merrily. "You will work sometimes for me. Deliveries. Not so neutral."

Tong Yi stiffened. The non-compete clause in his contract was really clear. Uncle Bei would happily pursue him for any perceived infraction. "I can't do that," he said. "If someone at *Huli* Transport found out…"

"No money change hands," See-tza pointed out. "Not real employee. Just deliver personal messages for me." Then she slid out from behind the counter and sidled up to him. "Unless you pay other ways," she added suggestively.

Tong Yi's mouth went dry. He was almost tempted, but he suspected that, too, would weigh on his soul.

"I don't want to get into trouble," he said, weakening. She wasn't really competition, was she? It wouldn't be like he was working for another delivery company.

See-tza laughed again. "You already trouble," she said. Then she shrugged. "Me? I like trouble. How about you?"

Tong Yi considered for a moment. See-tza seemed perfectly fine with him taking his time, thinking things through.

He wanted to learn magic. Desperately so. If he was honest with himself, he'd love to show up in the warzone and take his brother down. Show that he was finally better and stronger than his big brother.

More worthy and capable.

The more practical side of Tong Yi wanted to learn magic so he could defend himself, because he knew that someday, Quan Lo would come back to the human realm again.

Besides, Tong Yi wouldn't really be an employee of The Sweet Shop. He wouldn't really be working for another delivery company. He'd just be delivering messages for See-tza.

Or at least, that was how he justified it to himself.

"All right," he said slowly, nodding. "I would like to try this for one week."

See-tza clapped her hands. "Perfect! Let me get contract. You start tonight."

Tong Yi opened his mouth, closed it again, then slowly nodded his head.

He'd made his decision. He'd finally chosen a side.

The frog had finally landed—but not on the obvious lily pad.

Instead, he'd landed here.

In The Sweet Shop.

THE IMMORTALS' WAR

Here, wear this," See-tza said, handing Tong Yi a small silver medallion.

It immediately warmed Tong Yi's fingers. "What is it?" he asked. The magic in the coin made his skin tingle. It didn't have a lot of power, just a trace.

He hoped that learning to use it wouldn't involve another complicated magical spell. His brain *hurt* from all that he'd been trying to cram into it from the last three weeks, learning magic from See-tza at night, after working all day, delivering messages for *Huli* Transport. They'd already been working for a few hours that night.

They sat in See-tza's office, at the back of The Sweet Shop—the magic shop she owned. The office was the complete opposite of Ren Wu's office. Instead of being old and plain—with calendars two years out of date hanging on the cracked walls and a desk piled so high with papers and folders that Tong Yi could only see his boss through a crack—two pillows sat on the floor in the middle of the room.

That was it.

Each pillow was about a foot square, made of a soft, pale-green fabric. It had taken Tong Yi about a week to figure out how to sit on his pillow and hold himself so his back stopped hurting.

Tatami mats covered the floor itself, an auspicious eight in all. Nothing adorned the soothing, pale-gray walls. A single window stood opposite the door, up so high that the bottom of it reached Tong Yi's chest. A *shoji* screen covered it. A white radiator heater stood plugged into the corner. Diffuse light glowed from the ceiling panels, bright enough to do work, but not enough to make Tony Yi's eyes hurt.

Only as Tong Yi's *sight* and power grew did he realize that gray filing cabinets blended into the gray walls under the window, hiding in plain sight. Once, he'd even glimpsed a watercolor painting on the wall next to the door. The long scroll had been painted with white paint, an abstract that he couldn't make heads or tails of, that flickered and didn't remain solid.

The room probably hid other adornments that would only reveal themselves to Tong Yi as he grew stronger.

It made him despair sometimes, when he thought about how little he knew.

"Look carefully at the medallion," See-tza told him.

Tong Yi contained his sigh. Another damned test. It seemed to him that anyone who learned magic also learned to stop speaking clearly at the same time. Stopped giving out information freely.

He examined the silver piece. It was about the size of an American dime. Round. The edge ridged, with a small loop grown out of the top of it, to make it wearable.

When he ran his thumb across the surface, he felt markings. When he glanced at the piece, the metal appeared plain.

Tong Yi turned his head to the side, glancing at the far gray wall, then he turned back to the coin in his hand, trying to *see again*.

The markings slowly swam into focus.

In the center sat a large, modern character, *fu*, for good luck.

Around the edge swam eight ancient characters. They looked like squid or octopus, with long squiggly lines radiating out from a central body. Tong Yi recognized about half of them. Like all Chinese ideograms, in isolation, they could mean one thing, while in combination with other characters, they could form completely different words.

For example, he recognized the character *jiàn*, which meant *see*.

Tong Yi didn't know the characters on either side of the *jiàn*. Did it just mean see? Or did one of the other characters modify it, forming a word like *glass* or even *transparent*?

On the other side of the coin, he found his first name written in modern characters in the center. Underneath were three blank, raised squares. He'd seen something like that before, on a medallion a parent would give a child, with their birthdate engraved.

Why were his blank? Surely See-tza knew when Tong Yi had been born. Or was this coin to celebrate a different coming of age? Maybe when he became a full wizard?

"What is it?" Tong Yi asked again. Just reading the characters he could make out didn't tell him enough.

"It helps you build power," See-tza said. "Right now, small magic. You feel?"

Tong Yi nodded.

See-tza's human appearance faded and her cat features became more prominent. Her ears stayed the same—lynx ears growing up from underneath her hair on either side of her face, covered with soft, grey-and-white tufted hair. Her eyes changed, becoming a bright green, with an elongated pupil. And while she still stayed cute, her pert nose flattened and darkened, becoming more cat-like, and the teeth that peeked out from her smile grew sharp and pointed.

Tong Yi knew that if he looked down at her hands, he'd see claws springing out from the ends of her fingers. Underneath the lime-green blouse she wore, soft fur would coat her arms.

She'd never fully turn into a cat. She'd assured him that her final form was halfway between, with velvet-like fur that was also like skin, cat ears, eyes, and claws, but still upright and human.

And though See-tza had hinted more than once that he could see all of her if he was curious, Tong Yi really wasn't sure he wanted his first time to be with someone who wasn't human.

Particularly not someone with a tail, after she'd hinted about what she'd like to do with him.

While See-tza could do magic in her more human form, the more cat-like she became, the more magic she had.

Tong Yi braced himself. He squeezed the coin between his fingers tightly. What magic would See-tza throw at him this time?

The exhaustion that had been Tong Yi's constant companion suddenly doubled. Tong Yi had *no* energy left. He could barely sit up straight on his pillow.

The coin pressed between his fingers sent out a small, sharp spike of magic, warming Tong Yi's arm. He closed his eyes and *pulled*, drawing that spike up. Taking the source and using it, as he'd been taught.

His power increased. His exhaustion lessened.

He knew that if *See-tza* turned her full magical abilities on him, he'd never be able to fight her off. He wasn't sure if even Uncle Bei would be able to withstand her.

Her magic swarmed over him. Tried to push him down. Make him *bow*.

Tong Yi gritted his teeth. Put iron into his spine. Sucked up all the magic the coin could give him.

Refused to give an inch.

Gradually, the magical influence withdrew. See-tza let him win, allowed him to remain upright.

He panted with the effort to not just collapse. Slowly, strength flowed back into him, calming his pulse.

When Tong Yi opened his eyes, he saw his teacher smiling warmly at him. She'd become even more catlike, her entire face covered in light gray fur. "Very good!" she said gleefully.

Tong Yi nodded. "Thank you," he said, bowing his head low.

He saw the value of the coin now. It had helped him gather and build his own power. Wearing it, keeping it always on him, would help him build up even more.

And Tong Yi had learned that Uncle Bei had been telling the exact truth when he'd talked about magic previously. It wasn't necessarily ability, but *power*, that made the magician. Tong Yi could spend years learning spells, but until he built up the right level of power, he wouldn't be able to do anything with the knowledge.

"Here," See-tza said playfully.

Tong Yi took the proffered collar with distaste. He'd seen movies where people wore such things. He hoped See-tza wasn't being serious and wouldn't actually make him wear it. It looked exactly like a dog collar, an inch wide, made of padded brown leather. It had a silver loop in the front and a buckle in the back.

It had no magic, at least as far as Tong Yi could tell.

Tong Yi did *not* question his teacher. That would be disrespectful. He did raise his eyebrows, hoping she'd see and not ignore him.

"Don't you want to wear my collar?" See-tza said, her tone teasing.

"Honestly, ma'am?" Tong Yi asked. "I would prefer not to. Besides, it's too…obvious. It would be better if I kept the coin out of sight, under my shirt."

"You are very wise," See-tza said. Her cat-eyes sparkled with amusement. "Use this instead."

She handed him a long silver chain. It gleamed in the dim light of the room.

Tong Yi handed back the collar in exchange. The magic made the chain feel slippery in Tong Yi's fingers. "Thank you," he said again.

He glanced at the coin. It wasn't really a coin, was it?

More like…a tag. The kind which a beloved pet wore.

Bile filled the back of Tong Yi's throat.

Was he no better than a pet to See-tza? Her own messenger boy, at her beck and call?

But if he wanted to learn magic, his choice was to study either with her or Uncle Bei.

Who knew how badly the magician would treat Tong Yi?

He slipped the tag onto the chain, then put it over his neck, sliding it under his T-shirt, where it ended up in the exact center of his chest. Though the tag had been warm in his hand, it felt warmer now, against his skin.

See-tza's cat-like features faded, her human nose and eyes returning. "Very good. You wear always. Even in shower. You get stronger and stronger still."

"I will," Tong Yi promised.

He needed to learn as much as he could. As quickly as he could.

So he could walk away from all "teachers" and just teach himself.

Tong Yi focused on the small rock that sat on the sandy beach. See-tza had given it to him to practice on.

The sun had just crested the horizon that morning, casting a wide orange beam across the ocean on his right. Rocks protected his left side and behind him. No one could sneak up on him.

No one human, at any rate.

Tong Yi wore his usual T-shirt and jeans. His sandals sat some distance away. He knelt on a folded yoga mat, his toes digging into the cold sand. He'd borrowed his father's Vespa to drive out that morning.

See-tza had insisted that he get up before the dawn to practice his magic. According to her, he needed to start getting in touch with the elements. Water. Fire. Earth.

Because he was human, his magic followed different channels than hers. She *was* magic, it came naturally to her. He had to memorize spells and build up his own power reserve, instead of drawing power directly from the earth.

That morning, he was attempting a transformation—changing a rock into its component parts, casting it back into sand.

Much of the magic he'd been practicing had transformation as a base. Turning sand into glass. A cup of water into mist. A woven mat into a wide carpet. Dragonfly wings into blades.

The tag that See-tza had given Tong Yi a few days before had been very useful, now that he'd figured out more about it. He'd instinctively drawn any power from it when it spiked. Now, he was learning how to put power into it, to use it as a reservoir.

The more power he poured into the silver medallion, the more it took. Eventually, it reached its limit, and the power overflowed, drenching his skin.

How could he get the medallion to hold more energy? Did he need a bigger artifact? Or was his failure due to his lack of knowledge?

Tong Yi had put as much power as he could into the tag the night before.

Now, he concentrated on the stone. He sketched characters in the air, thrilled by the small amounts of fire and smoke he left behind, the images burning away quickly, tiny bits of ash drifting down onto the rock.

Once the stone held a fine coating of gray ash, Tong Yi started chanting. He called on the power of the earth, reminding the stone from where it had come. Where it was going. How it felt the call to change, to transform, to dissolve its pieces into tiny grains, to lose its solidarity to become one with the rest of the sand, to join its brothers.

Tong Yi didn't think the stone had a soul. Or at least, not one he might recognize it. It did have its own unique essence, however. He'd grown much more sensitive to those sorts of things.

He pulled power from the tag at the center of his chest, its warmth comforting.

Tong Yi repeated his chant. Then again. Poured everything he had into the spell he recited. Felt all the power draining from him.

When he finally finished, he didn't see any change in the stone.

Damn it! What had he done wrong?

Maybe the ash coating had been too thick? Tong Yi bent down and gently blew on it.

The rock underneath the ash crumbled into sand. The ash had only been containing the rock's shape.

Tong Yi raised his arms wearily over his head. Success!

Then he took a deep breath. But at what cost? Fuck, he was tired. He felt as though he'd just run all the way through the badland to the warzone and back.

Obviously, he needed to build up more endurance. So that a simple act like destroying a rock could become second nature, without using up all his reserves.

Tong Yi didn't want to think about how long that might take. He wasn't sure he minded, though. All magic fascinated him. Just like the non-humans did.

It would take him more than one lifetime for him to learn all that he wanted.

No wonder the ancient Taoists had always searched for the secret of immortality. Not just because they could live longer, but so that they could have more time to learn.

"Tong Yi! In my office. Now," Ren Wu called into the messenger break room where Tong Yi and Han Di sat, waiting for their next job.

"Uh oh," Han Di said as Tong Yi rose slightly. "What did teacher's pet do now?"

Tong Yi grimaced at his friend. "You have a very skewed idea of 'favorite' if you think I'm one." He shook his head, then forced himself to smile. "Or maybe I *am* his favorite, and he's saving me from the stench of your eggs."

Han Di made "tea eggs"—eggs hardboiled in tea and vinegar—on a regular basis.

"Those eggs make me strong!" Han Di called after Tong Yi. "Virile! Just ask any of the ladies."

Tong Yi snorted to himself and hurried after his boss. Han Di was charming and did flirt with every girl he met.

Tong Yi had never seen him be successful, however.

The air conditioning in Ren Wu's office must have been out. It wasn't merely warm because Tong Yi was nervous. Or so he assured himself.

The non-compete clauses in Tong Yi's contract with *Huli* Transport were very specific about his not working for another messenger company.

Delivering messages for See-tza wasn't technically breaking his contract.

It wasn't honoring the spirit of it, though.

And Tong Yi knew that by delivering messages for See-tza, he was cheating *Huli* Transport. The messages he delivered for her would be ones that normally she would contract the messengering service for.

He really hoped that wasn't why Ren Wu seemed so upset.

Tong Yi sat in one of the battered, green-plastic vinyl chairs on the far side of Ren Wu's desk. Had his boss actually been making some progress on his paperwork? The piles on the desk no longer towered, but had shrunk to merely a foot high.

When the war had first started a few months before, Ren Wu had looked completely exhausted. Tong Yi and the other messengers had worried that he never seemed to sleep more than a few hours every night and might expect them to follow his example.

Now, Ren Wu looked well rested. His dark skin was set off by the cream-colored polo shirt he wore, with the tiny emblem of a fox over the left breast pocket.

Ren Wu folded his hands in front of him on his surprisingly clean desk and asked pleasantly, not sounding at all as angry as he looked, "Can you tell me why Sun Hou-tse is asking for you by name to come pick up a message from him?"

Tong Yi could only blink. His confusion warred with his relief that he wasn't being fired. The Monkey King? Why? How? What?

Frequently, messages were delivered to the *Huli* Transport offices by magic or through a portal. Messengers were only used to hand-deliver the message to its intended recipient. Not all the time, of course. Messengers ferried important messages between clients.

However, this was the first time a client had ever asked for Tong Yi by name.

A client who had, as far as Tong Yi knew, never met him.

"I don't know, sir," Tong Yi said. "I don't know Sun Hou-tse. I've never delivered anything to him."

"Good," Ren Wu said. His anger dialed down considerably.

Tong Yi swallowed hard. He *had* to tell the truth. "Unless Houyi told him about me. Sir."

Ren Wu took a deep breath. "Go on."

"When I delivered my first message in the warzone," Tong Yi said hastily, "Houyi handed me a message to go to Sun Hou-tse. She seemed angry that I wouldn't immediately take it to him. She wanted me to hand-deliver it to him, instead of letting the office choose the messenger."

"I see," Ren Wu said. He nodded. His hooded eyes stared at his desk.

Tong Yi deliberately looked away, toward one of the cracked and scuffed yellow walls, the one with a "Year of the Dragon" poster on it that was at least ten years old, then looked back at Ren Wu, trying to *see again*.

Was Ren Wu magical? Strictly human, but a wizard like Uncle Bei? Or was he some other creature, like See-tza, and merely appeared human?

Tong Yi still couldn't tell. His boss did appear to be more magical than Tong Yi had originally assumed. But he still couldn't figure out exactly what.

Ren Wu looked up. The red light in his eyes faded. "I think it will be good for you to go fetch this message."

Internally, Tong Yi winced. Any dog or cat reference reminded him of the tag See-tza had given him the week before. He wore it, warm under his shirt, against the bare skin of his chest.

"And you should directly deliver the message to the next recipient," Ren Wu continued.

Tong Yi gulped. "What if they're both in the warzone?" Though Uncle Bei routinely held the portal open for ninety minutes now, finding two people in the warzone in that amount of time would be tricky, at best.

Ren Wu gave Tong Yi a wintry smile. "Then you'll just have to find your way out. Again." He paused, then added, "It will be easier this time. With all the magic you've learned."

Tong Yi stiffened. He hadn't told his boss—hell, he hadn't told anyone— about his lessons with See-tza. He'd told his parents he'd been picking up extra shifts at work, though they teased him about having a girlfriend.

"Don't worry," Ren Wu said, waving a hand at Tong Yi. "It hasn't done you any harm. So far. Just make sure that you stay focused on the job today. More magic…might mean more distraction. Until you learn to deal with it."

"I will," Tong Yi said fervently. "Thank you for the warning."

Tong Yi hated the warzone. Hated delivering messages there, despite the hazard pay. Hated knowing that his brother now lived there, in that crazed place.

Hated knowing that eventually, the war would end and Quan Lo would try to come home.

"Uncle Bei will give you all the instructions," Ren Wu said, dismissing Tong Yi. "Good luck. Safe travels."

"Thank you," Tong Yi said again as he left the office.

Uncle Bei had not been as friendly since Tong Yi had refused magic lessons from him.

Not that he'd ever been that friendly to start with.

But he wouldn't jeopardize a job for *Huli* Transport. He would continue to act like a professional, and would give all the information Tong Yi needed in order to fetch his message. Then deliver it.

Or die trying, which was always an option.

Hopefully training a new messenger would be more expensive than losing one.

When Tong Yi had started learning magic, one of the first things he'd done was to spend some time staring at Bing Xi, seeing if he could discern her magic. He knew that she was like See-tza—a fully magical being, transformed so she looked ordinary.

Was it a special ability of transformed beings that they could choose who saw them—either physically or magically? That was the only thing that Tong Yi could figure out. Because the motorcycle never appeared magical to him, at least not when he looked directly at her.

However, at night, when he sat on his bed and meditated as See-tza had taught him, letting go of the world and sinking deep into himself, more than once, an image of Bing Xi came to him. Not as a motorcycle or as Bi Qi, the horse, but as a woman, almost a goddess, tall and proud, wearing beautiful golden robes embroidered with the ancient Chinese ideogram for horse. Black and red ribbons were woven into her long hair.

Was that her *true* true form? The one she never showed anyone? Or was it just his imagination?

Han Di already gave Tong Yi shit about the ribbons he'd bought for Bing Xi. However, the other messengers would rarely drive Bing Xi now—said she was difficult to work with, stalling in the center of a busy intersection, or even fishtailing on dry ground.

Tong Yi had grown used to Bing Xi's "dancing" with him. He was even grateful for it. She'd taught him how to ride better, more defensively.

That afternoon, after finding out that he'd be going to the warzone the next morning, Tong Yi drove Bing Xi home. Masses of scooters and motorcycles gathered at each intersection. Tong Yi thankfully wore his helmet with a built-in filter, or else the stench would have been overwhelming.

Bing Xi, of course, didn't want to go directly to his parents' apartment. Tong Yi had been looking forward to napping all afternoon, possibly even catching up on his sleep, if that was possible. He had established with See-tza that they would not practice magic the night before he had to go to the warzone. He *had* to be well rested going there.

A few hours' sleep could mean the difference between life and death. The warzone was that dangerous.

However, Bing Xi kept tugging at Tong Yi, not wanting to turn into Hualien City's more residential neighborhoods.

Tong Yi knew that it would be better to give Bing Xi her head, now. She'd be better behaved in the warzone. Happier. That didn't mean that she wouldn't try to dump his ass if he didn't pay attention. But she'd be less of a brat about it.

Honestly, sometimes Tong Yi felt as though Bing Xi was a twelve-year-old girl, intent on teasing him to get his attention.

Instead of turning toward the beach, where Tong Yi had taken Bing Xi before, she headed for the highway, going north along the coast. To his right, Tong Yi caught glimpses of the ocean as they sped down the road, Bing Xi going faster and faster.

At least she wasn't trying to "dance" at these speeds, her wheels staying straight and true.

Tong Yi found he enjoyed the ride more than he'd thought he would. It reminded him of meditating. Sinking down into himself. Letting go of his thoughts. Drifting, almost. His reactions became instinctual. Shift. Change lanes. Speed up.

When they raced past the parked Red Zebra—a National Police car, painted with red and white stripes on the front and the back—Tong Yi hoped they'd not caught the patrol's attention.

No such luck. Bright blue and red lights started flashing behind them immediately, the car pulling off the side of the road, following them.

"I have to stop," Tong Yi told Bing Xi when she revved her engine as he started downshifting.

Bing Xi revved her motor once more, then subsided, allowing Tong Yi to slow down and pull over to the side of the road.

Tong Yi turned off Bing Xi's engine. He didn't want her getting any ideas about suddenly taking off. He backed her up onto her kickstand, then took off his gloves and his helmet, and stood, waiting.

The gravel on the shoulder beneath him glittered from the broken glass mixed in with the rock. A long-abandoned strip of shops sat a little ways back from the highway. It smelled strongly of urine and rotten wood. Ugly graffiti covered the corrugated metal that hung over the windows and doors. The roof sagged on the far side, the walls collapsing. Faded food wrappers, plastic bags, and other garbage lay piled along the foundation.

For some strange reason, it reminded Tong Yi of the castle at the southern gate, the palace his brother had built.

His magic tugged at him, getting him to turn his head and really look at the former shops.

No magical portal existed there, ready to take Tong Yi to some other place. Like his brother's "palace".

Currently.

Had one been built there? Recently? Like in the last week or so?

If the Red Zebra hadn't pulled up directly behind him, Tong Yi may have gotten off his bike and looked for evidence that a portal had been set up there at one point. Looked for a circle of characters outlined in ash.

He'd have to remember to ask Uncle Bei about it, the next day.

The officer sat for a moment. Tong Yi assumed he was running Bing Xi's plates.

All the messengers had been informed that if they broke any traffic laws while riding a *Huli* Transport vehicle, they were on their own.

Tong Yi sweat fiercely under the hot Taiwanese sun. At least while he'd been moving, there had been enough breeze to keep him cool in his company leathers, primarily brown with yellow accents. Now, he found himself steaming.

Finally, the patrolman got out of his car.

Tong Yi glanced back through his mirrors. No one sat in the passenger seat, so he only had one officer to deal with. Not that that made it any better.

"Nice ride," the patrolman said as he came walking up. He wasn't much taller than Tong Yi, despite his tall black boots. He had a round face with matching roundish eyes, a soft chin, and a small nose. His beige uniform deliberately mimicked the Army's uniforms. At least the volunteer ones.

"Thank you, sir," Tong Yi replied.

"It's registered to a *Huli* Transport?" the officer asked.

"That's the messengering service I work for," Tong Yi informed him.

The patrolman looked up and down the highway for a moment.

Tong Yi stiffened. There wasn't anything magical about the officer, at least as far as Tong Yi could tell.

But the man wanted *something*. A bribe? Tong Yi didn't have any money.

"How about you let me take her for a spin?" the officer asked after a moment.

Tong Yi blinked. He hadn't been expecting that at all.

He peered more closely at the patrolman. He was probably close to Tong Yi's age.

The man also had a cruel gleam in his eyes.

Would he deliberately wreck Bing Xi, given a chance?

Tong Yi gulped as his magical senses expanded.

That was *exactly* what the cop intended to do. To "teach" Tong Yi a lesson.

"I don't think that's a good idea," Tong Yi said. Could he persuade the patrolman to just give him a ticket instead? "I don't think Bing Xi will allow it."

"Cute," the patrolman said. "I suppose you also bought the ribbons across her handlebars? Like a couple of teenaged girls, braiding each others' hair?"

Tong Yi contained his snort, though he really wanted to laugh at the patrolman. "Not quite like that," he said. Bing Xi had rebraided the ribbons so they more closely resembled armor.

There wasn't anything magical or showy that Tong Yi could do to impress this cop, or to get him to back off. As a human, the patrolman wouldn't be able to see anything that was out of the ordinary.

Tong Yi could, however, lock the bike magically. Then, the cop could drop Bing Xi onto the ground, but that would be the only harm he'd be able to do. And Bing Xi could protect herself easily enough from that.

Tong Yi removed the keys from the ignition, then pressed his thumb against it.

The cop would never see the bright blue flash that enveloped the entire bike, magically protecting it.

The patrolman did, however, look uneasy as Tong Yi swung his leg over and got off.

"I doubt she'll even let you start her up," Tong Yi said, holding out the keys, "but be my guest."

The patrolman shook his head, clearing away his doubt. "Let me show you how it's done," he bragged.

Tong Yi kept his expression completely bland when the officer couldn't start up Bing Xi.

The patrolman forcefully stomped on the kickstarter again and again.

Bing Xi's engine didn't even turn over.

"You locked her down. Somehow," the cop accused Tong Yi.

Tong Yi merely shrugged. He did *not* reply with, "She just doesn't like you." Instead, he answered, "Maybe I'm just low on gas."

The patrolman looked back at the gauges.

Tong Yi knew that Bing Xi had more than enough fuel.

However, the cop replied, "Huh. I guess I pulled you over just in time. You are out of gas." He slid his leg off the bike, then deliberately pushed Bing

Xi over. "Have fun walking to the next town," he sneered as he made his way back to his Red Zebra.

Tong Yi sighed with relief when the cop finally pulled away. Only then did he right Bing Xi.

He'd been correct—the magical protection he'd put on the entire bike had prevented her from even a scratch.

Bing Xi started up with a growl.

Damn it. She was angry. He wasn't sure what had pissed her off more, the cocky cop trying to get her started, or that Tong Yi hadn't protected her better. Somehow.

As far as Tong Yi knew, he didn't have mind control over anyone. Particularly not anyone human. That wasn't how magic worked.

But maybe, maybe he could work more on his hiding skills.

What would the cop have done if he hadn't been able to find Tong Yi after he'd pulled over?

Thankfully, Bing Xi turned around easily, and they soon blasted back down the highway going the other direction, back toward Hualien City. At least they didn't run into more Red Zebras, and made it back to Tong Yi's parents' house without incident.

That night, after doing his meditation, Tong Yi thought more about Bing Xi. Who was she, really? A horse that transformed into a motorcycle? Some sort of hero, like Houyi? Or something else?

How could he protect her? Hide her from the bad people?

Though he knew, deep in his bones, that when push came to shove, hiding was not going to be an option.

Though Tong Yi hated getting up so early to go to the *Huli* Transport sales office, he did enjoy the quietness of the streets, how little traffic there was, how clear and cool the morning felt.

Before going to work for *Huli* Transport, Tong Yi had never considered traveling or working somewhere other than Taiwan.

He made good money, now. He'd almost finished paying off the debts left by his elder brother. He would soon be able to start saving all that extra money (and hazard pay). To do what, though?

Tong Yi didn't like to drink. Some of the boys he knew from high school went out to karaoke almost every night, drinking beer and whiskey until late.

He had no use for a fancy watch, or gold chains. He'd bought a serviceable used Honda motorcycle to replace the bike Quan Lo had stolen. He wasn't about to suddenly start wearing a suit, or even expensive shirts. T-shirts and shorts were good enough when he wasn't in his work uniform.

He did want to have his own family, someday. And his own house. He could just save the money. Worry about spending it later.

It wasn't as if Bing Xi really was his girlfriend, that he had to take out to expensive dinners or buy pretty things for.

Though he should probably get her something other than mere ribbons.

The alley behind the *Huli* Transport sales office looked the same, with a brick wall cutting the alley off about mid-way down the length of the block. Tong Yi paused at the end of the alley, peering closely at the wall.

Before, he could only see the magic in the wall when he got up close to it. Now, even from the end of the alley, the wall shimmered slightly. He couldn't see through it, but finally, he'd learned enough that he could tell it was something else. Something more than what it appeared.

Grinning, Tong Yi revved Bing Xi and drove as fast as he could for the wall, passing through it cleanly.

As he drove, he wondered if her insistence on speed was required. Could he just walk through the portal the wall represented?

He doubted it. He'd felt a slight barrier that he'd broken as he'd popped through. No one could casually go through the wall. There had to be intent.

Musing, Tong Yi slowed a little further down the lane where Uncle Bei stood.

Uncle Bei looked sourly at Tong Yi as he turned off Bing Xi, took off his helmet and gloves, then walked over to the wizard.

Uncle Bei appeared as he always did, in an impeccably tailored suit. The cloth was such a dark blue it appeared black. He wore a shiny green tie with white stripes running through it, and his usual red-jeweled cufflinks that held a tremendous amount of powerful magic.

Tong Yi waited while Uncle Bei peered at him, his dark eyes taking in all of Tong Yi's appearance, from uncovered head, across his leathers, down to his boots, then back up. He stared for a moment at Tong Yi's chest.

Directly at the tag hidden under Tong Yi's leathers and shirt.

The tag warmed. Tong Yi immediately pulled at the power it generated, pulling it into himself, strengthening himself.

Was Uncle Bei about to attack? Tong Yi tensed.

Finally, Uncle Bei nodded. "Let me know when you decide to stop playing at magic and want to learn real power," he said snidely.

"I will," Tong Yi told him solemnly. Not adding that it would have to be a cold day in Hell first before Tong Yi would turn to the lawyer for any sort of magical training.

"I suppose you don't know how to create a portal yet, do you?" Uncle Bei asked.

"I do not, sir," Tong Yi said. "But I'd love to learn. Oh, that reminds me. There was this abandoned string of shops up along highway 193. I didn't have a chance to look, but it felt as though a portal had been built there at some point."

Uncle Bei laughed at Tong Yi. Not in a kind way. "There are portals everywhere," he said. "They can be built anywhere. You're likely to run across remnants of them in every park and abandoned building you go to."

"Ah. I see. Thank you for teaching me," Tong Yi said gravely. "For correcting my ignorance."

Tong Yi maintained a solemn mien while Uncle Bei looked curiously at him again.

"All right," Uncle Bei finally said, seemingly mollified by Tong Yi's show of respect. "While it's good to note where other portals are being set up, you should *never* go through one of them. Remember, *Huli* Transport is *neutral* in all matters concerning the war. Going to the warzone through a non-neutral portal may mark you as a combatant."

Tong Yi's eyes widened. He hadn't considered that. "Thank you," he said again, more fervently.

Though he knew that what Uncle Bei said wasn't strictly true.

Huli Transport had chosen a side.

The side of law over chaos.

And Tong Yi was happy to be on that side as well.

Uncle Bei stretched his hands before him, as if he held a ripe moon fruit. He stared at the space between his widespread fingers, concentrating.

Power poured out from the wizard, cascading in waves over Tong Yi, causing him to shiver. Someone without the *sight* would have been able to feel it: they'd probably complain about an heir carelessly walking over their grave.

Tong Yi had originally thought that See-tza would have taken the wizard in any magical fight.

Now, he wasn't so sure.

A golden character formed between Uncle Bei's hands, lit with cool blue fire. The smell of burnt popcorn floated from it, making Tong Yi wrinkle his nose.

Excitement spiked through Tong Yi when he realized he recognized the character Uncle Bei had formed: the ancient Chinese ideogram for *run*.

Casually, Uncle Bei tossed the character in the air.

As before, a circle had been drawn on the gray stone patio that lay between two lines of trees in the other neighborhood beyond the alley wall. In the center of the circle sat the character *men*, meaning gate. It was about the size of Bing Xi. Uncle Bei had created that character first.

Around the outside of the waiting circle, more than two dozen other characters had already been laid out. The character Uncle Bei just generated flew directly to the next open spot on the waiting circle. Only a couple of empty spots remained.

Tong Yi had thought the lawyer had originally drawn the characters for the portal using red chalk.

Now, he realized how foolish that notion had been. The lawyer would *never* have gotten down on his knees and merely drawn the characters.

If the spell had required characters drawn on the ground, he would have had some minion do it.

Like Tong Yi.

"Can the characters only be formed this way?" Tong Yi asked as Uncle Bei gathered more power to himself, about to create the next character.

"Hmm?" Uncle Bei asked. He didn't reply until after he'd generated the next character. "There are many ways to create portals," he said, still sounding distracted. "Doing it this way ensures that the portal can hold more power. If you merely draw or paint the characters, the portal will close after only a few minutes. No way to hold it open."

"Then you'd have to create a second portal, wherever you landed, in order to get back home?" Tong Yi said. Would that take more energy? Or less?

"If you can," Uncle Bei said. "Some worlds are…less forgiving than others. Like the warzone. The land there is likely to drain your portal before you can even activate it."

"So how do people get back from there?" Tong Yi asked. Like Houyi. All her warriors.

"They have other ways," Uncle Bei said. He tossed the last character into the air. It spun lazily for a moment before it floated down into place, finishing the circle.

Was Uncle Bei showing off? Tong Yi wouldn't put it past him.

"Now, sprinkle the ashes like you did the first time," Uncle Bei instructed Tong Yi, handing him the same gray felt bag.

"What do the ashes do?" Tong Yi asked as he felt the weight of the bag. He'd expect ashes to be lighter, but these were surprisingly heavy. Maybe it was because of the magic.

"They *set* the characters," Uncle Bei replied. He paused for a moment, obviously searching for the right words. "When you draw the characters, you still have to fire them, somehow. Just pouring ash around them won't work. I fired the characters first. The ash holds them in place. Sets them against the concrete."

Uncle Bei narrowed his eyes at Tong Yi. "When you poured the ash for me the first time, you also poured what little magical power you had into it. Your desire for order and neatness mingled with the ashes. That gave the portal more stability. Remember, power hates to be contained. After a while, all portals dissolve because the power escapes. No matter how much of your own power you pour into it, eventually you can't power the portal enough to hold it open."

See-tza had said the same sort of things about power, though using different words, talking about the wild nature of power. How a free soul attracted it more. How forcing it to follow order would diminish it.

"I see," Tong Yi said. "It also made me very tired," he added. "I need to be on top of my game for this delivery. How would you advise me to pour the ashes today?" He hadn't expected Uncle Bei to talk with him about magic at all.

Or was Uncle Bei still showing off? Trying to prove that he'd be a more worthy teacher for Tong Yi?

Uncle Bei gave Tong Yi a very sharp smile. "I don't know. That depends on how long you want the portal to hold. The more power you pour with the ashes, the more stable the portal will be."

Tong Yi quietly sighed. That was the trick, wasn't it? If he gave more of himself, he'd have less power in the warzone.

But he'd also have more time there.

What was more critical? Time or power?

He didn't know.

He mentally flipped a coin. Not just any coin, no, the silver tag he wore. The side with his name came up first.

Fine. He'd use less power. Keep more of it for himself.

And hope like hell that he'd made the right choice.

"The portal will only be held for ninety minutes," Uncle Bei reminded Tong Yi as he put his helmet back on.

"I understand," Tong Yi said. "I will do my best to return before then."

He'd actually felt much better this time than he had the last time he'd poured ash for Uncle Bei, though he suspected he'd used about the same amount of power.

It appeared See-tza was right. He was getting stronger, magically.

But like any muscle, it took time to develop truly impressive strength.

Just creating one of the characters that Uncle Bei had done so easily would have left Tong Yi drained for a day or more.

He reminded himself he just had to have patience. Though Uncle Bei didn't appear to be that old, maybe only in his thirties, Tong Yi actually had no idea how old the lawyer was.

"See that you do," Uncle Bei said. He paused, then added quietly, "I know you've found another teacher. Possibly one that's more in line with your natural abilities. However, you will outgrow her. Faster than you realize."

Tong Yi blinked. Was Uncle Bei paying him a compliment?

Then the lawyer laughed sharply. "Not that you'll be able to challenge me for a few decades. If ever." He shrugged. "Still. Consider my offer. When you're ready for real power. You know where to find me."

"Thank you, sir," Tong Yi said. He bowed his head.

He still didn't think he'd *ever* take Uncle Bei up on his offer. As the lawyer had just said, See-tza's magic and training were more in line with Tong Yi's nature.

Sort of. Kind of.

He'd have to see.

"Good luck," Uncle Bei said after Tong Yi started Bing Xi up.

He didn't sound worried, did he?

"See you later, if you can make it back!" he called, stepping back and out of the way.

What the hell did that mean?

Tong Yi just shook his head.

He would come back. And through the portal, not via the badlands.

Just to prove Uncle Bei wrong.

Tong Yi shot through the portal at greater speed than usual. Bing Xi spun her wheels on the dirt and dried grass, bumping across rocks.

The *stench* of the place broke through Tong Yi's filtered helmet. He swallowed hard, bile building in the back of his throat.

What *was* that?

He slowed and glanced down.

Shit.

He'd landed in the middle of a battlefield.

Bodies lay strewn as far as he could see.

He sped up, desperately searching the horizon for a clear area. Away from the devastation.

More than a day had passed since the battle. He suspected that the land had sped up the putrefaction, added to the foulness as an expression of its general hatred.

Tong Yi tried to avoid the bodies as he drove on. The teeth and long snouts of the mole men, the *zhi ren*, lay sundered from their bodies. Arms and legs had been torn and flung as though a giant tornado had come through.

However, Tong Yi couldn't avoid the gore Bing Xi threw up with her tires, tearing out of there.

He shuddered as her tires spun and he felt the slap of the mud. He was never going to get the stench out of his leathers.

A line of rocks made him swerve. Then he realized they weren't rocks.

Heads of the mole men, the *zhi ren*, sat piled in a long row on the edge of the battlefield.

Opposite the heads of the mole men lay a second line. Humanoid heads. Interspersed with animal parts, cat paws and long horse noses, mule legs and huge panda-bear bellies. Plus pieces of garbage from the human world, like the empty struts of an umbrella that had eyes hanging from it. Or the refrigerator door with dead arms and legs splayed out.

Tong Yi grimly kept his eyes to the west, away from the ridge that he always associated with the badlands.

It wasn't difficult to guess that he'd landed where Quan Lo's men had fought the mole men.

Finally, Tong Yi drove past the debris of bodies. He kept going, wondering if he could outrun the stench. He slowed after a few moments more.

Damn it! Why did Uncle Bei drop Tong Yi there? Where was Sun Hou-tse? He was supposed to be in an encampment nearby.

Tong Yi turned to look back.

Ah hell. He was going to have to drive through all those bodies a second time when he returned to the portal.

He swallowed hard, determined not to throw up.

At least not until he got back to Hualien City.

He scanned the horizon again. There had to be an encampment nearby. Where?

Fortunately, he had some luck, and spotted it.

If the battleground ran north-south, and he was now in the center of the western side, there, on the south-west corner, stood tents.

Tong Yi pulled out the purely mechanical watch he'd purchased for his trips to the warzone.

It showed that he'd been there for eleven minutes already.

He didn't have long at all before the portal closed.

"Let's go," he told Bing Xi. "We want to fetch the message, deliver it, then get back to the portal before Uncle Bei closes it."

Bing Xi revved her engine and leaped forward, as if in agreement.

It took Tong Yi another seven minutes to reach the corner of the battlefield, going as fast as he dared. He couldn't avoid the smell when the wind blew the wrong way, but at least he could swerve around the shoals of bodies.

He only missed once or twice: The squelching sound of flesh under his tires was sure to follow him into his nightmares for years.

Houyi's camp had been made up of mostly brown tents, with a deliberate perimeter. Guards stood at the gate. The tents themselves laid out in ordered lines, with her tent raised in the very center.

Sun Hou-tse's camp had all different sizes of tents, some tall and thin, some squat and long. Brown, beige, and green seemed to be the predominant colors, but sprinkled in among them were also red, blue, and purple. The lanes between them zigged and zagged, as if a child playing in the park had laid them out.

Tong Yi slowed after he crossed into the camp. He took a deep, needed breath. The border was obvious to him, the pulsing hatred of the land immediately dulled. The air seemed cleaner there as well, the constant stench of death lessened. He found himself blinking.

When he looked over his shoulder at the battlefield, the bodies hadn't faded. However, the horror of it no longer seemed as intense.

How much of the gore from the battlefield was real? Did it affect him more because of his magical training? Or was the warzone playing tricks on him?

There wasn't any time to figure it out now. He needed to find Sun Houtse's tent. Would it be in the center? Like Houyi's?

That seemed too ordered for this mishmash.

Something made him look toward the southern part.

Wasn't the monkey king originally from the south?

Tong Yi swerved again, crossing the barrier of the camp so he could drive around it and get to the far southern edge quicker.

The hatred from the land pushed at him more softly, now. No sun beat down on him, but he felt warmer as well.

Most of the camp seemed to be abandoned. Tong Yi wasn't sure how he knew, but the tents sat empty.

Were the soldiers just off fighting in some other part of the warzone? Or had they all fallen?

Only a few soldiers sat outside of their tents, resting. Like the men in Houyi's camp, they wore ancient banded armor. Almost all the ones he saw wore the traditional straw sandals as well.

However, the soldiers weren't necessarily human. They had the faces of monkeys, like the best of Hollywood extras for those ape movies. They also weren't all men, either. At least half of those he saw were women.

Finally, Tong Yi saw a large, red tent. It was the traditional Chinese red, the color for weddings and joyous times. Red and green pennants flew above it, just like the ones above Houyi's tent.

Tong Yi slowly drove up to the main tent. At least guards stood outside there. Some sort of order.

Which side was the Monkey King on?

He reminded himself that *Huli* Transport was strictly neutral. They delivered messages to *all* sides.

No matter which side Tong Yi might personally align himself with.

Tong Yi pulled up in front of the red tent. He took a moment to turn Bing Xi off, rock her back onto her kickstand, then he magically locked the bike. The blue flash seemed much brighter here. Maybe there was just more to protect her against.

He took a deep breath as he approached the guards. They had monkey faces though their bodies were manlike.

"I'm from *Huli* Transport," Tong Yi announced. "Here to pick up a message from Sun Hou-tse."

The one on the right gave Tong Yi a grim smile. "So you're the messenger. We were told to expect you."

His eyes looked old, a brown faded to almost gray. Many wrinkles creased around his eyes.

Tong Yi fished out his messenger badge. The guard on the left held out his hand. He seemed much younger, with golden brown eyes. He put the badge in the palm of his strangely articulate ape hand, then brushed the top of it with long, brown fingers. His eyes glowed slightly as he looked at the badge.

Tong Yi tried to contain his patience. He didn't have time for this.

The guards had a musky, sour smell up close, like cats who'd stopped bathing. They both wore ancient armor, with brightly polished silver bands tied together with brown, red, and green ribbons.

Both had long swords strapped to their backs, with smaller knives tied to their calves and sharp daggers strapped to their arms. They wore the traditional straw sandals, though the straw was no longer clean, but bore the dirt and dust of the land.

However, they both had helmets that looked like battered bronze pots. Why were they so shapeless when the rest of the guards' armor fit them so well?

When the one guard finished examining Tong Yi's messenger badge, he looked up, staring directly at Tong Yi.

The tag resting against Tong Yi's chest warmed. Tong Yi tensed, ready to pull magic from the medallion if he was attacked.

Instead, the guard barred his teeth in what Tong Yi hoped was a smile.

"You go in now," he said, handing back Tong Yi's badge.

Funny, to Tong Yi it now felt as though the badge had *less* magic than it had before.

Did the examination by the guard drain it, somehow? Did it recharge itself, sipping at Tong Yi's power? That would make sense. Particularly if it was an artifact created by Uncle Bei. He wouldn't want to recharge the badges himself.

Tong Yi was going to have to pay much closer attention to the badge. Next time.

"Thank you," Tong Yi said to the guards. He bent his head and went through the door. He'd already been in the warzone for twenty-three minutes.

That left merely sixty-seven minutes before the portal closed.

And he'd have to go through that field of bodies again.

Tong Yi stopped just inside the tent, letting his eyes adjust.

Two figures stood in the center of the tent.

The figure on the left, Tong Yi assumed was the Monkey King.

The figure on the right grinned at him.

"Welcome! Welcome, my friend!"

It was the Monkey Man. The one who'd sold him the motorcycle that Quan Lo had then stolen.

The supposed cousin of the other messenger, Han Di.

The Monkey King and the Monkey Man shared a family resemblance. Both had flat faces, prominent jaws, and tiny eyes, as well as very dark skin. The Monkey Man's hair was roughly cut, as though he'd hacked it off himself with a knife. However, the Monkey King's hair was golden, with soft curls around his face.

They wore completely different outfits. The Monkey Man still dressed in his work clothes, a light blue shirt stained with grease and a pair of dark blue pants that hid the stains better. The ends of the pants, too, looked as though they'd been hacked off unevenly with a knife, just below his knees.

The Monkey Man still looked as wide as Tong Yi, though he barely came up to Tong Yi's chest. He stood in a wide stance, barefoot, displaying feet that were just as huge as his hands.

The Monkey King had roughly the same build as the Monkey Man, wide and short. However, the king wore beautiful red and gold armor. Instead of realistic bands of metal, it had a single breast plate, made out of red metal with gold filigree around the edges. He wore similar bracers and shin plates. His skirt looked Roman, not Chinese, made of wide strips of leather, tipped in metal.

"Ah, the messenger!" the Monkey King exclaimed. He grinned at Tong Yi.

For a moment, Tong Yi had the strongest feeling of being in the same room as See-tza.

He recognized it as being in the presence of a magical being,

How much of what he saw was part of the Monkey King's true appearance?

"I am here, as requested," Tong Yi said, using formal language.

He concentrated on the two…beings. The rest of the room held too many distractions. Brightly colored pillows lay scattered across the floor, with a gleam of enchantment on them, inviting those standing to sit and linger. The rugs soothed the eye and warmed the soul. Hanging strips of cloth separated the back of the tent from the front, a barrier that almost repelled Tong Yi.

His head already hurt from standing in this tent. The thick taste of magic coated the back of his throat, like burnt sugar. His ears hummed with a low buzz. His skin tingled.

Was this why See-tza's office stood so empty? Because of the effort it took to block out all the rest of the magic?

Surely she could have mundane furnishings. Or maybe she couldn't. Tong Yi had wondered if such a magical being automatically impregnated everything with magic. If this was why the Sweet Shop was so sweet.

Then the tag in the center of his chest spiked, sending warmth through his whole torso.

Without thinking about it, Tong Yi *pulled* at the magic the tag sent out.

Suddenly, all the magic in the tent receded.

What the hell had just happened? Of course it would take magic to repel magic. Was the tent *attacking* Tong Yi in some fashion?

The Monkey King's smile remained, but Tong Yi would swear it had just lost three degrees of warmth.

"So you know my cousin?" he asked, indicating the Monkey Man.

"We met once. Briefly," Tong Yi said.

He was going to have to tease Han Di about his cousin.

Or maybe not.

He didn't want to get his friend into trouble with the company.

"We did meet!" the Monkey Man said, bobbing his head. "You buy good bike from me. You give to your brother, then." His eyes gleamed.

Tong Yi almost opened his mouth to correct the man. But then he closed it. He hadn't given away the bike.

And as he'd said before, he had no brother. Not really. Not anymore.

"You have a message for me? Sir?" Tong Yi asked Sun Hou-tse. He needed to collect his message and be gone. Before the portal closed.

The Monkey King tilted his head to one side and examined Tong Yi. "I do. It is for Zhang Gua Lao."

Tong Yi nearly groaned. That was how this whole mess started. With him delivering that first message to the immortal.

The one who'd warned him about the war.

"Sir?" Tong Yi said as the Monkey King continued to merely stare at Tong Yi.

"I will give you the message directly," Sun Hou-tse said. "But I think you should deliver it on foot."

"Excuse me?" Tong Yi asked. He wasn't about to just leave Bing Xi behind.

"You should hand me your keys, now," the Monkey King said, holding out his hand.

The spike of warmth in the center of Tong Yi's chest from his medallion quickly cooled. He struggled to pull more power out of it. "You are interfering with a messenger from *Huli* Transport. You do not want to do that. The fines will be astronomical."

He found his hand slipping into his pocket.

No!

The Monkey King's eyes glowed red and gold, staring into his.

Tong Yi told himself that he could do this. He could resist this being. He tried to close his eyes, turn away.

His hand slipped into his jacket pocket.

"The fines only matter if your side wins," Sun Hou-tse replied.

"*Huli* Transport is neutral, sir," Tong Yi replied automatically.

Damn it! His hand was all the way inside his jacket pocket now.

"Don't worry about your girlfriend," the Monkey Man said. "I will take very good care of her."

"I will press charges," Tong Yi told them. He hadn't the first time with Quan Lo. This was a completely different matter.

This was no longer *family.*

"Only if you're able to catch me!" Sun Hou-tse replied gleefully.

Tong Yi found himself handing his keys over to the Monkey King.

"Please, don't," Tong Yi whispered. "Don't do this to me."

But he had no choice. He dropped his keys into Sun Hou-tse's waiting hand.

Tong Yi just hoped Bing Xi would forgive him.

Tong Yi blinked. How did he arrive here? He stood just past the border of the Monkey King's encampment. He still wore his leathers and his helmet. The stench of the battlefield to his right rolled over him, waking him up further. How did a cool breeze manage to find its way here? He shivered, chickenflesh rolling across his shoulders.

He immediately reached for his keys.

Damn it. He *had* handed them over to the Monkey King.

His hand closed around an envelope that rested in his pocket instead.

Slowly, Tong Yi pulled out the red envelope that held his message. The one he needed to deliver.

The one addressed to Zhang Gua Lao.

Tong Yi turned back toward the camp. Though it was only a few feet away, it seemed hazy, as though he viewed it through a heat haze.

He knew instinctively that Sun Hou-tse had closed his camp to Tong Yi.

The only way he'd get back in was after he'd delivered his message.

Bing Xi…hopefully she could take care of herself.

Then Tong Yi was going to demand his pound of flesh from the Monkey King. Plus any additional damages that he could think up.

Now, where to find the immortal? He must be here in the warzone, somewhere.

Tong Yi thought for a moment.

If the Monkey King had come from the south, Zhang Gua Lao came from the north. He was the eldest of the Immortals, and the most calm. The north had always been his element.

Tong Yi took off, running directly north.

He had less than fifty minutes to find the immortal.

Or die trying.

Tong Yi *ran* beside the long battlefield, heading north.

He hated running. He'd had to run regularly as part of his military service. Had never grown accustomed to it.

He had no choice, however.

Run he must. And as fast as he could.

The ruts in the land kept trying to trip him. Pulses of *hate* emanated from everywhere. The stench rolling off the putrefying bodies intensified. Ill winds blew awful smells at him, chilling what skin he had exposed.

Tong Yi tripped.

He put his hands out and *pushed* in that brief second, willing himself not to touch the awfulness of the ground beneath him.

He flew upwards instead.

What the hell?

Tong Yi came back to earth gently.

His magic had picked him up, prevented him from actually falling.

Could he somehow use magic to move more quickly?

Tong Yi bounced up and down on his toes. It felt wrong, somehow, to be trying a magic experiment when who knew what foulness Bing Xi was suffering at the hands of Sun Hou-tse.

Still. He tried taking a great leap.

Heart pounding, he rose off the ground, landing several feet away.

He paused, looking back again.

Maybe he could do this.

He took another leap. And another.

Soon, he *bounded* across the warzone.

He pulled power out of the very land itself. Channeled it explosively into every step. The medal on his chest grew warm as he poured in more energy, then pushed it out again.

The madness of it made him giggle. He moved like an anime character.

Anyone watching him would think him insane.

He kind of felt that way. Giddy with power. Pleased with every step that pushed him away from the land.

Normally, Tong Yi tried to live within the law.

Right here, right now, breaking the natural rules felt okay.

It took him much less time than he'd expected to get to the far northern side of the battleground.

Now, where was Zhang Gua Lao hiding?

Tong Yi closed his eyes, then rotated around in a circle, trying to *feel* his way.

Nothing.

He put his hand in his pocket, pressing his bare fingers against the red envelope. It would warm in the presence of its recipient. He tried again.

The first thing that drew him was at the very center of the battlefield.

The portal, he realized.

The second stood further north. The envelope didn't grow warm, but it did very slightly press against his waiting fingers.

There. A little north and east. If he drew a line down the center of the battlefield, then continued north, that would be the spot.

He checked his watch. Less than thirty minutes remained.

Would he get to Zhang Gua Lao in time? Then back to the camp with the Monkey King?

He suddenly realized that the Monkey King had planned this.

Tong Yi would have to abandon Bing Xi if he wanted to make it to the portal in time.

Sun Hou-tse should understand faithful service. Or at least the tales told about him implied that he did.

Tong Yi wondered if the stories were true. Or if those tales just told of a single aspect of the Monkey King. If they didn't display his true nature.

Which seemed to worship chaos, not order.

Tong Yi continued to bound across the landscape, heading directly toward that spot he'd identified. Whenever he stuck his hand in his pocket, he felt the envelope growing warmer.

He *was* going in the right direction.

However, his progress slowed. He bounded as far as he could with the next step, but it was half what he'd done previously.

Then half again.

No matter how he pushed, how high he tried to bounce, he could no longer make the same sort of progress.

What was wrong?

Tong Yi couldn't spend time trying to figure it out. Though it was already hopeless, he still raced against the clock to get to the immortal and back to his bike before time ran out and the portal closed. So he stopped trying to bound and changed to running.

At least he regained speed. For a short while.

Then he was forced to slow down again.

Damn it! Why couldn't he go faster?

Tong Yi sighed. He knew why.

One of the lessons that the immortal taught frequently was patience.

How could Tong Yi be patient and yet still approach the immortal quickly?

Tong Yi stopped, took a deep breath, and tried to release all his anger, all his urgency, all his haste with his breath.

He took three more breaths before he finally felt calmer. Despite how the land pulsed hatred at him, he still felt composed. Not frantic. Not calm, but approaching that.

He took a few more breaths, remembering his nightly meditations. That helped as well.

Finally, Tong Yi started walking.

He merely walked. He kept his pace leisurely.

Yet, it seemed as though he ate *li* with each small step.

Huh. Would this pace take him back to the Monkey King's kingdom more quickly as well?

He might have to try it and see.

Up ahead, a towering rock drew his attention. A white rock. It was at least as tall as a three-story house.

He gulped, dreading for a moment that it might be made of bone.

As he drew closer, the rock resolved itself.

It was Zhang Gua Lao's donkey.

It spotted Tong Yi and gave a loud braying greeting that hurt Tong Yi's ears.

Its breath smelled like fresh grass, stirring hope in Tong Yi's chest, warming the medallion there.

Zhang Gua Lao appeared beside the donkey. He wore a formal set of brown robes, edged with white, and with white cuffs. A huge brown leather belt was buckled around his waist, with a myriad of small bags hanging from it. He wore his black-and-white streaked hair in a bun with three long, red hairpins sticking from it.

He also stood as tall as a skyscraper, the kind they had in Taipei.

Tong Yi gulped. How could he talk with the immortal when he was all the way up there? How could he deliver his message?

Then the immortal started shrinking. His head came down so fast it made Tong Yi dizzy. After another moment, Zhang Gua Lao stepped out from behind one of his donkey's legs.

"Ah, my young friend. So good to see you! Welcome. You must come fishing with me today," the immortal said. He wore the same outfit as he had when he'd been taller.

"Maybe next time," Tong Yi said as he pulled the envelope out of his pocket.

"Oh, no. I insist," the old man said.

Tong Yi opened his mouth to protest, but Zhang Gua Lao had already turned his back.

"Come!" the immortal said imperiously.

"But, sir!" Tong Yi complained.

"Come," Zhang Gua Lao repeated without slowing down or turning around. "Do me this kindness."

Tong Yi sighed. All the tales of Zhang Gua Lao told of how he rewarded those who showed kindness or respect.

Hopefully, they didn't lie, and the immortal would help Tong Yi return to the Monkey King's camp in time.

A gray haze covered the land of the warzone, just a few paces from the donkey. The immortal didn't pause but walked right through.

Tong Yi helplessly followed. He needed to give the immortal his message.

He was already late, it had taken him so long to get here.

And what was happening to Bing Xi?

The haze washed over Tong Yi like a brief, wet mist. It cleansed his skin and his soul, washing away the grime and hopelessness. He suddenly took a deep breath, as if he hadn't for an age or more.

He found himself standing on the edge of a pond. Brilliant green trees rose up on either side, soft pines and gentle oaks. Fish plopped in the water under a brilliant blue sky. The air smelled sweet and felt soft against his cheeks.

Zhang Gua Lao was already sitting on the bank, his brown robes tucked up under his crossed legs. A bamboo fishing pole dangled a long line into the water.

"I'm so happy you're here!" the immortal said, patting the ground beside him.

Tong Yi sat, grateful that he didn't have to squat. He'd still not developed the knack of that. He took off his motorcycle helmet and placed it beside him. The envelope in his pocket put out a soft, warm heat.

The earth felt good under his bare hands. Welcoming and *right* in a way he'd never noticed before. This was a land that he'd relish walking slowly through, wearing only straw sandals so he could feel its goodness, the dirt coloring his feet.

While Tong Yi might sometimes still race and bound across such a land, it would be for sheer joy, not merely from haste.

Where was this place? Was it where the immortal actually lived? His home? Tong Yi wasn't sure. But it felt like a comforting place.

Tong Yi took the bamboo pole the old man handed him. It already had a modern hook on the end of it, with a squiggling worm baited there.

Tong Yi didn't look too closely at either. The worm glowed bright blue. It had a *presence* that surprised Tong Yi. It wasn't evil—that would have made him drop the pole. But it wasn't good, either. The hook itself had its own metallic gleam, shiny and new. Sleek and mean.

"Thank you, sir," Tong Yi said. He sneaked a look at his mechanical pocket watch, to see how much time he had there.

Less than thirty minutes left.

With a sigh, Tong Yi put his watch away, then followed the old fisherman's example, dropping his line into the water.

The quiet of the place stole over Tong Yi's soul. He found his breathing slowed even more, until it was like he was meditating. His worry for Bing Xi didn't diminish, but he found he wasn't in as much of a panic.

"So why are you here?" Zhang Gua Lao finally asked.

"Sir?" Tong Yi asked. "To give you this message," he added, reaching for his pocket.

"That is not what I asked," the immortal said sternly. "I know you have your job. And I realize that I asked you here, to fish with me. But you could have left the company, walked away from *Huli* Transport, after your first job, when the *fenghuang* attacked you. Or after the first trip to the warzone. What brings you back? And what keeps you sane? Why are you still whole?"

Tong Yi blinked, surprised. What did the immortal mean? He'd signed contracts. He liked his job, except for the parts he didn't. He had to support his parents, dig them out of the hole left behind by Quan Lo. He…

He could have left it at any time. His parents—his mother in particular—wanted him to get a safer job. A desk job. Preferably in a bank.

Tong Yi wasn't doing it for the money, no matter how much he might tell himself that.

An expectant air enveloped them as he rolled his reply around in his head.

This place encouraged the truth. A bluntness that Tong Yi had never experienced before. Almost American in nature.

Even more so than what he'd sometimes felt in the warzone.

"It's the world, sir," Tong Yi said. "There's just—there's so much more out there than I'd ever realized before. So much outside of the human realm that I want to learn about. To see and experience." The words tumbled from him. "I don't know if I'll ever be a great magician. I don't care." That surprised him. He hadn't realized that about himself. The words kept coming. "It just opens up another aspect, a new place to explore. More to learn about."

"Sounds to me as though you want to become a great traveler, or explorer," Zhang Gua Lao said.

"That isn't it," Tong Yi said, shaking his head. "I don't need to go see the world. I want to see everything here." He knew he wasn't making much sense. "Leaving Taiwan…I will do that someday. But this island, and its people, and the magic—it's all like an onion."

"Specialist then," Zhang Gua Lao speculated. "Not generalist or adventurist."

"Exactly!" Tong Yi said. He wanted to go deep, not broad, in his knowledge and learning.

To be an expert in everything for his city, his culture, his small portion of the world.

That didn't mean he didn't want to travel at some point.

He just knew that he would always feel homesick.

"You are a very special man," Zhang Gua Lao said. "Few learn their actual place in the world, where best to plant their feet and grow. It is my honor to make your acquaintance."

Tong Yi stuck his pole in the dirt, as Zhang Gua Lao had. He pressed his palms together and bowed his head. "The honor is all mine, sir," he replied.

And it was. He'd never realized his place before. How tightly connected he was.

How he'd travel and stray, but always come back home.

"If only the others felt as you did," Zhang Gua Lao said with a sigh. "We might have avoided the whole war."

Tong Yi couldn't help but stiffen. However, he turned and casually picked up his pole instead. "What do you mean?" he asked, trying desperately to sound bland and not to show how excited he was at the prospect of finally, *finally*, learning more about the war.

"Let me tell you a story," the immortal said.

"The Yellow Emperor originally formed the Middle Kingdom out of the mists of chaos," Zhang Gua Lao said.

Tong Yi tried to keep the confusion from his face. What was the immortal talking about? The land of the Middle Kingdom existed before the Yellow Emperor, didn't it?

"He carved out a space for his people, using rock and stone, the bones of the five sacred animals, and promises of the wind and the rain," Zhang Gua Lao continued.

Tong Yi had never heard of that. He knew that the Yellow Emperor had been a civilizing influence on the Chinese people. That he'd brought government and law to a lawless nation. Though some historians doubted that the Yellow Emperor had been an actual person, there were many, many accomplishments laid at his feet, like farming and mathematics.

The fish in the placid lake plopped, as if agreeing with Tong Yi. Soft breezes blew the trees beside them, rustling the leaves quietly. Sweet pine smells soothed Tong Yi's still urgent need to *move* and get going again, to go rescue Bing Xi. At least the breezes were cool here, and Tong Yi didn't find himself sweating in his leathers. Zhang Gua Lao also looked comfortable in his brown robes.

The immortal gave Tong Yi an indulgent smile. "I knew the young Yellow Emperor," he said confidentially. "Wild and full of ideals."

Tong Yi nodded, still confused but now full of questions. Tong Yi wanted to know more about the actual man.

"The Yellow Emperor brought law, true law, to the Middle Kingdom," Zhang Gua Lao continued. "His law was so powerful, so strong, that he was the first human to truly bind wild magic."

"So the Yellow Emperor was the first human wizard?" Tong Yi asked. This was awesome!

"In many ways, yes," the immortal said. "Instead of using the natural elements, which most wizards and magicians had done before him, he made *power* do his bidding, binding chaotic magic to his will. Since then, that is the path most men have followed."

"And chaos is still angry about that?" Tong Yi guessed.

"Exactly!" Zhang Gua Lao said. He beamed at Tong Yi as if he was a particularly bright pupil. "If you ask Zhongli Quan, whose fan stirs the seas in the east, he would tell you the war is about fishing rights. For his people's right to keep their catch and exploit their traditional territories, while the leviathans and other ocean monsters who rule those waters disagree. But if you ask Tieguai Li, he would tell you it's about power, and how the other immortals are using up all the magic in the world, leaving none for him or his kind."

Tong Yi blinked, confused again.

"Each of the immortals fights chaos in their own way," Zhang Gua Lao explained gently. "But in the end, the war remains the same. The battle between order and chaos. Chaos has never forgiven the Yellow Emperor for imposing order on it."

"It sounds as though all eight immortals are waging their own individual war," Tong Yi said slowly. Which meant…what a mess. And the other beings, as well. The heroes. And beings of legend. Were they fighting for themselves too? Like the Monkey King and Houyi?

"In some ways, they are," Zhang Gua Lao said with a sigh. The immortal sagged and looked older suddenly. "They fight without understanding how they are being goaded to fight. They battle without realizing that just by fighting, chaos wins."

Tong Yi shivered. "But they're immortals!" he complained. "Surely they know better." With horror, Tong Yi realized that Ren Wu had said the exact same thing.

Zhang Gua Lao gave a harsh, barking laugh. "Too many years of competition between them. Too much animosity. Too many humans now writing stories of us killing each other." The old man shivered. "We were once treated with respect. We taught morals to mortals, how to live good lives. We didn't war like the humans did."

Tong Yi shook his head. This land, this place, made him speak when he normally wouldn't. "You were paid too much respect, possibly."

The old man shot Tong Yi a quick smile. "True enough. Too much order is also a bad thing. It leads to all magic being stifled. The curious being ostracized. Those who are different becoming scapegoats. Villains."

"So this war is for nothing?" Tong Yi asked, the words tasting bitter.

Zhang Gua Lao shrugged. "It is teaching a new generation to fight. To decide what is important to them. To follow those choices all the way to the vicious end. Tell me," he continued, turning his dark eyes directly at Tong Yi, staring all the way into his soul, "did you mean what you said when you declared that you had no brother?"

Tong Yi wanted to deny it. Wanted to deny that he'd even said such a thing.

He could not, though.

"I did," he said. He swallowed hard against the bile that suddenly rose up. "I can't have a brother who is the opposite of me."

Zhang Gua Lao gave him a tight smile. "Ah, but that might be exactly what you need. His chaos to balance your order."

Tong Yi shivered. No. The immortal was wrong. The divide between him and his brother had grown into an impossible chasm that neither of them could cross.

If it was just the chaos and the war, that might be fine. But the drugs and the stealing, the way Quan Lo had abused their parents…Tong Yi wasn't certain if he could ever forgive him for that.

Or ever believe his brother if he claimed to be sober.

"We will see," the immortal predicted wisely. "Now, give me your message so that I might answer it and you might be on your way."

Tong Yi pulled the red envelope out of his pocket. He held his hands over his head and offered the message to Zhang Gua Lao, then sat back and waited.

Why was he so conflicted?

He needed to go rescue Bing Xi. To get back through the battlefield and to the portal. If it was still open.

But this place soothed his soul, brought him such tranquility. He felt reluctant to leave. Contentment flowed over him, keeping him rooted here.

He had his duty, though. And he wouldn't abandon a friend, a true companion.

"Here," Zhang Gua Lao said, handing Tong Yi back the envelope, this time folded into a tiny frog. He'd also changed the color of the envelope, from a deep, pleasing red to a bright green. "Please return this to Sun Hou-tse."

Tong Yi nearly objected. Then he shrugged. Since he had to go back to the Monkey King anyway.

But if Sun Hou-tse had another message, Tong Yi would *not* deliver it.

"And here," the immortal added, handing Tong Yi a bronze coin.

It felt warm and heavy against Tong Yi's hand. It had a small square cut in the center of it, like an ancient *cash*. The character for *ba*, eight, had been carved crudely into one side, and the other had the ancient character *ma* for horse.

"Go rescue your lady," the immortal said. "This will help. And consider your options. Chaos will not survive without order to fight against. But neither will order."

Suddenly, Tong Yi found himself standing on the edge of the Monkey King's camp. The coin in his hand flared brightly in the dim light. The camp no longer appeared hazy, but clear.

As Tong Yi hurried along the twisted lanes, he fished out his pocket watch.

He had thirty minutes. More time than he'd expected. The immortal *had* helped him with that too.

Maybe he and Bing Xi could get back to the portal before it closed.

Tong Yi took just a moment to verify that Bing Xi stood, seemingly unharmed, outside of Sun Hou-tse's tent. She stood stone still, colder than he'd ever felt her. Almost as though she'd become a statue.

Gods, what had they done to her?

There wasn't anything he could do about that now. He had to deliver his message, then get out of there.

Hopefully Bing Xi could still run, and he wasn't going to have to walk her back through the battlefield to the portal. If that was the case, they'd never make it back in time.

The guards waved Tong Yi directly through the entrance, not bothering to stop him.

He wasn't sure he would have stopped, not unless they'd pulled their swords on him.

Sun Hou-tse and the Monkey Man stood as they had been the first time he'd come into the tent. The Monkey King's armor looked the same, splendid red and gold.

Did the Monkey Man's shirt now have more grease stains on it?

Shit. What had they done to poor Bing Xi?

"You made good time," the Monkey King said sourly. "I suppose that old fool helped you."

Tong Yi shrugged. "I showed him a kindness," he said honestly enough. Was the immortal lonely? Did not enough young men go fishing with him? How many took the time to listen to the immortal's tales? To learn from his wisdom?

"*Hau*," the Monkey Man said, grinning. He looked very satisfied with himself.

Tong Yi wished that he had more magic, enough to wipe that smirk from the Monkey Man's face.

Dread settled deep in Tong Yi's bones.

The message in Tong Yi's pocket grew warm. "I do have a response for you, sir," he said. He drew the tiny frog out and held it in his palm.

When the Monkey King reached for it, Tong Yi moved his hand out of the way. "My keys," he insisted.

The Monkey King bared his teeth at Tong Yi. "What if I've decided to keep your bike?"

"That would be a very, very unwise thing to do," Tong Yi warned. "My motorcycle is *Huli* Transport property." While replacing a messenger would be costly, he wasn't sure that there was another creature like Bing Xi.

Tong Yi was almost looking forward to the havoc that Uncle Bei would loose on Sun Hou-tse if he insisted on keeping her.

"I know. And you still maintain that you are *neutral*," the Monkey King sneered.

Tong Yi's keys appeared in Sun Hou-tse's other hand. "Trade ya," he said.

Tong Yi dropped the frog into the Monkey King's outstretched hand at the same moment the Monkey King released Tong Yi's keys.

They felt…greasy. Gritty. Marked in ways that Tong Yi could only guess at.

He was going to have to get See-tza to teach him a cleansing spell.

Or maybe Uncle Bei.

"What is this?"

Tong Yi winced at the Monkey King's shout. His ears rang afterwards. He took a shallow breath, unable to breathe deeply, as if all the air had been pushed from the tent.

Tong Yi found that Sun Hou-tse stared directly at Tong Yi.

"Sir?" he asked, confused. That had been the message that Zhang Gua Lao had given him. What was Sun Hou-tse's problem?

"What am I supposed to do with this?" the Monkey King asked. He showed it to his cousin, who merely laughed at him.

"Stop it," the Monkey King told him.

That just made the Monkey Man giggle harder.

Sun Hou-tse looked in disgust at the green paper frog he pinched between long, brown fingers. "Here," he said, flinging the paper being at Tong Yi. "You take it. Since you're so enamored with the old man."

The frog landed in the center of Tong Yi's chest, exactly where his medallion lay under his leathers and shirt. He would swear that it clung there for a few moments before he plucked it off.

"Sir, the message is for you," Tong Yi said sternly, addressing the frog as much as the Monkey King.

"And I am pretending to be you, now," Sun Hou-tse said in a whiny voice. "I now deliver my message to you," he added formally.

Tong Yi recognized the ritual for what it was. That the message was now truly his. "I thank you for your duty," he replied, cupping the little frog carefully then sticking it in his pocket.

He bowed his head to both the Monkey King and the Monkey Man, then hurried out of the tent.

He had less than thirty minutes, now. Maybe only twenty.

If anyone could get him to the portal before it closed, Bing Xi could.

Tong Yi ran his hands across Bing Xi's handlebars, down the sides of her gas tank, sweeping up across the seat and down to the rear wheel.

She felt *cold*. He wasn't certain how or why, or what was causing it.

Tong Yi visually inspected her lines, but the brake and clutch seemed to be connected. Her engine looked clean.

It wasn't until he got to her gas cap that he realized the problem.

Bing Xi had a locking gas cap.

The key had been broken off inside the lock.

Cursing, Tong Yi pulled out his other keys. He called up a quick fire, running his fingers across them, warming and cleaning them.

It didn't take too much effort to pry out the broken off key, using the long, thin strip of metal attached to his father's Vespa key.

He blanched when he finally got a look at what now filled Bing Xi's gas tank.

Ice? No. He reached out a finger to touch it. Granular, like sand.

Then he brought it up to his nose to smell it. Even risked touching it to his tongue.

Sugar.

They'd filled her gas tank with sugar.

Goddamn it! How was he supposed to clean that out? He didn't have enough magical power. Just transforming a rock back into sand took everything he had.

How could he possibly clean sugar out of gas? Remove one element from the other?

He couldn't abandon Bing Xi. He had no idea what the Monkey Man might do to her next. He couldn't hide her. He didn't know how, or even if he could.

Could he clean out the tank? Maybe. If he had enough power.

Wait a moment.

Tong Yi reached into his pocket and pulled out the coin that Zhang Gua Lao had given him.

He had no idea why the immortal had given him such an artifact. What he was supposed to do with it. How he was supposed to use it.

He suspected that the old man hadn't meant for Tong Yi to use it to save Bing Xi, but to save himself.

As far as Tong Yi was concerned, saving Bing Xi *was* saving himself.

He thought for a moment, taking precious time composing his spell. He pulled lines from the other spells he'd learned, ancient rhymes and phrases.

Then he started chanting, asking the southern winds to blow clear, the fires to purify, the waters to wash clean and the earth to sanctify the ritual he performed. He asked for the gods to help and watch over him, the elements to grant their blessing. He pulled from his medallion, pulled all the power he'd put there and more, draining himself.

As smoke rose from the edges of Bing Xi's gas tank, Tong Yi pressed the coin down into the center of the sugar contained inside it.

Brilliant blue flames leaped out from around the coin. The sugar melted, dissolving slowly. The foul scent of burned sugar filled the air. Gas rose up around the sugar, a thick sheen of pearlescent colors waving across the top of it.

Tong Yi hurriedly closed the cap on the gas tank, then started Bing Xi up.

She growled, long and low. Shook herself, like a wet dog. Dirt that Tong Yi had assumed was normal flew from her tires, great gouts of skin and blood.

"I'm so sorry," Tong Yi whispered, running his bare hands across her handlebars again.

Her growl spiked louder.

"Let's get back through the portal," he said. "Then…then you never have to bear me again."

The growl subsided.

It was the least he could do, the best offer he could make, since he'd been forced to abandon her.

It would break his heart to never go dancing with her again, but he understood if she felt too betrayed to ever want him as a rider again.

"About time," Uncle Bei said as Tong Yi pulled to a stop.

Tong Yi turned Bing Xi around so she faced the portal and Uncle Bei. Then he slid her back onto her kickstand, but left the engine running.

Uncle Bei stood at the top of the portal, his arms and hands spread wide.

Tong Yi realized that Uncle Bei was drawing all the power that remained in the portal back into himself.

Did he store his power in the red cufflinks he wore? Maybe. It would make sense that Uncle Bei have such a powerful set of reservoirs. And that he had enough power to keep them from leaking over.

Could Tong Yi do that with his tag at some point? He knew he wasn't strong enough to hold all the power it might accumulate.

At some point, would he grow too strong, and need a bigger power source?

When Uncle Bei finished collapsing the portal, he turned and glanced at Tong Yi, then across the open space at Bing Xi.

"What the hell happened to your ride?" Uncle Bei said. He sounded worried.

Tong Yi looked.

The neatly tied ribbons along Bing Xi's handlebars had shredded. Her headlight had shattered, leaving broken teeth of glass sticking up. Long scratches marred her sides. Her front fender looked rusted and dented.

"Sir," Tong Yi said formally. "I wish to lodge a complaint against Sun Hou-tse. He forced me to give him my keys, to leave Bing Xi in his care while I delivered my message. While I was gone, someone put sugar in her gas tank, then broke the key off in the lock."

Uncle Bei blinked, then gave Tong Yi a sly grin. "I see," he said. He paused, then added, "Were they able to drive Bing Xi anywhere?"

"Not that I know of, sir," Tong Yi said. "I think they merely damaged her. Did her great harm."

"How did you clean out the sugar from her tank?" Uncle Bei asked.

"Zhang Gua Lao gave me a coin. I used that," Tong Yi said. He believed that the coin had done far more than his own spell.

"The immortal?" Uncle Bei clarified.

Tong Yi nodded, worried. What had he done wrong?

"You're safe here," Uncle Bei called out to Bing Xi, using a softer voice than Tong Yi thought the shark lawyer knew.

The bike shuddered. A haze gathered around it.

Tong Yi watched, horrified and mesmerized. What was Bing Xi doing? Was she merely fixing herself?

He tasted acrid magic in the air. Chills ran down his spine, spooling around his tailbone. He felt his own tag flare. He wasn't sure how to loan Bing Xi his power, but he gladly offered it to her.

It was the least he could do, since he'd betrayed her trust.

The motorcycle collapsed in on herself, shrinking down, the haze turning to an obscuring white mist.

Then strong winds came, carrying the sweet scent of jasmine and cherry blossoms. Tong Yi tasted spring on the back of his throat. Tears pricked his eyes as he remembered how he'd felt as a boy at the spring festival, watching the grand parades with his parents, holding the hand of his big brother.

When the clouds cleared away, a young woman rose up.

It was the woman of Tong Yi's dreams, the *true* form of Bing Xi, Bi Qi.

She wore a beautiful, old-fashioned, ivory-colored silk robe, embroidered with the ancient character for horse in black thread. Black and red ribbons tumbled in waves through her long black hair. She had an oval face with a long pointed chin, expressive dark eyes, and perfectly shaped eyebrows, like gull's wings.

Her smile stayed tentative as she licked her pretty pink lips. "Where am I?" she asked quietly. "What is this place?"

"It's a home for the *fei renlei*," Uncle Bei replied.

Tong Yi blinked, surprised. He knew he wasn't exactly in Hualien City anymore when he went through the alley portal, but he hadn't realized that it was a home for non-humans.

"Then I shall stay here, with the *fei renlei*," the woman announced. She turned her attention to Tong Yi. "I am Ba Xi. You may stay with me, here, if you want."

Tong Yi blinked, his back stiff with surprise. *Ba Xi?* Some sort of fragrant root? "Me?" He hated the squeak in his voice, but he couldn't help it. "Why me?"

"You broke the curse," Uncle Bei said softly.

"Curse?" Tong Yi asked, bewildered.

"He Xiangu, the immortal, cursed Ba Xi to serve all those who asked for service," Uncle Bei explained. "The curse could only be broken when Ba Xi finally sacrificed herself for another."

Ba Xi nodded. "Only the power of the coin you used from Zhang Gua Lao got us through the portal," she said. "I'd already used up everything I had."

"Thank you," Tong Yi said, bowing low to her.

"Thank you," she said in return. "You broke the curse."

"I did not," Tong Yi insisted. "You broke the curse. You gave yourself."

"You proved yourself worthy," Ba Xi said. "You came back. As you'd promised."

"I will always come back for you," Tong Yi said fervently.

Uncle Bei gave an exaggerated sigh. "Now that you've finished declaring your undying love, can we get back to business?"

Tong Yi sputtered. He hadn't just declared his undying love for Ba Xi, had he? He'd just told her that he was there for her. Not devoted to her.

That was different, right?

"Do you want to press charges?" Uncle Bei asked Ba Xi. "Against Tong Yi?"

Tong Yi managed to keep his mouth shut and not ask *what the fuck?*

Or was it because he'd left her? Was that why Uncle Bei asked that question?

"I could," Ba Xi said seriously. Then she smiled and winked at Tong Yi. "Except it really wasn't his fault. Sun Hou-tse did overwhelm him. There wasn't much he could do."

"Helpless human, huh?" Uncle Bei asked.

"Exactly!" Ba Xi teased.

"Do you want to press charges?" Uncle Bei asked Tong Yi. "For being forced into action against your will?"

Tong Yi would have immediately said yes, however, Ba Xi frantically shook her head no.

Uncle Bei caught the movement out of the corner of his eye. "You should not influence him in that fashion," he scolded. "You need to let him make up his own mind."

He turned back to Tong Yi. "You were forced against your will into committing actions you found abhorrent."

Tong Yi nodded. "And if I press charges, Sun Hou-tse will face a similar predicament?" he asked.

"He will," Uncle Bei said with relish.

Tong Yi narrowed his eyes. "The Monkey King claimed that he wouldn't be punished if his side won the war."

Uncle Bei scowled at him. "Technically, that's true. Not all of the punishments are cumulative. This sort of thing though…they could argue that we need to wait until the end of the conflict before it's enacted. And since he's a primary combatant, if his side does win, his punishment may be mitigated."

"How?" Tong Yi asked.

"Well, do you know that Sun Hou-tse was the one who inflicted the damage on Ba Xi? Or was it one of his assistants?"

Tong Yi sighed. He was certain that the Monkey King had immediately handed her keys over to the Monkey Man, and that he'd been the one to inflict all the damage on her. "His assistant."

He would have to ask Han Di later about his "cousin."

"So the punishment may be inflicted on the one who actually did the crime, instead of the one who ordered it done," Uncle Bei said slowly, "depending on the outcome of the war."

Tong Yi sighed. "Then how will Sun Hou-tse learn that what he did was wrong?"

Uncle Bei gave a bark of laughter. "You are so unswervingly naïve, little scholar," he said.

Even Ba Xi smiled at Tong Yi.

"You have twenty-four hours from now to decide what you want to do," Uncle Bei said.

"What would you advise?" Tong Yi asked the lawyer.

"As much as I hate to say it, I wouldn't press charges," Uncle Bei said slowly. "Not unless I was one hundred percent certain I could make them stick to the perpetrator. And the Monkey King is known for his wiliness."

Tong Yi nodded, unsurprised.

Before he could turn to go, he put his hand in his pocket and pulled out the little frog.

"Zhang Gua Lao gave this to Sun Hou-tse as a reply to his message," Tong Yi said formally. "Then Sun Hou-tse delivered it to me. I'm not certain if this message needs to be carried forward to another person or not."

"Oh ho!" Uncle Bei said with glee. "He passed it to you formally?" he asked, reaching for the tiny green paper creature.

"He did," Tong Yi said gravely.

Ba Xi came up and peered at the little frog that Uncle Bei now held.

"Tong Yi no longer has a ride," she said mischievously. "Shall we?"

"I think we should," he replied.

She ran one finger down the back of the intricately folded paper. It shivered and sparked.

"Very good," Uncle Bei purred. He put the frog down on the ground, then stepped back.

Tong Yi watched, fascinated, as the wizard pulled up power. It formed as a gray ball between his hands, about the size of a basketball.

Ba Xi made her hands like claws, positioning them on either side of the open space between Uncle Bei's hands. Then she pulled, stretching out the gray ball like cotton candy, making it longer, until it reached out more than a foot toward the front.

Then Ba Xi turned and faced the little frog sitting on the ground. She heaved the gray beam toward it, tossing it like a log, dropping it down onto the creature.

The big frog.

The much larger creature.

The *transforming* creature.

"Tong Yi," Uncle Bei called. "Set the spell. Fire it to make it permanent."

Tong Yi called up fire between his hands, casting it out. He assumed that was what Uncle Bei wanted. The tag on his chest grew warm and he pulled at the power, pulled at it continuously, throwing more flames and sparks from his fingers.

The magic struck the creature, baking it into place. Tong Yi poured everything he had into the constant flow of fire from his fingertips. Despite all the flames, he smelled the pond again, where he'd been fishing with Zhang Gua Lao, a warm, wet smell.

"Good," Uncle Bei declared. "Now pull back."

Tong Yi retracted his flames, exhaustion washing over him. A thick black smoke pooled above where the large frog sat.

When the smoke cleared, a brilliant, emerald green street racing motorcycle sat where the tiny paper frog had once been.

"This is now your ride," Uncle Bei explained. "Yours and yours alone. No one else will be able to ride him. It would take a great deal of magic to even steal him."

"When you learn how to properly work with him, you'll be able to fold the motorcycle back into a paper frog, and always carry him with you," Ba Xi told Tong Yi.

"Like how Zhang Gua Lao does with his mule?" Tong Yi asked, incredulous.

"Exactly!" Ba Xi said, clapping her hands.

Uncle Bei looked at them sourly. "You should have let him figure it out on his own," he said.

"No," she replied gaily. "The fun will be watching him learn."

Uncle Bei shrugged. "You have your ride, now. I will have new contracts for you to sign in the morning. If you choose, you will be able to lease your bike to *Huli* Transport when you use him for deliveries, when you are not required to drive a company vehicle."

Tong Yi blinked, surprised. This was now *his* bike? Not the company's? His own sweet ride that nothing and no one could steal?

"You'll be paid by the mile," Uncle Bei said.

"And a per diem," Ba Xi insisted.

Uncle Bei scowled, but agreed. "To cover wear and tear, as well as insurance and maintenance."

Tong Yi opened his mouth to ask who the hell he would bring his little frog to for maintenance.

Then he shut it again. He was certain there would be someone.

Hell, they might even be related to Han Di.

Tong Yi waited outside the *Huli* Transport messenger offices, in the alley in the back. His new motorcycle, Lu Wa, had been a little skittish that morning, leaping forward whenever Tong Yi pressed down on the accelerator, sliding around corners. Fortunately, Tong Yi was used to riding Bing Xi, "dancing" with her. Jumpy he could handle.

Ah. Ba Xi. So beautiful. He was going to take her out to dinner that night.

Okay, so maybe he was now officially dating his motorcycle. Or the woman who had once been his motorcycle. Though she wasn't a motorcycle anymore. She could still transform into one, or into a horse, at her discretion.

Would he ever learn the entire story about Ba Xi and the immortal He Xiangua? Had the immortal been jealous of the girl and her beauty? He Xiangua was the only female immortal of the eight. Or had Ba Xi been prideful, and not served the immortal when she'd asked?

Or had it been a bit of both?

Ba Xi had always been able to transform into a horse, as well as do magic. She wasn't entirely human. Just mostly human. It was good enough for Tong Yi.

The morning had dawned gray and humid, a promise of the coming monsoon season, though it was still more than a month away. It would turn hot, sunny, and humid before noon. The city smelled of its usual pollution, with that salty underlay of the ocean.

"Hey, Han Di," Tong Yi said as the other messenger came driving up. "Can I talk with you for a second?"

"Uh oh," Han Di said as he got off his motorcycle. "What kind of trouble have you gotten into now?" He gave Tong Yi a wide grin. Then he glanced at the bike Tong Yi rested against and gave a low whistle. "Sweet ride," he said. "If you can stand the color."

Tong Yi shrugged. He knew that Lu Wa's green made him stand out.

And in time, Tong Yi would be able to hide his ride when he needed to. Fold him up back into a little frog. Protect him in ways that he'd never been able to protect Bing Xi.

Though if he was being honest, Bing Xi hadn't needed the same level of protection that Lu Wa would. He was only a tiny frog, after all, though with tremendous heart.

Han Di glanced casually around. "Where's Bing Xi?" he asked. All the stalls were full, with Lu Wa taking up Bing Xi's usual spot.

"That's what I wanted to talk with you about," Tong Yi said urgently.

"What did you do now?" Han Di asked as they walked away from the other vehicles.

Tong Yi shook his head. "How well do you know the Monkey Man?" he asked.

"He's a cousin!" Han Di protested. "Family!"

Tong Yi merely raised an eyebrow and waited.

"Fine," Han Di said as he dug out one of his sweet clove cigarettes. "I'm not exactly sure. Cousin of a cousin sort of thing."

"He was in the warzone," Tong Yi said.

"No, really? How cool!" Han Di said.

Tong Yi narrowed his eyes at the other driver. Did he really have no idea? Or was he a much better actor than Tong Yi had suspected?

At least the tag in the center of Tong Yi's chest didn't flare with warmth, warning him of magic.

"The Monkey Man was hanging out with the Monkey King," Tong Yi said dryly.

Han Di gave him a cheeky grin. "Remember, *Huli* Transport is neutral in all matters regarding the war."

Tong Yi nodded. So Han Di at least suspected that the Monkey King was someone they'd normally be allied against.

"He hurt Bing Xi," Tong Yi continued.

"Who, the Monkey King?" Han Di asked.

His shock seemed genuine, but now Tong Yi was starting to doubt the other messenger's reactions.

"No. The Monkey Man," Tong Yi said.

Han Di grew serious as well. "You're not joking, are you?" he asked quietly.

Tong Yi shook his head. "Still trying to decide whether or not to press charges." Okay, so maybe that was an exaggeration. Probably. Maybe the Monkey King had ordered the Monkey Man to damage Bing Xi.

Or maybe he'd volunteered.

Han Di took a deep breath. "I didn't know the Monkey Man would do something like that, I swear," he said. "I really did expect him to provide you with a great bike."

Tong Yi grimaced. Had Han Di been taken in by the Monkey Man as well?

Possibly.

"Don't bring any of your other *friends* there, to him," Tong Yi warned. "He isn't…good."

"I won't," Han Di promised.

Tong Yi started walking back up the alley, toward the offices.

"You're not going to tell Ren Wu, are you?" Han Di asked as he came up from behind Tong Yi.

"Naw," Tong Yi said. "It's a family matter." It wasn't as though Ren Wu and the others didn't know that his own family was involved with the war. His brother being king of the southern gate and all.

"Thank you," Han Di said. "I owe you."

"Enough to stop eating your stinky eggs for a month?" Tong Yi asked slyly.

"A day," Han Di bargained.

"Two weeks," Tong Yi compromised.

"One week."

"Nope. Two," he said. "One week for Bing Xi, and one week for me."

Han Di took a deep breath. "All right. Two weeks. But we don't mention this again. Fair?"

"Deal," Tong Yi said.

"Now, tell me about your sweet ride," Han Di said, walking up to Lu Wa, his hands out greedily. "Ow!" he said.

Had Tong Yi just imagined that blue spark that leaped from the bike to the other messenger?

"He's still a little jumpy," Tong Yi explained. "Ask me again in a couple weeks."

"Growing mysterious with your power," Han Di said, nodding. "I like it."

Tong Yi wasn't certain what Han Di meant. Did he realize that Tong Yi was taking magic lessons? That he'd grown much more powerful than either of the other messengers?

He wasn't about to take Han Di to the side and ask him anything more.

Because while Tong Yi still liked the other messenger, he wasn't certain he trusted him anymore.

J-pop thumped from the speakers as Tong Yi entered The Sweet Shop. The bell hanging from the lintel rang merrily as Tong Yi pushed the door closed. The acrid smell of magic instantly coated the back of Tong Yi's throat, like burnt cotton candy. His skin tingled with the assault.

Without thinking about it, Tong Yi automatically *pulled* at the power around him. Magic saturated the air. Why not use it?

Instantly, the cacophony lessened. The brightly glowing candied treats dulled. His skin settled and stopped humming. Even the volume of the pop music turned down several notches.

Huh. Maybe he was learning more magic than he realized. His time in the warzone, and his time with Zhang Gua Lao, was paying off.

Ge Deng stood behind the counter on the left side of the door. "Hey, dude! Welcome!" The shopkeeper always greeted Tong Yi cheerfully. Then again, he welcomed everyone that way.

Ge Deng still wore his cat ears. It had taken Tong Yi a while to realize they *were* magical. Though they looked like plain fur on a plastic hairband, they swiveled on their own, like real cat ears, focusing forward or to the side, depending. Today, Ge Deng wore a black vest and looked like a traditional European shopkeeper. Or publican.

He also wore a white shirt with the sleeves rolled up, showing his sallow skin and hairless arms. His eyes were darker than Tong Yi's, almost black, and he wore his hair long and shaggy, like a pop-star's. He flipped his bangs back, a habit that sometimes made Tong Yi want to take scissors to Ge Deng's hair.

"Good evening," Tong Yi said, nodding at Ge Deng.

The day had been long but uneventful, just a handful of messages that he'd had to deliver. He'd had a lovely early dinner with Ba Xi.

She'd made him laugh. A lot.

Now, though Tong Yi was exhausted, he was here to do his duty. Deliver packages as needed by See-tza, learn even more magic.

A part of him couldn't wait to begin.

"Boss lady is waiting for you in the back," Ge Deng said seriously. "I'd go see her first. Then…" Ge Deng paused dramatically before he reached down beside him, bringing up an armful of packages.

Tong Yi sighed, then hurried through the shop aisles. At least he'd learned shortcuts and now knew how to get through the store quickly. The Pachinko games had stopped mesmerizing him and the circular sections no longer acted as a whirlpool.

Had they repainted the corridor down to See-tza's office? He didn't recall the walls having that blue tint before.

He paused, took off his sandals, then knocked politely on the door to her office.

"Come in!" came the cheery call.

Tong Yi pushed the door open.

Then stopped, amazed.

The walls suddenly shone with color. He'd always seen them as a boring gray. Now, they were filled with blue and green, like spring bamboo and freshly washed sky.

After he took a step through the doorway, he had to pause again.

How had he missed the sheer amount of *magic* in the room? Power swam through the air. It gleamed on every surface, even the plain tatami mats. See-tza herself glowed brightly.

Just as quickly, Tong Yi dulled down what he was seeing. It took barely a passing thought. He still felt the magic. But it wasn't as overwhelming.

He had learned to protect himself. Soon, it would be automatic.

"Good evening," Tong Yi said, bowing low after he'd seated himself on his pillow.

"So the student returns," See-tza said gravely. "Or has he?"

"What do you mean?" Tong Yi asked. Fear spiked through him. See-tza wasn't about to turn him away, was she? Just because he might, possibly, have a girlfriend?

"You aren't here to say goodbye?" See-tza teased.

"Why would I do that?" Tong Yi asked, still confused. "You have so much to teach me. There is so much more for me to learn!"

He remembered his conversation with Zhang Gua Lao. Tong Yi hadn't been kidding when he'd said that he was looking forward to learning everything.

See-tza nodded gravely. "True. But not many would realize that. Once they'd had a taste of true *power*."

Tong Yi shook his head. "I'm not sure what you mean." When had he tasted power? He'd always had to pull it up slowly from his medallion.

Honestly, that night was the first time he'd really felt the power all around him. He'd assumed it was because he was in a magic shop.

"Look at your tag," See-tza instructed him.

Tong Yi carefully pulled it out.

He still didn't know all the characters on the one side, the side that had *fu* for luck on it.

On the other side, the side with his name, he saw the date had been filled in.

"What happened?" he asked, fingering it gently. The date inscribed was two days before, when he'd come back from the warzone.

When, with Ba Xi and Uncle Bei's help, he'd set the magic around Lu Wa, bringing him to life.

"You have your sacred vehicle now," See-tza said. "I always suspected that your animal was the toad."

Tong Yi opened then shut his mouth again. He'd been born in the year of the rat. Wouldn't that be his animal? Where could he learn about the sacred animals of wizards and those with magic?

He nearly laughed at himself. He'd been a poor student in high school, cramming in enough to pass the standardized tests, then forgetting it immediately. He still probably was. Likely to only study what interested him until he moved on. Fortunately, there would be many, many things to interest him over the years.

Tong Yi finally told See-tza. "A man who knows his place in the world still knows there's a world he doesn't understand yet." He wasn't ready to abandon his studies with her.

See-tza gave him a bright smile. "You are wiser than your years. So our deal still stands? You deliver packages, I teach you?"

Tong Yi nodded. He paused, but he had to be truthful with her. "For now."

Because while he was certain that See-tza still had things to teach him, he was also certain that there was so much more for him to learn. Things that she had no idea about.

And he had made a promise to himself as well. That someday he'd be able to leave behind all teachers and parents, brothers and bosses, and be his own man. Do the things that he was meant to do. Start his own family. Teach his own children.

In the meanwhile, he bowed his head low to his first true mentor. "Can we begin?"

Girls' Night Out

Tong Yi cursed as Lu Wa splashed through another puddle.

Most of the time, Tong Yi would have said that having a little frog transformed into a motorcycle was an improvement over riding Bing Xi.

For one thing, Lu Wa tended to behave when they were stuck in traffic and didn't try to fishtail or "dance" with him. For another, when they were out on their own, while Lu Wa loved to jump and do tricks, Tong Yi never had to worry about him landing wrong. The little frog was always sure on his feet.

However, monsoon season had started. And Lu Wa *loved* puddles. He splashed through them as often as he could.

The leathers for *Huli* Transport mostly kept Tong Yi dry. And he'd added a protection spell to them, which helped.

But Lu Wa was *determined* to soak his rider. He couldn't seem to understand that humans didn't need water (or enjoy it) as much as little frogs did.

Fortunately, they were almost finished for the day. One more delivery for *Huli* Transport, then Tong Yi was officially on his own time. See-tza had no deliveries for him that night, and they had no magic lessons scheduled either.

Unfortunately, Ba Xi had made other plans as well, friends she'd made in her neighborhood. So Tong Yi was on his own.

Ba Xi had been welcomed by the *fei renlei* community, given an apartment and easy work translating ancient texts (in what had been her native tongue) into modern day equivalents. She fit in well there, though Tong Yi wondered sometimes if she longed for the olden times. She preferred staying in the *fei renlei* neighborhood to traveling through Hualien City.

Though maybe that would change, with time.

Tong Yi's parents would be shocked if he came home early that night, maybe had dinner with them. In the two months since he'd started dating Ba Xi, he'd rarely been home for dinner. Either he was working with See-tza after he'd finished with *Huli* Transport, or he was taking Ba Xi out.

Maybe it was time to go home for a while.

Tong Yi downshifted as they approached the southern-most pier for Hualien City. It was the least modern of the piers, smaller and built completely out of wood. The water that splashed through it was always freezing cold and inky black, no matter the time of day or year. While it appeared to be on this plane, Tong Yi suspected it actually straddled more than one.

At least this time, the message he carried went to the main warehouse just south of the pier, and not to one of the ships docked at the pier itself. He hated having to deliver there.

Tong Yi turned off the main highway, then pulled into the smaller alleys that ran between the warehouses clustered at the end of the southern-most pier. Modern, tall streetlights gave way to shorter, old-fashioned lamps that glowed orange in the misting afternoon rain. The smell of fish permeated the filter of Tong Yi's helmet. He swallowed, suddenly hungry for the ginger and fish-balls soup he could find at the eastern night market. Maybe he could pick up a large container and take it home for dinner.

It only took a few more turns before Tong Yi found the right warehouse. Bright golden numbers flared above the door of the building, numbers that he knew only those trained magically could see.

Tong Yi didn't really enjoy delivering messages to the *duchong* who worked at the warehouse. They were related to the larger sea monsters, though Tong Yi wasn't certain if they were the young of the leviathans or merely servants to them.

He'd delivered a package from See-tza to the *duchong* a couple of weeks previously, a large padded envelope that made slithering sounds. He'd assumed it contained ingredients of a magical kind.

The true appearance of the *duchong* had become clearer to Tong Yi as he'd gathered more power to himself and learned more magic. They were generally small, shorter than Tong Yi, with pale, translucent skin that always glistened, as if wet. No hair covered their bulbous heads. Their noses were mere slits and they always had their mouths open, as if in surprise.

He could never tell one from the other. Did they even have individual personalities? Or was it one giant hive mind? Usually, the messages he brought them could be delivered to any of them. Only rarely, like that night, did he actually have to find an individual among them.

After backing Lu Wa up onto his kickstand, Tong Yi pressed his thumb against the ignition to encase the bike in a magical protection spell. Then he walked slowly to the door. He only lifted the visor on his helmet and didn't bother taking the whole thing off. Once he got out of the rain he would.

A shiver ran down his spine when he saw the door stood partially open.

Why wasn't it locked, as always?

He sniffed, trying to see if he could smell any magic, but all he could smell was the stench of dead fish.

His skin didn't tingle with magic. He couldn't sense anything out of the ordinary. Nothing besides that door standing ajar.

Still. Something was wrong.

He drew power into himself, concentrating on filling his hands with fire.

Anyone who attacked him would get a lot more than they bargained for.

"Hello?" Tong Yi called as he pushed the door open with his shoulder, leaving his hands free. He peered into the darkness.

The smell of fish—dead fish, slowly rotting—rolled back over him. He swallowed against the bile rising in his throat.

He couldn't see much. Though he'd improved his ability to see in the darkness, he still needed a vague light source. Past the door, no light seeped into the warehouse, even from the skylights.

Very cautiously, Tong Yi gathered a small ball of flame in his right hand, then floated it up above his head.

Dead *duchong* lay everywhere. Slaughtered, their throats cut, black blood staining their pale skin. Bodies lay across the counter, on the desks, scattered across the floor. Papers also had been torn into bits and strewn about, looking like an odd snowfall. Drawers ripped out of cabinets. Locks burned out.

Tong Yi stood where he was, not daring to walk further into the massacre. He wasn't worried about the perpetrators still being there—the bodies had stopped bleeding some time before. He'd seen too many TV shows. He didn't want to mess up any evidence.

Though he wasn't sure who would investigate this crime. The leviathans? Some other magicians? Who would demand justice for the *duchong*?

A slithering sound startled Tong Yi. He froze, trying to determine where it had come from.

Was someone alive still? In this slaughterhouse?

A black snake's head peered out from behind the front counter.

Followed by another. And another. And another.

Tong Yi had no idea what the hell that thing was. Its body looked like a knot of snake bodies tied together. The way the snakes danced and intertwined, he couldn't count the number of heads it had.

Or the number of tails, each of which contained what looked like a poisonous stinger.

Tong Yi instinctively cast the fire that he'd been using for a light at the rolling predator.

One head stretched out from the rest, snagging the fireball. It continued to hold the fireball in its mouth, burning itself, while the others rapidly tore pieces away from it, swallowing the magic whole.

The entire creature began to glow brighter and brighter.

Tong Yi recognized his mistake.

The snakes couldn't handle the power they'd just consumed. They were night creatures, cold and hungry.

And stupid. Perhaps deliberately created without any minds or will.

The fire Tong Yi had thrown to them was the opposite of them. Light, hot, and strong.

Tong Yi slammed the door and ran for Lu Wa.

The building exploded behind him.

The blast picked Tong Yi up in a rough hand and flung him out, across the street, onto the hard wood of the pier, where darkness enfolded him.

Tong Yi's head pounded dully. Roaring filled his ears, like ocean waves during a storm. Bitter smoke coated his tongue. He coughed and groaned. *Ow.* That made his head hurt more. Slowly, Tong Yi pushed himself to his hands and knees, hawking and spitting. Great heat washed across his side.

The bright light of the fire burned to his right.

Something blocked it. A solid force that protected him from the worst of the flames.

It took Tong Yi a moment to realize that Lu Wa had moved on his own, and now stood between Tong Yi and the brightly burning building.

He wasn't sure how the little frog was actually shielding him. Was it the protection spell he'd done earlier?

It wasn't a great deal of protection. Just a small shield. It probably wouldn't help him much if the building exploded.

He was still grateful for the little frog's great heart. That Lu Wa had done what he could.

Tong Yi reached first for the message in his inner jacket pocket.

Stone cold. The recipient wasn't anywhere nearby. Probably dead.

Fortunately, *Huli* Transport had a protocol for that, though Tong Yi had never had to follow it before. Since the start of the war, other messengers had.

Tong Yi texted Ren Wu, his boss, first.

Client dead. Warehouse on fire.

Then he called Uncle Bei.

He realized his mistake when he lifted his phone to his ear.

He couldn't hear anything over the roaring of his ears.

Uncle Bei answered before Tong Yi could hang up. He could just imagine how annoyed the wizard would be.

Through the blast noise in his head, Tong Yi could make out the faint sound of sirens in the distance.

So he texted Uncle Bei instead. Same message he'd sent to his boss.

It took two tries, but Tong Yi pushed himself up to standing. Lu Wa helped, remaining more steady than a normal bike would have with a human tugging on it that way.

Somewhere in the back of his head, Tong Yi knew that he probably would have pulled a normal bike down on himself, using it to help himself up that way.

"Thank you," he told Lu Wa, though he couldn't tell if he was speaking out loud or not.

A part of him wanted to just leave. Get away before the cops and the fire patrol showed up.

He suspected that might be illegal, however. Though he didn't know what humans might see. Who they thought had run the warehouse.

So Tong Yi waited, leaning against Lu Wa, the fire baking him through his leathers.

Surprisingly enough, not two minutes later, Uncle Bei appeared suddenly beside him.

Uncle Bei looked more pissed off than usual. He wore an auburn colored suit that glowed in the brilliant light of the fire and a cream-colored shirt with his usual blood-red cufflinks. However, he didn't have a tie on.

Tong Yi had *never* seen Uncle Bei without a tie. Hell, he'd never even seen the lawyer loosen his tie.

Surely he hadn't been taking a day off?

Tong Yi merely shook his head when Uncle Bei asked him something. He could see Uncle Bei's lips moving, but he couldn't hear a sound. He pointed to his ears and shook his head again.

Uncle Bei grimaced but nodded. He quickly pulled power into his hands then raised them up, cupping Tong Yi's ears.

A flash of warmth pulsed through Tong Yi's head. He jumped, startled.

The bitter taste of magic coated the back of his throat, making him gag.

Once Tong Yi stopped coughing, he realized that he felt better. He could hear again—the sirens were much closer. And the cackling roar of the fire was no longer just inside his head. Plus, the pain had greatly diminished. He blinked, feeling the ache settle just behind his eyes instead of clamping down on his entire head.

"What happened?" Uncle Bei asked, speaking slowly, over-exaggerating his words.

Tong Yi contained his sigh. He'd been injured. He wasn't stupid. He quickly explained what he'd seen. The dead *duchong*. The snake-like creature. The way the snakes had exploded, setting the building on fire.

Uncle Bei turned to look at the burning building. "You do realize this is your fault," he said sourly.

Tong Yi nodded. "It was a setup, right? Any magic done inside the building would have made it explode?" That was probably why it had been so dark, too. So someone would cast a light spell.

And instantly blown themselves to smithereens.

"Possibly," Uncle Bei said grudgingly. "I just wish it hadn't been you."

Tong Yi waited for Uncle Bei to explain.

Bright lights flashed just to their right. The fire truck pulled up. Human shouts filled the night.

"It will be easy to prove that the building was rigged to blow," Uncle Bei said quietly as one of the firemen started trudging in their direction. "Even the humans will find that."

"But?" Tong Yi asked.

"But was it set to blow for just anyone delivering that message? Or for you?" Uncle Bei said.

The lawyer pushed himself forward to greet and schmooze the fireman approaching them, explaining that his client had accidentally set off the explosives just inside the door, that the firemen would find the building had been booby-trapped. That there still might be other traps in there, and they needed to be careful.

Tong Yi stood where he was, arms crossed over his chest, putting more weight than he probably should against Lu Wa, but his own legs would barely hold him.

The massacre he'd seen in the warehouse reminded him of the battlefields in the warzone.

He knew that the Monkey King didn't hold him in the highest regard.

Neither did Tong Yi's brother.

Had they finally decided to bring the war here, back to this plane?

There would be heavy consequences for that, he knew.

Astronomical fees, as Uncle Bei would say with delight.

Did they not care? Did they think they were that close to winning that it wouldn't matter?

If one of them had been behind this attack, had it all been a trap just for Tong Yi?

He doubted it. He wasn't that important, no matter what Uncle Bei might think.

Still. The warehouse had been a trap. Probably deliberately designed to destroy whoever set it off.

But created by whom?

"The trap wasn't set for you," Ren Wu assured Tong Yi the next morning. They sat in Ren Wu's messy office. Though the room had progressively grown less and less messy over the past months. The piles of folders and papers merely covered Ren Wu's desk. They weren't stacked over a foot tall.

The rest of the office still appeared plain and ordinary, with scuffed yellow walls that needed new paint, a calendar that was almost three years old now, battered metal filing cabinets just beyond the desk, the creaky visitor chair that Tong Yi sat in, the vinyl cracked and scratchy.

"If the trap had been set for anyone, it would have been set for Han Di," Ren Wu continued. He tugged at the collar of his dark-brown polo. His dark eyes peered out at Tong Yi, measuring his soul, as always.

Tong Yi stiffened. "What do you mean?" he asked.

"Han Di was supposed to deliver that message. He was the next one up on rotation. He got a flat, though, so called into the office and took the rest of the afternoon off. You were up next," Ren Wu replied.

Tong Yi kept himself very still. It wasn't that he thought Han Di would set him up that way. And he still liked the other messenger. Han Di made him laugh, all the time.

However, it had been Han Di's "cousin," the Monkey Man, who'd damaged Bing Xi. Who'd sold Tong Yi a motorcycle who had gladly become Quan Lo's ride.

Had the other messenger turned against his "family"? Had they decided to get revenge on him?

"So maybe that trap *was* for Han Di," Tong Yi finally said slowly.

"Possibly," Ren Wu said, nodding. "But really, almost anyone who walked into that building would have been killed. The light switch on the side of the door had also been booby-trapped."

"Ah. I see," Tong Yi said, taking a deeper breath and relaxing.

Whoever had set the trap had certainly covered their tracks, ensuring that the building would explode regardless of the person setting off the trap, magical or not.

That didn't sound like either his brother or the Monkey King. Neither of them struck Tong Yi as that thorough.

It would take someone like Uncle Bei to think through that level of detail.

That made Tong Yi shiver, to think that chaos had finally attracted that sort of ally.

"Do we know who set the trap?" Tong Yi asked after a moment.

Ren Wu shook his head. "Uncle Bei, of course, is looking for someone to sue." He smiled and rolled his eyes. Then he grew more serious. "It may have been a one-time thing. The *duchong* worked as a transport system as well. Possibly they weren't careful enough, took on a client they shouldn't have." Then he shrugged. "Or tried to cheat one."

"I will be careful," Tong Yi said solemnly. "Do you think—"

Ren Wu's cell phone rang, an urgent, screeching clatter.

Tong Yi knew that Ren Wu had several ringtones on his phone, each one personalized for the individual caller. He didn't know what his ringtone was. Uncle Bei's was the start of the Imperial March, from *Star Wars*.

This one—didn't sound good.

Tong Yi watched his boss carefully. Saw his eyes flare red. Finally (finally!) felt the tiniest wash of magic flow from Ren Wu.

It tasted of anger and flames. There and gone again.

What the *hell* was his boss, anyway?

Though the red light faded from Ren Wu's eyes, the fury remained.

"Wan Cho was in an accident this morning. She's okay. Someone cut the brake line on her bike." Ren Wu pushed his lips together tightly, as if he was afraid of what else he might say.

Tong Yi blinked, surprised. Everyone liked Wan Cho, the other messenger. She barely said anything to anyone. After she'd delivered her first message to the warzone, she had cut her hair. She still hadn't said much. But she'd stare at Tong Yi with unrelenting eyes.

Ren Wu nodded finally. He took a deep breath. "Uncle Bei may have been right." He lifted his head and stared through Tong Yi. "Someone wasn't out to get Han Di. Or you. They're after *Huli* Transport itself."

Tong Yi had never seen Wan Cho so angry. She *radiated* fury. He was surprised her cute, short hair wasn't standing up on end, like some sort of anime character's hair.

She wore her cream-colored *Huli* Transport shirt so tight there was no question that she was female. A black brace encased her left wrist. She looked like she wanted to smash it into the face of anyone questioning why she was there.

Instead of her regular sneakers, she wore heavy black boots under her casual brown slacks. Military style boots, with metal toes and a waffle sole.

Had she gotten those when she'd done her military training? They fit her well.

Her face looked fine, undamaged. But she leaned very carefully against the counter in the messenger break room instead of sitting down. When her brakes had failed, she'd plowed into a stopped car, flipping up and over the car, landing on her back.

She played a game on her phone one-handed, refusing to give up or take a day off.

The TV hanging from the corner of the break room silently showed a tennis match. Running commentary in Chinese ran across the bottom of the screen. Han Di had lost another bet, so his tea-and-vinegar eggs weren't stinking up the room. It smelled instead of the miso that Wan Cho drank, spiced with medicinal herbs.

Tong Yi split his attention between the game he was playing on his own phone, Wan Cho, and the open door. He needed to talk with Han Di, but the other messenger had been sent to the warzone that morning.

And he'd gone. Despite the fact that the reason he'd missed delivering the message to the *duchong* the night before was because his tires had been deliberately punctured with a very small implement. The tires could have gone out at any time during the day.

Possibly while Han Di was driving at high enough speeds that he might have crashed.

Tong Yi felt on edge, as if he was waiting for the other shoe to drop. Would the main office close the Hualien City branch if the attacks continued? Wan Cho wouldn't speculate with him like Han Di would have.

Finally, Ren Wu walked in. He looked sourly at Wan Cho, then glared at Tong Yi.

Tong Yi shrugged. There wasn't anything he could do about her being here. If he said anything, he was certain she'd chew his head off. With relish.

Besides, he sort of understood where the other messenger was coming from. He wasn't about to back down either, though he, too, had nearly been killed.

Ren Wu sighed and shook his head. "Contract run," he said.

Tong Yi nearly groaned. Contracts meant signing for them, giving proof of delivery. With blood.

One of the last contract runs he'd been on, the parties had signed and co-signed half a dozen documents. His thumb had been sore for two days from being constantly pricked, squeezing drops of blood out.

Wan Cho stared at Tong Yi, who shrugged. Her choice. She was the next messenger up in rotation. She got first dibs.

"I'll take it," she said. She pushed herself away from the counter. Wavered. Then stood up stiff and tall, marching over to Ren Wu and practically snatching the offered envelope from his hand.

Ren Wu remained in the break room for a moment after Wan Cho stalked off. "Will she be okay?" he asked, his eyes still watching her.

Tong Yi nodded, then added, "She will be. She will deliver her messages."

Or die trying.

That was in the contract all the messengers for *Huli* Transport had signed. Which looked more and more likely all the time.

Tong Yi sat in See-tza's office at the back of The Sweet Shop, sweating heavily though he held a ball of ice in his hands. See-tza had created it. Now he was trying to tear it apart.

The room glowed faintly with the magic they'd cast. The walls reflected power. Tong Yi used them as a measure of his own strength.

He couldn't believe that he'd once thought they'd been painted a plain, boring gray.

Now, they glowed with faint blue light, like the frozen ice ball. The hanging scrolls still hid their beauty from him most of the time, though occasionally he caught a glimpse of waterfalls or forests.

See-tza had claimed once that her walls held worlds.

Were the paintings actually portals to other places? Would he be able to use them someday?

And how much magical strength did it take to hold open a doorway like that?

The two green pillows that normally took up the center of the room had been casually thrown into the far corner, opposite the door.

Tong Yi stood in bare feet on the tatami mats. He still wore his *Huli* Transport shirt, as he'd come to work for See-tza straight from his job, though he'd changed into a pair of shorts. The muscles across his shoulders strained as he poured power into his hands, trying to tear apart the freezing ball.

See-tza had concentrated on their magical training since the attacks two weeks before. He hadn't made any deliveries for her. Which in his heart made him happy. He didn't like feeling as though he was cheating his primary employer.

See-tza stood serenely facing Tong Yi. She wore a cute pink top that day, tight enough to be distracting. Instead of her usual slacks, she wore a black skirt, pleated so it would flare up when she spun, which she'd done for Tong Yi more than once, teasing him.

She was about half transformed, her gray lynx ears rising up above her head, soft and tufted. Her face held most of its human features, though her nose had turned brown and melted down, her eyes had slitted pupils, and her teeth had grown sharp and pointed. She still had skin though, not fur, on her cheeks, and her fingers just had long fingernails, not claws.

Tong Yi felt as though he couldn't get a good grip on the ice ball. Every time he did manage to rip a chunk out, she replaced it before he could do more damage.

There had to be another way to tear the damned thing apart.

Unless…Maybe dismantling it wasn't the way to go.

Instead of digging into the ball, Tong Yi focused on compressing it. He sent his power into the ball, containing it. He didn't try to make the ball be less, just smaller.

The weight of the ice ball remained the same while it slowly shrank. The ice grew more dense.

At first, it had been the size of a melon.

Then it became the size of a grapefruit.

Then merely an apple.

When it was the size of a small grape, Tong Yi dropped the ball down to the tatami mats and without considering the consequences, stomped on it with his bare foot.

It felt as though a knife of ice pierced the bottom of his foot. The pain shot up his calf.

"Ow! Ow! Ow!" Tong Yi yelled, hopping on his other leg.

See-tza's merry giggles filled the room. "Oh sorry, so sorry, I know I shouldn't laugh. But you look so funny! So determined to win!"

Tong Yi glared at her as he tried to put his foot back down. Just touching it to the mat sent spikes of pain through the bone again.

Awkwardly, Tong Yi folded himself down, then fell the last few inches onto his butt.

See-tza giggled more.

Tong Yi gingerly brought his foot up. He wasn't limber enough to bring it all the way into his lap.

The skin felt cold to the touch. From just above the ankle all the way down the top of his foot looked pale, lifeless.

Then he realized the cold was spreading upwards. Fast.

Soon it would encase his entire calf.

Tong Yi swallowed down his panic. He could fix this.

He hoped.

He'd die if it spread to his heart.

He took a deep breath, calming himself. Then he began to warm his hands. He didn't want to call fire to them. That would be too much. Just the warm glow of a radiator. Soft.

It took as much effort to control the faint glow as it did to pour pure power and strength into his hands.

Huh.

Tong Yi's arms shook with the effort. He gulped when he realized the cold, dead skin had spread up his leg to just below his knee.

He cupped his leg and focused his attention on the fuzzy divide between the healthy looking skin and the pale white parts. He forced himself to go slowly. To apply gentle heat. To carefully push the cold down and away.

He took another deep breath when it started working and the ice receded. Pins and needles pricked his reawakening skin.

Tong Yi sweated as much as he had earlier, when he'd been trying to destroy the ice ball. But this time, he made good progress, all the way down.

The warmth stalled when Tong Yi reached his big toe. The rest of his foot had changed back to its natural, tanned color.

His big toe stayed stubbornly white.

Tong Yi increased the heat in his hands, but that just made the rest of his foot hurt. He tried less power, but that made no difference at all.

What was he doing wrong?

A soft sound made Tong Yi look up.

See-tza stood there with a sly smile on her face.

Oh. *She* was the one affecting his toe. Not the remains of the ice ball.

She tilted her head to one side, waiting.

Tong Yi silently sighed. "Can you help me?" he asked.

He always hated asking See-tza for anything. He didn't like that he wasn't strong enough to do everything on his own.

Though that wasn't quite it. He hated asking her for *magical* help. Hated the debt he was incurring. He knew that magicians frequently worked together, particularly for bigger spells. He'd been part of one himself when he'd helped *set* the spell for Lu Wa.

Tong Yi cleared his throat. Looked at her, then back to his foot.

Damn it! The cold was spreading again.

"You wanted something?" she asked innocently.

"Could you please stop pushing cold into me?" Tong Yi asked.

She twitched her nose. "Is that what I'm doing? Are you sure it's me?"

Tong Yi returned his attention to his foot. He'd been focused on his toe.

It took him a moment to realize that wasn't the problem.

It wasn't See-tza playing a trick.

It took a moment of painful stretching, but he brought his foot up further into his lap.

A sliver of ice pricked his skin on the sole of his foot. Where he'd stomped on the ice ball.

Warmth would take too long to melt the embedded ice. Fire would destroy not only the sliver, but his foot as well.

Tong Yi opened his mouth to ask for help, when he shrugged and just reached out with his hand. He flickered the end of the shard with his finger.

The sliver dislodged from his skin, gleaming as it tumbled through the air. When it landed on the tatami mats, it glowed brightly for a moment, then melted into a small puddle, about the size of Tong Yi's palm.

It was a lot of water for such a small piece of ice. Then again, Tong Yi had compressed the ice ball tightly earlier.

"Very good!" See-tza said, clapping her hands with delight.

Tong Yi took a deep breath and wiggled his toes.

Damn it. That had been close, though he didn't think See-tza would have let him be permanently damaged. Or die. Even in the process of teaching a lesson.

"Though it would have been fun warming you up," See-tza added flirtatiously.

Tong Yi contained his shiver. He knew *exactly* how See-tza wanted to warm him. She'd made her intentions clear. More than once.

Ba Xi would kill him if he cheated on her. Not to mention that she'd skin See-tza alive.

Tong Yi struggled to push himself all the way up to standing. His legs shook. He'd depleted what little energy he'd had.

Still, he was ready to continue if that was what his teacher demanded.

"We finished for today," See-tza told him. "Tomorrow night, I hire you as driver."

"Driver?" Tong Yi asked, surprised. Generally she used him to deliver messages, or small packages.

"Girls and I going out. Karaoke!" See-tza told him with a big grin. "You bring gold sedan here. Nine pm."

Tong Yi shook his head. "I can't just borrow the sedan," he said. It was one thing to use Lu Wa to deliver things for her.

It was quite another to take an official vehicle out on a job.

"No, silly. I *hire* you. Boss give you job in morning," See-tza said.

"Ah," Tong Yi said.

On the one hand, his curiosity pricked him. What would these friends of See-tza's be like? Would they be like her? Other creatures? Human? Wizards? He had no idea.

On the other hand, See-tza had already hinted how much more she'd like to see of him.

How handsy would she get if she was drunk?

"See you tomorrow!" See-tza said again.

Tong Yi pulled his strength together and gave See-tza as low a bow as he could manage. Then he tottered off toward the door.

Luckily, Lu Wa would stay steady and take him home safely.

Maybe only splash through a few puddles.

"And then the farmer said," Ba Xi paused dramatically. "'That's not my mule!'"

Tong Yi snorted with laughter. He'd learned early to stop drinking his tea and to put it to one side when Ba Xi started telling one of her stories.

Ba Xi giggled as well. She wore her waist-long black hair pulled back in a loose ponytail. She also wore a modern (and distractingly tight) black sheer blouse with red lace tucked in along the center plaque and around the cuffs. While she'd been beautiful in her robes, she could stop traffic in her jeans.

He wondered yet again what she saw in a poor human messenger like him.

"Would you like some more tea?" he asked after a moment of comfortable silence.

"Please," she said, holding out her cup to him.

They sat at the counter closest to the street in Tong Yi's favorite noodle shop. Rain lashed at the windows. Scooters and the occasional car splashed through the puddles. The comforting smell of seared soy sauce and noodles filled the tiny room. He wore his heavy leather jacket—like many shops, it didn't bother with heat during the few months it got cool.

Only one group of students sat with them in the shop, six of them clustered around tables pulled together in the center of the shop, busy with homework.

Since Tong Yi didn't have to go in until 3 pm that day he'd called Ba Xi for an impromptu late lunch. He assumed the change of his schedule had to do with driving See-tza and her friends to karaoke later that night.

Tong Yi poured tea into Ba Xi's cup from the small porcelain teapot they shared. She'd ordered a lovely, light jasmine tea that tasted like spring.

"This weekend," Tong Yi said after a moment. "Do you think…could we go out to dinner? With my parents?" He found himself sweating despite the cool air in the shop. His heart pounded in his ears.

"I don't know," Ba Xi said. She turned a teasing smile to him. "Are you sure you want to introduce them to a *fei renlei*?"

Tong Yi nodded seriously. "I do," he said. Though they were strictly human, and wouldn't necessarily see anything out of the ordinary in terms of magic.

"You do know that *sight* runs in families, right?" Ba Xi said. "One of them might see more than you think."

Tong Yi blinked. Though Ba Xi had assured him that she didn't read minds, she often responded as if she did.

Then Tong Yi shook his head. His brother, Quan Lo, probably had *sight*. Possibly, that *sight* was why he'd turned to drugs. Because he couldn't handle the non-human and magical things he saw. Had used the drugs to escape his expanding reality. Or possibly to explain it to himself.

But his mom? Or his dad? Neither of them had that much imagination.

"I would be delighted to meet your parents," Ba Xi said. "Though I have seen them before."

Tong Yi tilted his head to the side. When? Then he remembered.

"When I brought you home," he said. "As a motorcycle." On the evenings before he went to the warzone, he'd take Bing Xi back to his parents' apartment, rather than go to the messenger office early in the morning and fetch her.

Tong Yi was never certain how to refer to that period of her life. Uncle Bei had said she'd been cursed. Ba Xi didn't really talk about it.

"Exactly," Ba Xi said, nodding. "I'd see your father leave for work before you got up sometimes, tottering away on his ancient Vespa. I only saw your mother once, when she came home one night, late."

Tong Yi smiled at her. "But you haven't been formally introduced. And I'd like to do that." He shyly reached out and took her hand. "I'd like to introduce them to my girlfriend."

Ba Xi turned her hand in his so she could squeeze his fingers. "I would be delighted to meet your parents," she said formally. "And be introduced as your girlfriend." She paused, then asked, "Have you ever had a girlfriend before?"

Tong Yi shook his head. There were girls that he'd liked, girls he'd even taken out to tea, but no one that he'd dated.

Ba Xi squeezed his hand again. "Then this will be an extra special meeting," she promised him.

"Thank you," Tong Yi said. He paused.

Why was she doing this? She could have any man she wanted, human or otherwise. Should he ask her?

Before he could make a decision, Ba Xi turned her head and looked out on the street. "Is that Han Di?" she asked, slipping her hand out of Tong Yi's.

Tong Yi turned and looked. Yes, the other messenger had just parked and was walking toward the door.

Tong Yi waved at Han Di when he came into the shop. He acknowledged them, waving back, then hurried to the counter to order his lunch.

Han Di wore his *Huli* Transport leathers. He was probably taking a break between delivering messages. The ends of his longish hair were damp with rain. He tried to flirt with the girl behind the counter. She merely rolled her eyes at him.

Han Di took it in stride as always.

"So what are you two lovebirds up to?" Han Di asked as he came up with his large bowl of noodles and beef soup.

"Late lunch," Tong Yi said. He knew better than to protest about what Han Di called them.

Besides, Ba Xi was his girlfriend. He was going to introduce her to his parents and everything.

Han Di sat at the counter on the far side of Tong Yi, putting him in the middle of the three of them, then Han Di fell to ravenously eating.

Ba Xi pushed her leg against Tong Yi's to get his attention.

When he looked in her direction, she indicated with her chin that he should study the other messenger.

It took only a quick look for Tong Yi to realize that something was wrong with Han Di. He appeared pale under his normally tanned skin.

If Tong Yi gambled, he would have bet that the new wrinkles splaying out from the edges of Han Di's eyes and the corners of his mouth had been put there by fear.

Tong Yi looked away, blinked, then looked again, trying to "see anew," as his teachers had taught him.

The impression he gathered was illness and dread.

Something was desperately wrong with Han Di. The problem wasn't magical in nature however: No one had cursed Han Di or put a hex on him.

When Tong Yi turned back to Ba Xi, he nodded, then shrugged.

He wasn't sure what he could do for the other messenger. They all had their own problems these days.

Ba Xi gave him a sad smile, then pushed herself up to standing. "I have to go," she announced to the pair of them.

Then, in front of Han Di, she leaned in and gave Tong Yi a quick kiss on the cheek.

"I'll see you later," she said with a warm look.

"Always," Tong Yi replied automatically.

That earned him the most brilliant smile.

Ba Xi laid one hand in the center of Han Di's back. "Be well," she whispered softly.

Tong Yi wasn't sure that the messenger even noticed.

However, his shoulders relaxed slightly, as if Ba Xi had relieved at least part of his burden.

Han Di did look up from his food, his eyes following Ba Xi as she walked out the door of the noodle shop. "Damn," he said, shaking his head. "That's one fine woman. What the hell does she see in a shlump like you?"

Tong Yi made himself laugh, carefree, though Han Di's question struck a little too close for comfort. "Beats me."

He waited until Han Di had finished slurping his soup and had picked up his tea. "You didn't just happen to come here, did you?" Tong Yi asked directly. "I've never seen you here before." Tong Yi came to this noodle shop regularly enough that the counter staff knew him by name, and knew his usual order, too.

"You have talked about this place being your favorite noodle shop," Han Di said reasonably. "All the time. Particularly when I bring in my eggs."

"True," Tong Yi replied. He also realized that Han Di hadn't actually refuted his statement. "Well?" he asked after a few more moments when Han Di hadn't said anything else, but had just stared into the teacup he'd wrapped his hands around, staring as if it might give him some answers.

Han Di sighed. "I need your help," he said very quietly.

Tong Yi blinked in surprise.

Han Di admitting that he couldn't do something on his own? That he wasn't infallible?

Tong Yi bit back his teasing response when he saw how serious Han Di looked.

"What do you need?" Tong Yi asked.

"Magic."

Though Tong Yi loved his noodle shop, he didn't feel comfortable talking about magic there, so they moved two doors down to the Iron Kitty Teashop. The décor was a strange amalgamation of Hello Kitty and Iron Man. The menu hanging high behind the counter was the brightest pink Tong Yi could imagine, with gold and red letters and outlining.

The shop catered to both humans and non-humans, something Tong Yi suspected Han Di hadn't realized until they walked in and the other messenger saw a fox man sitting at the table just to the left of the door.

Tong Yi ordered his usual iced, avocado bubble tea while Han Di got a warm pot of traditional chrysanthemum. They sat in the far corner where the speakers playing J-pop were muted, and the lights dimmed appreciatively.

Though Tong Yi didn't stare, he noticed the other creatures taking refuge in the quiet and dark: the snake-man who lounged with his papers and his long tube of purple tea; the two girls—catlike and similar to See-tza though much less powerful—giggling over a video they watched together on a phone; and the usual tourist who didn't have a clue what was happening around her but who sat diligently writing in her notebook.

"Dude. You're going to have to take me out more often," Han Di said as he sipped his tea. A look of bliss washed across his face. "This is awesome!"

Tong Yi assumed that Han Di referred to both the tea and the shop. "You're welcome," he said. He was surprised that Han Di hadn't started seeking out these sorts of places once he'd realized that they shared a city with non-humans. Tong Yi had started exploring immediately.

He hadn't been lying when he'd told Zhang Gua Lao that he wanted to learn everything about Hualien City and everyone in it.

"So how can I help you?" Tong Yi asked after another moment. His own bubble tea had just a touch of sweetness added to the avocado. Mostly it was kind of bland, but thick and rich.

He'd learned early that casting magic took a lot of calories. He'd changed his diet to include a lot more fatty fish and other foods to compensate.

"You remember the attack on the *duchong?*" Han Di asked. He kept his attention on the teacup in his hands, not looking at Tong Yi.

"I do," Tong Yi said. He had no idea if anyone had ever figured out who'd done it, or why they'd been attacked.

"And Wan Cho's bike had been vandalized. And mine," Han Di said. He paused, then sighed. "Someone is after me."

"Why do you say that?" Tong Yi asked, not completely surprised, given how pale the other messenger was.

"Someone keeps messing with my bike," Han Di said.

"Really? What happened?"

"Something different. Every other day, every third day," Han Di said. "Like this morning. Came out and found a pile of shit on the seat."

"Damn," Tong Yi said. That was disgusting.

"My brakes kept locking up. Found out that someone had messed with the connections," Han Di said. "And my tires keep going flat."

"Have you told Ren Wu?" Tong Yi asked.

Han Di sighed. "Not directly," he admitted.

Tong Yi sensed that an entire story lay behind that. "What happened?" he asked quietly. "I won't tell anyone," he added after a moment. Except maybe Ba Xi, but he figured that went without saying.

"So the Monkey Man really *is* a relative," Han Di said. "He's a cousin of a cousin, or something. Came over for dinner the Saturday after you got back with Ba Xi. To the big family gathering. Asked if he could borrow my bike for a bit." Han Di shrugged. "I mean, I knew what he'd done to Ba Xi, but my parents were standing right there. What could I do?"

Tong Yi nodded. He understood Han Di's predicament.

If the Monkey Man had asked Han Di when they'd been alone, the messenger could have deflected the question, found a polite way to say no.

In front of family, however, Han Di would have been perceived as being a bad relative if he'd said no.

"He wasn't gone for long. And the bike *looked* okay when he brought it back. It just…" Han Di sighed. "It felt wrong, you know?"

"He'd done something magical to it," Tong Yi said. "Something that you couldn't see."

"How did you know?" Han Di asked. Then he nodded. "Because you're becoming a great wizard, right?"

Tong Yi couldn't help his snort. "Let me get back to you on that one," he said dryly. He was nowhere near Uncle Bei's league. Let alone See-tza's.

Although…the medallion he wore did have a date on it now, the day he helped create Lu Wa. And he didn't pull energy from it, not consciously, anyway. It was there, charged. It gave him a constant trickle of power that he used without thinking about it. He drew on it automatically.

"Anyway. I was supposed to go to the warzone the next morning," Han Di said. "But Uncle Bei stopped me when I drove up. Made me get off my bike while he examined it. He did…something. Some spell. A black oily cloud rose out of the bike when he was done."

Tong Yi shivered. That sounded bad. Like the Monkey Man had been trying to influence the nature of Han Di's bike. Corrupt it, perhaps.

What would have happened to Han Di had he ridden an afflicted bike to the warzone? Would it have killed him?

Or would riding a corrupt bike corrupt Han Di as well?

"A couple weeks after that, all three of us were attacked," Han Di said. "But someone keeps sabotaging my bike. I need to be able to protect it."

Tong Yi frowned, puzzled. "Why don't you just magically lock it?" he asked.

"Because I'm not a great magician?" Han Di replied, his voice dripping with sarcasm.

Tong Yi opened his mouth, then closed it again. "You were recruited to be a messenger because of your *sight*, right?" That was what he'd been told when he'd been approached.

Han Di nodded. "Yeah, yeah, and I've been through the magical training. That doesn't mean I know how to magically lock my bike."

Tong Yi thought back to how he'd learned. "Okay, when you drive the sedan, you remember how to lock that magically, right? So just do the same with your bike. Press your thumb against the keyhole. That should lock it."

"That's it?" Han Di asked. "You have to do something else."

Did Tong Yi do something else? Something he wasn't aware of?

He shrugged and took a sip of his bubble tea. "I think that's it. That was all I did. You should see a blue flash pop up when you do it."

Han Di shook his head. "I remember trying that once with the sedan. Nothing happened."

Tong Yi wondered if nothing had actually happened or if Han Di just hadn't been paying attention.

"Come on," Tong Yi said, standing up. "Let's go to the offices. I'll show you how to lock the sedan. Then you should be able to do the same thing with your bike."

"I haven't finished my tea yet!" Han Di complained. He stayed seated and looked up at Tong Yi. "Can't you give me a magical charm of protection or something?"

Tong Yi leaned over the table and spoke quietly. "I cannot. As I said before, I'm not much of a wizard."

"Yet," Han Di maintained. He lost his jovial smile and stared seriously at Tong Yi.

What did the other messenger really want? It wasn't just magical protection for his bike. Something else haunted him. Something he thought Tong Yi could help him with.

"Yet," Tong Yi finally agreed.

It would take him a long, long time to gather up the sort of power Uncle Bei used casually on a daily basis.

However, he was determined to try.

"So press your thumb here," Tong Yi said. He thought for a moment. "And *push*," he added.

"Push what? My thumb?" Han Di asked. He peered over Tong Yi's shoulder at the door of the sedan.

They both stood in the garage behind the messenger offices of *Huli* Transport. Neither had bothered checking in with Ren Wu just yet, afraid that they'd be sent off on deliveries as soon as they did.

The other stalls held a tiny electric car that didn't have any metal parts, for beings who couldn't stand iron, as well as an old-fashioned pedal cab. Tong Yi had seen it missing, though he was never sure who drove it, as the other messengers generally used one of the company motorcycles or the sedan.

The rain continued to slam down in buckets in the alley just beyond them, hiding everything behind a curtain of water. Cold wind blew in dampness, carrying the smell of the ocean. Tong Yi hoped that the rain would at least pause in the morning. After such a tremendous downpour, the sky was likely to be an incredible blue, everything washed clean.

"Don't press with just your thumb," Tong Yi said, "but with your will, too. You need to *will* it to be locked."

Or at least that was what he thought he was doing. Was it? Would that work for Han Di?

"Let me show you," he added. "Watch carefully."

Tong Yi pressed his thumb to the keyhole. He saw the blue flash of light momentarily encase the sedan, magically protecting it.

Then he turned to Han Di. "Did you see that?" he asked.

Han Di pressed his lips together. "I'm not sure," he admitted.

"Let me try it again," Tong Yi said. He pressed his thumb again against the lock, dissolving the magic.

Huh. He hadn't realized that he automatically gathered it back to himself, taking the power back into his medallion. It was a useful trick.

When had he learned to do that? He didn't recall anyone teaching him how to regather the power.

Maybe he was becoming a better wizard than he thought.

"I can't make the magic happen any slower," Tong Yi said. "You just have to be ready and *see*."

He rolled his eyes at himself. He was starting to sound like his teachers. Was that why magical beings didn't talk straight, or give direct instructions? Because it was frequently impossible to put into words what he did instinctively?

Tong Yi set the lock again.

Han Di saw nothing.

And again.

"Try looking out at the rain," Tong Yi finally suggested. "Just keep the car in the corner of your eye. Maybe you can catch a glimpse of it."

This time, Han Di gasped when Tong Yi set the magical protection.

"I saw it!" Han Di said excitedly. "There was a flash of blue light!"

"Good!" Tong Yi said.

They tried it a couple more times. Han Di couldn't seem to focus on the magic, but he could see the edges of it.

"So you need to keep practicing," Tong Yi said. "Keep paying attention to the strange lights that you barely see. So that eventually, you'll be able to look at them directly and see them."

"Sounds like a lot of work," Han Di said.

Tong Yi shrugged. "It's worth it." He paused, considering. "Okay, you try locking the sedan. Keep your head turned away, but *press* your will."

Han Di rolled his eyes at Tong Yi's instructions, but tried it himself.

Tong Yi concentrated on the sedan as Han Di tried to lock it.

A very faint shimmer rolled over the car. If he hadn't been looking for it, he would have missed it.

"You see! You did it!" he said, as enthusiastic as if his friend had created a strong lock.

"I did?" Han Di asked, puzzled.

"I saw it," Tong Yi assured him.

Han Di reached for the car. A tiny spark leaped up, but not enough to really deter Han Di. "It wasn't very much, was it?" he asked, sounding defeated.

"It was better than nothing," Tong Yi said. "You just need to practice."

"But I don't want to!" Han Di complained.

Tong Yi grinned. Han Di sounded like a twelve-year-old boy complaining about homework.

"Remember that first time we went through a portal? Uncle Bei said that we didn't have the power to build one," Tong Yi pointed out. "We, all three of us, have the *ability*. We just need to gather up enough power to do it."

"Can't you just give me a protection charm or something?" Han Di asked.

Tong Yi opened his mouth, then closed it again. He didn't know what Han Di's fascination was with charms. "I don't know how to create one," Tong Yi explained again, slowly. "And I'm not sure I have the strength, either. Magic is wild. Chaotic. It doesn't like to be caged."

Building a charm would probably take more power than he had, or could spend easily.

Han Di hung his head, looking defeated.

"Keep trying," Tong Yi told his friend. It was already past time for him to clock in. "We'll practice more later."

But Ren Wu had a job already waiting for Tong Yi, and by the time he got back, Han Di had already gone.

And left the sedan unlocked.

Tong Yi drove the golden sedan into the parking lot behind The Sweet Shop. The tall electric gate opened automatically as he approached. He assumed the car had a sensor that the gate recognized.

Only a few of the dozen spaces in the lot stood empty. The cars that gleamed wetly under the bright streetlights were all larger, American- or German-made vehicles, cars that he'd never be able to afford.

Tong Yi carefully slid the sedan into an open spot, then just as carefully got out. He couldn't afford to offend any of the rich people who parked here by accidentally banging his door into theirs. At least the rain had paused. He still fished out two large *Huli* Transport umbrellas for his guests from the trunk. Pausing, he locked the sedan, the blue flash bright in the dark night.

Maybe he should use less energy next time, dim down the light. He was going to have to try that. It would take more focus, as he'd learned.

Tong Yi hurried through the gate in the far corner of the parking lot. He wore a suit—white shirt with a skinny black tie, black suit with a tiny brown fox on the breast pocket, black socks and polished shoes. He suspected Ba Xi would call him very handsome, but he felt stiff and awkward. He much preferred jeans or his bike leathers.

The golden numbers above The Sweet Shop gleamed with their own bright light. Tong Yi tried not to stare at them—so many fours had to be bad luck. Even after all this time, the door handle still felt surprisingly cold when he touched it.

A boy-band ballad, sung in English, played over the speakers. The smell of magic hung heavy in the air, thick and sweet. He'd never grown used to how it coated the back of his tongue, like the time he'd tried that foreigner cheese and bean soup. Harsh lights shone down from the ceiling, making the shop as bright as day. The air felt dry and warm after the rain-soaked night.

No one stood behind the counter up front. That surprised Tong Yi. He'd wondered if Ge Deng actually lived there, as he'd been waiting in the shop no matter what time Tong Yi showed up.

"Hello?" Tong Yi called, fear spiking through him. He didn't sense anything wrong.

But he hadn't sensed anything wrong when he'd walked into the warehouse of the *duchong* either…

Tong Yi dropped the umbrellas and gathered fire into his hands. He took a step forward. Then another.

Everything seemed normal. The usual display cases with their magical goods. The neon signs urging him to buy now. The faint sound of the Pachinko machines off in the corner.

Suddenly, See-tza appeared out of nowhere, as if she'd stepped through an invisible portal. Tong Yi didn't allow himself to be distracted by her, but instead, studied the air around her. He saw a faint, glowing oval that winked out quickly.

It had been a portal, just not a permanent one.

He wanted to learn how to do that sort of magic so badly he could taste it, bitter and cloying.

Tong Yi extinguished the fire in his hands and turned his attention to See-tza. Then he stopped.

She looked *stunning*.

She wore a peach-colored shirt with long sleeves. White ribbons crisscrossed the sleeves, making a diamond pattern from bicep to just below her elbow. The cuffs were also white, as wide as his palm, and dripped down almost a foot. The blouse showed off See-tza's really nice chest and creamy skin. Expert makeup highlighted her green eyes and red lips. Her cat ears looked less real, more fake—possibly how a human would see them—sticking up from the silky curtain of black hair that fell to her waist. She also wore jeans and pointed black boots that gave her an extra three inches of height.

"Ma'am," Tong Yi said, bowing his head. "You look lovely."

"Thank you," she said, smiling at him graciously. "You look quite handsome yourself."

Tong Yi shrugged. It was a plain suit. Not custom made, not like Uncle Bei's suits. It hung long in the sleeves and always felt stiff.

"May I?" See-tza asked, reaching up with one hand.

Tong Yi nodded, though he was unsure what his teacher was asking.

See-tza brought her hands up and ran them down the front of his jacket, then up again to his shoulders and down his sleeves.

Tong Yi suddenly felt comfortable in his uniform. He looked down.

It was still a plain, black suit. But for the first time, it *fit* him. The jacket rested comfortably across his chest, the sleeves ended in the exact right place above his wrists. The shirt, too, fit better, the collar not too tight and not too loose, the material much softer.

"Thank you," Tong Yi said. How had she done that? Could he do that?

He was certain Uncle Bei did *not* do such a thing, that his suits were tailored to have this exact same effect.

Since he didn't have the money Uncle Bei did to buy bespoke suits, a little magic would go a long way.

"You're welcome," See-tza said. "It's only right that you should look good accompanying us tonight."

Before Tong Yi could ask about who else See-tza meant, the door to the shop opened.

Ba Xi walked in, carrying the night winds with her.

Tong Yi's mouth dropped open.

While See-tza was certainly beautiful, Ba Xi looked even *more* attractive.

Tong Yi gulped, finally remembering to close his mouth.

He'd seen Ba Xi's beautiful long hair tied up in red and black ribbons before. But he'd never seen her in that outfit before.

See-tza's blouse looked like a modernized robe. However, Ba Xi had gone for ultra-modern, with red-and-black patterned cloth pieces that shouldn't go together but did, forming a V-neck down the tightly-fitted front. Her sleeves were made from red gauze, showing off her pale, perfect skin underneath. She also wore jeans, though they were a deep green color, and stylish high heels.

"Wow," Tong Yi said as he stepped forward.

Ba Xi held out her hand to him. The only thing he could think to do was to bend over and kiss the back of it.

"Thank you," Ba Xi said. She brushed her fingertips against his cheek, giving him a brilliant smile.

Then she dropped her attention from him and turned her focus to See-tza. "My dear," she said, stepping forward.

The pair of them air-kissed both cheeks.

Tong Yi blinked, stunned. They *knew* each other?

The two women turned and looked back at Tong Yi. Both laughed out loud.

"He looks so surprised!" Ba Xi commented.

"Gaping like a fish," See-tza added.

Tong Yi gulped and nodded. "Where did you two meet?" he finally managed to ask.

Ba Xi shrugged. "We're neighbors," she said.

Of course. They both lived in the *fei renlei* neighborhood. How many non-humans lived there?

Tong Yi didn't know, but was suddenly curious and wanted to find out. There was so much to learn!

He waited politely while the women chatted, asking about each other's day, the work they were doing. Finally, when there was a pause in the conversation, Tong Yi asked, "Are we waiting for anyone else?"

"We are!" See-tza said. "And here she is now."

Tong Yi turned, wondering what other goddess he was going to have to escort.

Only it wasn't a *fei renlei*.

Wan Cho, the other messenger, walked through the door.

Tong Yi sat at the back of the karaoke bar sipping ginger soda. He didn't normally drink anything alcoholic and it was one of the few drinks he'd recognized on the menu. The rest of the "mocktails" had fancy names, and there was no way he was going to order anything he couldn't readily identify in *this* place.

The karaoke bar was north of Hualien City on highway 193. Not as far away as the abandoned strip of shops Tong Yi had been stopped at by the policeman. But quite a bit out of the city, on the ocean side of the road.

The building sat on an artificial cliff so it sat high enough to look out over the water. The karaoke bar was on the ground floor, while two more floors of clubs and dancing rose above it. It had been built recently, faced with shiny white and black stone. Inside, the motif continued, with black-and-white square tiles covering the floor, gleaming brass sconces holding bright lights, and red velvet curtains artfully drapped down the walls to soften the look.

The entire club was called "V", though Ba Xi and See-tza had argued if it was the English letter V or the Roman numeral five.

Of course, "V" was filled with *fei renlei*.

Tong Yi had never been there; then again, this wasn't the sort of place he'd sought out. He could name many of the teashops, restaurants, and markets that non-humans frequented. Not necessarily the bars, though.

Maybe he'd have to develop a list for those as well…

The karaoke bar had a traditional, western bar at the one end, where Tong Yi currently sat, nursing his drink (though *Huli* Transport would cover all his expenses for the evening). He sat on a comfortable-enough red-leather barstool, with brass trim. The bar itself was made of modern, black marble tile, shot through with white and the occasional sparkling line of gold.

A dark mirror hung against the wall. Tong Yi didn't pay attention to the reflections there, assuming that the magic in the mirror would try to trick him.

Long, lighted shelves stood in front of the mirror to the right and left, full of American brands of liquor, as well as many Chinese, and some Tong Yi had never seen before. He assumed those were just for the special clientele of the bar.

Maybe two dozen round tables lay scattered across the floor, each crowded with chairs. Most of the tables were full. The lights away from the bar were dim, so Tong Yi could barely make out the figures. He'd seen more than one *kitsune*, a couple of cat-like women, a creature that he assumed was mouse man, and other humans who were tinged with magic.

A raised stage stood on the other end of the room. Large TV screens hung from the ceiling, facing both the stage and the crowd. The words of whatever song was being played scrolled across them so the singer and the people being entertained could sing along, particularly during the chorus.

When the current woman finished singing, the MC moved into the bright spotlight that shone on the middle of the stage. He called the name of the next singer, who had been waiting at the foot of the stairs leading up to the stage. The MC handed her the microphone with a flourish. Then he stepped back, sliding into the shadows and disappearing.

The MC himself was human. Mostly. He had a broad, bland face that was forgettable. Tong Yi found himself surprised every time the MC stepped forward. He supposed the MC had cast a spell that enabled him to do that, so that whoever was singing felt as though they were in the spotlight though the MC still stood just behind them. He wore a pale linen suit with a beautifully contrasting pale green tie.

It took Tong Yi a while to figure out how people were signing up to go sing, how the MC knew who was next. The group closest to him chose their song and put their names into an app on one of their phones.

The three women he'd driven there had a table close to the stage. He was glad they'd sat so far from him, so he wouldn't be tempted to overhear their conversation. He watched them, however, from where he was seated.

It wasn't as if See-tza and Ba Xi couldn't take care of themselves. And Wan Cho could certainly handle herself. He was still ready to wade into the fray if something turned ugly.

Not that he could imagine that happening here. The crowd seemed very well behaved, just here to have a good time.

What could possibly go wrong?

"Hello, Tong Yi," came a warm voice from beside him.

Tong Yi jumped, startled. He turned his head slowly.

Uncle Bei stood beside him.

While Uncle Bei ordered a fancy whiskey that Tong Yi had never heard, Tong Yi tried to recover his wits.

Uncle Bei? Here? In a karaoke bar? Maybe he was meeting a client? He looked as though he was still working, wearing an impeccable tan suit with a red-striped, cream-colored tie, an off-white shirt, and his usual red-jeweled cufflinks of power.

When Uncle Bei raised his glass, Tong Yi silently raised his own class and clinked it against Uncle Bei's, still in too much shock to do much more than take a sip after the usual *Gan Bei* toast.

"This doesn't seem like your usual gig," Uncle Bei told Tong Yi.

"I'm still working," Tong Yi said. "Clients hired me to drive them here for the night."

Uncle Bei looked up over the crowd. His eyes focused in on the table with the three women.

"Girls' night out?" he guessed, giving Tong Yi his usual shark-like grin.

"Exactly," Tong Yi said.

"You won't mind if I join them, will you?" Uncle Bei said. "See if they'll make me an honorary girl for the evening?"

Tong Yi swallowed his own giggle. Uncle Bei? An honorary girl? That seemed like the furthest thing from Uncle Bei's usual style that Tong Yi could think of.

Still, Uncle Bei seemed to be waiting for Tong Yi's…approval?

"Be my guest," Tong Yi said, indicating with one hand that Uncle Bei should make his way over to the table.

Uncle Bei navigated the crowded floor easily. The women at the table appeared to welcome him.

Were they actually happy to see him? To make him an honorary girl for the night? Or were they too intimidated to stop him?

Tong Yi didn't know, but he suddenly suspected that it was no coincidence that Uncle Bei had shown up here this night.

The wizard was planning something. So were the women.

Tong Yi suspected he wouldn't much like it when he was finally let in on the plans.

Tong Yi's sense of dread built. See-tza, Ba Xi, Wan Cho and Uncle Bei appeared to be having a good time, along with everyone else. But the pit of his stomach kept turning over. He ordered another ginger soda and loosened his tie.

The floor of the karaoke bar was packed full, now. People, well, beings, stood along the edges and filled the bar. Tong Yi had given up his seat to a pair of young women who'd giggled and tried to flirt with him. He'd told them that he already had a girlfriend so they'd stop bothering him.

Now, Tong Yi leaned against the brass rail that separated the bar from the rest of the seats. He'd placed himself directly in the center, facing the stage.

Finally, the MC called See-tza's name, to have her come to the stage.

She looked lovely in the spotlight, the fresh-peach color of her blouse setting off her skin perfectly, her gray cat ears twitching, her long hair loose and flowing. She looked so elegant in her outfit, the perfect mixture of ancient and modern.

Tong Yi's stomach dropped. His palms started sweating.

Why was he suddenly afraid?

See-tza smiled directly at him.

Then she began to sing.

Tong Yi recognized the spell she wove with her song. Some of the other *fei renlei* had done it as well. Mixing magic with music, making the words dance, evoking a feeling beyond the song.

None had done it as well as his teacher.

Or maybe it was because the spell was for him.

See-tza sang a J-pop song, of course. Bouncy and full of life. Tong Yi thought he might have heard it before.

However, that was the song that most people heard.

Underneath was a second song, just for him.

He smelled the magic she cast, sweet like her shop, that chocolate candy coating that always left him hungry for more. Thick breezes wafted against his skin, reminding him of warm summer days on the beach. The lights gained a blue hue that he always associated with magic.

Rolled into the beat, strung throughout the notes, came the chaos of magic. The sheer beauty of it left Tong Yi breathless. See-tza showed him a steep path up the mountain, where too-aware lightning blasted either side of the trail he walked. Nothing tame grew there. Just wilderness, tangled trees, thorny bushes, shocking bursts of colorful flowers, sweet berries.

Tong Yi recognized it as the path she intended him to take to gather his magic. To live in harmony with the chaos, balancing power and structure.

His heart ached with the potential she showed him.

To live up high in that mountain with her. To dance in beauty and in light. To learn the secret name of every tree, every bush, every flower.

The crowd around Tong Yi erupted in noisy applause when See-tza finished, bringing Tong Yi back to the present, to the dark bar and karaoke stage. He suddenly remembered to breathe. He blinked away his tears, and gulped down the rest of his ginger soda, his mouth dry.

He didn't know if he could reach that height with See-tza. Gather that magic and power. He wanted to try.

Then Ba Xi got on the stage.

Tong Yi tried to prepare himself. However, he had no idea what Ba Xi would sing about. He wiped his sweating palms against his pant legs and loosened his tie a touch more.

Gulped again when Ba Xi directed her eyes at him.

The rest of the room faded away again.

Would she sing of love? Magic? Passion? Riding with the wind?

That she'd chosen a folk song didn't surprise him. For all that she dressed in modern fashion and used modern language, Tong Yi knew that at heart, Ba Xi was an old-fashioned girl.

Possibly as ancient as the immortals themselves.

The song turned out to be a moral tale of sorts, talking about how a faithful farmer would be rewarded for doing his duty, returning to the plow, sowing his seed and trusting in the weather, in the gods, despite all appearances to the contrary.

Ba Xi's words wove pictures in his mind. He saw the farmer toiling in his fields, stumbling behind his oxen day in and out. How he prayed for rain that never came. A son who never returned from the war. A wife to share the comforts of his bed, as his first had died in childbirth.

The farmer lived a hard life, poor from sunup to sundown. Danced at the feast days at the temple, always gave the nearby monks their portion of his grain. Paid his tithe to the lord of the region without complaint. Celebrated the good fortunes of his neighbors, though they'd gotten ahead by cheating. Never followed their example, despite their wealth, but instead, listened to his own heart.

The immortals rewarded the farmer for being a good and righteous man eventually, though it wasn't until he was an old man. He lived a more comfortable life after that. He never lived an easy life, however, despite how fulfilling it was.

Tong Yi felt Ba Xi's longing for that simpler time. When duty was clear. Choices, too.

The question remained though, carried on the last notes of the song.

Would Tong Yi remain faithful, as he'd promised? Would he always return to her?

Tong Yi clenched his hands into fists to hold himself back, so he wouldn't run to her. Take her in his arms and try to comfort her, calm her doubts.

He *would* remain faithful. No matter what magical heights he might climb to.

At least he had a clue why she was interested in him, now. Because of those promises.

And he also knew just how quickly she'd turn her back on him if he ever broke them.

Tong Yi was surprised when Wan Cho got on stage next. She wore a regular blouse, light blue and short-sleeved, that showed off surprising muscles in her upper arms.

Then again, Wan Cho rode the same motorcycles that Tong Yi and Han Di did. She would have had to built up some muscles to handle them.

Her jeans fit tightly down her strong legs. She wore them stuffed into her black motorcycle boots—plain and serviceable, not fashionable. She didn't look as stunning as the other two women. She was merely human.

However, her presence filled the stage once the MC stepped back, and her clear, sweet voice quickly stopped all other conversation.

She didn't cast a spell, not like Ba Xi or See-tza.

Tong Yi still had the feeling that she sang directly at him.

She'd chosen a popular Chinese song, one that Tong Yi remembered from when he'd been in high school. It told of the common love of a boy and a girl, how much they enjoyed doing ordinary things together like going to school, drinking tea, and staring at the stars at night.

Tong Yi knew that Wan Cho wasn't interested in him. Not that way.

She was, however, deliberately reminding him of the world beyond magic. The *fei renlei* were only a few compared to the hundreds of millions of humans. The non-humans shared all of this world. They had their own carved-out places, different planes. But the earth was for men.

While the *fei renlei* could be wonderful, fascinating, magical…the human world had its own wonders and its beauty as well.

Tong Yi sighed heavily when Wan Cho finished. He acknowledged that she had a point. She deliberately had soft-pedaled it, not trying to come across as strongly as the other two.

Humans were…merely human. They were not as special and different as the *fei renlei*.

However, at the end of the day, who would Tong Yi side with? Which world was more important to him?

Tong Yi shook his head and turned back toward the bar, intending to order himself another soda.

The girls had all had their say. It wasn't that they were all fighting over him, not exactly. He didn't have to choose one over the others.

Except that he sort of did.

See-tza and her wild magic would make demands on him that he wasn't sure he could fulfill while still keeping his promises to Ba Xi. His parents and the ordinary world had its demands as well.

The path he'd chosen was never going to be straight or easy. He had more to balance than he'd originally thought. More places where he could fall and fail.

Before Tong Yi could catch the eye of the bartender, the MC announced the next singer.

Uncle Bei.

Tong Yi wanted to hide. Not because he thought the lawyer would be a bad singer, that Tong Yi would be ashamed to hear him or be associated with him.

No. Tong Yi wasn't sure he wanted to hear what Uncle Bei had to say.

Tong Yi slid back into his spot resting on the rail that separated the bar from the rest of the karaoke room. He didn't recognize the musical interlude that played while Uncle Bei stood in the spotlight, ad-libbing like some kind of lounge singer, asking people how they were doing, complimenting one woman on her hair, commenting on the drink a man in the front row had.

Tong Yi swallowed hard. His stomach had retied itself back into knots. Even though he felt more comfortable in his suit, it still felt constrictive, like it was holding him in place.

Then the song began.

Uncle Bei sang in a surprisingly light tenor. Tong Yi had expected more of a growl than a crooning style.

Maybe Uncle Bei saw himself as a smooth-talking guy, like the old-fashioned American Rat Pack.

However, when the chorus came, Tong Yi realized that he'd been lulled into a comfortable state. That he hadn't been paying close attention to the words.

The chorus hit Tong Yi squarely in the chest. He finally clued in that the title of the song was "Witchcraft." It had been made popular a long time ago by an old crooner.

Like See-tza and Ba Xi, Uncle Bei sang a second song under the first, a spell intended just for Tong Yi.

The dark notes in the second song struck Tong Yi's heart hard.

Uncle Bei sang of great power, as well as the strength of character that it took to wield such magic. He told of blending and weaving the light and the dark, forging them together into something far greater than they were separately.

Tong Yi couldn't escape. He followed the wizard down shadowy trails, seeking the heart of magic, of power, of intricate incantations and spells.

Light existed in the halls of power. Light to be used, controlled, made to do the wizard's bidding. But darkness lived there too, the types of spells Tong Yi had been warned about, that would bruise his soul.

While See-tza had shown Tong Yi the mountain peaks and wild places, Uncle Bei took Tong Yi into human places, where men gathered power to themselves. To the ocean where the leviathan swam and bargained for magical artifacts. To the densest forests where strange creatures floated and harvested seeds from even stranger plants. To undgerground caverns and troll-like beings who built magical spells from leftover mechanical parts.

To the warzone seething with hate and death, to a land of clouds filled with sticky light, to golden palaces and darkest dungeons.

Uncle Bei showed everything to Tong Yi. The good and the bad. The powerful and those who'd been crippled by misusing their power. The ones who longed for better days, and those who created bad days for all.

By the time Uncle Bei finished, he had everyone in the entire bar singing along about how it was all witchcraft.

Tong Yi could only nod his head and agree.

Everything, *everything*, came down to that.

It was, indeed, all witchcraft, power, and magic.

How much did Tong Yi actually want?

"Tong Yi! In my office. Now," Ren Wu ordered.

Tong Yi sat up straighter in the chair he'd been slumped in, half-heartedly playing a video game while waiting in the messenger lounge for the next assignment. What did his boss want? Why was he so angry again?

Tong Yi hurried down the hallway to Ren Wu's office. He sat in the visitor chair Ren Wu pointed to and waited. The room felt chill with the rains they'd had that morning, the scuffed and plain walls suddenly no longer comforting.

Ren Wu glared at Tong Yi with red, baleful eyes. The force of his gaze felt heavier than magic. Tong Yi instinctively gathered power up in order to protect himself, but Ren Wu threw nothing but anger at him.

"Did you deliver this package to the *duchong*?" Ren Wu asked.

He waved his hand across the center of his surprisingly clear desk. Only a few piles of folders and papers sat on the edges.

A plain padded envelope appeared. Tong Yi stared at it.

Then a slithering sound escaped from the envelope.

Slowly, Tong Yi nodded. He vaguely remembered delivering something that made noise like that to the *duchong*. It had been a few weeks, though. "I think so," he replied.

Ren Wu heaved a huge sigh and sat back, deflating as his anger seeped out. The package in the center of his desk disappeared, leaving behind a faint fishy smell. "You're fired," he said softly.

"I…what?" Tong Yi asked, surprised. "Why?"

"Your contract states explicitly that your job is forfeit if you ever start delivering for another company," Ren Wu explained. "You didn't deliver that package for *Huli* Transport. You delivered it for someone else. And that package was why all the *duchong* were killed."

Tong Yi gasped, horrified. "See-tza had me deliver that package. I figured it contained magical ingredients from her shop."

"In exchange for?" Ren Wu asked sharply.

Tong Yi hung his head. "Magic lessons." He knew that delivering things for See-tza would eventually get him into trouble with his boss. "I'm sorry," he added quietly. "I didn't know. How…why did that delivery kill the *duchong*?"

Ren Wu nodded. "I've been willing to look the other way on your deliveries."

Tong Yi looked up at that, surprised.

"I knew about them," Ren Wu said. "I know about everything."

Tong Yi pressed his lips together, unwilling to ask anything more. Waiting to hear what Ren Wu would tell him.

"As I said, I was willing to look the other way. You weren't doing any harm. And quite frankly, See-tza's account is so small you weren't causing any financial harm, either. But," Ren Wu paused, "*Huli* Transport is *neutral*."

Tong Yi waited, tense, while Ren Wu gathered his thoughts, rubbing his hands together fitfully. Tong Yi knew that the company was neutral. That they delivered packages and messages to all sides of a conflict. Why were his "extra-curricular" deliveries not considered neutral?

"In addition to delivering to all sides, we also maintain a balance," Ren Wu said. "We make sure that power stays evenly distributed."

"Like some South American arms dealer," Tong Yi said starkly, bitterness flooding his mouth. He'd seen a documentary on that recently, how by keeping all sides armed, the companies supplying the guns maintained the conflict and kept the profits rolling in.

"Not exactly," Ren Wu said. "Though we are making a lot of profit from the war, we don't have a vested interest in keeping it going." He paused and gave a bark of a laugh. "The bosses aren't human, after all."

Tong Yi blinked at that. He'd never considered that angle before.

Then he shook his head. If what Zhang Gua Lao had said was true, whether the bosses were human or not wouldn't be the only reason why the war continued.

"By delivering that package," Ren Wu said, his voice now full of sorrow, "you changed the balance. The *duchong* and their leviathan masters were perceived of as too powerful. You brought the war here."

"The ones who killed the *duchong* brought the war here, sir," Tong Yi said firmly. While he'd take responsibility for some of what happened, he hadn't actually opened whatever portals were necessary for the killers from the warzone to come through.

Ren Wu gave Tong Yi a tight smile. "True enough, though that's a modern sentiment that not all share."

Tong Yi nodded. The more traditional way of thinking made everyone in the village responsible for what a single villager had done.

"I am sorry," Tong Yi said after another moment.

"I am too," Ren Wu said. "You were a good messenger. Delivered your messages without a lot of extraneous commentary or shyness."

Tong Yi knew that Ren Wu spoke of Han Di and Wan Cho, respectively.

Ren Wu pushed a folder across the desk. "Here are your exit papers. I wish you hadn't broken the rule so clearly, so that there might be some way around this."

"Thank you, sir," Tong Yi replied. He wasn't angry at Ren Wu, not really. Tong Yi had been the one who'd broken his contract by delivering messages on the side.

"Feel free to stop by later," Ren Wu informed Tong Yi as he perused his paperwork. "I must admit, I'm curious how far you'll go with your magic."

That made Tong Yi smile warmly. "I will," he promised.

He had no plans to stop by *Huli* Transport right away, however.

He needed to figure out where he'd land, first.

Tong Yi drove Lu Wa home to his parents' house. But there was nothing for him in his room. Nothing he wanted to watch on TV, no games he really wanted to get sucked into.

Instead, Tong Yi found himself walking through the neighborhood. The monsoons had paused that day, though he knew there would be more storms later that afternoon. Two- and three-story apartment buildings and houses lined the quiet street. Gardens with potted plants stood just behind the closed gates for many of them. Often, the pots lined the alley as well.

Since it was the middle of the day, not many people were out. He saw the occasional old man tending his potted trees, heard the loud shouts of a soap opera. Occasionally a scooter whizzed by, honking as it passed him, since there were no sidewalks in such a small street.

Tong Yi thought as he walked. What did he want to do next? He could maybe apply to be a full-time messenger/delivery boy for See-tza, but then how would he pay for his magic lessons with her?

Ba Xi had asked him once to move in with her, to the neighborhood of the *fei renlei*. But it wasn't as though he was paying rent to his parents, so that sort of move wouldn't necessarily decrease his expenses.

Tong Yi knew that at some point, he would probably live for a while in one of the *fei renlei* neighborhoods. Just so he could learn what they did there, how they lived.

He wouldn't stay there. He needed to keep at least one foot in the human world, as Wan Cho had reminded him.

But what was he going to do now?

Were there other non-human transport companies? He'd always wondered, given how the non-compete clause with *Huli* Transport had been worded.

A sense of *something* approaching brought Tong Yi out of his head. He looked around, surprised that he was now over a mile away from his parents' apartment.

A long, sleek, black town car pulled up beside Tong Yi. It growled with hidden power.

One of the mirrored glass backseat windows rolled down smoothly.

Uncle Bei grinned out at Tong Yi. "Want to ride with me for a while?"

Tong Yi paused, considering. He knew what Uncle Bei was actually asking, the subtext under the text.

Was Tong Yi ready to start learning magic from Uncle Bei?

Uncle Bei hadn't hid anything from Tong Yi when he'd sung about his magic at the karaoke bar. Human wizardry contained light spells as well as dark. There would be things that Uncle Bei would require Tong Yi to do that would bruise his soul.

Possibly darken it permanently.

Would Ba Xi forgive him for learning from Uncle Bei? Even for a short while?

Tong Yi would always come back for Ba Xi. He knew he would always be faithful to her. He'd walk away from Uncle Bei before he'd hurt Ba Xi.

The path that See-tza had laid before him was a lonely one. Not many humans would take it. It would lead to a solitary existence, living like a hermit up in the woods.

If Tong Yi was honest with himself, he already knew that type of life wasn't for him. As he'd told Zhang Gua Lao, his world was here, in Hualien City. Not high up in the clouds.

Tong Yi stared at Uncle Bei. He seemed honestly curious which way Tong Yi would jump.

He nearly snorted at himself when he realized that even before he'd helped create Lu Wa, Tong Yi already sometimes thought of himself in terms of a frog.

"I will ride with you for a while," Tong Yi finally replied.

Uncle Bei gave Tong Yi a smile of shark-like satisfaction. Tong Yi could already feel Uncle Bei weighing his soul.

"But I will ride with you for only a little while," Tong Yi clarified, making certain that Uncle Bei understood that this wasn't going to be a life sentence.

Uncle Bei peered at Tong Yi, considering. "For a while," he finally agreed, nodding.

How long would that while be?

Tong Yi couldn't say for certain.

Long enough for him to learn.

Not long enough for him to change into someone unrecognizable, whom Ba Xi could no longer love and support.

Tong Yi stepped forward, toward the open door.

Toward his new future.

Kiss. And Make Up.

A piercing scream reverberated through the dark hallway.

Tong Yi froze.

What the hell?

A long moan followed, shaking the very dirt beneath Tong Yi. The stench of burned flesh rolled around him, causing the torches in the dungeon hallway to flicker. The rough-hewn rock walls paled as the miasma passed, the brown stone growing ashen. Even the ceiling not far above his head seemed to drop down, dripping with poison.

Tong Yi couldn't help but gag, though he'd emptied the contents of his stomach much earlier, when he'd first stepped out of the portal and into the maze, immediately attacked by a creature hiding there, made up of a collection of rotting prawn heads, their long whiskers barbed and deadly.

Damn it.

He'd subdued the most recent creature who'd attacked him, the *suan long*. Brought the ugly creature to its knees. Smashed its mangled snout, cutting his fist on the scaled-over nostrils. Its acid still burned his chest, scarred his arms, and made his foot feel like it was on fire.

Another challenging roar reverberated through the hallway, gaining strength.

Tong Yi looked behind him, then forward.

Could he make it out of the dungeon? Through the maze and back to the portal before he had to face the dragon again?

Tong Yi doubted it. The damned acid-spitting dragon couldn't smell him: its own foul breath had destroyed its snout. It certainly couldn't taste anything over the bile of its deadly weapon.

Its tiny eyes could detect any movement, however, and its hearing was excellent.

Still, Tong Yi tried to run, though all he managed was a quick, limping gait. At least the dirt floor somewhat muffled the sound of his black motorcycle boots hitting the ground. His lungs hurt when he tried to take a deep breath—scarred, he suspected, from the poisonous cloud the *suan long* used.

The outfit he wore resembled the leathers he used to wear for *Huli* Transport, though these were done in shades of aquamarine and teal. Steel armor lined the chest, under the leather. Long tears marred the sleeves. A gash opened up the left pants leg from knee to ankle. At least he'd learned how to magically repair the cloth, as well as make it stronger for the next battle.

It wouldn't stop the dragon's acid, though.

Tong Yi knew better than to be optimistic that he'd escape without another fight. He just needed to get himself into a more strategic position. This hallway was death. It was too narrow and constricting. He needed more space in which to fight. To defend himself against the awful air.

While Tong Yi didn't think Uncle Bei would actually kill him in one of his training sessions, he wouldn't put it past his current teacher to maim him a little. Uncle Bei had done that once, letting Tong Yi suffer with a broken arm for a day before he'd healed him.

In the three months since Tong Yi had started training with Uncle Bei, his magical ability had grown by leaps and bounds. He was so much stronger now than when he'd started.

He was also very well aware of his shortcomings, and that taking on an evil creature like the *suan long* was pushing his abilities to the limit.

An empty space stood between the end of the hallway and the start of the maze, a non-symmetrical, roughly diamond-shaped room, maybe twenty feet across at its widest.

Tong Yi raced across the opening to the far end, close to the entrance to the maze. This would be as good a place as any to fight the acid-spitting dragon. He cast a ball of light up toward the ceiling so he could see better.

Rough rock walls made up the space. Soft dirt covered the floor. The air smelled stale and dusty.

If he looked closely, would he see cobwebs in the corners?

He didn't want to study the floor, though, afraid of the bloodstains he'd see there.

To his left gaped the dark opening of the maze. Smooth walls curved away from it, made out of brown bricks seamlessly fitted together. It would take much more magic than what he possessed to break those walls, dislodge that brick.

Tong Yi had nearly laughed when he'd first stepped into the maze and done an all-seeing spell that let him determine the nature of the full maze. A curved outer wall surrounded the interior walls, separating the maze from its surroundings. The maze itself was made up of tall walls that formed a shape similar to *shuangxi*, or double happiness, with many loops and two central long hallways.

Had the maze originally been set up as a trial for prospective husbands? For each to prove his worth to his wife-to-be?

He suspected that the maze had been separate, once. The walls and the feel of it were different than the rough rock walls in the rest of this place.

If Tong Yi could have explored this plane safely, he would have loved to figure out where the cracks were, to see if he could discover the line between where the maze ended and the dungeon began.

However, a careless wizard had opened a portal to a monstrous plane in the dungeon portion. Creatures infested both the maze and the hallways. Hideous beings, twisted out of legends and given flesh.

Tong Yi had been searching for the portal every day for a week, trying to find a way to close it. Most times, he'd barely gotten out alive.

He suspected that Uncle Bei probably could have found the opening and closed it in a day.

However, Uncle Bei considered the fighting good practice for Tong Yi. The wizard thought of this plane as a training ground for his young apprentice.

The *suan long* roared again as it flowed into the open space, the sound hurting Tong Yi's ears. Iron-colored scales covered the dragon, hammered and full of dents, as though it had been forged by a mad blacksmith. It moved like a bad dream, cloudy and dangerous. Three long claws at the end of each leg gripped the soft dirt floor, the nails biting into the ground.

Still, Tong Yi couldn't help but see the grace in it. The way it pooled itself opposite him. How its long, sinuous body undulated, its whiskers flowing elegantly through the air.

Had the dragon had a different nature once? Something that didn't spit acid, but lived among the clouds instead? Since its own acid breath had damaged its snout, he wondered if the weapon wasn't natural, but had been forced on the creature.

It didn't matter. The creature's eyes whirled yellow and angry. It didn't talk or try to impart wisdom, but just attacked. A sickly yellowish cloud of acid rolled toward Tong Yi.

Tong Yi had his magical shield ready, protecting himself from the awful breath. He knew it wouldn't block the acid, just prevent it from reaching him initially. He'd already made the mistake of stepping in it.

As the stench rolled over him, he wished again for his filtered motorcycle helmet.

Though he wasn't sure the filter would have lasted long here, that the horrible cloud wouldn't have burned it out.

He'd tried casting fire at the damned dragon at first, but that hadn't done any damage. He'd tried water and ice as well.

Stupid thing seemed impervious to everything but a physical attack. Tong Yi had surprised it by reaching out and smacking its snout.

He knew he wouldn't surprise it again.

Tong Yi gathered up the dirt of the soft floor around him. He compressed it into a hard rock and threw it, striking the dragon in the center of its chest.

Yay! Score one for the good guys.

The dragon shook its head, confused.

It really wasn't used to, or prepared for, physical attacks.

Could Tong Yi conjure up a magical spear or lance? He didn't want to get up close and personal with the stupid dragon again.

Before he could figure out how to do that, the dragon attacked again.

But this time, it followed Tong Yi's lead.

It moved with startling speed, stretching out across the room before Tong Yi could defend himself.

And smacked him hard with an open-handed claw.

Tong Yi had a moment, while flying through the air, of wondering if Ba Xi would miss him.

Then the ground came up, knocking the breath out of his chest, darkness overtaking the world.

Tong Yi woke but lay exactly where he was, staying perfectly still.

Where was he? Was he in the dungeon still?

He took a deep breath. Without pain.

No. He'd been moved. Healed.

Or he was dead and just a ghost?

Did ghosts breathe?

"I know you're awake," came Uncle Bei's wry voice, "so if you're finished with your little nap…"

Tong Yi forced his eyes open. The ceiling of Uncle Bei's magical conjuring room came into focus—a dark ceiling, like a night sky, with a sprinkling of stars that formed no constellation that Tong Yi could ever find. The stars never stayed in one fixed position, but they didn't rotate like they should in a normal sky. He'd given up trying to figure the logic of the stars out.

With one heavy hand, Tong Yi rubbed away the grit around his eyes. He took another deep breath, glad that Uncle Bei had cured his scarred lungs. He swallowed and wriggled his toes. Yup. All there.

Slowly, Tong Yi pushed himself upright, folding his legs under him so he sat cross-legged on Uncle Bei's cold stone floor. His whole body felt heavy, sluggish. As though he pushed against deep water instead of air.

The off-white walls of Uncle Bei's conjuring room had been toned down, the light barely illuminating the tall, modern drafting table Uncle Bei used for assembling ingredients and writing spells. Cubbyholes lined the wall above the desk, filled with herbs, roots, and other magical ingredients. Long shelves stood against the far wall, stacked with scrolls and books of incantations. The room smelled of the ginger tea that Uncle Bei favored, a comforting scent.

The room itself was square, maybe eight feet on a side. It did, but didn't, exist as part of Uncle Bei's modern apartment in downtown Hualien City. A single portal led to it, through a hidden door. Tong Yi wasn't sure if he could get into the room on his own—and he wasn't sure he would ever want to, either.

Tong Yi realized that he still wore his torn and stained leathers. He grimaced as he very carefully lifted one arm. Ew. They stank of broiled flesh and acid. *He* stank.

"What happened?" Tong Yi asked as he slowly lowered his arm. He heard the words drip out of his mouth; again, moving at maybe a quarter of his natural pace.

"Why didn't you kill the *suan long* the first time you faced it?" Uncle Bei asked. He knelt on a comfortable pillow that floated about a foot off the floor. He looked at ease sitting that way, in his designer jeans and white, long-sleeved shirt. The red cufflinks winked with power. No tie. His nose and chin as sharp as an anime character's. His black hair still standing at attention, not daring to relax, even in Uncle Bei's off hours.

Tong Yi had still never quite managed to figure out how to balance floating as Uncle Bei did, perfectly still and content without the earth holding him steady. The cold stone of Uncle Bei's floor would just have to do.

He considered Uncle Bei's question. Then he shrugged. While Uncle Bei waited, Tong Yi gathered his thoughts together. "Do what's necessary," Tong Yi finally said. "No more. No less."

That had been a big part of the lessons that Uncle Bei had been teaching him. Tong Yi had started down that pathway on his own. He'd realized he was wasting magic, and had started pulling back. For example, instead of using a sharp spike of power to protect Lu Wa, his motorcycle, Tong Yi had figured out how to just use a small push. When he used magic to punch open a door, he'd learned how to use just the right amount of force.

Uncle Bei nodded, his mouth held in a grim line. "You needed to do more. You needed to kill the creature. The first time you encountered it."

"I know that now," Tong Yi replied. He was too tired to control the sarcastic tone that filled the words.

"Do you?" Uncle Bei asked. He sighed. "I didn't expect to find a killer instinct buried deep inside you, just waiting to be freed. I did, however, expect you to value your own skin more," he added sourly.

Tong Yi wasn't sure how to reply to that. He'd disappointed his teacher. Again. As usual.

"I will strive to do better next time," Tong Yi said eventually, as Uncle Bei appeared to be waiting for some sort of answer.

Uncle Bei shrugged. "At some point, it won't be a test or a training exercise. I won't be there to rescue you. I hope you have enough sense to rescue yourself. Or to actually do what's necessary."

With that, the lawyer stretched out his long legs, landing gently on the ground, then stood up, as graceful as a cat.

Tong Yi oh-so-slowly pushed himself up to standing. He shivered in the cool air of the conjuring room. It took him three tries but he managed to run his hands down his jacket and mend the worst of the holes there. He needed to at least appear intact so he could ride home without a cop pulling him over for indecent exposure.

When Tong Yi looked up, Uncle Bei studied him, as if seeing him for the first time in a while. "You go sleep for three days," he ordered.

Tong Yi felt a smile crack his face, as if he hadn't smiled in years. "Thank you, sir."

"Then you're going to have to work on cleaning up that dungeon," Uncle Bei casually tossed over his shoulder as he walked out the door.

Tong Yi contained his groan. How the hell was he going to do that? He'd barely survived this last battle.

At least he had three days to think about it. Plan how to do it.

Or to figure out how to tell Uncle Bei that he was giving up magic for good.

The next afternoon, after a solid twelve hours of sleep, Tong Yi still felt as though his thoughts had to push their way through the cotton that stuffed his head. He made his way slowly from his room in his parents' apartment down to the kitchen.

No one sat at the table in the eating nook, of course. It was the middle of the day, and both his parents worked—his mom, teaching business English at the local college, and his dad, selling insurance downtown. The room smelled of garlic and chicken stir-fry—probably what his parents had eaten the night before. Tong Yi didn't turn on the light, but instead allowed the sunlight to filter in from the window over the table.

Tong Yi shuffled over to the refrigerator. Ah. Leftovers. Breakfast of champions.

He heated up some fish stew, dumped it over the rice and chicken mixture he'd found in a different container, then heated it all together. It smelled strange, garlic and chicken and fish, but his stomach wouldn't care.

Without thinking, Tong Yi tried to lift the steaming hot bowl from the microwave, burning his tender fingers.

Damn it.

He glanced behind him. Then he took a deep breath and listened with his ears and his magical senses.

No one else was there, either in the apartment or even in the apartments on either side. No one watched from outside the window. No one was spying on him, that he knew of.

Fuck it.

Tong Yi sent out a thin thread of magic—formed into a puff of air—to pick up the too-hot bowl and carry it to the table.

He couldn't help but grin. He always felt such guilty pleasure when he used his magic for mundane tasks.

There weren't any strictures against using his magic that way. And he knew that even if a human saw him do it, they wouldn't *really* see what he'd done.

It just wasn't *necessary*—he could have gotten a towel to pick up the bowl instead.

And he did try, no matter what Uncle Bei thought, to only use his magic when necessary, and only the necessary amount.

Tong Yi collapsed into his usual chair and started shoveling food into his mouth. It tasted sweet and salty, mixed up in a good way. He was going to have to try this combination again.

He knew he needed to eat. His body was still healing from the attack, no matter how much fixing Uncle Bei had done.

How bad had he been? Probably pretty bad, given how slow he still felt.

And speaking of slow…He cautiously slid his bowl to the side, off of the note waiting for him.

It was from his mother, reminding him of his father's birthday the following day. He would be turning forty-three, a respectable age.

It was good his mother had reminded him. Tong Yi had the date set in his phone, of course. But would he have remembered to check it?

What were they doing to celebrate?

Tong Yi knew his mom had already made plans. He hoped fervently that he'd taken notes already and put them into his phone as well.

However, there was something else.

Tong Yi had a nagging feeling suddenly.

He finished slurping up the remains of his soup and went searching for his phone.

He hadn't made any plans, had he? He knew better than that.

He gulped when he finally did fish out his phone.

Damn it. Lunch. Ba Xi. In…ten minutes.

He didn't have to check his bank accounts to know that there wouldn't be a lot more lunches with her. He'd been living off his savings, his parents supporting him while he "studied" with a great lawyer. He was going to have to get another job. Soon.

Tong Yi ran his hands down his shirt and his shorts, changing his clothes instantly to a dressier, hunter green polo shirt and khaki shorts with solid shoes. He ran his fingers through his hair, though he knew his helmet would mess up whatever he did to it now. Then he raced for his bike.

Lu Wa would welcome the challenge of getting him there in time.

And fortunately, Tong Yi could always eat.

Tong Yi realized his mistake as soon as he entered the restaurant.

Not only was it a place that catered to the *fei renlei*, Ba Xi wasn't by herself.

Tong Yi thought about immediately turning back around and walking out the door. Just for a brief minute. He should strengthen the spell on his outfit. There would be many creatures here who could naturally see through the illusion, would know what he wore, that he wasn't actually very well dressed. Particularly for a human.

But Ba Xi had already seen him. Her eyes narrowed but she still beckoned him back to their table.

Damn it. Of course she knew what he really wore. And realized that he'd forgotten about their lunch until the last minute.

The lunch where she was going to introduce him to her friends, the new girls she'd met since breaking the curse.

Tong Yi would rather go back to Uncle Bei's dungeon and fight a dozen acid-spitting dragons than to meet Ba Xi's friends and not be appropriately dressed. For her friends to get a bad impression about him, to think he was a slob.

Could he just duck out for a moment?

He couldn't.

He could only walk forward and into battle.

Hopefully, she would let him make it up to her later. Somehow.

The restaurant itself specialized in *hua gua*—cook-it-yourself meats and delicacies in a boiling pot of oil (or soup) set at the center of each table. Tong Yi had been to the human equivalent of such restaurants with both his family and friends. It made eating together easy, because everyone could get what they wanted to cook. The only thing the group had to decide on was the flavor of soup they'd used to cook their meal in, or if they would forego the soup and use oil instead.

Bright white lights shone down on the two-dozen round tables that filled the entire floor of the restaurant. Laughter and lively conversation echoed off the hard walls and eternally chipper red-and-gold touristy decorations. Chairs covered with yellow, vinyl cushions surrounded each table. The room smelled of warm soup and sharp chives.

Along the far end of the room stood a long, gleaming buffet. Packed ice formed a small hill down the center of it, with buckets of raw ingredients sticking out of either side.

Tong Yi hurried past the half-full tables on his way to see the…girls. Ba Xi looked lovely, of course, dressed in a tight black T-shirt with red piping around the sleeves and along the scoop neck. Her friends, the three of them, wore similar modern clothing, T-shirts and plain blouses.

However, Ba Xi was the only one who appeared human. Mostly human. Tong Yi knew that she preferred that form, particularly since she'd been cursed and could only appear as a horse or motorcycle for centuries.

One of the others who sat the furthest from Ba Xi appeared to be the same race as See-tza, a cat-like being, with furry ears rising above her sleek black hair, large, green cat-eyes, a smaller black nose and great long whiskers. The one sitting directly to the left of Ba Xi looked part fox, with a cute snout and red fur ears.

The other, sitting on Ba Xi's right…Tong Yi wasn't sure exactly what she was. She looked human. If he was being honest, she appeared more beautiful than Ba Xi.

However, he could see the bright yellow seat *through* her.

Was she a ghost? She picked up one of the tiny teacups with the name of the restaurant emblazoned in bright red and gold, then held it in her palms as if warming her hands.

So she wasn't a ghost, but she wasn't fully in this plane, either.

Tong Yi had no idea what she was. He'd have to ask Uncle Bei about her later.

All of the women turned to face him, staring critically at him. He gulped but still marched directly up to the table.

He couldn't change his outfit. He didn't have time to strengthen the magic that hid his appearance. He didn't know if anyone did, even Uncle Bei. Tong Yi could only be clever enough that Ba Xi would forgive him. Eventually.

Tong Yi bowed low and held the position for a few moments. Sweat started pouring down his sides.

"Ladies," he said, straightening up. He cleared his throat, trying to hide how his voice shook. "Ladies," he said again. He took a deep breath, then looked at each of the women, as direct as a foreigner. "I apologize for my lateness. As well as my appearance." At least his voice didn't squeak as he spoke. He kept his hands firmly behind his back.

This was something else Uncle Bei had been trying to teach Tong Yi, how to appear as more than he actually was. Uncle Bei claimed that he used that with clients all the time, bluffing his way through a case, getting the other side to blink. Though Uncle Bei was a great wizard now, he stressed that he hadn't always been.

That if Tong Yi wanted to be a great wizard someday, he had to start acting like one now.

"You are not dressed appropriately," Ba Xi said, her voice stern despite her smile.

The other women nodded. "I'd send him back home and make him change," the cat-woman said.

The ghost woman shook her head. "He should redo the spell until we are all satisfied." She spoke as if her words weren't uttered there, but someplace else, and carried on a soft wind. It made it very difficult for Tong Yi to understand her.

"I think the punishment should be left up to our hostess," the fox woman said sternly. "She is the one who invited him here."

The way the fox woman looked down her snout told Tong Yi exactly how low her opinion was. Not just of him, but possibly of all humans.

"Yes, what would you have him do?" the cat-woman said, eagerly turning her face toward Ba Xi. Tong Yi instantly disliked her. He'd seen See-tza in a "playful" mood before, when, like a cat, she seemed to enjoy torturing her prey.

The ghost woman nodded as well. "That seems fair," she proclaimed.

Something about her reminded Tong Yi of Zhang Gua Lao.

This wasn't He Xiangu, was it? The immortal who had originally cursed Ba Xi? All her legends said that she'd grown too light for the earth as a mortal and had floated away.

Tong Yi gulped again. Would Ba Xi ever forgive him?

Ba Xi looked at Tong Yi, then at her friends, then over her shoulder at the long buffet of delicacies. "Since he's dressed no better than a serving boy, I proclaim that he shall serve us all through our meal."

Tong Yi held himself still for a moment. She wanted him to do what? Did she think that little of him? Or was she just that angry?

Then he bowed his head, acquiescing. "I would be delighted to fetch your food for you this afternoon," he said graciously. "For all of you."

So what if his girlfriend didn't consider him any better than a messenger boy?

He'd failed her.

This would just be the first step in raising her opinion of him.

Hopefully she'd allow him to make additional steps.

As Tong Yi hurried back to the buffet table to get more items for the women, he decided he might have the best girlfriend in all the worlds.

Instead of having to sit uncomfortably and make small talk with these women, he had an excuse to continuously leave the table.

It might have offended Uncle Bei, the great wizard, to play waiter. But it gave Tong Yi the chance to do something, be useful, and not to be completely awkward.

"And some of those feelers, too!" the fox woman called.

At least as the afternoon had progressed, the restaurant had gotten less crowded, so Tong Yi didn't have to wait as long for special delicacies from the chef, or in the long line at the iced buckets of delicacies at the buffet table.

The women had certainly lived up to their end of the bargain, sending him back again and again to the buffet. He hadn't bothered to sit down, but instead, played his role of personal waiter to the hilt, filling their teacups before they emptied, fetching water, asking the chef to raid his pantry for even more delicacies.

The two waitresses working at the restaurant had agreed to allow Tong Yi to wait on the table, particularly when he'd explained that Ba Xi was his girlfriend and he was in the doghouse. They found it romantic that he would work so hard to get back into her good graces.

In the meanwhile—Tong Yi tried not to be squeamish about the raw ingredients he gathered. Most of it was normal fare that he'd eaten at places like this, such chicken pieces (including beaks, butts, and feet), more types of seaweed than he recognized, many types of fish, eel, cuttlefish, octopus, as well as thin slivers of beef, lamb, and goat.

However, non-human types of food also appeared on the buffet table. Like the feelers the fox woman favored: long black whiskers, each about the diameter of his pinkie finger and three times as long, that still moved sluggishly against the ice. Great gelatinous eyes from a sea creature Tong Yi couldn't identify, each bigger than his outstretched hand. Short, stubby, pale pieces that looked like human fingers to him, and that crunched as if they still had bone in them.

Tong Yi was just as happy that he didn't have to try all the foods the non-humans ate with relish. Though he'd told Zhang Gua Lao that he wanted to explore everything this world had to offer, he'd also come to realize he had some limits when it came to the non-human world.

Finally, the women appeared to be finished. Tong Yi tempted them further with red-bean-paste pudding, laced with vanilla and chocolate swirls and topped with candied peanuts.

Plus more tea, of course.

They all appeared to be sharing a private joke when Tong Yi came back from carrying their dessert plates to the kitchen.

"So, how did he do?" Ba Xi asked. She gave him a smile that warmed his heart.

Perhaps he wasn't completely in the doghouse.

"He did try to bring us everything we requested," the fox woman said, sniffing. "Even if he was occasionally sluggish about it."

Tong Yi kept a pleasant smile plastered on his face. He couldn't help it if there had been a line at the buffet table and sometimes he'd had to wait.

"I agree," the cat woman replied. "He was adequate to the task." She gave him a calculating smile. "I think whether you forgive him or not should depend on additional tasks you assign him."

The way she licked her lips reminded Tong Yi of See-tza, along with her sexual innuendo.

He tried to keep his shiver at bay, but suspected he'd failed when the cat woman just laughed at him.

"I think making him perform more tasks is a splendid idea," the ghost woman said. "He needs to perform at least two more great feats before you let him back in your heart." She continued to speak the most formally of all of them, while her words sounded like she whispered them.

"Thank you for your guidance," Ba Xi said, nodding toward her friends. "I agree that he must perform additional tasks. But he did do well today, making up for his appearance and his tardiness."

"Thank you, my lady," Tong Yi said, bowing his head toward Ba Xi. "Ladies," he added, nodding in their direction as well.

"I think he should—" the cat woman began.

Before she could finish, Ba Xi interrupted. "I will have to think on what my knight needs to do. Come up with an appropriate plan."

"As you wish," Tong Yi said gravely, thankful that she'd keep her own counsel and wouldn't listen to the torturous plans the cat woman surely had in mind.

"Now, you may go," Ba Xi said.

Tong Yi paused. He'd woken up as he'd been serving the women, and though he was still tired, he'd remembered the dinner birthday party his mother had planned for his father.

Ba Xi added. "I will see you tomorrow, as we planned," she said.

"Thank you," Tong Yi said gratefully. Of course, he could make excuses to his parents about why his girlfriend wasn't there, that she'd had to work or some family matter had come up.

It would still be better for all of them if she was there.

Tong Yi walked out of the restaurant beaming. He was starving. He realized that he'd used up what little reserves he'd had, and was exhausted. He'd have to trust Lu Wa to get him home safely.

But he'd managed to keep his relationship with Ba Xi alive, and that was worth it.

Tong Yi carefully drove Lu Wa through the quiet streets of the *fei renlei* neighborhood on his way to pick up Ba Xi, to take her to his father's birthday party that night. Tong Yi always found the non-human neighborhood so peaceful. It wasn't as if he'd suddenly stepped back in time, though the streetlights always struck him as old-fashioned, and very few modern cars, scooters, or motorcycles ever drove beside him. Instead, people walked or rode bicycles here. He'd even seen more than one pedal cab.

Evergreen camphor trees, as well as beautiful pines, lofty Japanese maples, Empress trees, and palm trees lined the street, like columns outside a castle. A few Western-style individual houses sat tucked away behind paved courtyards full of statues, fountains, and potted plants. Most houses, though, were connected, generally part of a larger complex that took up an entire block, the outside walls solid and plain, while the inside of each faced a beautiful garden.

Ba Xi lived in a complex like that. Each unit stood two stories tall, with a gray tiled roof with the ends of the four corners lifted slightly, like a temple. Clay animals stood guard on each corner of the roof. Tong Yi knew they were more than just decoration: a small trickle of magic flowed through them, keeping them aware.

He wasn't sure exactly what they'd do if they felt the house was under attack, but he also didn't want to try anything to find out.

The round gateway to Ba Xi's complex appeared locked and barred, as always. Tong Yi had learned the trick of driving through it with Lu Wa. Unlike the barrier wall that blocked the back of the *Huli* Transport sales offices from the *fei renlei* neighborhood, this gate needed to be approached slowly, and on foot.

Tong Yi parked Lu Wa beside the gate, off the street. He still hadn't managed to refold the motorcycle back up into a tiny frog that he could always carry with him, but he believed he was close.

He knew he had to be careful: he didn't want to undo the magic spell that Ba Xi, Uncle Bei, and he had used to originally turn the paper frog into a motorcycle by accident and turn the motorcycle permanently back into its paper form.

He just needed to loosen the spell for a bit.

It had recently occurred to him that he needed to do the opposite of setting the spell.

Instead of using fire, he needed to use water.

Tong Yi backed Lu Wa up onto his kickstand, then stood beside the motorcycle for a moment, calming his thoughts. The night carried scents of jasmine incense and the sweet smell of pine. Crickets chirped softly in the background. Frogs belched their song.

Tong Yi felt himself relax, the buzz of the human world fading.

Could he do this? Could he make Lu Wa transform? Did Tong Yi want to do this here, now?

Better here and now when he could get Ba Xi to help him, than later when he desperately needed to carry the motorcycle away with him.

It was easy for Tong Yi to call fire to his fingertips. It had become his first defense. But he needed to think along different paths, to do what was necessary, as Uncle Bei had instructed him.

While Tong Yi could call up a ball of water or ice, he knew that would be too much. Instead, he brought up just a few drops of water to his hand. He spread his fingers and caused them to drip onto Lu Wa's seat.

The motorcycle shivered.

Was that a good thing? Or a bad thing?

Tong Yi forced himself to take another deep breath and flung more water at the bike before he started his quiet chant, encouraging the little frog to fold itself up, find its way to safety. Come and sit next to his heart for a while.

It had surprised Tong Yi to learn that while many spells had intricate rhymes and stanzas he'd had to memorize, most magic operated on an intuitive level. Like how he'd cleaned the sugar out of Ba Xi's gas tank: learning the basic lines of magic from the major spells, then combining them to fit the task at hand.

He hoped that one day he'd be able to create major spells, like Uncle Bei. However, learning bits and pieces suited him.

Lu Wa shivered again, then began to shrink down.

Tong Yi grinned. Finally!

Lu Wa continued to lose mass, folding in on himself, until a tiny green paper frog sat on the concrete in front of the gate.

Tong Yi reached over to pick up the frog.

The weight staggered him.

Damn it! How was he supposed to pick up a tiny paper frog that still weighed as much as his motorcycle? How was he supposed to account for that? He'd thought that the form was what mattered.

Tong Yi sighed. Of course, there was always something else to learn.

And if he didn't hurry up and figure out something *right now*, he was going to be late to pick up Ba Xi. And lose what few points he'd picked up by serving her and her friends at lunch the day before.

Tong Yi first tried a feather-type spell, with chants that he might use to make an item light enough to fly.

Didn't help. Actually seemed to flatten the paper frog, make it hug the ground more tightly.

What did Tong Yi need to use? A wind spell? That didn't seem to be right.

A fox man on a bicycle passed through the street, nodding at him.

Should Tong Yi just give up? Turn the frog back into a motorcycle?

No, he wanted to impress Ba Xi with something. He didn't know what other tasks she would set him, but he needed to keep upping his game with her. He had to give her reasons to stick with a mere human like him. Promising to always return for her couldn't be enough.

Besides, he wasn't certain how to change Lu Wa back into a motorcycle. Would it take more fire?

Tong Yi sighed. Maybe more water…

He called up another sprinkle of water and sang his chant again about the little frog finding safety, hopping back to its hearth.

Tong Yi startled and nearly squealed when suddenly the paper frog leaped up in the air and landed in the middle of his chest, only weighing as much as the folded envelope.

Tong Yi shook his head. He'd been so stupid!

He'd been trying to treat Lu Wa like an inanimate object. To force his will on the machine.

He needed to remember that a little frog still lived at the heart of the great motorcycle. Tong Yi would *never* have been able to just pick him up.

Not until Lu Wa decided he wanted to move.

Tong Yi plucked the frog from his chest and held it in the palm of his hand. "I'm sorry," he said formally, bowing his head.

Lu Wa, like Ba Xi, needed to be treated like a partner. Like a being who had a will of his own.

The large front fingers of the little frog clutched the skin of Tong Yi's hand. Tong Yi hoped he'd been forgiven.

But now, he needed to collect Ba Xi and return to the human world for his father's birthday party.

Tong Yi sighed with contentment as Lu Wa sped down the highway, heading south of Hualien City. Ba Xi rode behind him, her arms clasped loosely around his waist, her head resting against his shoulder blades, her warm weight welcome across his back.

She'd been delighted that he'd figured out how to work with Lu Wa, had learned how to get him to fold up into a paper frog. It had even earned Tong Yi a kiss on the cheek, and an extra pat for Lu Wa when he'd reformed into a motorcycle. (The way the little frog had sprung back up into the great machine had made Tong Yi wonder if Lu Wa, too, had been trying to impress Ba Xi.)

With great reluctance, Tong Yi signaled his turn to exit the highway, heading for the restaurant his mother had chosen for his father's birthday party. It stood just south of the city, on the ocean side of the highway, and was known for its great seafood.

Tong Yi wasn't certain who else would be at the party. Some of his dad's co-workers, his Aunt Kun Gu (his dad's sister), maybe even the older couple who lived just up the street.

His grandparents wouldn't be there. Normally, they would have made the trip down from Taipei, but they'd scheduled a holiday long before the event had been planned (plus, his father was only the second son). His dad's older brother probably wouldn't be there either: he'd joined the navy, and as far as Tong Yi knew, was still deployed in the strait and wouldn't be back to the island for a while.

Tong Yi doubted that Quan Lo would be there either. No one had heard from his older brother for months. It had been a nice break.

Was Quan Lo dead? Had he been killed in the warzone? Tong Yi really didn't know how the war was going anymore, though he knew it was still being fought since Uncle Bei still had to create portals to the warzone frequently enough.

And he'd not seen any more evidence of his mistake, of the war coming here, to this plane.

Uncle Bei had hinted that at some point, Tong Yi should return to the warzone as a combatant. Fortunately, he hadn't pressed the matter.

Tong Yi was pretty sure he never wanted to go back.

He sighed again as he carefully turned onto a side street. If it hadn't been such a great obligation, Tong Yi would have been tempted to keep going down the coast, keep driving with Ba Xi. Not that he wanted to go someplace private and do inappropriate things with her. They were only dating. But the way the moon shone on the water, the quiet of the night, the happiness he felt with her, made him not want to stop.

Lu Wa appeared to be taking just as much care with Ba Xi as Tong Yi did, slowing down and taking the curves in the street more gently than the little frog normally did.

They pulled up to the brightly lit restaurant. A giant neon-fish appeared to be leaping above the name of the restaurant. Broad picture windows looked out over the street. Many people filled the tables inside. Tong Yi assumed the restaurant took up the entire ground floor, from the front to the back, and that his family would have reserved a room with an ocean view.

Two valets in white shirts with black vests, slacks, and ties lounged on the street. They wouldn't bother parking a motorcycle. Not that Tong Yi would have let them touch Lu Wa, or that the motorcycle would have suffered them to drive him.

Just up the street Tong Yi found a place to park, sliding in carefully. Ba Xi climbed off. Tong Yi's back suddenly chilled as her warm weight lifted.

Tong Yi backed Lu Wa onto his kickstand, then pressed his thumb against the keyhole. The blue light that sprang up was subdued compared to the magic Tong Yi used to use.

He grinned. He really was learning. And Lu Wa had his own defenses as well. No one would bother the little frog.

Tong Yi slid both their helmets into one of Lu Wa's bags, passing his hand over that and locking it as well. Then he stood for a moment, breathing in the air from the ocean.

Ba Xi nodded. "This is nice," she said quietly. "Maybe this weekend we can go on a picnic up in the hills, away from people and crowds."

"I'd like that," Tong Yi said, shyly taking Ba Xi's hand.

She squeezed his hand in return, warm and comforting. "I shouldn't be nervous, right?" she said.

"They already love you!" Tong Yi protested. "Though they do wonder what you see in me," he added, trying to keep the bitterness out of his tone. His parents' comments about what a lovely girl Ba Xi was and how she'd seemed out of his league had stung Tong Yi, striking far too close to home.

However, the fact that Tong Yi had such a lovely girlfriend, as well as was currently studying with a lawyer, had made his parents show him a bit more respect. Even if he wasn't getting paid and his savings were running low.

Maybe it was just his imagination, but they appeared to be happier with him and not so disappointed.

Ba Xi gave Tong Yi a brilliant smile. "I know that your parents really like me. It's just…something feels off. Maybe it's the breeze. Carrying a foul scent."

Tong Yi nodded, uncertain. He lifted his head and sniffed. The wind brought the smell of dead fish, long rotted. Underneath that lay the salty smell of the water. The breeze blew softly against his cheeks. He didn't sense trouble, though.

"Come on," Ba Xi said. "Or we'll be late."

"You're right," Tong Yi said. They walked hand-in-hand up to the door of the restaurant. A man in a fine suit opened the door for them, welcoming them as if they were royalty.

The restaurant itself was surprisingly noisy, particularly after the quiet of the night. Tong Yi felt himself shrink slightly.

Fortunately, he'd been right in his assessment. His family wasn't sitting in the main part of the restaurant where it was loud and boisterous, but in a private room in the back. The hostess led them there, down a narrow hallway decorated with brightly painted metal fish that appeared to be leaping in and out of the blue and white waves painted on the wall.

Tong Yi breathed a sigh of relief as the noise diminished. He knew that the party itself would be noisy, but that would just be family.

The silence that greeted Tong Yi and Ba Xi when they stepped into the room surprised him. Then he stopped. Cursed silently.

Of course, nothing had been wrong outside the restaurant.

It was all wrong in here.

Quan Lo sat beside his parents.

"Brother!" Quan Lo said loudly into the quiet room.

Tong Yi nearly pulled fire into his hands, readying himself for violence. Ba Xi placed her hand on his arm, stopping him from doing something monumentally stupid.

Like attacking his brother in front of his parents without provocation.

A round table nearly filled the room, covered with a red tablecloth. A large wooden lazy-Susan took up most of the center of the table. Floor-to-ceiling glass windows covered one wall of the room, with the dark ocean outside. A "Happy Birthday" sign hung just in front of the glass, done in brilliant gold ideograms. Cheery red posters covered the other walls, advertising the specials of the day and healthy meals for all.

The other guests sat uneasily at the table, unsure of the currents that even the humans could feel. As Tong Yi had figured, besides his parents, there were a few of his dad's co-workers, the neighbors from down the street, and his aunt. They wore conservative party clothes, suits and nice dresses with sweaters.

Quan Lo looked as mad as ever. He wore a white poet's shirt similar to the one Tong Yi had seen him wear in the warzone, with baggy sleeves tied at the wrists and with laces down the front, left inappropriately open, exposing far too much pale skin. His black hair had gotten longer and still needed a good washing. His features had always been sharp, but now, his nose looked as though he'd had plastic surgery done to it. It seemed smaller than before, and pointed up in the air.

Beside Quan Lo sat the cat-woman whom Tong Yi had seen in the warzone. She also wore a white laced shirt, though it was tied much too tightly and hung too low across her barely covered chest. She also wore a dark green vest that accented her breasts instead of covering them.

Tong Yi could still see the cat ears poking out from her hair. What did the humans see? Did they see them at all? Or did they think they were fake ears, attached to a plastic hairband?

Tong Yi stepped up to the round table, defiantly keeping Ba Xi's hand tucked up against his arm. "Quan Lo," he said quietly.

The name rippled across the table, and the side conversation of a couple of his dad's co-workers stopped.

Tong Yi would not acknowledge this man as his brother. Not anymore. His brother had died in the warzone. This stranger might share a history with Quan Lo, but Tong Yi no longer considered him family.

Quan Lo narrowed his eyes at Tong Yi. "I haven't seen you around much, messenger boy," he said.

Tong Yi shook his head. "I left the messaging business," he stated clearly. "Studying at a law firm, now. Perhaps you remember Uncle Bei."

Quan Lo would know the type of things Uncle Bei was teaching Tong Yi. Tong Yi couldn't explain that to his parents. And he wasn't about to disappoint his mother and her fondest hopes that he was studying to become a law clerk.

"You're studying with Uncle Bei?" Quan Lo said. He broke into a great grin. "I didn't know you had it in you, brother! Come, sit beside me and tell me all about that old shark. And introduce me to your cute girlfriend. You remember Kitty, my right-hand man?"

Tong Yi bowed his head politely. "We were never formally introduced." Then he glanced over at his mother, who sat looking very worried. His dad, too, didn't appear very jovial. "After I say hello to my parents, first."

Quan Lo frowned at that, obviously disappointed that Tong Yi hadn't said "our parents".

Tong Yi quickly hurried around the round table, brushing past the bright red tablecloth. "Happy birthday!" he told his father, bowing his head as his father stood up.

They didn't hug or shake hands like foreigners did. Particularly not in front of guests. Tong Yi wanted to show how much he respected his father.

Ba Xi, however, walked straight up to Tong Yi's father and kissed him lightly on the cheek. "May your days continue to multiply and be full of wealth and happy dreams," she said.

Quan Lo laughed loudly. "You sound like an old peasant woman!" he proclaimed.

Ba Xi gave him a frosty smile. "Proper manners never go out of style," she told him.

Kitty snickered at that. "You can claim they're manners now. Just wait until the claws come out later."

Tong Yi sighed. This dinner was going to be the longest of his entire life, he just knew it.

He leaned past his father to kiss his mother on the cheek. "I hope your days go well, too," he said.

"Thank you, dear," his mom said. She gave a quick glance to her right, where Quan Lo sat in the seat of honor.

Tong Yi waited. Would she ask for his protection? For him to sit next to her? Would she disgrace her eldest son that way?

"It's good to see you," she added, squeezing his hand then letting go.

Tong Yi swallowed against a dry throat, the anger bitter in his mouth. Of course she'd give Quan Lo every honor. Despite the fact that he'd stolen from them time and again. That he still used drugs. That he was evil.

Quan Lo was the eldest son. That was all that mattered.

No matter what he did to shame them.

"Come on, Ba Xi! I don't bite. Not unless you ask really nicely," Quan Lo said.

Tong Yi shivered. He remembered how his brother's jaw had distended when he'd swallowed down the message Tong Yi had delivered to him in the warzone.

Kitty sat to the right of Quan Lo. He leaned over her and patted the chair to the right of her, indicating that Ba Xi should sit there. The rest of the guests at the party had restarted their own quiet conversations, though Tong Yi knew they'd be listening with great curiosity.

There wasn't anything he could do to help his father's reputation with his co-workers. None of them would even ask about Tong Yi the next morning. They'd all make delicate inquiries about Quan Lo, however.

How inappropriate would Quan Lo get with Ba Xi? While she could defend herself, Tong Yi didn't want to make it necessary. He squeezed Ba Xi's hand, then held her back so that he could make his way around the table and take the proffered seat.

Ba Xi sat beside Tong Yi, on his right side. She gave him a warm smile and patted his arm. Tong Yi took a deep breath. He could do this. He could face this battle. He wasn't completely alone.

Plus, his brother wouldn't be worse than the acid-spitting dragon he'd faced earlier that week.

Probably.

"You entertain the old man for a while," Quan Lo instructed Kitty as they changed chairs so the brothers sat next to each other.

"How are you, brother?" Quan Lo asked, leaning close and talking quietly.

His breath stank of rotten fish and the strong whisky he'd been drinking. Up close, his skin appeared pale and smooth, like wax. Tong Yi didn't slide his head any closer to his brother's, afraid that there might be bugs in his filthy hair.

"I am well, thank you for asking," Tong Yi replied. He'd mostly recovered from his run-in with the acid-spitting dragon, having spent the last day sleeping, eating, and not doing anything more strenuous than play games on his phone.

Though Tong Yi didn't want to engage Quan Lo at all, he still felt obliged to ask, "How are you?"

At least Quan Lo didn't appear to notice that Tong Yi didn't call him brother.

"Doing so well! My kingdom is growing," he bragged. "I have more subjects than ever! You should come back to the castle and visit sometime."

Tong Yi nodded politely but without commitment. There was no way in hell that he'd go back to the warzone if he could help it, and certainly not to visit his brother.

"And you'll have to bring your lovely girlfriend," Quan Lo continued. "Where did you two meet?" He peered at Ba Xi, who sat having an animated conversation with her dinner partner on the other side.

"Delivering messages," Tong Yi said blandly. He'd told his parents that he used to see Ba Xi at work and had delivered messages to her. It wasn't the truth, but it was close enough.

"She seems familiar," Quan Lo said after a moment, shaking his head.

"She gets that a lot," Tong Yi replied dryly.

A waitress came into the room, delivering the first course. The scent of a lemony fish soup filled the air. She placed a large serving bowl full of the soup on the lazy Susan that took up the center of the table, along with bowls and spoons for people to serve themselves.

Tong Yi looked back at Quan Lo.

His brother had leaned over to Kitty and was kissing her deeply, his tongue down her throat.

Damn it! When was Quan Lo going to stop rebelling? Start acting like the elder son?

Never.

This evening just confirmed it.

"For our honored guest!" Tong Yi said loudly, spinning the lazy Susan around so the bowls and soup stopped directly in front of his father.

His father sat up straighter, ignoring the display taking place beside him. "Thank you," he said, glancing over at Tong Yi and nodding.

Dad took his portion of the soup, as was proper. Mom would eat last, as she was the official host for the event.

"Ah, birthday boy! Eat up!" Quan Lo said.

Before Tong Yi could spin the lazy Susan away, Quan Lo moved it toward him. He served himself and Kitty before allowing Tong Yi to move it again.

At least his brother had behaved himself. This round. Soup remained for the rest of the guests. Tong Yi wouldn't put it past Quan Lo to use magic to make it appear as if no food was left.

Tong Yi served himself and Ba Xi, then the other guests took their serving.

"God, I hate human food," Quan Lo muttered as he stirred his soup. "It's so…dead."

Tong Yi glanced over at the bowl. Nothing appeared to be wrong with it. And it smelled heavenly, like sweet seaweed and grilled fish, with a sprinkling of lemon.

Kitty looked over Quan Lo's shoulder. "I agree. Human food is just awful," she said softly. "Should we liven it up some?"

Tong Yi didn't like the look of mischief that crossed her face. She pointed a finger at the large serving bowl.

"Kitty. This is my father's birthday party," Tong Yi said sternly. "Behave yourselves." He pulled at the power in the room, ready to block whatever magic Kitty or Quan Lo might throw.

Quan Lo pouted at Tong Yi. "We wouldn't have hurt anyone. Much." Then he narrowed his eyes, his gaze zeroing in on the tag that Tong Yi still wore under his shirt. "Oh ho, little brother! You have been getting stronger!"

The medallion instantly grew much, much warmer. Tong Yi sensed Quan Lo trying to pull power from it. Without thinking, Tong Yi cut him off, not allowing him to access it.

Quan Lo grimaced at Tong Yi. "You shouldn't do that," he said. "I always get what I want."

Tong Yi opened his mouth, then closed it again, not replying, though given the look that Quan Lo shot him, he wondered if his brother heard his words anyway: *And that's always been your problem.*

"Eat," Ba Xi said quietly, putting her warm hand on Tong Yi's arm.

"Thank you," he said, turning to her gratefully. No matter what happened with his brother, he had to remember that he wasn't alone. At least, not now.

He suspected though, that come the end, it would be just him and Quan Lo.

Rolling his eyes, Tong Yi removed whatever the hell enchantment Quan Lo had placed on the desserts being served. He figured he would be the only one who saw eyeballs instead of lychee fruit, but the magic would still make the humans uneasy about them. The iced red-bean paste and coconut milk no longer swam with maggots. And the sweet rice and jack fruit no longer smelled like rotted mangoes.

Tong Yi hadn't been sure if his brother had been testing him all through dinner, seeing how quickly he could counteract Quan Lo's spells, or, which was much more likely, he had found amusement in tweaking his younger brother's nose all night.

Quan Lo had never been one for tests and plans. That had always been Tong Yi.

At least he'd managed to survive dinner without blowing up at Quan Lo. He'd kept their arguments to quiet voices and muttered whispers. Tong Yi couldn't save his father's reputation, or change what his co-workers would think about the eldest son. All he could do was to minimize what they saw or could say about him.

Quan Lo glared at Tong Yi when he realized his spell had been neutralized. Tong Yi couldn't help but be pleased at how cross his brother seemed.

But then Quan Lo gave Tong Yi a smile that sent chills down his spine: predatory and triumphant.

"Birthday boy!" he said loudly enough to shut down most of the other conversations taking place in the room. "You must open your presents!"

Tong Yi sat, shocked. Foreigners did that sort of thing, opening gifts in front of the giver. It wasn't appropriate for his father to do so. There was no way for either the giver or the receiver to save face.

"I don't think we should do that here," Mom said.

Tong Yi felt his eyebrows rise. His mom had just spoken up against Quan Lo? She *never* did that.

"I insist," Quan Lo said. "Please, Daddy. At least open mine." He plucked a red envelope out of the air and handed it to their father.

Tong Yi stiffened. The humans at the party would all think the envelope had been sitting on the table beside Quan Lo. They wouldn't have seen it just appear.

He tried to sense what type of magic lay on the envelope. Would his father be trapped, somehow, just by opening it? Most spells didn't work on the truly mundane.

And given his parents' reactions to the evening, Tong Yi would bet that if the *sight* ran in his family, it had come from his mother's side. She'd shaken her head and blinked more than once after Quan Lo had changed the food, before Tong Yi had changed it back.

However, the envelope didn't appear to have any wisps of magic emanating from it. It seemed perfectly fine.

Tong Yi's father looked over at his mother, as if checking in.

"Are you certain that this is the appropriate time?" Mom asked sternly, surprising Tong Yi more. When had she grown so firm?

Tong Yi knew better than to hope, though, that his mom would deny her eldest son anything.

"Of course, Mommy!" Quan Lo said blithely.

Mom waited, allowing the silence in the room to grow uncomfortable.

Finally, Quan Lo responded. "It's fine," he insisted. "Trust me."

That was the *last* thing that either of Tong Yi's parents were likely to do with their eldest son.

Quan Lo refused to back down. He shoved the envelope forward, into his father's face. "You'll like what's inside here," he said in a sing-song voice. "Promise."

Tong Yi glanced over at Ba Xi. He raised his eyebrows in question. Did she sense anything amiss with the envelope?

Ba Xi shrugged. It seemed she couldn't sense anything either.

It shocked Tong Yi when his mom looked at him next. When had she started to trust his judgment?

Slowly, Tong Yi nodded that it was all right. He didn't like it. But it would be better to take the envelope than to start an all-out battle with Quan Lo. Particularly in front of strangers.

However, Tong Yi readied a powerful water spell, just in case. The humans could always blame the fire alarm sprinklers if he had to use it. And water would dampen any fire or smoke effect.

His dad reached for the envelope and held it gingerly, as if afraid it would bite.

Tong Yi gulped when he realized the envelope had suddenly gained weight and girth.

Carefully, his dad opened one end of the envelope and slid out the contents.

Money.

Possibly a hundred blue one-thousand New Taiwanese dollar bills.

"To pay for dinner," Quan Lo smirked. "And to cover my debts."

Tong Yi pressed his lips together. He had paid off all of the debts that Quan Lo had accumulated, the credit card bills he'd run up. His parents had never had that kind of cash.

It stung badly that Quan Lo had suddenly showed up with the money. Particularly since Tong Yi was certain that his parents wouldn't think to pay him back, or to credit him at all for keeping the debtor off their back.

Tong Yi sent out a tendril of magic to make sure that the bills were actually there, that they weren't magically marked or manufactured and would suddenly disappear at the most inappropriate moment, embarrassing his father.

But the bills still seemed real and mundane, not spoiled at all.

"Thank you," Tong Yi's father said gravely. "It is good that you have finally taken responsibility for your debts." He handed the envelope to his wife without looking at her, keeping his gaze firmly on his eldest son. "If you can continue to prove that you are recovered from your illnesses, we may consider inviting you over for dinner. But not before."

Tong Yi blinked, shocked. Had his father just acknowledged that his eldest son had problems? And that he was no longer welcome at their home?

Maybe they really did like Ba Xi. And Tong Yi's studies with Uncle Bei.

"But who will take care of you if your eldest son isn't there?" Quan Lo whined.

"Tong Yi has been doing an excellent job as our son," Mom suddenly spoke up. "You could learn from him."

Tong Yi snapped his mouth shut. His mother couldn't have delivered a more deadly insult, suggesting that the younger son might be better at something than the eldest.

"Tong Yi," Quan Lo said, shooting an evil glare at his brother. "I see."

Quan Lo sat back in his chair, brooding while the party finished. His malevolence boiled around him, like a dark cloud.

Tong Yi wasn't sure exactly what conclusion his parents had come to about their eldest son. That they'd rebuked him in public still shocked Tong Yi.

Maybe there was hope for his family yet.

Despite the late hour, Tong Yi stood beside Ba Xi in her kitchen, sipping tea. Only the light above the stove was on. The rest of her apartment lay in the dark. Outside the walls, the night pressed in quietly around them. The sweet smell of jasmine tea filled the small room.

The kitchen was surprisingly modern, filled with gleaming black and chrome appliances. The stovetop took up three feet of counter space, a large grill making up most of it. A sleek rice cooker stood next to it. The black marble countertop had flecks of gray and silver running through it, making it seem lighter than it was. The cabinets were made out of a darker wood, while large, reddish-brown tiles covered the floor.

Beyond the open kitchen stood a small living room. It didn't surprise Tong Yi that Ba Xi had only marginally decorated, that most of the space stood empty.

Between the two windows stood a large, old-fashioned fireplace. White-painted bricks made up the mantel, while ancient flagstones formed the hearth. The only thing Ba Xi had put on the mantel was a very small picture of Tong Yi, in a tiny, oval frame.

A single end table stood underneath one of the windows overlooking the courtyard of the building, with a beautiful white and pink orchid in a green pot standing in the center of it.

A futon couch took up the center of the room, covered with the brightest orange cloth that Tong Yi had ever encountered. The couch had been very comfortable the times they'd sat on it, holding hands, and occasionally, kissing.

Soft gray color covered the walls. It changed subtly with the light, growing much brighter and more white during the day, then darker, turning to a slate gray, at night.

To the left of the kitchen stood a closed door, leading to Ba Xi's bedroom. Tong Yi had never been in it, but he'd glanced through the door a couple of times when it had stood open, and knew that the walls in there were painted in shades of ivory and dusky rose. The bed took up most of the room, with four tall posts in the corners of it and white gauze hanging from them. It looked very romantic, and Tong Yi hoped that one day, soon, he'd be able to experience it.

"During dinner, I talked with Gan Ou, one of your father's co-workers," Ba Xi said after a few more moments of peaceful quiet.

"What did he say?" Tong Yi asked, trying to be polite. He was too tired to experience more than the slightest passing of fear.

"Before we arrived, Quan Lo had talked about moving back home with your parents," Ba Xi said.

"Why would he do that?" Tong Yi wondered. "Is the war actually going badly? Does he want to leave the warzone?"

"That isn't it," Ba Xi said. "I think he wants a home base, here, on this plane. So he can spread his filth more easily. And move his drugs. That money wasn't tainted with magic, but with drugs and blood."

Tong Yi couldn't help his shiver. "I see," he said. He sighed. "I can't let him move back in." Maybe after the package he'd delivered to the *duchong*, the combatants hadn't been able to move the war to the earthly plane. Maybe they needed a better place to operate from.

Ba Xi took a sip of her tea. "I know." She sighed. "I'm afraid of what you'll have to do to stop him, though."

Tong Yi contained his own sigh. "Is there anyone else who could stop him? Who will?"

"While there are others who could," Ba Xi said. "No one else will."

"And?" Tong Yi asked as the silence grew expectant.

Ba Xi shook her head. "You haven't let the magic of Uncle Bei taint your soul too badly," she said.

Tong Yi blinked. He'd known that had been one of her concerns, that the darkness of Uncle Bei's magic would change him. He was glad that he'd managed to continue to find the light. That Ba Xi still found him attractive.

"However, your brother is a whole other matter," Ba Xi continued.

"I would only do what was necessary to stop him," Tong Yi said gravely. He didn't want to kill Quan Lo. He didn't want to kill anyone.

Ba Xi pressed her lips together for a moment, considering her words, before she finally responded. "And what if *necessary* is too much? If that changes you? Blackens your soul forever?"

"I will still always come back for you," Tong Yi said fervently. He had no idea what else to say. Dealing with his brother wouldn't make him break his promises to Ba Xi. "I will always be true to you."

Ba Xi shook her head. "I know you say that. I know you believe that's true. But what if the person making that promise is no longer there?"

Tong Yi didn't know how to respond to that. "I won't let it change me too much," he said, though he heard the hollowness of his words. Magic had changed him so much already. He easily saw how more magic would mean more changes.

"I know you'll try," Ba Xi said, giving him a small smile. "I can only pray that it's enough."

Tong Yi nodded grimly. There really wasn't much else he could promise. He would be the one to deal with his brother.

Or die trying.

Tong Yi drove Lu Wa through the quiet streets of Hualien. He loved the softness of the night, the bright lights of the human city. While the *fei renlei* neighborhood was deliciously peaceful and a wonderful escape, he also loved the life of his fellow humans, the tight streets.

Lu Wa was rarely restless, needing to drive like Ba Xi, so Tong Yi was able to go directly home. He could tell that his motorcycle felt anxious, however. A touch jumpy.

"We'll go on a long ride tomorrow," he promised the little frog. "Go to the beach. Play in the sand."

That seemed to settle his motorcycle a little, though it still seemed skittish as Tong Yi pulled up to his parents' apartment building.

Tong Yi got off the bike and sniffed the air. He didn't smell any magic. Only the occasional motorcycle or scooter passed on the street. Most of the buildings around him were dark. The night air still felt soft and humid.

"Do you want to come with me?" Tong Yi asked Lu Wa. Tong Yi patted the seat gently, then left his hand there on the warm vinyl. He wasn't sure if he should fold up the motorcycle and carry it with him or not. If that would help settle the little frog.

Lu Wa seemed to consider the question. It gave a shudder and appeared to shrink slightly under Tong Yi's fingers.

Tong Yi took that to mean that Lu Wa wanted to go with him. He called up some water, sprinkling the seat.

Lu Wa shrank down in the blink of an eye. Tong Yi didn't know that the bike could transform that quickly. But it felt to him as though the motorcycle wanted to hide.

"It's okay," he assured the little frog as he plucked him off the ground, then carefully put him in his shirt pocket. The frog stirred a bit before it settled, its long fingers spread out over Tong Yi's chest.

What was wrong? Tong Yi didn't know. But he readied himself for an attack as he walked in the door of his parents' apartment.

Nothing seemed amiss. The darkened living room looked the same as always, with the couch taking up much of the center, the flat-screen TV hanging on the wall in front of it. Just beyond the couch on the shelves, the family altar still held its place. All the figures stood there, along with a small bowl of rice and a second small bowl of fresh water.

Tong Yi slid more magic into his hands, letting them glow slightly as he approached the darkened hallway, then up the stairs toward his room.

He stopped at the top of the staircase and sniffed.

A very, very faint trace of magic wafted through the air.

Not Tong Yi's magic. But someone else's. Magic with a bitter tinge, more sour than sweet.

Tong Yi glanced at the door to his parents' bedroom. It was firmly closed and he didn't sense anything wrong behind it.

His own bedroom door, however…

The door stood ajar, not how he'd left it. And the smell of that foul magic flowed strongly from it.

Tong Yi readied his fire and pushed the door open with his foot.

Nothing appeared to be wrong. The narrow bed jutted to his right, sticking out from the middle of the wall, the covers messy. Beyond that, sitting next to the windows on the far wall, squatted his desk, a modern wooden piece of furniture that he'd bought himself when he'd started studying magic seriously. On the other wall stood a tall dresser. He'd kept most of his old school photos on top of it, and had only recently added a couple of pictures of himself and Ba Xi.

Where was the scent of magic coming from?

Tong Yi looked around the room a second time before he finally noticed that a red envelope sat on his pillow.

Someone had magically delivered a message to him.

Must be a very poorly trained messenger who didn't wait for his recipient. Or the person who'd sent the message hadn't considered it very important.

Tong Yi lifted the envelope off the bed using magic, without touching it. It didn't grow heavier when he flipped open one end, unlike that envelope with the money in it that Quan Lo had given his father.

A single piece of paper was enclosed. Nothing else. Tong Yi didn't sense the magic increasing as he slid the paper out, still not touching it.

Lu Wa pressed harder against his chest. Tong Yi nodded and put on his gloves before he finally touched the paper with his hands.

> *You have insulted my honor and my pride.*
> *I can no longer abide by such disgrace.*
> *I challenge you to a duel.*
> *Tomorrow. Noon.*
> *In the courtyard of the Palace of the Southern Gate.*
> *Sincerely*
> *Quan Lo*

The paper flared abruptly, catching fire. Tong Yi jumped, startled. He caught at the ash before it fell and set his bed on fire.

Goddamn it! How was he going to handle this? He didn't want to face his brother in a duel. He wasn't even sure what that meant.

He had a sneaking suspicion, though, that he really wasn't going to like it when he found out.

Tong Yi dragged himself out of bed when his alarm went off, swearing. Though he'd slept, he'd had nightmares all night, dreams of chasing a deadly paper dragon through darkened dungeon hallways, its long tail shedding sparks as it fled. Until it finally turned and faced Tong Yi, growing as large as Zhang Gua Lao's mule, brilliant white and about to explode with disease.

Uncle Bei had responded to his text the night before, telling him to haul his ass over to Uncle Bei's apartment and meet him early. Tong Yi trusted Lu Wa to get him there safely, as his own eyes were barely open. Fortunately, there never was much traffic that early in the morning.

Uncle Bei opened the door to his apartment fully dressed in a navy-blue suit with subtle blue pinstripes running through it, a brilliant white shirt, his usual cufflinks of power and a tie with bold golden stripes interspersed with much smaller black and white stripes.

"What happened?" Uncle Bei asked. He took one look at Tong Yi and whistled up a cup of tea, sending it sailing directly into Tong Yi's waiting hands.

"Thank you," Tong Yi said as he stepped across the threshold and into Uncle Bei's apartment. It had a lot more furniture than Ba Xi's apartment: besides the couch and two armchairs made of a dark brown leather it also had bookcases lining three of the walls. A TV stood on a filing cabinet against one wall. To the side of it was a sliding glass door, leading to Uncle Bei's deck.

The room always smelled of bay rum cologne, leather, and cloying magic. Today it also smelled of the rice and chicken that Uncle Bei had had for breakfast. To the left of the living room was a small kitchen that was generally immaculate: Uncle Bei rarely cooked.

Tong Yi explained about his father's birthday party the night before, the money Quan Lo had given his father, how he'd wanted to move back home, and then the challenge he'd issued.

Uncle Bei nodded, steepling his fingers in front of him and bowing his head for a moment, deep in thought. "He plans to bring the war here," Uncle Bei finally said. "To spread chaos through his drugs."

"That's what we thought," Tong Yi replied. The tea had woken him up, cutting through the morning fog.

"You have to stop him," Uncle Bei said.

"How?" Tong Yi asked. "I don't want to fight him."

Uncle Bei smiled grimly at him. "Too bad. He's chosen you for the portal."

"What portal?" Tong Yi asked. When Uncle Bei didn't reply, Tong Yi added, "And what's involved with a duel?"

Uncle Bei shrugged. "Duels don't have many rules around them. At least, not magical duels. Basically, it's you and the challenger, fighting in the style they've chosen. Which could be practically anything. Like creating beasts to fight each other. Or maybe fighting with swords. It's rarely actually throwing magic at each other." He paused. "Because he's chosen the time and place, you will have some advantages, such as setting limits to the conflict."

"So I don't have to kill him? It won't be a fight to the death?" Tong Yi asked, hopefully for the first time in a while.

"That's correct," Uncle Bei said slowly. "But you also need to ensure that you do what's necessary to stop him. Or he's going to keep coming after you, again and again."

"I see," Tong Yi said.

"I don't think you do," Uncle Bei said. "Quan Lo won't stop unless you kill him. He hates you. And you now stand in the way of the war effort for his side. He has to eliminate you. Just because you set terms in the battle, and specify that you don't have to kill him to win, doesn't mean that he won't be trying his damnedest to kill you."

Was this what Ba Xi had been talking about? That what was necessary might be too much for Tong Yi's soul? Would change him too much?

"What happens if I don't stop him?" Tong Yi asked.

"More drugs on the island," Uncle Bei said. "Corruption. Prostitution. Chaos spreading. Your parents will be the first casualty."

Tong Yi gulped. He hadn't thought of that. But Uncle Bei was right. Quan Lo didn't respect their parents, not like a dutiful son should.

"I'll go fight him," Tong Yi said slowly. "And I'll stop him." He wasn't sure how. There had to be some other way than fratricide.

"Good luck," Uncle Bei said. Then he gave Tong Yi his shark-like smile. "Just be like me for a while. You'll get it done."

Tong Yi blinked, surprised. That was actually useful advice. If Tong Yi could channel his mentor, see the world through his eyes…

Tong Yi hardened his heart and looked out over the room. The warm leather furniture grew darker, heavier. The pure white of the walls grew starker. Haze covered the windows looking out over the city. Contrasts grew. Right and wrong. Black and white.

It was an easy world to fall into. To divide us and them. Brother from brother.

Tong Yi longed for that simplicity.

But the world held grays. And off-whites. And tans. As well as burgundy and blue and green.

Color seeped back into his vision.

Was that really how Uncle Bei saw the world? That starkly? With very few victors, and many, many enemies?

Tong Yi appreciated Ba Xi's concerns more fully, now. Once he started seeing the world that way, it would change him greatly. More so than he could imagine.

He shook his head. There had to be a better way.

"It's your decision," Uncle Bei said. It sounded as if he still stood a long distance from Tong Yi.

Tong Yi came all the way back to the day. Uncle Bei looked at him, studying him intently, as if trying to see which way Tong Yi would jump.

Tong Yi shrugged. He didn't know, and wouldn't, until the time came.

"So how do I get to the warzone?" Tong Yi asked.

"I can't help you, I'm afraid," Uncle Bei said. "Part of my non-compete clause. Can't open portals to the warzone on my own. Only as directed by *Huli* Transport."

"Then how will I get there?" Tong Yi asked. "And get back?" Panic struck him.

"It's always easiest to build a portal on a site that already had one," Uncle Bei said slowly. "You said you might have found one, north of the city, up along the highway?"

Tong Yi nodded, remembering the abandoned strip of shops.

"You could easily build one there," Uncle Bei assured him.

"I could? Really?" Tong Yi asked, surprised.

"Really. Do you think I would have taken you on if you didn't have some promise?" Uncle Bei asked dryly.

Tong Yi opened his mouth, then shut it again. He'd never built a portal himself, but if Uncle Bei thought that he could…

"How will I return?" Tong Yi asked. He needed someone on this side to hold the portal open for him.

"You could ask that girlfriend of yours," Uncle Bei said slyly.

Tong Yi took a deep breath. He hadn't wanted to involve Ba Xi in any of this. He hadn't even told her of the duel challenge.

It appeared he would have to, though.

"Thank you," Tong Yi said, bowing his head low to his mentor and teacher, returning the teacup to him.

"Good luck," Uncle Bei said.

"I'll need it?" Tong Yi couldn't help but ask. Okay, so maybe some of Uncle Bei had already rubbed off on him.

"You will," Uncle Bei said with his shark grin. "And if you do survive, I expect you back here by Friday. That dungeon won't clear itself."

Tong Yi shook his head. Of course Uncle Bei would keep pushing him.

Tong Yi just hoped that he proved himself worthy.

A black figure stood beside Lu Wa. Tong Yi exited Uncle Bei's apartment building and walked quickly down the sidewalk. He thought about calling magic up into his hands. The day seemed bright and sticky, a lot of moisture in the air. Tong Yi considered calling up water instead of fire.

However, he held himself back.

He really didn't want to fall into Uncle Bei's world where everyone who hadn't proved themselves a friend was already considered an enemy.

The figure resolved slowly into Ba Xi, who appeared to be talking with Lu Wa. She looked up as he approached.

She wore a long jacket made out of red velvet with a swirling pattern burnt in it, showing the black mesh underneath, so the color changed between black and red as she moved. Underneath that, she wore a light red blouse, with jeans and black boots. She had her hair pulled severely back into a tight ponytail braided with red and black ribbons.

"What are you doing here?" Tong Yi asked, hurrying forward, holding both hands out to take hers. "Are you hurt?"

"I could ask you the same," Ba Xi told him dryly. But she still leaned forward and gave him a kiss on the cheek.

"Why are you here?" Tong Yi asked again when he pulled back and she continued to just study him.

"A little frog told me you were here," Ba Xi said.

"Ah," Tong Yi said, nodding, though he wasn't exactly sure how that worked. Did Lu Wa have an affinity to Ba Xi, because of who she was, what she had been? Or did he just like her, because she was Tong Yi's girlfriend?

"Did he tell you about the challenge?" Tong Yi asked.

"He did," Ba Xi said.

Tong Yi wasn't sure why so much sadness tinged her words. "Uncle Bei said I have to go stop him."

"I know," Ba Xi said, nodding. She shivered despite the warmth of the morning, crossed her arms over her chest and looked away.

When she didn't say anything more, Tong Yi asked, "Will you help me?"

Ba Xi gave him a single sharp nod.

"Will you hold the portal for me?" he asked softly. He wouldn't ask her to transform herself into her magnificent motorcycle form, though a part of him missed that side of her.

She gave him a tight smile. "That I will do," she said, sounding relieved.

What had she thought he would ask her to do? He wouldn't have asked her to do his duty. That would have been unfair.

Then he thought about Uncle Bei. He wouldn't have hesitated to ask Ba Xi, or anyone else, to do this work for him. To either kill Quan Lo, or to help Uncle Bei kill him.

Maybe that was what Ba Xi had also been afraid of—that Tong Yi would stop asking, and would just expect her to help. That he'd stop shouldering his own duty.

He vowed he'd always ask, and never just assume.

Would that be enough?

Tong Yi drove carefully up highway 169, obeying the speed limit, getting passed by the other bikes and cars. He didn't want to get stopped by a Red Zebra again. The sun shone down brightly on the ocean to his right. He wished that he could just keep going up the coast. That he and Ba Xi were going on a picnic, maybe up in the hills, away from everyone for a while, as they'd talked about.

Hopefully when he got back, that would be one of the very first things they'd do.

Ba Xi rode behind him on Lu Wa. He'd asked how she'd gotten to Uncle Bei's apartment but she'd just given him a mysterious smile. "I have my ways."

Tong Yi had learned that there was more than one entrance into the *fei renlei* neighborhood. He assumed there was probably more than one exit as well. It wouldn't have surprised him if there was a portal close to Uncle Bei's apartment building.

It didn't take long at all to reach the abandoned strip of shops. Tong Yi nudged Lu Wa reluctantly off the highway. He drove the bike up, along the side, then eased it through the tall weeds, rocks, and garbage back behind the buildings.

The stench of decay, rotten fish, and stale magic rolled over Tong Yi as soon as he lifted the visor on his helmet. He looked over his shoulder at Ba Xi. She wrinkled her cute nose at him. "Ugh," she said distinctly.

That at least made him smile. They got off the bike, then he asked Lu Wa to shrink down again. The little frog leaped from the ground to his jacket as soon as he'd transformed, landing in the center of Tong Yi's chest, over his medallion.

"Do you want to ride in a pocket?" Tong Yi asked, bending his head awkwardly so he could look at the frog.

The paper figure shook its head.

He wanted to stay right where he was.

Did he think he was going to act as a type of shield for whatever Tong Yi was about to face?

Tong Yi had no idea.

All he knew was that for such a small frog, Lu Wa certainly had the largest heart of anyone Tong Yi knew.

Tong Yi used magic to pull off the pieces of corrugated metal nailed over the back door of one of the stores. It took some power—not because the thing had been nailed down efficiently, but because something magical held it in place.

The ugly graffiti that covered the metal piece faded as Tong Yi pulled it to one side. Without thinking, he immediately absorbed the power being released.

Ba Xi looked at him funny when he tossed the metal away.

"What is it?" he asked. He needed all the power he could get before this battle.

"Be careful what you absorb," she said. "Sometimes power is tainted."

Tong Yi nodded. He knew that. Both Uncle Bei and See-tza had explained the need for caution.

But it took a lot of power to taint magic that way, and to have it maintain that flavor. Nothing here was that powerful.

In the warzone, he'd have to be a lot more careful, though.

The stench of rotten oranges, dead fish, and mildewing wood rolled out through the dark opening, underlaid with the cloying smell of tainted magic.

Tong Yi called up fire into his hands and stepped forward. He could tell that Ba Xi thought about going first, but let him instead.

She was probably stronger than he was magically. But it wouldn't have been right.

Would he always feel that way?

It wasn't difficult for them to find the site of the former portal. It had been formed in the northernmost shop. Cracks of light streamed in through the plywood and corrugated metal that covered what had once been wide front windows. All the garbage had been pushed to the edges of the square room, leaving the center bare.

The room itself wasn't large. It took Tong Yi a moment to realize that the faint lines on the floor marked the edges of tatami mats, that the room itself held four and a half mats, which made it about eight feet square.

Uncle Bei had been right—the portal created here had only been used one time, and burned up in the process. Black characters, drawn with ashes and smeared with blood, formed a wide circle in the center of the front room. Dark sigils also danced across the walls. The smell of feces made Tong Yi want to gag.

"This is it?" Ba Xi asked. "This is where you want to create a portal?"

Tong Yi sighed. "Here," he said. "That way, if I don't make it, and this portal becomes a weak point…"

"The opening between the planes is already at a weak joint," Ba Xi said. "As opposed to weakening a healthy joint."

"Exactly," Tong Yi said, relieved.

"Let me clear this up, then," Ba Xi said. She looked expectantly at Tong Yi.

It took Tong Yi a moment to realize that she wanted him out of the way. He ducked behind her, knowing better than to make a joke about never getting in the way of a woman and her housecleaning.

Bright light filled the dark space, burning away all the filth and cobwebs, cleaning the walls of their dark signs. The scent of orange blossoms came with it, refreshing and cool.

The characters in the center of the room stayed put. Their color grew darker, a pure black. Some of them wiggled, then lined up more truly with their neighbors, the circle growing more symmetrical.

Tong Yi marveled at Ba Xi's command of magic. He'd always known she was powerful, though she generally preferred to do everything by hand and not use magic. She didn't blast the space. She left the garbage along the edges of the room. She just did what was necessary.

As he hoped to.

When Ba Xi finished, the space fell back into dimness, with sunlight still streaming through the cracks in the metal and plywood covering the front windows. However, the room felt lighter and more airy, as if she'd chased away the shadows who'd also taken up residence there. The air smelled fresh and sweet, and Tong Yi could smell the salt of the nearby water as well. Glowing characters filled the center of the room, the magic making the hair on Tong Yi's arms stand up.

A familiar, swirling blue-and-gray oval sprang up in the center of the room. The middle of it reminded Tong Yi of his nightmares, black and endless.

"How long can you hold the portal for?" he asked Ba Xi.

"I'll actually do something better than merely keep the portal open," Ba Xi told him. "I will give you a way to call me. So that you don't have to worry about time." She pulled a coin out of her pocket and handed it to him.

Tong Yi nearly swore. It was the same coin he'd used to clean out her gas tank, so long ago. The coin that Zhang Gua Lao had given him.

"Thank you," Tong Yi said fervently. "I swear I'll bring this back to you." He assumed it had strong sentimental value for her, not just great magical power. He paused, then asked, "Uhm. How do I use it?"

Ba Xi laughed at him. "I could tell you to swallow it when you're ready to come home," she teased. "But it would be too messy getting it out of you."

Tong Yi gulped at that. That sounded…painful.

"Just hold it in your hands and tell the coin that you wish to see me again," Ba Xi told him. "If you're on Lu Wa, that will help."

"Thank you," Tong Yi told her again.

After a moment, he reached his hand for her arm.

She let him pull her in. In her boots, she stood as tall as him.

The kiss started gentle and grew fiercely possessive on both their parts.

"Come home to me," Ba Xi said, pressing her cool forehead against his.

"I will," Tong Yi promised.

She smiled at him and stroked her hand along his face, her eyes shining with tears as she shook her head and stepped back away from him.

"Why doesn't Uncle Bei let the messengers of *Huli* Transport just call him like this?" Tong Yi asked as he grabbed his motorcycle helmet. "Instead of holding a portal open?" He thought he knew the answer, but he wanted to make sure.

"You have to have an affinity to someone for them to be able to call across planes," she said. She paused, then added, "There is a downside, though. If… If you change too much over there, I won't hear you."

Tong Yi blinked. Ba Xi was taking a huge chance on him, that he'd come back to her, as himself.

Tong Yi didn't want to ask, but he had to. "Can Lu Wa find his way out through the badlands?"

"He can," Ba Xi said. "I told him how."

"Thank you," Tong Yi said. "I hope he never has to use that knowledge."

Ba Xi merely gave him a sad smile that told Tong Yi just how little hope she had that he'd come back to her with his soul intact.

As there was nothing left to say, Tong Yi bowed his head to her, low and with great respect, then he turned and entered the portal on foot.

It was only midway through that he realized he hadn't asked for her token to wear into battle.

But she hadn't offered any ribbons, either. Just the coin.

As he'd always suspected, it was just going to be him and Quan Lo at the very end.

The warzone hadn't changed. The sky still bled that awful shade of purple, like an old bruise, along the edges of the boiling, iron-gray clouds. Deep, rutted earth made up the ground, pulsing with enough hate to set Tong Yi's teeth on edge. The staleness of the air struck him as odd—it was as if the plane needed the air recycled, and that hadn't happened in a while.

Tong Yi glanced around, trying to place himself on the broad, flat plain. To his left stood the long ridge of mountains, the direction he'd always designated as east. To his right stood an endless open field that possibly went to the very edge of the world, the direction he'd designated west.

Just behind him stood the portal, burning warm and *human* in a way he hadn't ever really thought about. It was not of this place. It led the way home.

He couldn't help his small cry of dismay as the portal winked out of existence.

He'd always had to rely on a portal to take him home, on it staying open long enough for him.

He made himself stand up straighter. He would be able to call it open again. He had to trust himself, trust Ba Xi.

He turned around and nearly jumped out of his skin.

Zhang Gua Lao stood there, with his paper mule unfolded and standing beside him. The immortal looked much the same as he had the last time Tong Yi had seen him, wearing a formal brown robe edged in heavy white satin. A large brown-leather belt around his waist had numerous small bags hanging from it. Straw sandals were tied to his feet, and his long black hair, streaked with white, had been done up in a knot on the back of his head, held in place by two long hair sticks.

"So, what do we have here?" the immortal asked. He reached forward before Tong Yi could stop him and plucked Lu Wa from his chest.

"Sir," Tong Yi said, forcing himself to take a deep breath, willing his pounding heart to at least slow down. "That originally had been your message to Sun Hou-Tze."

"I see, I see!" the old man said, nodding. He placed the frog in the center of his palm and examined it carefully for a moment. "Very clever, indeed." He bowed his head. "And a pleasure to meet you too," he added.

Could Lu Wa talk? And Tong Yi just hadn't learned how to hear the little frog yet? He was going to have to investigate that. And soon.

"Thank you, sir," Tong Yi said as he took back the paper frog.

"Go on," Zhang Gua Lao said, stepping back. "He wants to change. Let me see."

"All right," Tong Yi said with a grin. Then he paused, considering. This was really the first time he'd tried to perform this type of magic here in the warzone. What would be different? What did he need to compensate for?

Or did he need to do anything different? And just trust that Lu Wa wanted to show off for the immortal?

It took almost no effort for Tong Yi to call water up to his fingertips. He hadn't realized before just how much *power* this land held.

The warzone called to him, to those parts of him that had grown stronger, that held more magic.

It was…disturbing.

He remembered the first time he'd been to the warzone, how he'd been the last one to find the portal back home.

How long it had taken for the warzone to truly disturb his soul.

Was that because of the power it represented? And how he recognized it, unconsciously?

He suddenly understood why Quan Lo stayed here, wrapped in so much power, even if it wasn't pure and clean.

Tong Yi shook his head and pushed those thoughts from his mind as he concentrated on Lu Wa. "Come to me, little one," he said softly as he sprinkled a few drops of water onto the back of the paper frog. "Come bear me."

Slowly, much more slowly than ever before, the little frog grew and changed into his other self.

Tong Yi studied the motorcycle. It had subtly changed, as Bing Xi had when she'd come here.

His tires had grown narrower, with the tail hiked up, so Lu Wa appeared more like a dirt bike. Both fenders had extended downward. They'd also grown wider, so they protected the wheels more. The body had remained the same sleek green shape, though the seat had shrunk, as if Lu Wa never expected to carry more than one rider now.

In addition, the headlight had changed, growing round and bug-eyed. The only comparison that Tong Yi could come up with was that Lu Wa's headlight now looked more like his frog eye.

Then the headlight blinked.

Or was it winking at him?

Tong Yi felt much better, knowing that the little frog could see everything as well.

"Lovely, just lovely," Zhang Gua Lao said, leaning over to pat the headlight. "And you, too."

"Thank you?" Tong Yi said, confused about what the immortal was complimenting him on.

"Come. Walk with me a little while," Zhang Gua Lao said.

Tong Yi reached for Lu Wa, but the immortal stopped him. "No, leave him here. They have a lot to talk about," he added conspiratorially.

Tong Yi nearly asked who but then he realized that Zhang Gua Lao meant his mule.

"You okay with that?" he still asked Lu Wa.

The bike gave a happy shiver.

"All right," Tong Yi said. He wasn't certain how he knew Lu Wa was happy, but he was.

Tong Yi turned and walked beside Zhang Gua Lao, in the direction he'd always called west, directly opposite the tall range of rocks behind him.

"So you go to battle your brother," Zhang Gua Lao said after a few moments.

"I do," Tong Yi said grimly. He still didn't want to. Still didn't want to have to kill Quan Lo.

Still wasn't sure exactly what he was going to do, either.

"It is always sad when brother fights brother," the immortal said solemnly.

"I agree," Tong Yi said. "Do you see some other way?" he asked, hopeful.

"I do not," Zhang Gua Lao said with a heavy sigh. "How much do you want to bet that you'll win?"

"I beg your pardon?" Tong Yi asked, not sure that he heard the immortal correctly.

"Will you win?" Zhang Gua Lao asked more plainly.

"I...I don't know, sir," Tong Yi admitted. He wanted to win. That much he knew. And not only that, he had to win the *right* way. He had too much to lose if he didn't.

"You know, the Yellow Emperor had much more confidence when he went up to battle chaos, to bind it to structure and order," Zhang Gua Lao said sourly.

"I'm not the Yellow Emperor," Tong Yi replied, stung. Of course the Yellow Emperor had more confidence! He also had more power.

"He didn't have more power than you," Zhang Gua Lao said, as if Tong Yi had spoken out loud.

"Sir?" Tong Yi asked, confused. "How could that be?"

"This war is about power, as all wars are at the heart of them," Zhang Gua Lao said. "Who controls it. Who has more of it. And who has less."

"I see," Tong Yi said, though he really didn't. What was the old man driving at?

"You and Quan Lo represent a microcosm," Zhang Gua Lao continued, "almost the entire war, its culture and its parties, in miniature."

"We do?" Tong Yi asked. How could that be? Was the war about drugs or something?

Then he thought back and realized what the immortal was saying.

Quan Lo represented chaos, disrespect, sex and drugs and rock and roll and all those things foreign to their native culture.

Tong Yi stood for tradition, family values, for being a dutiful son no matter the circumstances, for respecting his elders, for always asking and never assuming.

"I do see," Tong Yi said grimly.

"Will you win?" Zhang Gua Lao asked again.

Tong Yi realized that the immortal wasn't asking lightly. His answer had weight, particularly in this plane.

"I will," Tong Yi finally responded.

He didn't add the words that rang clearly through his head.

Or die trying.

Tong Yi raced across the warzone on the back of Lu Wa. In some ways it was easier to drive Lu Wa than Bing Xi here—Lu Wa never tried to fishtail across the rutted earth.

In other ways, it was more difficult. Lu Wa took every opportunity he could to leave the earth, to jump high from one rut to the other.

Tong Yi didn't scold the little frog, though he'd been tempted to once when he didn't land as straight as he should have and they nearly rolled. However, Lu Wa had been more sedate after that, not quite so enthusiastic.

Tong Yi figured that Lu Wa just needed to get some of his nervousness out of his system before they met up with Quan Lo. Just in case his brother declared some sort of race or something as the duel challenge.

The castle finally appeared on the horizon. Tong Yi didn't slow down as he approached it. It, too, hadn't changed much, still looking like a child's nightmare made out of trash. It had the same feel as the empty strip of shops where Ba Xi had created the portal: covered with graffiti and leftovers from construction sites and garbage heaps.

Only one tower stood on the left side of the castle. It looked as though it had been built out of pieces of modern appliances, like refrigerator doors, stovetops, and dishwasher racks. The rest of the castle appeared to be crumbling under the weight of all the trash heaped on it, the chair legs sticking out of the walls covered in leftover plastic bags, the picture frames filled with fast food wrappers, and the drawers of the metal filing cabinets overflowing with papers.

Tong Yi couldn't help the thrill of hope that raced through him. Were things not going well for Quan Lo? Was that why his palace was getting covered with so much garbage? Was Quan Lo, and his side of the war, already losing?

The front courtyard of the castle held two rickety wooden sets of bleachers. On the right, packed tightly together, sat mole men, cat-like creatures, and others that Tong Yi couldn't easily identify.

A single sad creature stood on the bleachers on the left. He looked like the joker from a deck of playing cards brought to life: thin as paper, with only half a face, though his clothes were brightly colored in purple and green. He raised a flag when Tong Yi entered the courtyard.

His cheering section. The joker. Of course. The opposite of all that Tong Yi stood for, a wild card representing chance and luck, not order and law.

Tong Yi scanned the ground between the two bleachers. Sand had been brought in, gray and silky smooth. It would make driving more difficult, as Lu Wa wouldn't be able to get good traction.

However, Tong Yi didn't see any magical potholes, or other traps that he might fall into. The area, for all it sickened his sense of right, was clean.

Quan Lo rode Mei Fuang out of the castle entrance, across the small dirt bridge over the moat. He wore his typical peasant's shirt, jeans and boots. His helmet looked like polished steel, with great metal pieces rising on either side, like bird wings.

The motorcycle's sleek lines had grown more gaunt, though she didn't look frail, just wiry. The blue of her gas tank had stayed an incongruously pretty blue, shiny and metallic.

Did she also have a hidden soul? Could she, under other circumstances, have transformed into another creature? Or was she just as she appeared, a motorcycle driven by a madman?

Tong Yi would never know.

"Brother! You've come!" Quan Lo called out cheerfully. He used magic to amplify his voice over the roaring of the crowd.

Tong Yi did the same. "Your honor demanded a duel," Tong Yi said. "Mine requires a victory."

Loud catcalls greeted his declaration. Tong Yi shrugged.

He refused to always channel Uncle Bei. But sometimes, it might be necessary.

"A victory, brother?" Quan Lo said, obviously taken aback. "Then come! Let us engage in joyful battle! May the best brother win!"

"No, we will not," Tong Yi said, holding his place and not moving. "Not until we establish the rules of loss. And victory."

"Victory is your head on my pike!" Quan Lo said.

Tong Yi merely shook his head. "What is the battle?"

"Jousting!" Quan Lo declared joyfully. A lance appeared in his hands, pointed directly at Tong Yi's heart.

A second lance appeared, sticking out of the ground beside Tong Yi.

"Two out of three falls?" Tong Yi asked as he plucked the long pole from its resting place. It had been made out of a polished wood, with a wider base than tip. It would shatter with too much force. "And then this duel is over? We are finished?"

"Very well," Quan Lo said petulantly. "But I don't promise not to *accidentally* drive over you!"

"Ditto," Tong Yi replied. He hefted the lance under his right arm. "You got this?" he whispered to Lu Wa, hoping that for the most part the little frog would be able to steer himself.

Lu Wa shivered, determined.

"Then let's do this," Tong Yi said.

Or die trying seemed more and more likely.

The crowd on the bleachers cheered, the sound deafening. The sky above the brothers boiled more angrily, as if disappointed they were no longer paying any attention to it.

Tong Yi revved Lu Wa's engine from his end of the arena.

Quan Lo did likewise, an angry, buzzing sound.

The two brothers raced toward each other.

Tong Yi tried not to gag as he drove closer to the filthy water of the moat circling the castle.

He pulled at the power in the air, the power of the land, building himself an effective shield against his brother's lance.

Thunk!

Quan Lo smacked his lance against Tong Yi's. They both shivered under the forceful impact. Tong Yi held onto his seat, but just barely.

Quan Lo stayed on his bike as well.

In the split second after the collision, Tong Yi tried to guide Lu Wa to the side.

Mei Fuang veered toward him. She would have struck them head on if Lu Wa hadn't leaped away at the last moment.

Tong Yi barely got his bike under control before it ran into the bleachers at the far end. He spun the bike around, spitting sand and gravel on the watchers, their jeers making his head ring.

"What the hell is wrong with you?" he called angrily to Quan Lo. "Jousting means hitting each other with these!" he added, holding up his lance. "Not running our bikes into each other!"

Quan Lo laughed and shrugged. "I can't help it if my beast is more determined to win than yours."

Or she has a death wish.

Was that why she appeared so skeletal? Did she regret her choice of brother?

Tong Yi shook himself and rolled his shoulders. His arms still shook with the combined force of their lances. Only magic had helped him hold on.

He patted Lu Wa, who also shivered, though Tong Yi wasn't certain what his bike was feeling. Anger? Fear? Determination? Some combination of all of those?

At least he didn't have to worry about which bike had the biggest heart. He knew that would be Lu Wa.

Now, how could he unseat his brother during the next attack? How could he apply structure to his brother's chaos, and make the magic roll with him?

Tong Yi studied Quan Lo as he lunged forward, trying to spot a weakness. He didn't see anything obvious.

At the last minute, Quan Lo shifted his target from Tong Yi to Lu Wa, attempting to spear the motorcycle's rear wheel.

Tong Yi saw the move as it unfolded.

He urged Lu Wa to jump again.

As they passed, Quan Lo reached out and shoved Tong Yi to the side, trying to throw him off.

"Hey!" Tong Yi shouted, barely righting himself again. Was that fair?

Then he realized he hadn't dictated how the other had to be thrown. So of course, Quan Lo would use everything in his power, not just his lance.

Very well, then.

As they approached the third time, Tong Yi threw his lance in front of him, like a spear. Once in the air, he transformed it from a long lance into a short, stout log.

It landed directly in front of Mei Fuang's front tire.

Quan Lo went up and over the front of his bike in slow motion.

Tong Yi knew Quan Lo wouldn't be hurt. Hell, he probably enjoyed the flight.

When Tong Yi turned around, his brother stood in the center of the field, his hands on his hips. "So that's the way it's to be, brother?"

Tong Yi shrugged. "First fall goes to me," he proclaimed loudly.

"Two out of three!" Quan Lo reminded him.

Tong Yi nodded. He'd agreed. Just because he'd made Quan Lo take the first fall didn't mean that Tong Yi had won the battle.

However, Mei Fuang wouldn't rise again. She'd bent the front forks that held the wheel.

Tong Yi got off Lu Wa and brought up water to his fingertips, encouraging the machine to shrink down. He picked up the small frog from the sand and slipped it inside the front of his leather jacket.

Though Tong Yi knew that technically he could still ride his brother down, that wouldn't be fair.

And if Tong Yi represented law, he had to be bound by those limits.

Quan Lo merely grinned at him as a large sword appeared in his hand.

"Won't you dance with me, Tong Yi?" he called.

Tong Yi shivered, remembering the last time Quan Lo had used that phrase, back in their family's kitchen, when he'd been so high.

"First blood?" Tong Yi said as he called his own sword to his hand. He'd rarely had to fight with one. He'd preferred magical battles instead. Both Uncle Bei and See-tza had insisted that he learn the basics of sword fighting, however.

"First death," Quan Lo said nastily, charging.

Tong Yi remained where he was, calm and certain that Quan Lo couldn't strike him until the new terms of their battle had been agreed upon.

Quan Lo stopped abruptly less than three inches from Tong Yi. The stench from his breath flowed down. His skin still appeared pale and waxy. Sweat dripped freely from his greasy hair, staining his shirt. His eyes whirled yellow and mad.

Tong Yi stood his ground. He hated that he still had to look up, physically, at his brother. Chickenflesh covered his shoulders and back, causing him to shiver, but he refused to back down, or even take a step back.

The brothers stared at each other. Hatred flared between them like a living thing, crackling with electricity.

"Not a minor scratch," Quan Lo said, breathing hard. "Serious cut."

Tong Yi swallowed hard. This was about to turn even uglier than before.

"If I agree, and I win, you never get to challenge me again," Tong Yi stated clearly. "You stay here with the endless war, never returning to the earthly plane."

"And if I win, I take your place on the earthly plane," Quan Lo said, clearly triumphant.

Tong Yi wasn't sure exactly what that meant. Was Quan Lo a doppelgänger? Could he transform himself into someone else? Some*thing* else?

It didn't matter. Tong Yi had to win.

"You're on," Tong Yi said, though he still wasn't exactly sure what he was agreeing to.

"Ah, brother, your Ba Xi is going to be such a sweet ride!" Quan Lo crowed as he took two steps back and readied his sword.

"She'd know the difference," Tong Yi told him flatly.

"No, nom she wouldn't," Quan Lo assured him. His features flowed and Tong Yi suddenly found himself staring at the face he saw in the bathroom mirror every day. "Hi, little one," Quan Lo said shyly.

Damn it! Quan Lo sounded exactly like Tong Yi. And the innocent feeling he projected was perfect too.

Quan Lo could *not* be allowed to win this fight.

Even more was at stake, now.

Tong Yi stood with most of his weight on his forward foot, his left. He didn't bounce, though nervous energy coiled through all his muscles. He kept his left arm raised, holding a magical shield, round and silver like a coin, embossed with the character *lu*, for order.

He felt like a great warrior from one of his video games, standing with his right arm behind him, long curved sword raised high. His right foot, too, stood solidly behind him, ready to absorb Quan Lo's first blow.

Quan Lo started in a similar stance—left foot in front, left arm with a shield, right arm and sword behind. The shield was covered in constantly twisting snakes.

He swung his right arm wide, landing a solid blow on Tong Yi's shield. *Wump.*

Tong Yi had expected sparks, or even lightning when they clashed.

Instead, it felt like all space-time warped around them. A wash of power rippled out, like a shock wave.

Tong Yi pivoted his hips so he could bring all his power into his swing. He tried to focus his energy along the edge of the blade, to cut through his brother's shield.

Another solid *wump* echoed out from their contact, rippling across the screaming onlookers, warping the sound to monstrous howls.

Quan Lo quickly swung again, the strength of his blow forcing Tong Yi onto his back foot.

Tong Yi rocked forward just as fast and struck again with his blade.

Quan Lo let the weight of the blow swing him to the side, pivoting in a circle, his momentum carrying him through, landing a solid strike on the side of Tong Yi's shield, knocking him forward, out of position.

Tong Yi stumbled and turned quickly.

Quan Lo struck again, forcing Tong Yi back.

Damn it!

All the magic in the world wouldn't sustain Tong Yi, or let him win this fight. Already his muscles ached, his arms tired from the blows.

He tried to imitate Quan Lo, letting the next strike carry him in a circle.

However, Quan Lo was twice as fast as Tong Yi anticipated.

Before Tong Yi could get all the way around, his brother rose in the air behind him, striking out with a foot that landed square in the middle of Tong Yi's back.

Tong Yi flew forward, dropping his sword and shield as he landed on the dirt.

He was in trouble.

Tong Yi forced himself up, spinning around, sand flying from his clothes. He called his sword and shield back to him.

Quan Lo floated high in the air, his arms and legs spread in a martial arts pose that he'd probably learned from Dragonball Z.

"Do you yield, brother?" Quan Lo called out triumphantly. "Because the next time I strike you, you'll feel the cut of my blade, not the bluntness of my fist."

"Never," Tong Yi called through gritted teeth. He *pulled* power from the land, his medallion, and Lu Wa, then flowed up into the air.

He took a similar stance to the one he had before, left arm and shield forward, right foot and sword back.

Quan Lo deliberately yawned, then struck at Tong Yi's shield with three successive blows that forced Tong Yi back.

Tong Yi narrowed his eyes. So that was how it was to be?

He *pulled* even more magic to him, willing it to flow into his leaden limbs, trying to move as quickly as Quan Lo.

To no avail.

Quan Lo laughed as he struck Tong Yi's shield repeatedly, driving him further and further back.

The crowd below them jeered all the louder.

Finally, Tong Yi jumped past Quan Lo and landed on the ground a short distance away, panting.

Quan Lo preened for his court while Tong Yi gulped stale air.

Damn it! Quan Lo couldn't be that good. He looked unwinded, as though he hadn't been fighting at all.

Tong Yi narrowed his eyes and stared hard at his brother.

Gone was the sweat from earlier. Quan Lo appeared as fresh as when they'd first taken the field.

Tong Yi pushed himself into the air again like an anime fighter, sword out this time, instead of holding it behind him in a proper stance.

Quan Lo joined him, still joyful.

This time, Tong Yi bashed Quan Lo's sword, not his shield.

Quan Lo quickly struck back, as if they were both working with fencing foils instead of heavier Chinese *dao* blades.

Tong Yi knew that getting closer to Quan Lo was dangerous. Still, he pushed forward for two more blows before he dropped down and swung out with his foot.

It went *through* Quan Lo's leg.

Tong Yi dropped all the way to the ground, growling.

Quan Lo wasn't really here. The image Tong Yi saw was just a projection.

No wonder he was such an amazing fighter.

When had Quan Lo made the switch? When had he stopped fighting with his own body, and started using a simulacrum instead?

Probably during the first fall, when he'd gone flying through the air. The fake Quan Lo had landed on the ground of the arena, while the real one had flitted away somewhere safe.

No matter.

Tong Yi *had* to take the fight to Quan Lo, to where his brother was actually hidden.

Tong Yi closed his eyes and sought out his brother. He'd been trained by *Huli* Transport to find people, to help him deliver his messages.

He didn't have much time before the image struck him again.

As the mirage drew closer, Tong Yi *felt* the difference. From inside the castle came a magical beam, directed at the image of Quan Lo, maintaining it.

Quan Lo was inside.

Tong Yi ducked under the figure and took off, great leaping bounds, over the moat and into the darkness of the castle itself.

The crowd behind him jeered, calling him a coward. The image of Quan Lo crowed loudly, chasing after him.

Tong Yi put them all out of his mind.

He had to find his real brother.

And dance with him one last time.

As Tong Yi suspected, Quan Lo was in the tower. It gave him the clearest view of the field they'd been fighting on. It also explained why the specter continued to leap so high in the air.

The soft dirt under Tong Yi's motorcycle boots muffled his pounding footsteps as he raced through the darkened hallways. He kept his sword upright, making it flame brightly like a torch to help him see. Stale air filled the corridors—no fresh winds had blown here in some time. More garbage lined the walls, not just leftover car-wheel rims, truck lights, and empty TV frames, but fast food wrappers, rotten fruit, fish skeletons, and rotting shrimp shells.

The ghostly figure of an ancient temple guard "protecting" the stairs didn't stand a chance. Tong Yi brushed by him as if he didn't exist.

Then he realized his mistake. He'd walked right into a sticky web. Long strings covered his bare face. Glistening silver strands coated his arms.

Was it supposed to hold him? Stop him? Or just annoy him?

Tong Yi kept going, wiping his face clear. The stairs were also made of dirt, twisting to the left as they climbed. He shuddered when he saw faces embedded in the walls, human-like figures with their mouths and eyes wide open, as if screaming in horror.

They weren't really human faces—just pieces of junk arranged to look that way.

Still, Tong Yi tried to keep his eyes forward.

Lu Wa suddenly warmed against his chest. Tong Yi glanced down.

Damn it! The web he'd passed through had spiders in it. Lu Wa was gobbling them up as fast as he could, zapping them with his power, but Tong Yi knew the little frog couldn't get them all. He took another moment to stop and brush the…creatures…from the front of his leather jacket.

Then realized his mistake when he leaned over to brush at his pants and a sword went whizzing over his head.

Goddamn it!

The specter of Quan Lo floated beside him. "You can't find the treasure in time to save yourself!" he crowed.

"You're wrong," Tong Yi said flatly. "I have the power of the Yellow Emperor behind me. The power of Confucius and law. You…you have nothing."

Quan Lo appeared to falter at that.

Tong Yi contained his smile. Yes, channeling Uncle Bei did have its uses.

Instead of engaging further with the simulacrum, Tong Yi *used* it. He pulled at the power directing it, following it back to its source.

The figure of his brother floating before him faded.

Tong Yi took a calculated risk and raced *through* the figure. It shocked his skin, as though he'd touched a live wire. While he didn't drain any power from it, it didn't take any from him, either.

Down the hallway filled with excrement and rotting garbage. Nasty symbols danced on the walls, figures writhing, meant to distract anyone coming this way.

Tong Yi pushed his way through the door into Quan Lo's…bedroom.

It looked almost identical to Tong Yi's, back on earth. A long narrow bed stuck out of the middle of the wall on the right. A desk squatted in the corner, and a tall dresser stood beside the door.

The main changes were the windows—instead of a small opening, the entire wall opposite the door held wide open windows, facing the battleground, as Tong Yi had suspected.

The other difference was the light. It seemed brighter here than in the rest of the castle. White and pure.

Was this where Quan Lo kept the remains of his soul? The parts of him that hadn't been corrupted yet?

Tong Yi *pulled* at the power in the room, willing himself to see beyond whatever illusion Quan Lo spun up.

The walls shimmered and the air changed, growing misty and clammy.

Tong Yi felt as though he'd just stepped through another portal.

Quan Lo lay on the bed, gasping. His skin was pocked, no longer smooth and wax-like. His hair looked the same, greasy and long. Sweat drenched the soft mattress Quan Lo lay on.

At the same time, a great light shone out from the figure, soft and warm. When Tong Yi touched the light, tasted it with his magic, he found the essence of his brother.

They were no longer merely in the castle.

They had moved into the essence of Quan Lo, the room that held his soul.

Did Tong Yi have such a room as well? Or was this all just metaphor? A dream within a dream?

"Brother," Quan Lo croaked, reaching up a frail hand.

Tong Yi was shocked. His brother was a mere shell of his former self. Tong Yi could see his ribs through his poet shirt, the bones in his hands, the way his skin stretched across his sharp cheekbones and chin.

It looked as though Quan Lo had been on a month-long drug binge. And maybe that was what living in the warzone felt like to his brother's soul.

Tong Yi looked at the sword in his hand. If he cut his brother, as they'd agreed…Quan Lo would stay here. Destitute. Unable to leave. Possibly even when the war ended.

Could Tong Yi condemn Quan Lo to that?

Or was there another way? Could he kill the sickness in his brother without killing his brother himself?

Mirages flickered through the room. Dancing cats from the cartoons they'd watched as children. Sinuous snakes from nightmares. Scary clowns.

And hospital rooms.

Suddenly, Tong Yi saw an IV stand, looming tall beside his brother's prone form. Luminous drugs dripped through the tubing, flowing into Quan Lo's arm.

Tong Yi thought he understood the dreamland's message. What Quan Lo's soul was trying to tell him.

Quan Lo, himself, wasn't sick.

The sickness came from what he'd put into his body.

Tong Yi could stop this. Could stop Quan Lo from using. Stop him from spreading his filth.

It wasn't all that hard, really, for Tong Yi to reach out with the tip of his sword and carefully touch the center of his brother's chest.

Then he *pulled*.

Tong Yi sucked up all the magic in Quan Lo's system. Vacuumed it out of his heart. Scrubbed his blood clean of it.

Cut off his *sight*.

Until Quan Lo was merely human. Mundane. Unable to touch magic, ever again.

The room shimmered. The air grew stale and foul.

They'd left that pure dreamland, the cleanness of Quan Lo's soul.

They stood back in the castle.

Quan Lo blinked, shaking his head. "Where am I?"

"Flophouse," Tong Yi said blithely.

"Whoa," Quan Lo said, turning his head from side to side. How much of the walls of the palace could he see now? "What a trip," he murmured.

"Let's get you home," Tong Yi said, lifting his brother easily. Though Quan Lo was taller and bigger than Tong Yi, he'd lost a lot of weight.

Would Quan Lo stay clean? Tong Yi didn't know.

But at least he had a chance, now.

It was only after Tong Yi had put Quan Lo on Lu Wa that he realized his mistake.

The world expanded in front of him when he looked up. The warzone sprang to life in brilliant colors, as though Tong Yi had just taken drugs. The castle's walls smoothed out, the broken figures taking on more pattern and sense, changing from garbage to art. The air changed, growing rich and fecund.

He swallowed his sudden urge to laugh manically, to leave Lu Wa behind and bound across the warzone on his own, to go back into the castle and proclaim himself king.

What Tong Yi had taken was his brother's power instead of his life. He'd absorbed it. Swallowed it whole.

Filth, chaos, and all.

And now that power tainted his own soul.

Ba Xi's coin held no warmth. No light. No magic.

Tong Yi squeezed it hard between his thumb and forefinger, calling her desperately. He stood astride Lu Wa, one arm around an unconscious Quan Lo, keeping him upright. He'd driven away from the castle before it had collapsed in on itself, its denizens falling apart, breaking into scrap pieces even as they fled. Tong Yi knew he had the power to maintain them, to keep them whole, but he couldn't. Not unless he chose to stay here, to fill his brother's place.

Damn it! How was he going to get home? He couldn't open a portal here on his own, could he? Was he strong enough, now? Could he force the land to his will?

And that was part of the problem, wasn't it? Tong Yi had done what was necessary. Only that, no more, no less. Just taken his brother's magic. Not his soul. Uncle Bei would be proud of him.

Ba Xi would never speak with him again.

Tong Yi looked out over the colorful horizon. Green rivers of rocks ran through the ruts in the ground. Tiny yellow flowers sprang up between the rocks. His tainted soul urged him forward, to go explore, set up his own castle of might.

He shook his head.

To the right lay the badlands. The rocks that marked the border looked washed in subtle hues of red and orange, no longer a plain gray. He knew Lu Wa could get him through those, jumping over the tighter spaces.

But what of Quan Lo? He was merely human, now. Would he make it through that desolate place beyond the rocks? He needed medical attention. Tong Yi didn't like how his brother's breath rattled.

The hatred of the land seemed muted, now. All Tong Yi felt was its power. Saw its brilliant, mad colors. Felt the appeal of its insanity.

What did Quan Lo feel, however?

Tong Yi placed the coin on Lu Wa's gas tank while he considered his options. He couldn't build a portal here. The land was jealous of its power. It wouldn't allow him to steal enough to form an opening. The portal would fizzle before he completed the spell. The land itself would blow sand and dirt over the characters he drew. He'd never be able to move fast enough to create the portal, then drive through it.

Could he build one in the air? He considered the possibility, flaming characters in a circle above his head. Lu Wa could certainly jump through such a hoop.

Hell, the little frog would probably like that.

Lu Wa shivered between Tong Yi's legs.

"What is it?" Tong Yi asked, looking down.

The coin, Ba Xi's coin, that he'd placed on Lu Wa's gas tank, had started glowing.

It grew brighter. More blue.

Then the circle of light expanded.

The coin floated up, off the gas tank. It stood on end, the circle turning into a familiar oval of blue and black.

The coin had turned into a portal.

Tong Yi noticed with a grin that it didn't touch the earth. That Lu Wa would have to leap through it.

Sadness still struck his heart that he hadn't been able to call Ba Xi himself. That she was forever cut off from him. His soul had been tainted by his brother's power.

No matter.

He had his brother. His family was together again.

That had to be enough.

The tinkling bell over the door of The Sweet Shop sounded the same as always to Tong Yi as he stepped into the cool, air-conditioned shop. J-pop still blasted from the speakers, mingled with the endless pinging of the Pachinko games. The sugary smell that coated the back of his throat didn't seem as bitter as it once had: maybe he was more magical, or possibly, more bitter and cynical himself.

The magic inside Tong Yi stirred, like sand being blown on a beach. Tong Yi clamped down on it, unwilling to spend the time to determine how pure the impulse was, if his magic wanted to do something chaotic or lawful.

Ge Deng stood behind the counter, as always. He wore a bright, red-and-white checked shirt, like a tablecloth for a picnic. His cat ears swiveled toward Tong Yi, then away again. Instead of the usual affable greeting, Ge Deng called out urgently, "Boss! Company!"

Tong Yi stopped, surprised. Was he no longer welcome here?

See-tza appeared beside the counter with a puff of sweet jasmine incense. "Oh! Tong Yi! How good to see you!" she said, stepping directly in front of him.

Tong Yi realized that she'd just barred him from going further into the shop.

"See-tza," Tong Yi said, bowing low to his former teacher.

He blinked, surprised when she returned his bow, treating him like an equal.

"What can my humble establishment do for such a powerful wizard as yourself?" See-tza asked. She was all smiles, wearing a particularly lovely deep-purple shirt under a black vest, with black jeans that showed off her curves.

However, Tong Yi had the definite impression that she wasn't pleased to see him. Maybe it was the way her cat ears kept flicking back and forth.

"I'm not sure what you can do for me," Tong Yi said slowly. He'd come here with the intention of seeing if See-tza needed anything delivered. He needed a job. His savings were almost wiped out.

Uncle Bei had said that he'd be glad to welcome Tong Yi as a student again. However, he couldn't help Tong Yi set the boundaries he needed. Didn't understand how Tong Yi's soul was now tainted. Couldn't understand why Tong Yi was reluctant to use his greater power.

Though Tong Yi had found it useful to channel the lawyer now and again, he knew that if he continued studying with Uncle Bei, that he'd become a pale imitation of the lawyer.

Tong Yi needed to find his own path. Despite how thrilled his mother might be if he went on to become a lawyer.

See-tza peered curiously at him. "You need ingredients for a great spell?" she asked.

Tong Yi shook his head. "I thought maybe we could have tea sometime," he said, his voice sounding weak even to his ears.

See-tza gave him a real smile, finally. Not the one she reserved for customers. She clapped her hands and nodded. "Yes! Tea! Next week," she added firmly.

"Okay," Tong Yi said. "I'll call you." Would she pick up the phone? Or would she always be "busy"?

"Please do," See-tza said. She seemed sincere.

Tong Yi was about to turn to go when he felt a wave of magic wash over him. He blocked it automatically, pushing it easily to the side. It didn't even cause the hair on his arms to stand up. If anything, it was like he'd just walked past a weakly blowing fan. There hadn't even been enough power for him to bother trying to absorb it, use it.

"What was that?" he asked, puzzled. It didn't anger him that See-tza would throw magic at him. Just confused him.

See-tza gave him an odd look. Then she nodded, as if she'd come to an important conclusion about him.

"You are strong," she said slowly. "Much, much more power than you know."

Tong Yi blinked. He had known that he was stronger, at least twice as strong, since absorbing Quan Lo's magic.

As See-tza appeared to be waiting for a reply, Tong Yi finally said, "I know."

See-tza tilted her head to the side. "You do not know. Not yet. Such a spell of magic, that I sent you, would have pushed you to your knees, before."

"Really?" Tong Yi asked, surprised.

"Really," See-tza said. "You control all that power well. But…"

"But?" Tong Yi prompted when she didn't continue.

"You find something to do with that magic, first," See-tza said. "Then come back to see me."

Tong Yi opened his mouth, then closed it again. "I see," he said, though he didn't really. After another moment, Tong Yi bowed to his former teacher again. "Thank you for continuing to educate me," he said.

He'd hoped that she'd give him a job. Was he too powerful for that, now? Though he had no desire to be merely a message boy, not ever again.

With a sigh, Tong Yi walked out of The Sweet Shop.

He would go back there. When he had need.

Not before.

He shook his head and nearly walked into the woman coming toward him.

"Sorry," he said, automatically reaching out his hands to prevent her from falling.

Then he froze.

Ba Xi stood before him.

How had Tong Yi forgotten how beautiful Ba Xi was? Though she haunted his dreams, she never looked as dazzling as this—a goddess in human form—with perfect skin, gull-wing eyebrows across an intelligent brow, her neck as graceful as a swan's. She wore the front of her hair down, curling on either side of her face, while the majority of it was pulled back and tied up with black and red ribbons. A black jacket set off her creamy skin, and the red and white blouse matched it.

Already her sweet perfume floated over him, making his gut ache.

"I'm sorry," Tong Yi said stiffly. He bowed his head. Though *Ba Guan* Street was normally crowded, the sounds of the traffic died away as he looked at her, the peace of the *fei renlei* neighborhood emanating from her.

"It's fine," Ba Xi said softly. She appeared to be drinking in his appearance with hungry eyes.

Or maybe that was just his imagination, what he wished for.

"It is good to see you," Ba Xi added. "You look well. Strong."

Tong Yi nodded. "So do you."

"How is your brother?" Ba Xi asked.

Tong Yi blinked, surprised. Why would Ba Xi ask about him? "He's doing much better," Tong Yi told her. "He'll be released from the hospital at the end of the week. We nearly lost him, more than once. The doctors replaced all his blood twice. Some strange disease kept trying to infect him. But he's healing, now."

Quan Lo watched the world with haunted eyes. He frequently stared at Tong Yi, as if looking for the magic he could no longer sense.

The first time Quan Lo had woken up clear-eyed, he'd asked for paper and charcoal pencils. He spent most of his time drawing now. Sometimes Tong Yi recognized the figures his brother drew: Kitty, the man made of clothespins, others.

But Quan Lo also drew fantastical bridges going off to nowhere, wings carrying hearts in a rainbow, Mexican fighters riding unicycles while squaring off in a ring.

According to the doctors, he'd never fully recover, be who he'd once been. His brain had been too fevered for too long. The simplest tasks frustrated him now, like how to read (though he could still draw characters), how to work the remote for the TV, even how to operate the call button for the nurse. His personality had also changed. He'd grown shy in front of strangers, tongue tied in front of his parents, even had developed a stutter.

Quan Lo had a good chance of staying sober, however. He lived for his drawings, now. He might make a good living at it.

Tong Yi was determined to do everything he could to get Quan Lo set up on his own, to help him relearn human things and reintegrate into society. However, Tong Yi suspected that he might have to look after his brother until the end of Quan Lo's days.

"I'm glad your brother is better," Ba Xi replied. "It's good that he's recovering. That you have your family, now."

Tong Yi swallowed against a suddenly dry throat. He heard all the words Ba Xi didn't say, could never say.

How in the end, Tong Yi had chosen his family over her.

That she understood his sacrifice.

Even if it meant that they would never be together.

Tong Yi felt as though a door in his soul had just closed, that pathway cut off.

He'd chosen a different trail, away from her. Though he'd love her for the rest of the life, they could never be together. He had to make his own way, now. Away from his old teachers and friends.

For a moment, he felt light-headed. Giddy, even.

The loss still cut at him, but he was free, now.

"Thank you for understanding," Tong Yi told Ba Xi. "For everything."

She gave him a sad smile. "You're welcome," she said. "I wish you and your family much joy and happiness through the end of their days."

"I wish the same for you and yours," Tong Yi replied formally.

And he did.

Magic stirred again in Tong Yi's soul as he walked down toward where he'd parked Lu Wa. He had no doubt that whatever his magic prompted him to do—whether it was lawful or not—he had the strength to handle it. Endure the consequences. Make it right, if he had to.

He had his family now.

It was enough.

Tong Yi walked out of his parents' apartment building early in the morning. Not as ridiculously early as when he'd been delivering messages: the sun had already come up, and the heated, humid air was just a promise of what was to come later that afternoon.

In the alley directly across from his parents' apartment stood an older man. He wore a white T-shirt that showed a muscled chest, with a pair of brown, cropped pants and sandals. Blue reflective wraparound sunglasses hid his eyes. His white and gray hair was shorn short, sticking up all over his meaty head.

The man smiled at Tong Yi when he saw him.

Tong Yi approached the man slowly. Magic emanated from this being, as well as from the pure white motorcycle he leaned against.

"Good to see you, Tong Yi," the man said.

Tong Yi narrowed his eyes. The man seemed vaguely familiar, but he couldn't place him.

"Good morning," Tong Yi replied cautiously. The chaotic side of his magic needled him, demanding that he attack immediately.

The more lawful side waited to be provoked first.

The man slowly lifted his sunglasses so Tong Yi could see his eyes.

With a shock, Tong Yi realized it was Zhang Gua Lao. The motorcycle he leaned against was his mule, transformed.

Tong Yi grinned at the immortal. "It is good to see you as well, sir," he said as he stepped closer.

The smell of pine and soft incense floated around him, settling his soul. At the same time, his skin buzzed with magic.

"I came by to thank you," the old man said.

"For what?" Tong Yi asked, perplexed.

"You did what was necessary," Zhang Gua Lao explained. "You re-tamed chaos. Reset the bonds."

Tong Yi shook his head. It didn't feel that way inside of him. He constantly fought himself, the urges to break out, be wild, do the unexpected.

Plus, just the night before he'd had a nightmare where he'd dreamed that the immortal had been dressing him in the Yellow Emperor's robes while Quan Lo knelt behind him, in chains, weeping.

Zhang Gua Lao shrugged. "It might not feel that way," he said, as if Tong Yi had just told him all of his difficulties. "But because of you, the war is falling apart. The combatants are negotiating instead of fighting. By breaking the hold of the southern gate, you broke the will of many of the fighters."

That thrilled Tong Yi's soul. That his actions had some meaning. That he'd saved more than just his brother.

The old man dropped his sunglasses back down over his eyes. "Come on. You need some fun."

"I was going to go visit my brother…" Tong Yi said. He was reluctant to not stick with the schedule he'd set. Quan Lo needed structure.

So did he.

Zhang Gua Lao waved his hand.

Suddenly, the pair of them stood with their bikes on an empty highway beside the ocean. It reminded Tong Yi of the place where he'd first found the immortal, fishing in a stream. The air smelled clear and clean. The pavement looked new, a long, unmarred black ribbon that stretched to the horizon. The sun shone down on them, soft and warm, turning the sand golden.

"I'll make sure you get back in time." The immortal swung his leg over his motorcycle. It instantly came to life, and he revved the engine. "Wanna race?"

Tong Yi grinned. The immortal was right. While he, too, needed structure and stability, he also needed to have fun. For a moment, he remembered how he'd gone bounding across the warzone.

"You're on," Tong Yi said.

In the few moments while Lu Wa transformed from paper into metal, Tong Yi marveled at his luck. Here he was, about to race like a mad fool with one of the eight immortals. His own magic was powerful enough that his former teacher turned him away. He had found his own path, his own middle way, his own life.

Now, he just had to live it.

Lu Wa happily jumped to life, his engine roaring.

Then they all were off, racing down the road as if death flew after them.

Tong Yi sat in the living room of his parents' apartment, dully flipping through channels on the big TV. The afternoon air pressed in hot and humid, the air conditioner fighting to keep the room cool. His brother would be home the next day. Tong Yi had already fixed up his bedroom, stocked it with all the art supplies he could think of, as well as cleaned the rest of the apartment.

He didn't know what to do with himself. He knew he needed to get a job. His savings would run out fast.

He'd already started looking for another position, but nothing interested him. He wanted something that dealt with both the human and non-human worlds. And possibly something that involved his magic as well.

Working at a shop on Hai'an Boulevard just didn't have the same appeal as it once might have, though he was getting desperate enough that he might apply.

The tiny picture Ba Xi had kept on her mantel had appeared on the top of his dresser that morning, carrying the faint smell of jasmine with it.

He knew he couldn't be with her. That they'd never have lasted. Despite how powerful he'd grown, that path was no longer open to him. He'd changed too much to be the person she needed him to be.

His heart still ached no matter how much logic he tried to use.

A knock on the door stirred him out of his self-reflection.

He gasped when he saw Ren Wu, his old boss, standing outside. He looked like he normally did, in an ivory polo shirt with a tiny brown fox embroidered on the left pocket, brown pants, sandals.

"Come in," Tong Yi said, holding the door open. "It's good to see you." He took a moment to look at his old boss with new eyes, as well as new magic.

Ren Wu *did* have magic. Not anywhere near as much as Uncle Bei, or even Tong Yi, now.

However, Ren Wu didn't store any of his magic on him. It all came from deep within himself. He didn't augment his power in a medallion like Tong Yi wore, or like Uncle Bei's cufflinks.

No wonder Tong Yi had never been able to figure out Ren Wu. He could have been a powerful wizard. However, he'd chosen a different path.

Interesting. Maybe he could talk with his old boss about magic.

"Can I get you some tea? Water? A beer?" Tong Yi asked, leading Ren Wu back into the living room.

"Thank you," Ren Wu said. "Some tea would be lovely."

"Follow me," Tong Yi said, leading his old boss back into the kitchen.

The kitchen still felt like the most homey room in the apartment. Light filtered in through the frosted glass window over the eating nook in the back. The light over the stove was on as well. Breakfast dishes sat drying in the rack next to the sink. The refrigerator hummed quietly to itself. Tong Yi filled the electric kettle with bottled water, then plugged it in.

"How are you?" Ren Wu asked.

"Better," Tong Yi said, nodding. And he was. Recovering, but slowly. Trying to find his balance between the chaos he'd absorbed and the structure of his own soul. Figure out what was normal for him, and what wasn't.

"Good," Ren Wu said with a grin. "Busy?" he asked.

"Not really," Tong Yi said slowly.

"I may have a job for you, then," Ren Wu said with a grin.

Tong Yi narrowed his eyes. "Delivering messages?" he asked, disapprovingly. He really didn't want to go back to his old job, his old habits.

Ren Wu laughed. "Oh no. I have something much, much better for you."

Tong Yi cruised with Lu Wa through the quiet streets of Hualien City. It was early morning, before the regular rush of traffic, just before 7 a.m. The day had dawned bright and clear, with the promise of great heat later that afternoon. Gulls called from the beach just a few blocks away. Delivery trucks lumbered ahead of him.

He checked the address he had again, circling the block when he'd realized he'd driven past it. He finally pulled up across the street from the ordinary-looking house.

A middle-aged woman walked up to the gate as Tong Yi backed Lu Wa up onto his kickstand. She nodded at him.

It took him a moment to realize that this was the teacher he'd met the day before. Yet another of Han Di's "cousins". She'd been hired by *Huli* Transport to keep an eye out for special students.

Extraordinary ones.

A young schoolgirl exited the gate and happily greeted the teacher. She had her long hair in two braids, hanging down off her shoulders. Her school uniform consisted of a white, short-sleeved shirt, and a beige-and-red set of bib overall shorts.

The teacher indicated that they should walk across the street to where Tong Yi waited.

He got off his bike when he saw them coming, then deliberately used a sharp spike of magic, pressing his thumb against the ignition, to lock and protect the bike.

The girl startled at the flash of blue.

Tong Yi smiled at her. "You saw that, didn't you?"

She nodded slowly, hugging her books in front of her chest.

The teacher made the formal introduction. As Tong Yi bowed, he sent out another deliberate flare of magic.

The girl gasped, then she grinned at him.

"I can explain those things that you see," Tong Yi told the girl. "Let's walk together for a while."

The girl looked back at the teacher, who nodded, giving her approval.

Deliberately, the girl started walking quickly down the street, as if daring Tong Yi to keep up with her. He stretched his legs and ended up beside her, while the teacher followed them a few steps behind, like an old-fashioned chaperone.

Tong Yi had no idea where the girl would end up in the *Huli* Transport organization, whether in the school Ren Wu had set up with Uncle Bei, if she'd become a messenger, or just a sales person, dealing with the *fei renlei.* He couldn't sense her power, her potential.

No one could. It would be up to her to decide.

He would, however, help her transition into the world of magic.

The more youngsters he could recruit, the less chance of another Quan Lo forming.

Though in some ways, Tong Yi was still a messenger boy, at least now he was delivering the right messages. Finally.

ABOUT THE AUTHOR

Leah Cutter writes page-turning fiction in exotic locations, such as a magical New Orleans, the ancient Orient, Hungary, the Oregon coast, rural Kentucky, Seattle, Minneapolis, and many others.

She writes literary, fantasy, mystery, science fiction, and horror fiction. Her short fiction has been published in magazines like Alfred Hitchcock's Mystery Magazine and Talebones, anthologies like Fiction River, and on the web. Her long fiction has been published both by New York publishers as well as small presses.

Read more books by Leah Cutter at www.KnottedRoadPress.com.

Follow her blog at www.LeahCutter.com.

Never miss a release!

If you'd like to be notified of new releases, sign up for my newsletter.

I only send out newsletters once a quarter, will never spam you, or use your email for nefarious purposes. You can also unsubscribe at any time.

http://www.LeahCutter.com/newsletter/

Reviews

It's true. Reviews help me sell more books. If you've enjoyed this story, please consider leaving a review of it on your favorite site.

ABOUT BOOK VIEW CAFÉ

Book View Café is a professional authors' cooperative offering DRM-free ebooks in multiple formats to readers around the world. With authors in a variety of genres including mystery, romance, fantasy, and science fiction, Book View Café has something for everyone.

Book View Café is good for readers because you can enjoy high-quality DRM-free ebooks from your favorite authors at a reasonable price.

Book View Café is good for writers because 95% of the profit goes directly to the book's author.

Book View Café authors include Nebula, Hugo, and Philip K. Dick Award winners, Nebula, Hugo, World Fantasy, and Rita Award nominees, and *New York Times* bestsellers and notable book authors.

www.bookviewcafe.com

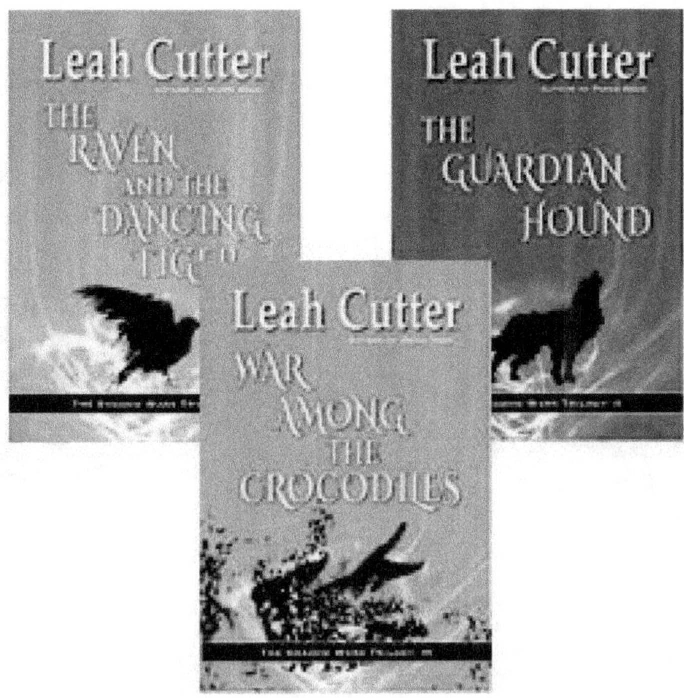

Read the three books of the Shadow Wars trilogy, about the shape shifters who hide among us and their battles with those who would destroy humanity:

The Raven and the Dancing Tiger
The Guardian Hound
War Among the Crocodiles

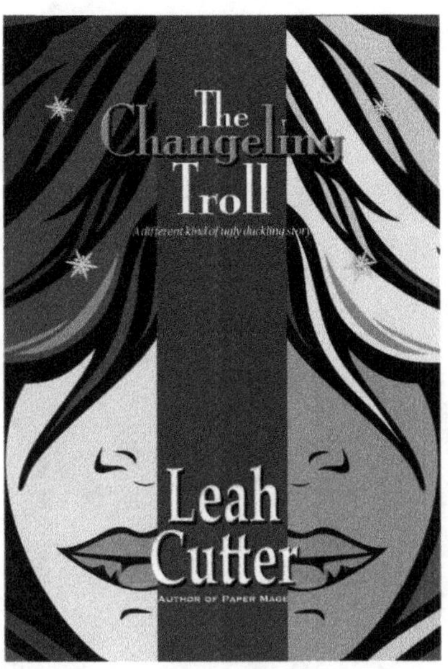

Piles of books line the floor of Christine's living room, threaten to take over every surface in her apartment. Christine escapes into her stories every chance she gets. Because magic only happens in fairy tales. Right?

After losing a bet with her brother, Christine forces herself to leave the sanctuary of her apartment and go to a real bar. Listen to a live band. Maybe dance.

She hates all of it with a passion—the noise, the music, the people. Then the impossible happens. She meets her identical twin.

The Changeling Troll—the first novel in a new-adult, urban fantasy trilogy—turns the ugly duckling story on its head in this enchanting, whimsical tale.

www.ingramcontent.com/pod-product-compliance
Lightning Source LLC
Chambersburg PA
CBHW070436120726
47910CB00003B/803